S0-CLQ-650

BAKER'S DOZEN

KATHLEEN NORRIS

BAKER'S DOZEN

Short Story Index Reprint Series

BOOKS FOR LIBRARIES PRESS
FREEPORT, NEW YORK

Reprinted 1970 by arrangement with
Doubleday & Company, Inc.

INTERNATIONAL STANDARD BOOK NUMBER:
0-8369-3649-3

LIBRARY OF CONGRESS CATALOG CARD NUMBER:
71-130068

PRINTED IN THE UNITED STATES OF AMERICA

TO JACQUELINE

A small ambassadress by happy chance
May hold, within a sunburned hand and puny,
The key that locks to all the charm of France
Les Etats-Unis.

And such is Jacqueline, whose red-gold curls
Will bob someday above two nations' story,
Writ for, as e'en for other little girls,
Ma nièce adorée.

So, Jacqueline, take which language you prefer,
And as with "*être*" and "being" you make merry,
May Heaven be kind to you. I mean may *Dieu*
Te garde, ma chérie.

Contents

BAKER'S DOZEN

Second Choice

A BLEAK, miserable afternoon, belonging properly to no season of the year. Otis Livermore, deceived by the heat of April's last day, had walked to the office this morning in his thin, shabby, summer suit. Now, walking home in the grimy windy twilight, he felt cold as well as tired and a little dispirited. May was coming in with thoroughly disagreeable weather.

The house, when he reached it, looked as dreary as the day. No matter, Otis reflected, for they were moving away tomorrow. It was a frame house, it needed painting. It would have painting now; it was to be thoroughly renovated; he had heard that there was to be a garage built when the new tenants, and the new rent, commenced their reign.

He and Ellen had always loved this house. They felt bitter now about what was a practical eviction. They had found it, with what excitement, during a Sunday walk five years ago, when Margaret was a toddling three and the second child's birth some months ahead.

And Ellen had said that if she could have this house, in this lovely neighborhood, with the open fireplace and the wonderful big closets and two bathrooms, and hardwood floors—but it was too good to be true! It would be seventy-five dollars, just as sure as he was born.

What a day that was! When they found it was forty . . .

Well, mused Otis, in the dusk, noticing that the dead and gone hollyhocks had left ugly stains on the side wall and reflecting that nothing made a house look more desolate than to have the windows bare, well, Ellen's guess would have been more moderate in these days. The new tenant was paying eighty; and eighty was too much for the Livermores, and they were moving away tomorrow.

The door opened as he pushed back the garden gate, and a little girl of eight came flying to meet him. Margaret had been a wonderful baby; strangers had often stopped her father on Sundays to admire her. And she still had her moments of looking exquisite. But tonight she looked dirty and tumbled and her grin showed missing teeth.

She made a leap for her father and with her greeting struck weary horror to his heart.

"Daddy, the Fuller boy was throwing rocks, and Patsy was there, and he hit her, and Mother had the doctor!"

Otis Livermore gathered his first-born under his arm and took the steps between him and his front door in bounds. It opened, and he was met by his wife, a slender, tired woman in a draggled and dirty gingham dress, with her fair hair in an untidy mop.

The kiss they exchanged was like a countersign almost automatically presented in time of stress.

"What happened?" Otis asked tensely.

"Nothing serious," Ellen Livermore answered quickly and soothingly. "She's all right! Her head was cut, and there was a good deal of blood. . . ."

"Her head cut!" he breathed. They were running upstairs together. Now they were in their own dismantled and dirty bedroom: the old "body Brussels" had been ripped from the floor and ridges of dust lay upon the boards. On the couch lay Patsy, her beautiful baby face still tear streaked, her expectant black eyes fixed upon her father, and her dark mop of curls crossed by a hideously professional-looking bandage.

Otis, his face paling, fell on his knees beside her and encircled the precious little limp figure with his arm.

"What happened!" he said again. The exquisite baby lips began to tremble. "No, no, my darling," he said, his cheek close against the little girl's cheek, "you mustn't cry any more!"

"No harm done whatever," Mrs Livermore said with great cheerfulness. "Doctor Brewster was lovely; he put in two stitches, and she was Mother's brave, darling girl."

"The Fuller boy?" Otis asked grimly, glancing at his wife.

"Well, they were all throwing rocks!"

"And, Margaret, why weren't you looking out for your little sister?" he asked sharply. "Don't you think that you are about big enough——"

"She was having a music lesson, Otis," the mother interposed quickly. "Miss Pfingst came, and there was one more lesson paid for, and—ah, now you hurt our feelings, Daddy," Ellen broke off as, at her defense, the older child began quietly to cry. "Tell Daddy what Inga did, dear!" she distracted Margaret tactfully. The little girl began to strangle with laughter through tears.

"She—she ran after the Fuller boy and she caught him by the arm, and he—he began to cry!" she hiccupped.

"And she talked to him in Swedish, Otis, you would have *died!*" his wife added in eager amusement. "I was rushing into the house with Patsy, frightened to death, of course, but I had to laugh——"

"Well, I'm glad you could find some amusement in it," Otis, tired and depressed and angry, said disapprovingly. "The Fuller boy has thrown his last rock at my child," he added quietly. "I propose to see Fuller right now——"

"Oh, Otis," his wife interrupted again. "That is part of it. Inga and the boys all yelling made such an uproar that they really did bring the police—that fat policeman who always talks to Patsy. And he asked me—he came while I was telephoning the doctor—he asked me if she was in her own garden when it happened, and of course I said yes, and he took the boy to the station house. It's enough to kill Mrs Fuller.

Inga says—as well as I can make her out—that they've got the boy home now but that they've got to appear in court on Tuesday before Judge Ransom!"

Otis sat back on his heels, miraculously soothed. Between the Fullers and the Ransoms there existed an old feud. Serve them right: they never punished the boy, they never disciplined him. Now Judge Ransom would tell them just what decent people thought of a boy who threw rocks at baby girls!

He had breath for other matters.

"You got the carpets up—good girl. Are you dead?" he said rather than asked, glancing about the room.

"Yes, I am. They got here at three," his wife answered with a long-drawn breath. The scene she had been dreading for exactly two hours was over: Otis knew about the accident. She could descend to other affairs herself. "Not too much p-i-t-y," she spelled lightly in warning.

"Yes, I get you." Otis got to his feet.

"I wish Patsy felt well enough to come down because I think Inga has a nice supper," Ellen remarked casually. Patsy remained languid, looking thoughtfully at the little apron that was stained with water and blood.

"I don't know but what she'd better have milk toast in bed," Otis added artfully, "I brought a box of dates, but I don't know——"

"Oh, Daddy!" Patsy said, sitting up briskly and aggrievedly. "I'm well! Doctor said that I could jump froo hoops tomorrow, didn't he, Muv?"

"I believe she could ride down on your back, Daddy—there's the bell now!" Ellen said. "I am so dirty and so achy and so utterly worn out," she added wearily.

"Don't clean up, don't change!" he urged her hastily. "Come just as you are. Let's eat."

"I don't know what there *is* to eat," Ellen commented, following him downstairs. "I told Inga *anything*. . . ."

"Bread and tea will taste good to me!" her husband answered, resolutely cheerful.

But even bread and tea were not to be, it appeared, immediately available. Inga had placed upon the table boiled potatoes, two end slices of bread, canned corn swimming palely in milky juice and yesterday's mutton, cold and dry.

"This isn't a very nice supper for you, Daddy," Ellen murmured. "She *will* not boil these potatoes long enough!" she added despairingly.

"Am I to cut this up for Margaret?" Otis asked dispassionately, eying an uninviting plateful.

"Certainly, dear, what did you suppose you were to do? Inga, have you tea? Haven't you hot water? Please put it on right away, and bring us more bread, please. Every night since she *came,*" said Ellen in an undertone as the maid clumped out, "we have had tea. But I suppose if it was ten years instead of ten months she would have to be told!"

"Perhaps if you went into the kitchen just before dinner and simply made a few suggestions," Otis began. Color came into his wife's tired face.

"Perhaps if you had packed all the china and the little girls' clothes and swept the entire lower floor and assorted linen and kitchenware and been delayed by a serious accident, you would not find that so simple," Ellen thought of replying. But instead she was silent, helping corn through a dazzle of tears.

Inga came in for money: there was no more bread, but she could get it while the kettle boiled.

Otis' ready hand went into his pocket, and he managed to convey nothing but mild curiosity to his wife as he said:

"Haven't we a bill at Kelly's?"

"I paid it, Otis. I didn't want it to run over into this month."

"That's right!" They loitered over their supper, waiting for the bread and tea. The fifth person at the table, Ellen's big, gentle, kindly mother, came to the rescue of the languishing conversation.

"How did the Westmarket house look to you today, Otis? Did you get out?"

"Yes, I ran out at noon, Gramma. It looks—*fine.*"

"Paperers gone?"

"Oh yes, and the bedrooms look nice and clean. It looks"—Otis halted again on the word, brought it out firmly—"*fine.*"

Ellen, handing him at last his hot and fragrant tea, sighed.

"For heaven's sake," he said, turning to her with a sort of humorous and affectionate impatience, "for heaven's sake, cheer up, old girl! I know you hate the house; I'm not crazy about it myself. But since we've *got* to get out, and since we are lucky enough to find *anything*——"

"Yes, I know!" she interrupted with an effort to be reasonable. "But somehow I cannot seem to get up the slightest interest in that house. I've always said I would never live in the Westmarket district. And when I think of the window-box house . . ."

For she and Otis, in this unwelcome search for a new abode, had of course found the ideal one, at three times their maximum rent. "The window-box house," as they called it, had been unbelievably artistic, unique and fascinating. Of course it had no furnace, and it was small, and it was a hundred and fifty dollars a month. But oh, how they had discussed it, and how they had wanted it, and how shabby and commonplace and cheap it had seemed to make the house in the Westmarket district, to which they moved tomorrow!

"Seems like you always find a place to spoil the place you have to take," said Ellen's mother consolingly.

"I know," Ellen said. "But oh, the brass knocker and that gallery and the back yard—we could have had all our meals there!" She sighed, unconsoled. "And then the man telling Otis that he thought they'd take anything on a lease!" she persisted.

"Oh, say, the Baker baby has come!" Otis said suddenly. Ellen was interested. What was it?

It was a boy, Otis said. The woman whose children were both girls felt a little jealous pang as old as civilization. A man-child born to spoiled, idle Ethel Baker, the young wife of the young vice-president and junior partner of Otis' firm. Of course it would be a boy—didn't Ethel Baker always get everything she wanted! Lifelessly she changed the subject.

"Did the lost check turn up, Otis?"

A worried look came into the man's face.

"Nope—that is the darnedest thing!" he answered, shaking his head. Ellen apportioned dates to her daughters with a dull sense of weariness and grievance. Ethel Baker had a son, the lost check, for which Otis was responsible, had not been found, and they were moving to the Westmarket house tomorrow.

Her hands felt grimed and sore from packing. The dining room, with the outlines of picture frames clearly shown upon the faded wallpaper and with a clutter of excelsior and papers and strings upon the floor, looked dreary in the dull light. But it was even worse when Inga suddenly flooded it with harsh electric radiance. Ellen had taken away the familiar lamp shades; there was a pyramid of books, a pile of curtaining, behind Otis' chair.

"Early to bed tonight for everyone?" the man asked, feeling better after his meal. "What time do the vans get here?"

"Otis," his wife answered regretfully, "I had to leave the glassware for you, and some of the bric-a-brac. They only brought one barrel, and I was just starting to ask Kelly to send me another when poor Patsy got hurt."

"Well, that's all right!" He got bravely to his feet, cast off his coat, looked about challengingly.

"Clear this away, Inga, and put the linen into that basket in the kitchen," Ellen said, also rising. "Don't touch that with your sticky hands! It's a shame to have left this for you. If you would just go up with them, then I will come up and finish them off," she added, addressing maid, children, husband and mother in turn. "I'll help you, Inga," she added when Mrs Cutting had herded the protestant little girls to the stairs, "and then I can help you, dear!" she finished, to Otis.

They went at it courageously, although Ellen knew he was tired, and she herself actually ached with stiffness, soreness and chill. He bent and straightened himself tirelessly over the cases; Ellen brought the finger bowls and the Canton jar and the Dresden shepherd and shepherdess.

"Horrible bleak weather!"

"Nasty. Hand me those newspapers."

"Here's Margaret's dear little silver mug, Otis, the one Bert sent. Remember how excited we were! I suppose they're terribly pleased that it's a boy—the Bakers, I mean. Remember how we always spoke of Patsy as 'Bobby,' before she was born? Here's this stein again; the Youngers gave it to us. We both hate it and I suppose we always will, but one can't deliberately smash a thing that is whole. Dear me, I wish I could forget that window-box place. I would feel so different if we *wanted* to move! I've always loved this house—I remember moving in here. Of course we shall like the Westmarket place. . . ."

Thus Ellen, working as she mused. Otis was equally inconsequential.

"The idea is to pack 'em snug, no use putting in packing if they can flop around. When was that chipped? By golly, whatever we lose, I hope it isn't these carvers. It makes a dinner party go, I give you my word for it, to have a man able to carve without half killing—— Sit down, Mother, we'll all be dead this time tomorrow night. Might as well rest while you can! Take that shelf paper off and give it to me, Ellen; it's just the rough sort of stuff I want in here. Whew! I'm warmed up now. I suppose we set great value on these what-you-may-call-'ems, do we? Priceless, eh? All righty, what you say goes. . . . Nope, it's a funny thing about that check. I had it. I think I gave it to Redding. Red says he doesn't remember it at all. Worries you—thing like that. I've got to go down tomorrow—I'll get away early!"

"Oh, Otis!" His wife straightened her aching back, stood looking at him aghast, an oily brass lamp in her dirty hands.

"I've got to, dearie, I'm sorry! We've got to eat, you know!"

"Oh, eat!" said Ellen Livermore in a bitter undertone as she wrapped the lamp bowl in newspaper. "I wonder what it would feel like, just once, not to have to think of economy!" she mused. "The man came in today to take out the telephone, the month was up yesterday. I asked him to leave it in. I was actually telephoning the doctor, but he said—it's perfectly reasonable, I suppose!—that you had notified them that you were giving it up. Then about the vans: those men stood about spitting and deliberating today whether they could get our furniture into two vans. I wanted to scream at them, 'Oh, bring three vans then!' but of course that meant sixteen dollars——"

"I left the light on because the children want to see you," Mrs Cutting, who was untangling brown and white and pink strings at Otis' request, observed at this point. Ellen, wondering if she could get up the stairs, started lamely for the doorway. She had a mental vision of herself kissing the little girls, extinguishing the light, taking a hot, curative, restful, leisurely bath, laying out clothes for the morning, gathering a few overlooked medicine bottles into readiness for quick packing tomorrow and going to bed after a thorough cold-creaming of her face, brushing of her hair and straightening of her bedroom.

Instead she carried each daughter a drink, inspected Patsy's bandage in anxious ignorance, tried to look into a small ear to find the pain of which Margaret complained, heard prayers, found Patsy's bear and the pink shell Margaret had taken to bed with her every night for seven years, turned out the lights and lay down "for just a second" close to the delicious warmth and the affectionate little arms of the older child.

Otis waked her, heavy, chilly, aching, an hour later, and

in an agony of weariness she stumbled into bed. Her last thought was that she wished she might sleep through the dreadful day to come. The suitcases, and Donny . . . where was his chain? . . . And where was the strap for the hamper? . . . The big picture . . . and Inga had smashed the lovely vase . . . it lay in a smudge of opalescent dust at the foot of the stairs . . . where their feet had been pulverizing it since ten o'clock. . . .

B-r-rr-rrr-! That was the alarm clock at six. Otis moaned, but Ellen, fresh and clean, could laugh at him as he struggled for another nap.

"Dearie, for heaven's sake, shut it off!"

"But you must wake up, it's moving day!" she told him, proceeding with her dressing at the bureau. Buttoning a clean blouse, she stepped to the window and saw his drowsy eye following her. "It's a perfectly glorious day!" she encouraged him.

"Well . . . ya-a-ah! . . . that's lucky," Otis commented, rolling over upon his back. "Are you dead? You ought to be," he yawned.

"No. I will be, of course, but I feel gorgeous!" Ellen answered, briskly busy. "Come down just as soon as you can, to give us a good start," she said, leaving the room, "for the vans get here at eight. Kishums mudder because it was so beautiful!"

The last remark was to Margaret, who had come in barefoot in her little pajamas to have her usual morning snuggle with her father. This child, who had brought them not only her beautiful self, but also father- and motherhood, was sure of her touch upon these two adoring hearts.

"Patsy woke up in the night, and her head hurt," she said, "and she went into Gramma's room, and they're both asleep!"

Ellen, with an exclamation, fled; the day had begun.

"Where is my list?" she said thirty-seven times in the next three hours. The list was accompanied with the gold pencil she had won at a bridge party; the pencil did not work well, and the list was written upon the bottom of a small cardboard soapbox.

It began "make men set up Mother's bed," and rambled on through "cleanser, ammonia, have gas turned on, order wood and coal, get cleaning woman in neighborhood, milk, spoons in lower sideboard drawer." Every five minutes Ellen searched for this list, finding it on the top rail of the gate or weighted by the stove handle on the kitchen table. She added "notify postman" and "telephone Otis when movers get here."

Otis regretfully left at half-past eight; Ellen wandered through the dismantled rooms. The little girls fluttered in great satisfaction among these familiar dull possessions so mysteriously made interesting; it was settled at about half-past nine o'clock that Gramma was to go with the children to the new house, accompanied by Inga, who could do nothing here and might at least sweep there. Inga, however, interposed a request to stop and see her mother. Ellen, who was accompanying her own mother to the car at the corner, granted the request uneasily.

"But, Inga, why do you take all your things, just to see your mother?" she said, eying the straw suitcase and the large bundle which contained all of Inga's worldly possessions.

Inga, looking shockingly unservantlike in her green suit and white-topped, dirty shoes, smiled sagely under her pink hat. She went away without remark; Ellen laughed philosophically.

"I think she'll turn up," Mrs Cutting said reassuringly.

"Now, Mother dearest, you won't overdo and get too tired?" Ellen begged, one strong young arm about the broad figure.

"I was thinking I might order some groceries in?" the older woman questioned.

"Well, you see, that's the annoying thing! They didn't get

their checks at the office yesterday, and Otis was short, paying two months rent in advance and everything—rugs cleaned and all that!" Ellen explained. "He told me that he'd just as soon draw it from the bank, but it seemed so unnecessary. So he's to meet us at the house at twelve and bring me some money, and we'll all have a pickup meal then. The movers said that they would have us all in at eleven, but I believe I'll telephone them," Ellen mused doubtfully. "I can't understand why they don't . . ."

She smiled farewell at the three dear faces, but her own face was sober as she walked back to the house. The postman arrived. Ellen recognized in the Guaranty and Trust Company's envelope the arrival of her mother's monthly check—five minutes too late to be of use! The postman wrote down the new address: Ellen said they would miss him. Something in his jaunty reply made her wonder if he expected a tip in farewell. She went into the house uncomfortably thinking about it.

Nothing to do but wait. Ellen found a lemon on the sink and after a look about the empty hooks and drawers cut it open with an abandoned dustpan. She was cleaning her grimed hands with it in cold water when the movers arrived at eleven.

Uproar set in. They shouted, perspired, came and went. The furniture, set about the sidewalk, looked unspeakably shabby and forlorn. The ice-cream freezer, standing between the stained and chipped enamel of the wicker crib and the drop-leaf mahogany hall table, looked as aristocratic as either.

Bright sunlight flashed from the mirrors into the faces of interested passers-by. The day was still, warm, perfumed with spring leaves and blossoms.

Ellen began to feel very hungry. A cup of tea! But both stoves had long been grimily and sootily disconnected. The kitchen was simply wreckage.

"Don't you eat lunch?" she asked the redfaced man who

was always shouting facetious things at the others for her benefit.

They'd get the loads packed first, he answered heartily. Get something on the way to the other house. He took off his oily cap and from a piece of paper stuck within it read the Westmarket Street address carefully to her. Ellen again wandered away, pondering upon tips. There were five men here. Would they all expect tips?

At twenty minutes past twelve Otis arrived, hot and angry. Her complacent mood vanished before his first glance.

"Ellen, what's the trouble? Thought you were going to meet me at the new house?"

"Well, you can see . . . !" Her fire rose quickly in answer to his own. "They didn't *get* here until eleven!" she explained, hurt. Otis was instantly rude to the redheaded one who had been so nice. The redheaded one promptly retaliated.

"I thought you were to meet me, I thought it was all understood," Otis reproached her when they were alone in the kitchen. "You were to have the gas turned on and get some food in! I was just there. Your mother and the girls are there—they've had no lunch! You—you just knock the ground from under me when you fail me this way."

"Otis, will you *kindly* tell me what I could do?"

"Well, perhaps you couldn't!" His tone was pacifying, she knew he was hungry. "You'd better come with me and get something to eat and leave them to finish this up," he arranged hastily. "Been down cellar?"

"No, but they have." Otis rushed down to the cellar, came up hurriedly.

"Say, there's a big box of pots and china and so on down cellar!" he announced to the movers. They stopped short with the dissembled piano, looked doubtfully at each other, shook their heads.

"You oughter told me that, lady," said the fickle redheaded one reproachfully.

"Come on, we'll get lunch!" Otis urged her when the men had clumped in a body downstairs.

"But Otis, if they can't get it in!"

"They'll get it in, all right," he reassured her comfortably. "Now we'll get a taxi and go straight to the gas company and get that off our minds! Then we'll get Mother and the girls and go to one of those oyster places, near Westmarket Street, and get some coffee and oysters. Does that sound good? And then you can send your grocery order——"

"Don't forget to give me some money, Otis! Had Inga turned up?"

"I'll give it to you now. No, but she will. I don't think this is going to be a hard move at all. Your mother is pleased with the place."

Ellen laughed happily as she scrambled into the taxi. This was action at last!

"What is it?" she asked anxiously as, simultaneously with her discovery that it was twenty-five minutes to one, the taxi stopped.

It was nothing—the driver opened the engine hood. Nope, they were all right. They were off again. Had they better stop at the gas company's office? Otis thought they had.

"My poor starving babies!" Ellen murmured, following him into the clean, wide, deliciously cool and orderly office. Information, Rebates, Bills; this was the wrong man, this was the right man.

Complications again. The house in Westmarket Street was not piped for gas. Ellen denied this eagerly, had seen the pipe in the kitchen.

"Yes, madam," patiently explained the man with the sharp yellow pencil. "But we've got to tie you up with the main."

Ellen glanced at Otis. Would that be expensive?

No charge at all. It could be done this week. The man with the pencil was obliging: suggested that they use their coal stove for a few days. Ellen angered Otis by the simplicity with which she explained that they had sold their coal stove because the kitchen in the new house was so pleasant and big that she meant to make a sort of dining ell, with white furniture, in the east windows. . . .

Otis was frankly cross when they returned to the taxi, but these blank walls brought out what was best in Ellen. He was to leave her, the furniture would arrive all right, they would manage somehow, she would buy a kerosene stove if necessary, it would all turn out right, Otis must grab a sandwich somewhere and get home that afternoon as soon as he could.

"It 'll take them a month to get the gas pipe in!" said Otis despairingly.

"No, it won't, now, just be patient!" his wife answered, conscious that heat and hunger and fatigue had started a headache and longing only to pay this stupid man the two dollars and ten cents for his wretched car and get on a Westmarket trolley and get to her mother and children.

"You'll kill yourself," Otis said, sulky, discouraged, affectionately concerned, "and then I'll have myself to blame for the rest of my life!"

"No, I won't!" she answered bravely from the step of the trolley. But the glare of the bright day and the brazen jarring of the gong made her feel that her head would split. She stumbled to a wicker seat. The woman next to her had a pound of coffee in a paper package. Ellen caught the delicious smell. She felt a lifetime away from comfort and food, rest and order.

Otis was later than he had hoped, not getting to the new house until night after all. He approached it somewhat timidly. Quarter to five o'clock, and he had hoped to be able to help Ellen with all the hardest beginnings of getting in!

What did rich people do when they moved? Went to hotels, of course, or to Bermuda or Florida.

"Hoo-hoo, Daddy! Come in here and see how nice we are!" It was Ellen's voice, such a heartening, gay, delightful voice! Otis' spirits took a sudden upward leap; he sprang through the scattered boxes and crates and upturned chairs of the wide, old-fashioned hall and found her in the dining room.

"Say—you—are—a—wonder!" said Otis Livermore, looking about him, and at his wife, and beyond her into the big parlor. "Say, it isn't going to be so bad!" he commented, still a little unsure of her mood.

"It's going to be perfectly sweet!" his wife answered, dropping into a chair and waving a tack hammer as she spoke. "Of course you don't get any idea of the drawing room yet, but Mother and I held the curtains up—we couldn't wait—and they are *perfect!* And look how the sunlight comes in through those long windows, Otis. Isn't that lovely—sort of old-fashioned and hoop-skirty? The chairs always crowded the old house, you know, but they just fit in there."

He sat down, wiped his forehead, fitted Patsy in between knee and shoulder.

"Say, you are wonders!" he said thankfully, admiringly. "I feel terribly about not coming home sooner, but I had to go lock the old house——"

"It didn't matter. I got this colored woman and her husband, and we got beds up. Really we've done practically nothing, but we can take our time now. And the men are actually digging in the street. Of course that's the way things ought to be done, but somehow—with those big corporations one doesn't expect anything! Things are *much* cheaper here in the markets, Otis. Mother and I strolled over to them before the loads came. You'd be surprised! Of course we shall miss the second bathroom. But there's that washroom at the back; I believe we could put a bath in there . . . paying only thirty-seven dollars rent, you know. . . ."

"It's darned easy to get to," Otis said. "I got on a Westmarket car today at ten minutes to twelve, and I was here at seven minutes after! What about the stove?"

"Well, you'll *die*," said Ellen, "but there's a little laundry stove in the laundry, and I'm going to have that connected tomorrow—or she said if her husband came in she'd send him to connect it tonight, didn't she, Mother? And meanwhile—look!"

A little fire of wood and papers and small rubbish was burning in the dining room's old-fashioned coal grate, and now Ellen drew from it a covered big saucepan. A delicious odor drifted into the room.

"This is your dinner. It's stew; it's been simmering here since three!" Ellen said triumphantly. "We're going to have a great many expenses, moving in, and there's no sense in your spending six or eight dollars every night for our dinners. We have fresh milk and coffee and a cake——"

"Isn't she the greatest!" said Mrs Cutting. And Otis could only agree, grinning, that she was.

They led him about from discovery to discovery. He began to express a feverish eagerness to take off his coat and help.

"We found that check!" he said suddenly.

"Otis Livermore!"

"Yep. It had caught on the top of the partition between Redding's desk and the next desk. He and some of the fellows throw them over sometimes. The janitor found it. I forgot to tell you!"

"I knew they would!" Ellen said, magnificently scornful, and when he asked if by any chance Inga had come back she answered quietly that of course she had.

"Red and I had quite a talk this afternoon," Otis added presently. "It gave me something to think about too."

But Ellen was not listening. She wanted to show him how exactly Mother's bed fitted its alcove and that the wideness of the back porch would allow the little girls room for a table and chairs, even beds, if they wanted to try it.

And would he go get a loaf of graham bread? The grocer had not had it, but there was a lovely bakery in the middle of the block. No, Ellen thought he had better not wait for the little girls. All right, all right, they could go, they could go! They had been very good all day, and if Mother could find them anything half clean to wear they might go.

She led them into the new bedroom, the sparkling clean windows pierced by shafts of pleasant spring light from the slowly sinking sun. It seemed enormous after the compact modern little house they had left today. But it already looked homelike, Ellen thought, and to the chattering children it was already "Mother's room." She debated wildly: where were their clean linens?

Not in that trunk—not in that trunk. Ellen dropped upon her knees before her bureau, tore open the lower drawer, felt for the rustle of tissue paper.

Just to please Otis she would put them into their new frocks, the delicious, demure, soft, dark blue linens Aunt Mollie had made them. White socks, a touch of the brush to the dark curls and the thick fair mane, the wide dark hats pressed over blue eyes and black, and they were ready.

"Daddy, do these girls look nice enough to go for bread with you?" Ellen asked, leading them down. The father's face lighted as if by sunshine.

"Well, say—*say!*" he stammered. "Say, where 'd we get these outfits?" he asked with a look for his wife nothing short of fatuous in its pride. He walked off into the streaming sunshine, a little girl in each hand. She and her mother watched them go, then Ellen began to set the table.

"Well, we're *in!*" she said with a thankful sigh.

"That's the main thing," Mrs Cutting, covering shelves with white paper, brisk and strong at sixty, answered comfortably. "With the girls growing up and having their friends in, the extra sitting room is going to come in very well!" she added. "I don't know where you get your strength from, Ellen, you ought to be worn out!"

Ellen came behind her, locked her arms about the broad figure and laid her cheek against her mother's shoulder.

"So nice to have you with us, Mummy! It seems to make everything so much easier!" she said.

Later they sat on the steps. The blue linens should long before have been back in their tissue paper and their wearers sound asleep, but the occasion was a happy, irregular one, and when the ridiculous picnic supper was over everyone was too tired to unpack, and yet willing to prolong the happy hour.

Mrs Cutting rocked and dozed in the dimness of the porch; Ellen had the upper step, Margaret beside her. Otis sat below her with Patsy drowsy in his lap. The spring day was over, but the air was still warm, and twilight lingered on indefinitely in the pleasant and unfamiliar street.

"We shall be quite sheltered here all summer, Otis. The house facing sideways really gives us a good deal of privacy."

"I thought of that."

"It doesn't seem such a terrible neighborhood. That nice woman in the grocery told me that people were really beginning to restore these old brick houses now. I don't believe it 'll retrograde, I think it 'll improve!"

"I shouldn't wonder!"

There was silence again for a while. Then Ellen asked, quite as naturally as if he had just mentioned the subject:

"What did Redding say that interested you?"

"Oh? Oh yes. Well, I don't know how I feel about it. I thought I'd talk to you. Red says that old Baker retires next year, and there 'll be a general shift, and he wants to go into business for himself and wants me to go with him!"

"Otis!"

"Well, what do you think?"

"Oh, I don't know what I think!" But she was tremendously excited. "Just as you and poor Paul planned before he died," she mused. "Well," she added hardily, "you designed every inch of the Sterling Building, and you did practically all the Olympic Club!"

"That's what Red says."

"Oh, dearest, it would make up for that bitter disappointment about Paul last year!"

"It would—well, I bet it 'll work out!"

"Otis," said his wife after a dreaming silence, "wouldn't it be remarkable, someday, if we remembered sitting here on the steps and talking about—about Redding and Livermore, Architects!"

"Livermore and Redding, Red says," her husband answered with a grin. "He puts up two thirds of the money, about four thousand. But he says I put up the brains!"

"But is it so serious?" She was impressed.

"You bet your life it's serious! No, I'd rather have tried it with Paul," Otis said thoughtfully. "But I'm not sure but what Red is the better businessman."

Ellen Livermore mused silently for a while. Upon her charming face a smile deepened slowly.

"Darling, I'm so proud of you!" she burst out suddenly.

"If we do it—and we may not—you can thank yourself," said Otis. "I certainly wouldn't try it if we were taking money out of the bank for rent every month! But I can swing this place. . . ."

"The window-box house," said Ellen after a silence, convincedly, for the first of one hundred times, "would have been idiotic. I see that." After a while she murmured, "This child is asleep!"

"This one too," he said. And in an undertone he could say at last: "Did you ever see them look so gorgeous as they did today in those blue dresses? There was a regular riot in the bakery—people turned in the street to look at them."

"Darlings!" Ellen breathed against the fair little head that was so heavy against her shoulder. "I wonder what we ever did to have such children. I remember thinking that Margaret was the most wonderful child that ever was born, but in some ways Patsy's so loving . . . and so winning . . ."

"Remember being just a mite disappointed when the doctor said it was another girl?"

"Don't remind me of it," Ellen said soberly. "I remember the excitement, and no nurse, and the doctor there only five minutes. But from the minute I saw that dark little head she was my Patsy-baby, and I wouldn't change one of her curls for ten boys!"

"Lord, I feel sometimes that we never wanted a boy. My little girls—I don't know, as they trotted along beside me tonight they were so—so sweet, somehow. Boys go to girls' houses, but girls make a home—they make their own circle."

"The truth is, human beings don't know what they want," Ellen summarized. She kissed the blond head. "I thought I wanted to marry Lew Hungerford," she said, laughing softly.

"You bet your life you did, and for five or six years too!" her husband reminded her.

"Two or three years, dear! It was one part Lew and three parts the money and the house and the motorcars," Ellen countered. "Not that it mattered to you, engaged to Cora Hackett!" she added neatly.

Her husband chuckled heartily in the dusk.

"Lord, how crazy I was about that woman!" he mused. "She was a beauty too. Oh yes, she was! She's married again, by the way. I saw her brother; he tells me that both she and Yates have married again. She's in France."

"And where do you suppose the little Yates boy is?"

"I don't know—in school somewhere. She has no use for a boy of ten."

"Poor little lonely fellow! Otis, think what they miss, not loving him and taking him to circuses and tucking him up at night!"

"Think of Margaret, there, in boarding school!"

"Oh, don't!" Ellen shuddered against the heavy little body. "We *must* carry them in!" she said.

"In three minutes. But we'll only be young once, Ellen,

and they'll only be little once. It's so pleasant, sitting here," the man pleaded boyishly, shifting the sleeping baby lovingly. "I'm dog-tired, I'm going right to bed, but I love to sit here and talk about what we want to do to the house, and the girls, and going into business with old Red, and—I don't know—the things we might have done and didn't do!"

"I wouldn't walk across the street now to talk to poor old Lew Hungerford," Ellen said thoughtfully. "My dear, the plans we've made, the worries and the successes, and the day Margaret was born . . ." she added tenderly, her hand upon his thick brown hair. "I wouldn't give one of them up for anything in the world!"

"You—you kind of think you'd have me again, Ellen?" her husband asked, youthfully and a little gruffly, as he drew the caressing hand down to his lips and kissed the tired, slender fingers.

"I kind of think," she answered in her deep, humorous voice that was shot with rifts of real feeling, "I kind of think that if I was Ellen Cutting again, keeping books for Baker and Barnard, Architects, and if I could do what I pleased, that I'd marry the same man again and have my oldest child Margaret and my next one Patricia, and that exactly ten years later I'd move to the southeast corner of Westmarket and Wheeler streets!"

Her voice shook, and the fingers she had laid over his eyes were suddenly wet. They both laughed awkwardly and a little shakily.

And then it was time to go into the house and lock doors and put the children to bed, with Margaret's inevitable drink, and the pinning of blankets over restless Patsy, and time to wind the clock and peep in upon Mother for good night, and speak to Inga, who was eternally astonished by the thought of breakfast, and for Otis to brush his shoes, and Ellen her masses of dark hair. It was time for the Livermores, in short, quite ordinary young Americans, in a quite ordinary street, to settle down in the new home for the night.

No Party

HE SAW THE LOOK in her eyes that always made his heart stand still, and was quick in concerned apology.

"Babs, I hurt your feelings!"

"Oh no—no," she said, smiling through a mist, trying to talk with great bravado. "It's nothing! It's only that I want Christmas to be nice! If Mother's coming, and Aunt Grace and Uncle Potter and Tim and Mary, everything will have to be—*nice*. And—I don't know, it seems to be specially hard this year; more than I can do!"

An added shadow deepened the shadow that was already dark on Stan's young face.

"I don't know; maybe it's *that?*" he said hesitantly. Barbara smiled more brightly than ever.

"No, I don't think so!" she said. And suddenly she was crying, crying outright, with her throat choked and hurting and her breast heaving and her eyes flooding tears. She put her elbows on the table and hid her face with her hands.

Stan watched her for a minute. Then he moved his chair about the table and put his arm about her, and she shifted her young slender body so that her arm could creep around his neck and her wet face touch his. And for a moment they clung together, the man's face sober, the woman making no sound.

Then Barbara sat up and dried her eyes and blew her nose and said not quite steadily: "I'm sorry to be so silly!

"We can put Mother in the dressing room and Tim and

Mary in our room, and Aunt Grace in the spare room, and we can sleep on the davenport," she said, regaining self-control with every word. "I'll get those curtains up this week. And we'll have to buy a cot for Mother."

"I wish to goodness they weren't coming," Stan said simply.

"So do I," Barbara agreed. She repeated the phrase with deep fervor. "Oh, goodness, I wish they weren't! Wouldn't it be easy?" she said. "I simply ache when I think of it—turkey and wreaths and Carrie washing china! There's no *end* to it!"

"I suppose we've got to go in for the turkey and the wreaths?"

"Oh yes, and mince pie and pumpkin pie. And flowers on the table. But imagine Uncle Potter and Aunt Grace coming all the way from Bound Brook! It seems so silly. I never would have asked them if I had dreamed they'd come. And Mary! I should think she'd want to stay at home in that gorgeous new house and entertain *us*."

"We can call it all off," Stan suggested tentatively.

"Ah no, we can't do that, Stan! We let ourselves in for it."

"We let ourselves in for it," he said gloomily, "before the bottom dropped out of everything!"

To this Barbara could only answer with a subdued, "Yes, I know."

He had a pencil and an old envelope; he began to figure.

"Thirty dollars ought to do it," he said. "Funny how thirty dollars look when you haven't got thirty dollars! Six of those insignificant little fives——"

"Thirty!" she echoed, shocked, as his voice dwindled away. "It won't be that. More like ten."

"No, counting up Carrie for a couple of days to help you, and the cot and mattress, and presents for them all, I suppose, it 'll be thirty at least."

"Well, I'd have to send them something anyway. Oh,

Stan," said Barbara, passionately in earnest, "isn't it a shame the way things cost money! I'm getting so sick of money. I hate just the look of it in my purse, and the way it goes down! I ask you for twenty, and the first thing I know it's one five and some change. Why haven't people learned to get along without *money?*"

"Yep, it's tough," he agreed absently.

"Doesn't the budget—I've been so strict about it," she said wistfully; "doesn't the budget do any good?"

"Darling, it isn't anything you could help or I could help. When we married I had about three thousand of my father's debts to pay off. Maybe we should have waited—well, anyway, we didn't wait. Then came your mother's operation, about six hundred there. Then we struggled out somehow, except for that last five hundred, and bought this house."

"But that was an actual economy, Stan!" the woman said eagerly. "Thirty-eight fifty for rent, with two bathrooms and our gorgeous back garden!"

"Thirty-eight fifty plus twenty for mortgage, and insurance on top of that," Stan reminded her. "It's more like seventy. Call it seventy, and call the table another seventy."

"Sixty, Stan. I said two dollars a day."

"Yep, but you didn't count in flowers and Carrie."

"No, I didn't count in flowers and Carrie. Call it seventy. But even so," Barbara said, rallying, "that's only a hundred and thirty out of three hundred!"

"Car thirty-five," Stan said, writing it down.

"Is it that much?"

"Just about. We owe Duffy about a hundred for tires and repairs and so on, and I pay ten on that now and then."

"But add that up, Stan. That's only a hundred and seventy-five. That leaves a hundred and a quarter. That ought to be *oceans!*" Barbara argued, worried.

He looked at the figures, finished the sum off with two firm little naughts in the decimal places and a hard dot.

"Movies, telephones, carfare, clubs, books, clothes,

lunches, doctor, dentist, electricity," Stan recited. "Out in Phyllis' pantry the other night," he added, "it seemed nothing; my glasses fall on the floor and smash and everyone laughs and it's nothing! But when I go to Peyser it's fourteen dollars. But all this and the budget and Christmas wreaths aren't the thing," he went on with a deep sigh that tried to dismiss the subject, and in a more cheerful tone. "The thing is that we're about seven hundred and something over the line, and I've got a note that has to be picked up on the eighteenth—that's Friday."

"Seven hundred! I thought it was five and that we cut it down?"

"It was five, and we did cut it down. And now it's seven hundred, and five thousand to the bank."

"You and Fred Baker. The loan, you mean?"

"Yep."

"Well, that's business of course," she said, sighing. "But how did our household bills ever get up to seven hundred again, Stan? It's so darned discouraging," Barbara lamented. "And if—if," she recommenced with a timid glance at his serious face, "if it should be that—a baby, I mean? But it seems so silly after eight years! For so long we sort of feared, and sort of hoped, too, I suppose?" She stopped with a questioning look. "We *did* hope, Stan, in the beginning?" she asked, wanting his confirmation.

He did not look at her. He was making a careful line of little eights that might have been the microscopic prints of a baby's curled foot.

"Oh, sure we hoped!" he said, clearing his throat. "And even now—if it's coming along . . ."

"But what a *time!*" she wailed, her cheek against his again. "It means money, more doctor's bills, and my being laid up, and Carrie here, and hospital expenses and clothes and everything!"

Stan went back to his seat, looked vaguely around him, put two fresh pieces of bread into the electric toaster.

"Yes, I hope it isn't so," he said gravely. Barbara reached for his cup, jammed in the plug that started the coffeepot to bubbling again. She poured the clear hot stream steadily, but no sooner had she passed the cup than she put her elbows on the table again, covered her face with her hands and burst into bitter crying.

This time Stan did not go to her. He went on steadily with his toast and coffee.

"Don't cry, Babs," he said wearily. "We'll get out of this. People do. It's just that it all seems to come at once. Have some hot coffee, darling."

"Coffee makes me feel—horrid." She was suddenly composed, sobered by the spreading realization of real trouble. "That's one of the things that makes me feel pretty sure," she said. "The way coffee smells."

"You ought to go see Stubbs," Stan said with the quiet air of one to whom an extra burden or two make small difference. He laughed without much mirth. "I've got to see Pickering at the bank today," he added. "Why don't you see Stubbs?"

"Because I don't want him to say it's true," Barbara answered, tears showing wet on her pale cheeks. "I've always," she said thickly, "I've always wanted a baby. But to have you worried and be worried myself and to feel so—so *rotten* all the time . . ." Tears impeded utterance, and she was still.

"I never have felt much enthusiasm about it," the man stated quietly. "I've never been near a small baby; perhaps that's the reason. I want *you,* the way you used to be, always laughing and always confident. I want to be free of this accursed feeling that we've got to get money somewhere—money! God knows, I hate it. If we could once get clear!

"But now," he went on somberly, as she was silent, "now with five thousand to raise somehow . . . ! I've been to everyone I could think of, explained it. I've said that Fred and I went into it together and that the very day the poor old fellow was killed we'd been taking stock—we'd begun to see our way clear for the first time since the crash. We'd be in the black now, we'd be on easy street if Fred hadn't gone. Peggy wanted to sell out of course; I had to take over Fred's stock. . . . Well, maybe they'll renew. But Pickering had a young fellow at the office all yesterday morning, going over books, and he told me frankly—I would have liked to punch his face in for him!—that he didn't feel that he could make a very good report."

"Stan, would it help if we rented this place and moved into three rooms somewhere? I could cut our table down to—well, fifty. Forty, maybe. I'd do anything," Barbara faltered with a trembling lip.

He glanced up gravely; glanced back at his pencil tip again.

"If there's any chance of complications in July," he reminded her without smiling, "you'll need room. You'll need the back yard for wash. We wouldn't get enough out of making the change to make it pay. Nope, we'll have to stay here."

Barbara looked into space, and it seemed to her that life was a wearisome tunnel of despair.

"Could you find time at noon to get a bed of some sort, and a mattress?" she presently said, arousing herself to a consideration of the practical side of the matter. "I'll have to get the Chesterfield down from the attic. Oh, wait—I think there's a cot up there!"

"The Chesterfield? Oh, Lord, yes! I suppose your mother 'd be wild if we didn't have that in full view."

"Well, she made such a fuss about giving it to us. Stan," Barbara asked timidly, "shall you feel very sorry if—I'm not sure, you know—but shall you feel very sorry?"

Again he sent her a brief, unsmiling glance.

"Well, I don't suppose either of us will be *glad,* exactly," he said simply. "It seems a bad time. I don't know; maybe we'll get caught up sometime and maybe we're the sort of people who don't. But somehow I think you and I are the sort that would keep abreast of the current—you're economical, and I don't drink—if we once got *even*. And if Pickering renews my note we'll begin to hack something off that seven hundred; we'll begin with the new year, Babs, and see what we can do."

He kissed her kindly, abstractedly, and went away, and Barbara sat on for a long while, not thinking, merely feeling. The coffee cooled in the pot; the shiny toaster grew cold; the voices of children running to school died away into morning silence.

After perhaps twenty minutes of this she got to her feet. The dining room was a cheerless litter of newspapers and breakfast things; the kitchen, of course, was worse, with the omelet pan blackened and crumbs all over the table. Barbara went slowly to the wide davenport in the sitting room and sank down upon it, pulling a pillow under her head.

She could see disorder from here too: ashes in last night's trays, dust in a fine gray film on the rungs of the chairs, the card table up and strewn with cards. And she could think of a hundred other disorders; her bedroom one wild confusion; the front steps plastered with wet leaves; milk bottles were accumulating in streaked ugliness on the back porch; the bathroom was all wet towels and spattered water; garments for the cleaner heaped on the spare-room bed; notes and telephone calls lay neglected on her desk.

The processional went by her discouraged spirit dreamily; she seemed as unable as she was unwilling to stir hand or foot. The only thing in the world that she wanted to do was lie here and rest, rest eternally, and let the dust and the dishes and the disorder pile themselves up as fast as they liked in every direction.

Just why had she let herself in for this awful Christmas scramble? she wondered. What stupidity had made her think that she would have energy or interest to go through with one quarter of it? Every necessary detail, as she thought of it, washed over her with a fresh weariness. The whole house must be gotten into order; she and Stan would have to sleep for one night at least on this couch; or maybe Aunt Grace and Uncle Potter would mercifully decide to go back to Bound Brook late on Christmas night? No, they wouldn't, on account of Uncle Potter's bronchitis.

The house must be very warm. Wreaths. Red candles. Canned mushroom soup; turkey; cranberry jelly. And the terrible old Chesterfield and the cot must come down from upstairs. Perhaps Johnson, the furnace man, could do that. A tip to Johnson.

"Christmas," she thought, "will be on a Saturday—a week from next Saturday. I'll see about the curtains this afternoon. I wish I could lie here forever. Ten o'clock. Oh dear. Cool coffee smell is sickening. That horrible old doctor smoking a cigar in the next garden! Sickening. Nobody ought to be allowed to smoke cigars. I'm probably going to have a baby. And we're in debt. Stan has never noticed children; he's not glad. I'll love it, I suppose, when it comes. Hospital in July, broiling hot. I shouldn't lie here and lie here and lie here like a log. I'll make a start anyway, and get those dishes into the kitchen."

She brought her feet to the floor, sat on the couch, staring into space, her head hanging a little sidewise. Moments went by. Her face felt fuzzy and warm and she swallowed with a dry mouth. After a while she toppled over sideways and drew up her feet and shivered and closed her eyes, hunching her shoulders, digging her head down against the pillow. A little drift of sleep went over her. . . .

"What do women do when they have five or six small children and feel this way?" she said half aloud when the noon whistles blew. And again she dragged herself to a sitting posture and felt a wave of vertigo lessen and increase and lessen again, and managed to wander to the kitchen and put her hand on the eggy frying pan.

In the next ten days she achieved much more than she would have dreamed possible, but at the cost of continual fatigue. It was amazing to Barbara that anyone could be so tired all the time, and never get a full night's delicious rest, and never want a meal, and never catch up, and yet somehow live. The weather was cold, dark, sunless; furnace pipes clanked all day. When she went out to shop she walked carefully, partly because she felt tired and partly because the streets were slippery with frozen streaks of old snow.

Windows were putting on silver and red; bells and stars were everywhere. Draggled Santa Clauses with wire-netted pots appeared on the corners; women in furs carried bundles and laughed as they crowded in store aisles and searched for places in the omnibuses. Dark came swift and early. Carrie was in Barbara's kitchen almost every night now. It meant money, money, money, but there was so much to do, and Barbara herself felt completely unequal to it.

The Chesterfield came down from the attic, various chairs and tables being shifted about to accommodate it in the sitting room. Wreaths went up in the windows; Carrie climbed on a chair and lifted down the creamy Lennox plates with their borders of fruits and leaves. Napkins were counted; glasses washed. Barbara found the right present for her mother, for Aunt Grace; she was not so sure of Uncle Potter or of Tom, and had nothing for Mary, when the day before Christmas dawned in a furious cold windstorm with petals of heavy wet snow falling from time to time.

Carrie had planned to do all the bedrooms this morning, put towels and flowers and last touches everywhere upstairs and then descend to the lower floor and "rampage." Some earlier employer of Carrie's had evidently used this word in some connection with a tremendous effort, and to Carrie it expressed an occasion that demanded the tying up of her head in a thin-washed strip of old flour sack, the opening of drafty windows, the distribution of buckets of hot water, cakes of sand soap, boxes of fluffy powder, brooms, mops, brushes. The mere thought of such things on this howling cold morning made Barbara feel weary, but she tried gallantly to do her share; clearing the dining-room table so that Stan, when he came home that afternoon, could put in the extension leaves, piling dishes in the sink, standing dreamily with her hand under the running water, wondering why it was not hot this morning.

A large grocery order came from the market; the big, limp, cold turkey, the bottled tomato juice that Uncle Potter had to have on all occasions, celery, red cranberries in a damp bag. Snowflakes were caught here and there on the cans and packages; the delivery boy was breathless, his face wind-bitten. Barbara felt the packages cold and wet in her fingers as she put butter and sugar and pumpkin into their places.

Wind shook the kitchen windows, rattled them in their frames. The Smedburgs' washing, over the fence, stood out straight in the gale, straining on the line. The world was so bare of leaves that Barbara could see shabby back yards and garbage barrels and children's broken red and yellow toys far up the block. Dreary, dreary Christmas Eve!

Suddenly, in mid-morning, Stan was in the kitchen. It was still in confusion because Barbara had decided to get the turkey dressing started, and cook the cranberries, and make her piecrust, and then clean everything up at once.

So the percolator was there, crusted with lines of dried coffee grounds, and the egg cup and the cold broken rolls and the sticky spoons. The dishpan was full of tea towels that Carrie had set to soak, and the onions, thoughtfully set to boil today to save the house odors tomorrow, were drenching the kitchen in their own particular smell. Eggshells were in view; the little white enamel garbage can was open to show orange skins and onion peels.

Barbara paled, facing her husband.

"Stan dearest, sick?" she managed to say. She sat down slowly, one hand pressed hard on the table.

"No, no, no," he said, smiling. But he looked a little pale, too, and seemed slightly out of breath. "No, but you look sick," he said anxiously. "Gosh, what a terrible day!"

Tears came into Barbara's eyes.

"I tried some hot tea and it didn't work," she said. "I've been feeling—sort of—rotten."

"Couldn't manage any breakfast after I left?"

"No, it didn't seem to appeal." The colorless lips smiled.

"And you didn't eat any dinner," Stan said, half to himself.

"No. Couldn't."

"You ought to be in bed." He glanced at the cluttered table. "Can't Carrie do all this? Or we can call the whole thing off!"

"I'm not doing anything, really. Carrie's rampaging upstairs, that's why the house is so cold. I'll be all right. Mother's on her way, and to put off Uncle Potter and Aunt Grace would hurt them; they're that sort. And after all," Barbara said with a wan smile, "our oldest will probably inherit the fighting spirit. Darn him anyway!" she added whimsically, with an expression of nausea. Stan did not smile.

"I wish we hadn't let ourselves in for this," he said.

"It's only a party, darling, like all others, and it 'll be over like all others. All day Sunday I'll lie in bed, and you can bring me cups of scalding hot thin malted milk. I've a right to cravings now, you know, and I'm busily craving thin hot malted milk."

"Then for heaven's sake let me fix you some!"

"We don't happen to have any at the moment. Carrie's going to get me some at noon. Stan, what brings you home?"

He had seated himself at the table opposite her; he looked at her with a smile that held compunction and appeal and affection.

"Needing you, I guess, my dear. I had to see you."

"Pickering?" she asked. "He won't renew?"

"He says he can't." There was an odd gentleness in Stan's manner that frightened Barbara. "He told me that a week ago," he said.

"You never told me!"

"I wanted to see Bagshaw, and I wanted to see the federal loan fellows. No go," Stan explained simply.

Her eyes were round with apprehension.

"Then . . . ?" she asked on a suspended breath.

"Yep, it's curtains! It's good-by to Thomas Stillman and Son. I simply can't swing it," Stan said.

"Stan, you told them that you're to get the German things?"

"Yep, told them everything. I said that once I get those two agencies I'm set. I've all but cleared it now; I can't fail. By June I might actually be making money—I would be! But it's no good."

A silence, during which they looked fixedly at each other.

"What will you do, Stan?"

"Turn everything over to them, go through a liquidation."

"And what 'll *we* do?"

"Start over, darling. We'll find a room somewhere, I suppose, get a gas plate. I'll probably go in with Butler or the Vardells."

"You said the Vardells were crooked, Stan!"

"Well, *I* won't have to be."

"But why not Butler?"

She saw the hard red come up into his face.

"I was talking to Harwood Butler at the club Sunday," he began slowly and stopped. Barbara flushed quickly too; she did not follow up the suggestion.

"I'll love our room and our gas plate!" she said stanchly. And suddenly she began to cry.

Stan watched her somberly for a moment. Presently he said:

"I wish I could save you some of it. I hate to have you cry. It means everyone knowing, and selling this place, and selling a lot of our things, too, I suppose. And July."

"And I wish I could save you, Stan," Barbara answered, recovering her self-control almost as quickly as she had lost it. "Meeting men and explaining and all the details! But we can't, my darling, and we'll just have to go through with it. We'll have each other."

He came around the table to kneel on one knee beside her, and put his arm about her.

"My God, I love you!" he said. Barbara kissed him thoughtfully, her lips soft and warm against his eyes.

"That's all that matters."

"Look here," said Stan then. "I've got to go down to the bank; they close at twelve today. But I'll be back. Anything I can bring you?"

"Bring yourself. I don't know how much lunch you'll get, but we'll manage something. Carrie's going out for lunch; she has to take her boy to the doctor, but I'll have something for you. Is it frightful out?"

The windows and the gale rattled an answer.

"It's awful!" Stan said. "The wind is like a saw, cutting into your face. There's hardly anyone in sight downtown. But I can stay home this afternoon and help you; we'll get the cot downstairs. And by the way, tell Carrie I'll bring the malted milk. I'll be home before she is. What time is your mother coming?"

"Around four. She'll probably want to go to a movie and take us to dinner somewhere, but I'm ready here if she'd rather stay in, and Carrie 'll be on the job. Kiss me again, Stan. I'm not in the least afraid. We just have to—to tighten our belts, that 'll be all. And I'll—I'll get through July with flying colors. I'm the kind that's terribly sick and then has a ten-pound boy."

"Just the same . . ." he began dubiously. Then he stopped short, smiled in answer to her shaken smile, and was gone. The wind, swooping up over the kitchen with a shriek, drowned out the quick slam of the door.

Stan was out in the harsh whirl of it, pulling his hat down tightly, glancing up at the moving leaden clouds overhead. It might bring in a white Christmas, this fury of airs;

tomorrow might be as calm as midsummer, with sun shining coldly on fresh snow.

Wind. Boys with hard, wind-bitten faces, and square small bodies buttoned into mackinaws, were running and screaming and blowing horns; not many other folk were abroad. Shopping women in the department stores would make a general resolve to "get everything here and have lunch here." Small children would be kept within doors. He thought of the old persons, warm and idle in the handsome big memorial home, as he walked briskly past it. They would be thinking of presents, turkey, candy, like the children they were again.

He was kept waiting at the bank. His card, he thought with shame, sent in to one of the vice-presidents, would tell the story; there would be no hurry about seeing Stillman. Stan sat on a wide polished bench and watched hurried men signing vouchers, cashing last checks. Girl clerks came in and moved slowly in the long queue at the receiving window; money from Christmas sales must be deposited at once.

At one o'clock he was out in the rising fury of the elements again. Snow was flying now, scudding white along dirty gray sidewalks. The air was raw and fresh; it smote his face and hurt his lungs. He stopped at a drugstore for the malted milk; considered a sandwich and some coffee. Barbara would only want the hot drink; his lunching now might save her some trouble.

But no, she would be all ready for him, poor darling. Stan decided to walk home; a taxi meant forty cents; there was no convenient surface car, and the buses were wet, miserable scrambles and jammings at half-past one on Christmas Eve. He took the twenty blocks briskly, approached his house eagerly. It would be good to get in out of the battering wind, to shut the door and hear the gale howl defeated over the roof.

Exactly when a sense of terror supplanted his aimless thoughts, exactly when the crowd and the fire engines and the banners of smoke that were being snatched away into the wild wind smote simultaneously upon his senses, he did not know. He knew that it was the house next door—or on the other side—no, it was *his!*

He was there, slipping through the ring of spectators, gripping the arm of a thin, gray-mustached fireman. The man, plying a hose, shouted back.

"I can't hear you!"

"It's my house! Everyone out?"

"There wasn't anyone in except a colored woman! She's out—over there!"

Stan, without consciousness of purpose or movement or feeling, was beside Carrie, who was screaming aimlessly and holding the goldfish bowl. Upon seeing Stan she dropped it with a smash, her shriek turning to words.

"We ain't save nothin'! We ain't save nothin'! She gone burn to de groun' *dis* time! She sholy burnin' smack to de groun'!"

"Carrie, where's my wife—where's Mrs Stillman? Where did she go?"

"She's out, Mr Stillman," a neighbor woman whom he knew said in a deep man's voice. "The men went through all the rooms. Carrie here said that she was in the kitchen. She's out. She's probably gone somewhere to get out of the wind. My God, how fast it goes!"

The fire was making a great roaring noise, water was hissing, voices were shouting above the chunking, incessant choking of the pumps. Stan went around to the back of the house, brushing by several much-occupied men with a ladder who were hurrying in the opposite direction and who shouted at him to keep out and be unusually quick about it. He did not hear them at all. He heard his own voice saying in a low, natural tone, "She went upstairs to find the cot and lay down. She went upstairs and lay down and fell off to sleep. She'd had no breakfast, she didn't eat any dinner last night——"

He went into the kitchen and saw the turkey big and cold and neatly sewed now, ready in a pan. The fire was sucking and roaring at the front of the house; pink tongues of flame were busy with silky black charred wood in the dining room. It had gotten a good start, all right! Stan thought. The front stairs were awhirl; he went up the back stairs, remembering as he did so that the agent who had sold him the house had made a great point of the two bathrooms and the two stairways.

The spare room was all peace and quiet, with roses on the bureau, but in his own room fire was busily eating at Barbara's dressing table, and water drummed in a hard stream against a closed window black with wreathing smoke.

"Nothing to this!" he said aloud. "I'm all right!"

The upper hall was filling fast with choking smoke; the attic door was open. Stan took the stairs in three leaps, reached its shadowy space and emptiness. It was warm up here, and she'd probably been cold, poor little thing! Curled down like a kitten, sound asleep, she was lying on the cot, with an old fur coat over her.

Stan lifted her, coat and all. It was all done in a flash, for the air was not quite breathable now, and there were crackling noises overhead that meant the front of the roof was going.

"Stan, I can walk!" Barbara said in his ear, in a whisper, as they went down the narrow stairs. But in the hall below she choked and stumbled against him, and he caught her up again.

"Here, keep your arms in the coat. It's terrible out!"

The front stairway was blazing now; there was fire close overhead, screaming in the wind. Stan ran to the back stairway, but smoke poured as from a funnel when he opened the door; he could not face it. Barbara was clinging to him.

"We're all right, Stan!" she said and fainted. Stan flung her on the spare-room bed, opened a window and shouted to two firemen who were dragging the refrigerator into the yard.

"Get a canvas—we have to jump! Get the hose around to this window! It's getting very hot," he said loudly, not daring to turn around. "God, what a noise fire makes! The front roof is going to fall in, I imagine."

Down below they were running around the corner, dragging a hose; they were circling about a spread canvas ring—God bless them, but firemen were quick! The ladder, better wait just a few seconds for the ladder, and the gentle big arm of this red-faced giant in the rubber helmet, lifting Barbara down. All very simple; he was even laughing as he jumped into the canvas, staggered to his feet on the blessed solid earth.

"I thought my wife might have gone up to the attic for a cot. I went up for her. Is she all right?"

Of course she was all right! They held the crowd back, and Barbara, huddled warmly in the old coat, rested in the garage, in a salvaged armchair, and breathed deep and called herself contemptuous names.

"Stan, what happened?"

Stan's face was pale under grime and sweat, but he smiled.

"Nothing much. But I guess ten twenty-two is a goner!"

"Heavens, look at it burn! Did I faint, Stan?"

"You'd not have had a chance in the world," the deep-voiced neighbor said, "if your husband hadn't rushed in there! That colored Carrie of yours told them everyone was out."

"You were up in the attic, Babs."

"Oh yes—yes, I remember. I'd gone up to see if the cot was there. It was Christmas Eve—I remember."

"I'd just come back with your malted milk."

"Oh, Stan, how strange! I might have been . . ." She sat silent, watching the flames in the wind. Everyone had drawn back now; everything that was going to be saved from the Stillman fire was saved. Great tongues of red were leaping from the upper windows; the entire front of the house had fallen in. Hoses played and hissed in the wind. The drawing-room chairs, soaked through their tapestries, were speckled with wet flakes of snow; boys were walking curiously about the piled china; two small girls importuned Barbara in shrill, polite little voices:

"Kin we have your goldfish, Mrs Stillman? Our brother picked them up and we have them in a jar. We'll bring them up very carefully!"

"Look at the utter rubbish they've saved!" Barbara said presently on a feeble laugh. "Those old tennis rackets from the rubber closet! I wonder if Mother's portrait—that was the only valuable thing we had . . ."

"Seem lak aind de worl'!" moaned Carrie.

"You're coming right over to my house and lie down!" said the deep-voiced neighbor.

"No, thanks so much. Mr Stillman's gone to telephone for a taxi; he'll have made some arrangement for tonight." Barbara was still a little dazed. She stood up, and Stan wrapped the coat about her, and they went slowly to the waiting taxi through a fringe of sympathetic onlookers.

"Ah, it's terrible—Christmas Eve! Poor things. Christmas Eve, too!" Barbara heard the murmur on all sides.

They got into the taxi.

"I've got a room at the Baxter; it's comfortable and it's clean," Stand said. "I'll go out after a while and buy nightgowns and toothbrushes and things. And then when I come back we'll telephone your mother and Uncle Potter——"

Her pale, dirty face, under the soaked hair, was suddenly alight.

"No Christmas party!" she said with a great relieved sigh. "No turkey, no effort! I can go to bed and simply lie there —lie there forever!"

"Well, that's the silver lining then!" Stan said, his face turned about to look anxiously, lovingly at the face on his shoulder.

"Were we insured, Stan?"

"No, but the guarantee company is, so that's all right. Do you feel all right, my sweetheart?"

"Wonderful. Stan," said Barbara, "this is Trot's fault, and the first thing I'll do when he comes is give him a slap on his bad little face! If I hadn't been so ill I never would have gone to sleep in the attic, and then, when it started, I'd have been right there to turn in the alarm."

"Be careful how you threaten to slap my son," Stan said in an odd voice, looking out at the Christmas streets. "I'll not stand any bullying of Thomas Stanford Stillman, junior."

She straightened up, her face almost frightened, her eyes stars.

"Stan?" she whispered, a tremble of joy in her voice.

"I thought of him," Stan said, still looking away from her. "I said to myself, 'Your dad's got to begin taking care of you right now, Tom!' It was for both of you I went up those stairs."

She was strangling him, laughing and crying, her face hidden against his chest.

"Oh, Stanny, that's all I've wanted you to say! That's all I've been waiting for," she sobbed. "I wanted you to love him! Oh, I don't care now! I don't care about anything now! One room, and no money, so long as you love me, and we both love him!"

"Well, don't cry about it, honey!" he laughed. But there were tears in his own eyes. "Lord," he said, "there's nothing to it. I'll get a job. Things will be all right. I suddenly realized today what it means to a man to say 'My wife and the baby.' What do we care what anyone else thinks about us?"

"Oh, we don't!" Laughter had won the day; a few casual onlookers stared at them oddly as, disheveled, dirty, strangely clad, yet laughing, they went into the hotel.

She was in bed, sweet and clean, infinitely at peace, sipping a long glass of hot malted milk when he came upstairs from some telephoning fifteen minutes later. Stan sat down beside her to make his report.

"I caught your mother; she'll be down tomorrow and then she's going on to Bound Brook. I got Mary, and she and Tim are all agog and she's sending you some things. And your Aunt Grace said immediately that they couldn't have come anyway, as Uncle Potter has bronchitis, and she'd make her Christmas present a check. Now I'm going out to buy a few things, and at about seven I'll take you to a dollar table d'hôte at Roullier's and a movie afterward."

"Stan, do you feel most extraordinarily *free?*"

"Funny feeling, isn't it? I feel—well, equal to anything!"

"And the Chesterfield is burned!"

"Oh, I'm sorry. They saved the Chesterfield. It was one of the first things I saw, with four boys sitting on it on the sidewalk!"

"Well, you can't have everything!" Barbara said, and they both laughed.

"It takes a thing like this to make you realize that nothing matters except that we're together," Stan presently said, sobering.

"Ah, doesn't it?" she said. And for a while neither spoke.

"Stan, I've a Christmas present for you," Barbara began then, out of a peaceful silence. "I was going to wait until tomorrow, but I can't. I'll give it to you now."

"You haven't got it with you?"

She nodded, childishly mysterious.

"Uh-huh."

Stan looked at her curiously. She had rummaged a hand beneath the pillows; she brought it out with the fist tightly closed.

"You know that old coat that's been up in the attic ever since we moved, and that you wrapped about me?"

"Yep."

"Well, that was Aunt Florence's best fur coat, twenty

years ago, and she gave it to Mother, and Mother gave it to me when we drove up to Canada last March."

"I remember."

"Look what was caught in the lining—it had slipped in between the pocket and a seam. I found it there—oh, fifteen minutes ago!"

He looked at it; glanced at her, a little at a loss.

"A pin, eh?"

"It's my Aunt Florence's ruby; she left it to me," Barbara said.

"It's handsome. I guess it's kind of old-fashioned, isn't it?" Stan said, puzzled by her manner.

"Oh, terribly old-fashioned. It's fifty years old, that setting," Barbara agreed, studying it. "She left it to me in her will, you know, and then we never could find it. We finally decided that she had either lost it or sold it for Liberty bonds, as she did the necklace. Sparkle, dear, it's Christmas Eve!" she said to the pin. "She was very mysterious, Aunt Florence; you never knew her," Barbara continued dreamily. "She died before I ever met you. Well, there's your Christmas present!" she added, thrusting it into his hand.

"But, sweetheart, I couldn't wear it! Someday we'll have it set for you." Stan laid it on the bed.

"Defective, that's what you are," Barbara said compassionately, polishing the great stone on the counterpane, holding it to the light. "I went with my aunt once to see about insuring this," she said. "She never would insure it; she was very tight. This was twenty years ago; I was about nine. But the value they put on it at Gorham's was nine thousand dollars. And rubies have doubled in value since then."

Stan stared at her. At first the look she gave him in return was all mischief, but that changed. She put her slim hand, ring and all, into his, without moving her eyes from his face, and he saw the laughter merge into a mist of tears, into the tenderest look that any man ever can win from any woman.

"From Tommy and Mother, with Christmas love," she

whispered. Stan knelt down by the bed and lifted her hand to his lips and laid his black head against her shoulder. And she gathered it there and cradled it as if she loved the feeling of mothering her big man for a few seconds.

In the plain little hotel room that smelled of wood smoke there was silence, but down in the street Christmas laughter and Christmas bells were beginning to ring together.

Prisoner's Base

FORD LOOKED so savage as he came in that Dina did not dare say anything to him, much less mention what was really on her mind. Instead she put dinner on the table—the one o'clock dinner of sausage cakes and hot biscuits, sweet potatoes and stewed tomatoes, apple jelly and fig pudding. Ford liked hearty, hot, greasy food on these chilly spring noons; sometimes he would eat three or four doughnuts while he was waiting, and fall upon his meal with his appetite apparently unaffected.

Today he did not have to wait; Dina was ready for him. She sat down opposite him, eating little herself but watching keenly to see that he had plenty of butter and that the cream and sugar were handily placed for him.

"You cook these?" he presently asked, with his mouth full.

She nodded yes, anxiously adding a question: weren't they all right?

"Sure they're all right," Ford said. "Cash don't do any cooking, does she?" he added suspiciously.

"I don't believe she knows how to cook."

"That's not what I asked you."

"No," Dina answered quickly, apologetically. "Poor old Cash, she just clears up."

"I don't want any murderer seasoning my food!" Ford said.

"I don't know that they proved anything on her, Ford. She denies she was there at all that night. She says she wasn't allowed to put her witness on the stand."

"They all say that." Ford's first wild savagery of appetite

was a little appeased now, and he attacked his second helpings more slowly. "Can't trust any of 'em!" he said, picking his teeth with a rotary movement of lips and tongue.

"I suppose you can't." Ford Huddleston was warden of the prison whose shadow lay across Dina's dining table, and her kitchen and her bedroom. Its great brick walls rose above their lives like barriers between them and all the rest of the world. At their meals they talked about little else than the prison, and at other times they talked hardly at all. "How's that Mexican girl?" Dina asked.

"Got her in a jacket."

"Ah, poor thing. More coffee, Ford?"

"I don't know why you always ask me that. I always take it, don't I?"

Dina said nothing as she poured the smoking amber fluid into his big cup. She had talked only to half-crazed Lily Cash, her convict washwoman, that morning; she would have been glad of some little interest or distraction in a fresh conversation. But Ida Snow, the wife of Ford's assistant, had gone to visit her folks in Cleveland, and there were no other women near. Larkin Flat, the town, was two miles away.

"Oh, I had a letter from California," Dina presently said. She said it deliberately, bravely, but with a fast-beating heart.

"How d'you mean, you had a letter from California? That don't make sense."

"Well, I meant from—from Lin's folks. I knew you didn't like me to talk about 'em much."

"I suppose you got to tell me Chester is O.K.," the man sneered, wiping a walrus mustache after a long draught of coffee. "Head of his class in kindergarten and getting on fine. All right, I know it."

"Lin's brother Thomas is coming East as far as Chicago," the woman said. "He and Het are driving. He said he'd bring Chester and leave him here for a month, if you're willing."

"What's the big idea taking him out of school?"

"Oh, this wouldn't be until vacation, Ford!" Dina was so

eager that her color fluctuated painfully, and the thin hand on the table trembled. "This wouldn't be for 'most two months!" she said.

"Well, no use getting excited about it until the time comes."

"I don't know, Ford. It's April now, and those California schools close in June."

Ford Huddleston scowled, staring away into space. He finished picking his teeth and took out his pipe. Dina rose and got him matches and an old leather bag of tobacco. She sat down again, anxious and eager, her eyes glued to his face.

"No," he said suddenly. "I don't want him here!"

"Oh, Ford, don't say that, if it was just for a month! He'd have such a good time here."

"I'm not thinking of him. I'm thinking of you. I don't propose to have my wife forgetting everything else but a kid of five. When you had him you hadn't any use for me."

"That's not true, Ford," she pleaded mildly. "But he was only a baby then, he wasn't four. And the understanding—the understanding was," Dina stammered, made bold by desperation, "that he was to be with us."

"You mean before we were married?"

"Don't you remember, at Cousin Julia's? 'Member saying that he'd be just like your own boy?"

"Yep . . . Well, fellers say funny things when they're after a woman."

"But he's been in California seven months now, Ford, and that's an awful long time in a little boy's life."

"They're good to him, ain't they?"

"Well, I guess they are. But I never knew Lin's folks. I guess his brother Tom's kind enough. He's a doctor, and he don't live at the ranch with the old lady. But since he and his wife are willing to bring Chester along with their children he must be kinder goodhearted." Dina stopped; her voice sank to a note of wheedling. "He won't be any bother to you now, Ford," she said. "He's getting to be a big feller. If I had him here for a month seems 's if I could go on. He——"

"Seems 's if you could go on?" the man echoed. "What you talking about? What are you going to do if you *don't* go on? You women can talk more like fools than anything I ever saw! What more do you want than you got? Your husband run off and left you, didn't he?"

"He might of come back, Ford. He was killed in a log jam. That wasn't his fault."

"He wouldn'ter come back! His kind don't. He was through, all right. He'd had enough of his own kid whining and crying around, I don't know why I should put up with it! His folks said they'd take the baby——"

"Because you wrote 'em, Ford! You wrote 'em a year ago. I never would of! I never had had him away from me even for one night till you and I were married. I never thought I'd have to give him up. When you and I first began going together——"

Dina stopped and assumed a good-humored smile. When she spoke again it was lightly.

"Anyway, if I could have him for July this year," she said, "I'd send him back to Lin's folks in August without saying a word."

The man—he was a large, gross man whose two-days growth of heavy black beard, added to the effect of the straggling mustache and thin disordered hair, made him look unkempt—was watching her thoughtfully as he chewed on his empty pipe. He was in his shirt sleeves and vest; his big figure bulged shapelessly at the belt. His small eyes were narrowed into a suspicious smile.

"Better leave him where he is," he said comfortably.

"Oh, Ford, but it's such a chance to see him and feel like he's mine again!"

"Yes, well, that's just what 'll upset you and get you half crazy again, the way you were last fall. No, you leave him be, where he's lucky. He don't miss you by this time, and he don't need you. I know more 'n you do about things like this."

"But don't you remember, Ford," Dina said patiently, in

desperate courage, as he fell into self-satisfied musing, "the Sunday we fixed it all up that we were going to get married, that you and I walked past that corner house, back in Somersville, and you says, 'Wouldn't you and your kid like a home like that? Won't you do it for Chester's sake?' Don't you remember that, Ford, when I was sick and couldn't go on teaching?"

His small eyes moved over her ruminatively. Again he worked his tongue to clean his teeth.

"Nope," he said flatly. "All I know is, we gave the kid a fair chance. It didn't work. When his grandma wrote from California I happened to open the letter, and I wrote her. She said she'd gladly take him. I don't know what more you want."

"Yes, but I don't even know if he's well or not, Ford! This letter this morning is only the second I've had."

"Listen," the man said. "One man walked out on you because you were always sniveling and whining. You look out you don't find yourself looking for a job again!"

He got up and walked into the adjoining bedroom. Dina could hear the bed creak as he flung himself down upon it. In another few seconds his heavy deep snoring sounded throughout the cheaply built house.

It was a one-story house, one of a row of five. Two of them were empty; a third was the Snows', temporarily deserted now; a fourth occupied by bachelor assistant wardens; and the fifth, the largest and the corner building, was the Huddlestons'. To all five the prison walls supplied a back fence, and from all five the great rise of the northwest wall shut away the late afternoon sun.

Two miles from the prison the little prairie town of Larkin Flat lay open and level, crossed by railroad lines, boasting only a few two-story buildings, only a few trees. In the summer it sent a dazzle of alkaline dusty heat to the white sky; in the winter it was bare, brown, beaten down by rain and broken up into mudholes that reflected the homely little frame houses and the bare whips of the cottonwoods. Here and there, in a cottage yard, some homesick woman had planted geraniums and marguerites, but water was scarce at Larkin Flat, and gardens did not flourish there.

The town, forlorn as it was, however, was a haven of coziness and comfort compared to the prison that was reached by a bare stark ribbon of highway across the prairie. There was no green at all here; there was nothing here but the harsh squareness of unrelenting cement and brick, of barred windows, of clanking doorways within doorways, of cold sanitary smells of carbolic and antiseptics and hideous warm smells of cheap food, bodies, defective plumbing. There was a sack factory, a storehouse, a flagged gray yard for exercise and for the desolate activities known as "sports," and there was the row of five gray-painted cottages—that was all. One of the big buildings housed the electric chair and the row of cells for the condemned.

Dina was not an imaginative woman. Her years were but twenty-nine to her husband's forty-eight; her type had been, and in many ways still was, girlish, simple, confiding, uncritical. She was a little woman with pale gold hair and a transparent skin; tears, wakeful nights and hours of hard work and harder worry had shadowed her blue eyes and robbed them of color, and constant thought of her child had given them an eternally anxious, asking look, but she was still, in some odd unchangeable way, a comfortable, an essentially wifely little creature, and she managed to make homelike even the dreary environment in which she found herself.

But she wondered sometimes how it all had happened. How had she happened to marry Ford? Even sick, penniless and with little Chester to care for, it must have been a strangely blind hour that saw her promising herself to the big, blustering, conceited man. She had known Ford Huddleston to be one of the idlers, one of the bullies of Somersville—green, tree-shaded Somersville, with the big elms arching over it, and the good Sunday dinner cooking so decorously in Cousin

Julia's house; Somersville with green trees and gardens, with women sauntering home from club afternoons and baking smells floating from kitchen doorways.

Nothing good had ever come of the Huddleston blood. And yet Ford had seemed to be making an effort to be worthy of a wife; he had stopped drinking, he had been wonderful to little Chess. . . .

Then the prison appointment had come. Why? What had Ford ever done in his forty-five years except hang about drinking places, gamble, brag of his political influence? Why, quite suddenly, had this last boast been made good and he been appointed warden at Larkin Flat Prison? Ford, with powers of everything short of life and death in his hands! Dina and he had been married on the strength of the new job and had come together to this hideous place more than two years ago.

One hundred and fourteen men in his power now, and the possibilities of graft and abuse and favoritism and bribery infinite! He could drink all he liked now, and still he would be obeyed. Nobody could talk back to Ford in these days.

Dina roused herself from musing, began the usual clearing away; she stacked the dishes neatly in the sink, darkened the dining room just as Cousin Julia always darkened hers after a meal; set about dishwashing and dinner preparations methodically. Corned beef and cabbage for dinner, reheated biscuits and blackberry roll. The meat had been simmering all morning, filling the house with its gluey, unsalted smell. Dina took down from a shelf a jar of blackberries of her own preserving, poured the black liquid contents into a bowl.

It was just then that the telephone rang sharply, and at the same moment the voice of the prison siren rose in a great shriek and swept above the house like a shrill howling wind, bringing Dina's heart into her mouth with terror, and bringing Ford forth from the bedroom still half asleep, his face florid where it had touched the pillow, his fingers fumbling with vest buttons. He snatched the telephone.

"Who is it?" he shouted more than once. "How long ago?

What the hell have you fellers been about that you leave it wide open?

"It's Pool!" Ford said to his wife, hastily concluding only the essential part of his redressing. "Five fellers' time was up this morning, and we let 'em go. Luke says they think he slid out when they did."

"He's got a good chance then," Dina contributed, half to herself. She couldn't help it; when they escaped she always hoped they'd get away. "Murderer, Ford?"

"Killed a feller that got fresh with his sister. I don't know what it was——" Ford rushed away, and Dina followed him to the door and stood there, staring out at a world so bare and level that even a cottontail could hardly expect to escape across it in any direction, especially with the siren sweeping it with a wild alarm of warning, and the townsfolk running to their doorways two miles away to share the excitement of a getaway.

"I wonder where he is; they'll kill him if he's a lifer," Dina thought, her heart hammering. "Oh, poor fellow, poor fellow, what could he possibly do? Where can he go? They'll get him, and Ford 'll talk to him that awful, awful way he does. . . ."

She went back to her kitchen; knelt down. She was a praying woman, though there was small encouragement for trust in God here. Now she very simply asked her Father not to let Ford talk to the man the way he always did; not to say, "Well, by the time we get through with you you won't feel like running so fast! Tie him up, Luke, and let's have a little party to celebrate his getting away!"

Standing up, opening her eyes, a little dizzy, she saw a mud-spattered, dirty man in stripes standing in the kitchen door.

Dina was not frightened for herself; men in stripes were a commonplace with her. But a swift protective pity for him tore at her heart.

"For God's sake go give yourself up while there's time," she said in a sharp, furious whisper.

The man was staring at her.

"Say . . ." he stammered. "What do you know! *Say!*"

She looked at him now, and her knees grew weak, and her mouth filled with salt water. Dina sank slowly into a chair, never moving her eyes from his.

"Oh, my God in heaven!" she whispered.

He had a cup of water at her lips; she swallowed some with an effort that brought tears to her eyes. Her look did not leave him.

"Say, what a break *this* is!" he said. "Dina!"

"Lin," her lips said without sound. She sat staring at him weakly, broken.

"What are you doin' here?"

"I'm—I'm Huddleston's wife."

"Oh, my Godfrey!" Lin said. She remembered the old oath. "I bin here two months," he added. "Funny I never saw you."

"I don't go over much. I'm in the women's end a good deal, but Ford don't like me to see too much of the men."

"You ain't married to *Huddleston,* Dina?"

"For 'most three years now."

"You haven't had much of a break with your husbands, I'll say that," the man said after a pause. The siren was still now; the world very still. A chicken looked in the kitchen door, clucked reproachfully, went away. Dina panted; she was very pale. "You got a divorce?" the man said.

"There isn't any divorce if you're a Catholic," she reminded him, speaking vaguely, almost apathetically. "We thought you were killed, Lin, when the jam broke. The boys came back and said you and old Cap Cutter and three of the Portygees were washed right down the river. They found the bodies and there was a funeral. Then I took Chester and went to Cousin Julia's for a spell."

"I didn't go back," he said. "I wanted to get out. I was sick and Chester was sick all the time. I've paid for it, Dina. I've never had a happy moment since. I've wanted to go back and tell you I knew how mean I'd been. I always thought I'd make good and then come get you."

"How'd you come to murder anyone, Lin? Ford says it was someone insulted your sister. And when 'd you take the name Pool?"

"Curt Pool," he said. "I never done it, Dina."

"They all say that."

"But this was a frame-up. Dina, where's the kid?"

"Out in California with your mother."

"No?" the man said. And into his sallow, haggard young face a strange light suddenly came. "Is that right? Did you take him there? She's got a nice little prune ranch up in the Santa Cruz range; it's just about a living for her. Is he there?"

"Ford sent him. He can't stand Chester. When we were married he said he'd always give him a home——

"Lin," Dina said, interrupting herself in sudden agitation as the siren began to whine again high up in the sun-washed air of the chill spring afternoon, "you've got to get out of this and I don't know how I can help you! They'll shoot you down like a dog if you put up any fight, and there isn't a place between here and Larkin Flat that 'd hide a cat. What 'd you do it for? You can't get away with it!"

"I gotter have clothes," the man said.

"There isn't a thing—he'd kill me if I helped you, because there was three escapes and that Baretti thing last month, and he's scared to death of his job!" the woman said. "He isn't going to let anyone else get away. Oh, why did you do it?"

"Lissen, Dina. If I can get to Larkin Flat for the five train —it's after three now—I'm all right. I'll get West to Ma, and she'll hide me away until things blow over. Huddleston ain't anxious for any more breaks to be reported from Larkin Flat. Get me an overcoat anyway, can't you?" He came nearer, and she remembered the look in his eyes and the tones of his voice. "Look," he said. "Whether they get me or not, here's something I want to know. Will you forgive me, Dina? If I get away I'm going to do different now. Honest I am. I'm going out to Ma's and run her place for her, and try to give the kid a break. Will you just say that you aren't mad at me?"

She looked at him, trembling. June color flooded up under her fine skin and a young light softened her tired eyes.

"I've always loved you, Lin," she said thickly, very low. "You weren't ever unkind to me. You were sick, and Chester was sick—— Oh, my God, that's Ford!"

She broke off in a terrified whisper and went quickly to the dining room, closing the kitchen door behind her. Ford had thundered up the front steps to the barren little porch; three or four guards were with him.

"See anything of him?" he shouted.

"Run this way?" Dina called back.

"Sure he did. The boys seen him. He was hiding in the storehouse; he'd tunneled into it somehow. They knew he was in there for an hour; they didn't think he'd dare make a break for it. But he run out, half an hour back, when the siren began! Circle the house, boys, and look through the Snow place," Ford directed in an excited shout.

"He may be in one of them empty houses!" one of the men called.

"Oh, where is he? Where could he get to?" Dina's frantic thoughts ran. "The flour barrel—under those quilts in the closet—up attic—there's not room to stand up there, but he might have swung himself up through the trapdoor and be lying flat. He's fighting for his life now, sure enough! I guess you're wishing you'd let well enough alone now, Lin."

"Didn't see nobody?" her husband demanded, following her into the kitchen now as the men forged to and fro like hounds on a scent, their voices echoing up and down Warden's Row. The siren was silent again, and all other noises sounded loud.

"I was out in the kitchen, Ford. You know how awful that siren makes me feel!"

"He's a tough bozo, all right!" Ford was searching the closets, the laundry; he leaped down the cellar stairs. "He dropped his gun as he ran," he said. "So we're not going to have any trouble with that baby!"

Dina stood still on the kitchen doorstep, with the great walls of the prison rising to shut off her vision a hundred feet away. The zoom of the mail plane sounded far overhead; that meant three o'clock. It would come to earth in twenty minutes at Ridley, nine miles away. The free, graceful thing flashed white against a whiter sky; twinkled in the cold spring light. Dina's eyes followed it westward until the harsh roof line of the prison shut it from sight. Oh, to be in it, to be up in the clean cold air, to be anywhere but here!

At any second they might find Lin now; at some one of these ghastly seconds they would find him. They would drag him in, helpless and whining. "Aw, have a heart, Warden, you'd have done the same thing!" Lin would perhaps be muttering as he was hustled over to the jail again, to such limited mercies as Luke and Ford chose to extend. They had hosed Baretti until he was half conscious and then flung him into "solitary" until he raved and frothed and died—but no, there was no use being sorry for the men in the prison, there was nothing to be done about it, it was just that way!

The hunt went on. Men ran across the little back yards of the Row, jumped fences, looked down from upstairs windows, called back and forth. Ford ran to the prison, came hurrying home again. Dina thought that she never had seen him in a worse state of excitement and anger.

"If he don't show up pretty soon I'll get the dogs from Plaquette!" he said, jerking the telephone dial about with his fat forefinger.

"How'd he make the break, Ford?" Dina was sure, by this time, that Lin had somehow gotten himself into the attic. Impossible to think how he had managed it in the few minutes between her seeing Ford and his violent entry into the kitchen, for a dozen men were scouring the place now, and every garage and chicken house and porch corner had been turned out; but somehow he had managed to hide himself. She attempted to engage Ford in conversation as often as she could; wherever he was, time was an important consideration to Lin.

"He must have got into the storehouse when the men went out this morning. We let five fellers go today; they made the noon train from Larkin Flat, and he probably fooled himself he could get away with 'em. But nix. Luke checked 'em—they don't put anything over on him! This feller Pool—he's a lifer —got himself into the storehouse through a window in the back that's been blocked up for years," Ford went on, his eyes searching the open space before the Row as he and Dina stood on the front porch, his voice absent minded and lowered to little more than a growl. "He shoved the boxes around and squeezed in. Maybe he thought he could live in there for a while," he said. "Luke didn't miss him until the boys come back from lunch and then he asked Harry, and they scouted around a little—I was over here—and they seen his legs through the front window of the storehouse. But he run through and jumped out the back window—they didn't know it was there—and by the time they got Red and Tex he was running this way. He got behind this row of houses all right, and Tex come for me—I was just back in my office—and I says, 'No rush, boys, a flea couldn't get away cross these flats, and we'll do this thing right,' so we went down and checked 'em all over and locked 'em up. I don't want no more trouble here," the man ended. "That business last month didn't do me any good. When we get hold of Mr Curt Pool he'll wish he hadn't been quite so tricky."

Dina saw the three o'clock train pull itself like a shining little snake free of the village. Two miles away, every inch of the road open to the merciless prison inspection, and Conway, the stationmaster, vigilantly on the lookout. No, no hope there! She had talked to Lin ten minutes ago; no man could make two miles in that time—no man in prison stripes, with his sinister history written in his haggard face and terrified eyes.

"I should think he'd kill himself," Dina said, wondering if

he had, in one of the empty rooms of the two untenanted houses. Was that going to be the end of Lin Forrest, the lean, good-natured boy who had bought her a Florodora sundae at Witting's so many years ago, and had walked home with her, and told her that she was the cutest-looking girl he had ever seen? Poor Lin, who was just getting a start in the lumber mill when Chester had arrived, and times had gone hard, and Lin's health had given way. He hadn't been able to eat or to sleep; he had grown depressed and cross; "getting you and the kid into a mess like this!" And then had come the terrible wet day of his leaving her, and a week later the log jam and the sullen rush of the swollen river, and six men—and Lin among them, swept away in a jumble of raging, coffee-colored water and churning logs—logs leaping into the air, logs standing on end, logs hammered together as they had gone roaring down toward the rapids.

Weeks afterward, with their clothing torn and washed away and their faces obliterated, some of the men's bodies had been found. There had been a funeral, with Mrs Lin Forrest as one of four widows. To no one, least of all to terrified little penniless Dina, had it occurred to doubt the finality of that hour.

"But I surely liked that lumber town," Dina thought, staring at the bare prairie and the twinkling distant roofs of Larkin Flat. "The big trees, when they were wet, and the way the smoke smelled, and taking our lunch up to the falls in the summer."

"Got him!" Luke, the guard Dina especially disliked, shouted at this moment. He charged past the Huddlestons, husband and wife, thundered across the porch to the kitchen. Dina and Ford followed him. "He's up here in your attic, Mis' Huddleston!" Luke shouted.

"He can't be," Dina said. "I was right here in my kitchen all the time the siren was blowing!"

"He's here, all right!" the man repeated. "Looka the—looka that trap door!"

"Ford!" Dina caught at her husband's arm. "Don't let the boys shoot at him! You've got him—he can't get away. If you kill him there 'll be an investigation, and after all that trouble last month that won't do you any good. Robertson wrote you he wasn't any too well pleased——"

"Get out of my way!" Ford shouted, jumping up on the gas stove, extending big arms toward the trap door. But he had heard her. "Don't shoot, boys," he said as the other guards gathered in an excited group in the kitchen. "He ain't got a gun. If he gets funny with his fists knock him out, but we don't want the governor over here again. You picked up his gun, didn't you, Tex?"

"Red did," Tex answered in a soft thin wheeze oddly at variance with his gorillalike person. "He din' have nothin' in his hands when he run."

Ford mounted the ladder someone had brought and placed beneath the trap-door opening. With that strange unimaginative courage that had before this surprised Dina in him he thrust his head up into the dusty darkness above.

"We got you, Pool!" he called. "Come on down here. You can't get away with it!"

"Maybe you have and maybe you haven't, Huddleston!" Lin's voice sounded from somewhere under the low raw pine shingles. There was a crash of glass. "You ain't any more anxious to have more trouble here than I am!" Lin added. Ford withdrew a dusty head, yelled incoherently to his men. "He's out on the roof—he's got away. Get out there, some of you—get a move on—hold onto this ladder, Tex——"

They all rushed out to the front of the house again, Dina following. She ran down past the forlorn straggle of the garden, looked up at the roof. The guards were swarming along the Row from porch to porch now, yelling at the man's figure that was running fleetly from roof to roof above their heads. The five cottages stood close together. The man ran up the slope of one roof as if it were a little hill, ran down the corresponding slope and lightly jumped the five-foot space between the gutters to repeat the performance on the next roof. He was swifter than the clumsy tumble and scramble of the guards below; he reached the empty end house, sprang from its roof to that of the garage, bounded to the earth and was clearly to be seen running like a deer across the slight rise of the bare field beyond.

Lost, of course, but how he ran! Lin had been a famous runner years ago, and he had a hundred-yard start on his pursuers now. Dina thought of the plane that had moved so steadily westward half an hour earlier. Ah, if it had been against the cold white afternoon sky now, and had swooped down toward that straining figure, what an escape there might have been!

But there was no plane. There was only the open stubbled prairie bleak before the first breath of spring, and filled with mudholes where the men had dug rocks or played their cheerless ball games. Twice she saw Lin fall; both times he was up and away again like a hare, but both times the panting, shouting, cursing following of the guards was closer.

"Don't shoot!" Ford had bellowed after them. She went back into the kitchen and knelt down and covered her face with her hands. No hope, no chance for him. No God to pray to! Lin to be soused with icy water, punched and beaten, flung into the bitter exile of "solitary," and her little Chess, who so loyally loved his mother, who couldn't believe that "Mom" was sending him away even for a visit—little Chess seventeen hundred miles away! And herself presently to listen to Ford gloating upon the capture of his prey, and to serve corned beef and cabbage for supper.

"You couldn't do anything about this, God, and I'm not going to bother asking You," Dina said. The hunt was over now; they were bringing Lin back. She could hear their voices; she looked from her kitchen window and saw them crossing the field, the muddy figure walking uprightly enough, but tightly gripped by the big hands of Charlie and Red. "No, Lin, you couldn't make it; you never had a chance," she said.

She stuck a fork into the corned beef that was gently turning pink and gray, in the frothy, slowly boiling water. Dina was a good cook; that was all Ford wanted, and a woman. His meals had to be hot and prompt and hearty, and his wife hard working, silent, capable, and at night affectionate—there was Ford's whole idea of a mate.

The siren again; three short blasts. Silence, and then three more. That meant that the fugitive was captured. That screamed to all the farms and villages within reach of its hideous voice that there was no more danger from the runaway; wives could turn their children loose in dooryards again, and small boys go off to pastures to bring in cows. He was caught. Warden Huddleston was a darned fine warden in spite of that cruelty story last month. A lifer got loose today at noon and they landed him before four o'clock. . . .

Blackberry roll for dinner. Dina stooped toward her flour barrel, scooped up the sifter. Blackberry roll. "Oh, God, I hope they aren't going after him with the hose. God, help him! I went over to Mrs Goldberg's when Chester was born, and Lin came creeping in—he was crying. There never was a mean bone in his body. . . .

"Don't I remember how funny his face looked with tears all over it, and I wiping them off with my hand! Didn't it feel good lying there, and hearing Chess fussing! And the smell of tea when Linda Goldberg brought me in a cup. That was a long day. Four o'clock in the morning when Lin and I walked over to Goldbergs' and got Joe Goldberg out of his good warm bed. . . .

"Ford's certainly having a good time with Lin now. Well, if they kill him, like they did Baretti, there 'll be an investigation this time, sure enough! You'll not feel so good, Mr Ford Huddleston, if the governor comes over. . . .

"I wonder what Ford 'd do to you, Lin, if he knew what I'm thinking? If he knew I was remembering that day I wore my cross-barred organdy and my white hat, and we walked from the church down toward Mill Lane, and you took the key of our cottage out of your pocket? You said, 'Now don't you get scared, Mrs Forrest, I'm just the same Lin's been keeping company with you for three years. I haven't waited for you this long to scare you now. You and I'll get dinner together like we have at Julia's dozens of times. . . .'

"Seven years ago. My Lord, that seems more than seven years ago!"

Five o'clock, and Ford due home for dinner any minute. Lin was lucky if he had been flung, cold and muddy and supperless and aching from blows, upon the black verminous floor of the solitary cell. But it took the boys a lot of time to wreak their vengeance upon anyone who broke jail; they liked excitement, they adored a hunt, but none of them enjoyed the necessity of sounding the siren that notified all the surrounding country that another man had evaded their vigilance and was making a desperate rush for freedom. The "caught" siren was always sounded with especial fervor and repeated with what, to Dina at least, was nauseating gusto.

The telephone rang. The sheriff and the station agent and the authorities generally wanted to know if Pool had been captured. Yes, they got him, Dina answered patiently. They had him fifteen minutes ago—half an hour ago. Mr Huddleston was still over at the prison but they probably weren't answering that telephone now; it was after five, and there wouldn't be anyone in the office. She began to wish feverishly that Ford would come home, ending the episode, ending the horrible suspense of not knowing what was happening to Lin.

"I guess I'll stop praying," Dina thought.

A sudden new doubt assailed her. With Lin living—living beaten and soaked with cold water and flung into solitary confinement, it was true, and subsisting on water and dry bread, yet still alive—what was her status in Ford Huddleston's house? What could Ford do to her if he ever discovered that she was deceiving him, that she had not been genuinely a widow at the time she and Ford had married?

"He couldn't put me into jail, I should think. It wasn't my fault. The priest married Lin and me and read prayers over Lin's body with the rest of the boys that were drowned when the jam broke. Maybe I ought to get away. I've got 'most two hundred dollars saved. I always thought I'd use it for Chester's education, but it 'd get me someplace Ford couldn't find me. But if he found out he'd be meaner 'n ever to Lin. . . ."

It was almost six o'clock; the table was set and the supper ready when Ford's heavy foot sounded on the porch. The spring night had closed down dark and chilly, and Dina had lighted a fire in the black iron "airtight stove." Her kitchen was brightly lighted and warm, but the passage was dark, and at first she could only see that a man was with Ford; he was bringing someone home for supper.

The man followed him to the kitchen door; a lean man, with a rather white face and gentle sad blue eyes, and long clever hands. A man whose brown hair was wetly brushed, and who was clothed in worn garments obviously never selected to fit his thin breadth and his inches. Lin.

Lin. Dina stood staring, the color ebbing from her face. She was too completely stupefied to disguise her amazement, but fortunately Ford, who was in a boisterous, jovial mood, saw nothing.

"Got enough dinner for two hungry fellers?" he asked.

"I got plenty, I guess." Dina said in a third attempt to speak.

"This is Tom Mack, the feller we were chasing today."

"I thought it was Pool you were chasing."

"Well, we did too!" Ford said with a forced, hearty laugh. "Come in, Mack," he said. "Set down. Yes," Ford expanded it with relish as his shapeless, gross body itself expanded comfortably in a big chair, "we certainly got things balled up today. Mack's time was up this morning, and he left the pen with the others."

"Oh, 'sat so?" Dina said politely, setting another place. Her face was pale and her hands were shaking, but she did not look at Lin, and Ford never really looked at anyone. "Where's —where's Pool?" she asked.

"Well," Ford said, taking his knife from his pocket and paring his nails, "he's got away. He must be hiding out round here someplace, in some barn or silo, and I ain't going to make any fuss about him. We'll get him. The sheriff 'll have to know. I'll stop in and talk it over with him tonight, but I don't want the boys to blow the siren again. It does nothing but frighten the women. We'll get him, all right."

"Mrs Huddleston looks like she'd like to know how I got back into rocks, after I was let out," the visitor now said. It was Lin's remembered voice, and now that he had abandoned the hideous filthy striped prison apparel the men called "rocks" he was indeed Lin again, only older and thinner; he was the man she had loved so eagerly years ago, after her lonesome and bewildered girlhood—indeed, the man she loved still.

"Pool stole his clothes while he was washing up down at the canal," Ford explained. "Get a move on, Dina," he remonstrated. "Can't we eat? I've got to get Mack, here, to the seven-ten."

"I was discharged with four other fellers this morning," Lin explained, falling upon the corned beef with vigor. "Warden, here, drove 'em over to the noon train, but I walked. I been shut up for a year, and it felt good to me to walk where I liked again."

Dina moved her trusting, weary eyes to his face questioningly.

"I got a year for being mixed in with a gambling racket," he said.

"You weren't a lifer, then?" the woman asked mildly.

"No, but Pool was. And Pool worked a break while we was busy getting the boys discharged this morning," Ford said. "He must have hid in them cotton woods where the maller bushes are, down at the canal back of the grain elevator, and when Mack, here, stopped to wash himself and clean up he stole Mack's clothes. Mack had to get back into the rocks or go naked, and he come back here to explain to me and borrow some clothes." Ford gulped down masses of hot meat smeared with mustard, forkloads of steaming cabbage, wiped his dripping mustache. "Then what 'd you do, that you got caught in the storehouse, Mack?" he asked.

"Well, I followed Red in there when he went in for some beans. I wanted to talk to him," Lin explained. "But the minute he saw the rocks he went out again, and the door slammed and shut me in. Red and Tex and some of those others stood guard, and they sent for you, Mr Huddleston. I was afraid they'd shoot, and I wasn't sure they'd seen me, so I lay low. Well, after a while I saw the back window, and I thought I could sneak round here and explain, but the boys seen me and it was all up. Maybe," Lin added, with an apologetic smile for the warden, "maybe I shouldn't of been so scared. But I ran without thinking what I was doing——"

"You should of yelled that you wasn't Pool," Ford said genially. "But you boys get so you can't look no one in the face!"

"I know. But when you've been in the pen awhile you sorter lose your guts," Lin apologized simply. And as Ford's bullhead was lowered over a second mammoth helping of food he winked at Dina.

"Where you goin' now, Mack?"

"I'm going West. I've got a wife and kid—well, my wife ain't there just now," Lin said. "But I'm expectin' her to join me," he added.

" 'Sat right? Know you was sent up?"

"Does she know I was in the pen? Yep, she does," Lin answered after a moment. He split open a fifth biscuit. "Home cooking surely does taste good, Mrs Huddleston," he said.

"I guess it doesn't make any difference to her," Dina said. "If she thought you were dead she might of married someone else, but as long as you were living she'd know she was your wife."

"In that case—if she thought a man was dead, and married again—a woman would just have to leave a letter for the second man, explaining that she was no bigamist," Lin said. "And get out. He wouldn't have no claim on her."

Ford was not listening.

"Ain't there something else?" he demanded.

"There's a blackberry roll. Wait a minute." Dina carried plates into the kitchen, came back with the smoking pudding and the graniteware coffeepot. The men finished their dessert hastily; it was quarter to seven now, and the dirt road to town was filled with mudholes. Ford went around the corner to get the car; Lin and Dina had a moment together on the porch.

"How'd you get him to bring you to supper?" the woman asked in a quick, furtive undertone.

"Oh, the boys had turned the hose on me and they were getting pretty rough. I guess he felt a little ashamed, and nervous maybe, on account of Baretti passing out on him last month. He don't want any more trouble."

"Why'd you do it, Lin? You're smarter than he is. You didn't have to hide in the storehouse and make that getaway. All you had to do was walk into the office and say, 'I'm Mack.' "

Ford had driven the muddy car to the floor of the garden twenty paces away; Lin was leaving.

"All right!" Ford yelled.

"Say this over to yourself until you understand it, Dee," Lin said hastily, shaking hands in farewell. She remembered the little name of their early days together, and the little shack at the lumber camp, and the smell of wood smoke and wet redwoods, and her heart began to dance in a way it had long forgotten. "Say this over till you get it," said Lin. "Pool is a friend of mine and a good feller; I've known him seven years. He done what he did—well, never mind that, but there was reason! He killed a skunk, and his wife's dying of tuberculosis, and there's children. He's got a hide-out up in the Canadian woods where they'll never find him. He's got a name fixed and a place and everything. And his brother-in-law is the mail pilot—get that? The mail pilot that went down at Ridley at three-twenty, see? I had to keep things going until three-twenty. After that I knew he'd be all right. He had four hours to walk nine miles. We swapped clothes at the canal, and I spattered my face with mud. I took care they wouldn't recognize me——"

"Come on!" shouted Ford. Lin ran lightly down the steps, waved a hand from the car.

"See you again someday, Mrs Huddleston!"

"See you again!" Dina echoed. She leaned against the door-post and looked up at the wheeling stars in the dark blue sky of spring; there was a new moon and she thought it seemed friendly, as if it was smiling down at the tired little woman in the shabby kitchen apron in the shadow of the big prison. When she brought her eyes to earth again she felt as if she had been praying—really praying, not just making herself say the words of prayers.

The lights of the town twinkled on the prairie, two miles away. Dina could see the train pull in, a caterpillar of little lights, could see it draw away again, toward the Far West.

Lin was on his way West now, on his way to the mountains and the redwoods, and the frosty mornings green and shadowy, and the long summer days scented with tarweed and prunes. Chester was out there, little slender, anxious, affectionate Chester in his belted sweater and stubby little shoes, waiting for "Mom."

"Gee, it is certainly one sweet night tonight. I guess we are going to have spring early after all!" Dina said aloud. "I guess it does you good to pray even when you've kinder stopped for a while," she said.

Yesterday

THE GIRLS KNEW that they were late, but they hoped for a little luck. They avoided the street door above its flight of impressive stone steps and thick balustrades, and went in at the side of the house, where there was a narrow passage between the den and the library. The musty smell of both rooms met here, and added to it was the odor of rubbers from the slope-ceilinged closet under the stairs. Charlotte and Isabel ran up the back stairs and noiselessly opened a glass-paneled door in the upper hallway, gaining their room breathless and panicky just as the big cuckoo clock on the stairs and some of the lesser clocks began in their various chimes and tings and gongs to strike six.

They began as rapidly as possible to take off their street attire, too desperately in a hurry even to laugh or exchange a word. Isabel wore under her brown cloth coat a suit of black serge lined with a bright scarlet silesia. The skirt flared in five wide gores; the hem, which touched the ground, was reinforced with a brush-braid binding; the jacket was many-seamed and fitted close, with a score of darts, to Isabel's rounded young figure.

Revealed, when she took off these garments, were her full petticoats, flounces of embroidery on flounces of muslin, and her corset waist, snugly buttoned over the corsets themselves, and the ribbed long shirt under the corsets. Isabel took a house dress from the closet; it was challis, blue and pink flowers on a cream ground with a design of ribbons in the pattern, and yards and yards of narrow blue ribbon binding bretelles that went over the shoulders and the double flounce of the skirt. She began to work on its myriad hooks.

"Listen, are you going to?" she demanded of Charlotte at this point.

Charlotte, brushing a heavy crop of light brown hair, gave a nervous giggle.

"Nobody's coming in," she offered.

"No. But it might get Papa accustomed to it," Charlotte said and both girls burst into laughter.

"Here it is," Isabel said. She took from a hiding place under ranged linen garments in a lower drawer a small pad made of gauze and filled with cornstarch. "If you will, I will!" she told her sister daringly. They looked at it and at each other.

"He'll kill us. He said only bad women powdered," Charlotte said, hesitating. She leaned over her sister at the bureau and boldly padded her face with the starch. Her freshly washed, shiny young nose took on a softened bloom. "I love it!" she said.

"You'd have to wipe about half that off," Isabel said, eyes wide, scandalized fingers touching her cheek.

"Oh, I know. We were just fooling, Mamma," Charlotte said with an apologetic laugh. Her mother had come into the room.

"Not a very nice sort of fooling!"

Mrs Buckminster was a large, generously built woman, dressed in dark blue silk with a trimming of bands of lighter blue velvet. Her plainly knotted gray-brown hair was wet from recent combing. Her eyes were small but kindly; on the level plateau of her forced-up breast a small watch was held by a silver ribbon pin. "Give me that, Isabel," she said, reaching an imperious plump hand for the powder puff. "You know how Papa feels about that. I don't see why you girls want to be so silly! Do you think any man respects a woman who makes herself common with paint and powder?"

"But, Mamma, your face shines so when you wash it!"

There was a passageway with a basin of chocolate-and-pink marble between the enormous bedroom and the adjoining chamber. Isabel was standing there now, washing herself vigorously with hot water and soap.

"But if that's the way God intends us to look, dear?"

"But you curl your hair and Lucy's hair in rags every night, Mamma, and surely God doesn't make you do that?" Isabel was looking over the red-and-white stripes of the fringed towel. Her mother glanced at her and said simply:

"Isabel." Charlotte gave her sister an uneasy glance; Isabel began to search in the closet for her slippers. There was a silence. "Why were you so late, girls?" the mother presently said, her displeasure waning on one score only to rise on another.

"We were in before six."

"Not much before six. Papa came up here looking for you around five."

Oh, this was bad. They had hoped that not even Mamma would notice their lateness! Now Papa was on the warpath!

"Did you stop at Miss Muzzy's?"

The sisters exchanged stricken glances. They had forgotten. Their mother spoke with a deceptive gentle patience.

"What were you doing, girls, that you forgot that I wanted her next Tuesday and Wednesday?"

"Mamma, I'm sorry," twenty-two-year-old Charlotte said penitently.

"And how sorry would you be if I said that as a punishment you could not go to Geraldine's on Saturday?" Mrs Buckminster said in a quiet, judicial voice. Isabel spoke impetuously.

"You couldn't do that!"

Her mother looked at her with slightly narrowed eyes.

"I *couldn't?*" she asked pleasantly, almost archly.

"Oh, but, Mamma, listen! It's to be a spiderweb party, and Gerry has the partners and everything arranged!"

"That wouldn't make a mother hesitate to do what she felt was best for her children," the older woman said.

"Ah, but, Mamma, you won't! Mamma, truly it wasn't six when we came in," Charlotte, who was her mother's favorite among eight daughters, said daringly. She leaned her fresh face and the crown of her hair against her mother, hugged her laughingly. "It's the only party we've been invited to since Clara's," she pleaded.

"I will wait and see," Mrs Buckminster said judicially. But she was softened. "It may not have been six o'clock," she went on. "But it was dark, or almost dark. See, it's black outside now. What sort of girls go about without an escort in the dark, do you think?"

"Was Papa mad?"

"He wasn't very pleased. That Lieutenant Browne wrote you, Charlotte, and Papa naturally wanted an explanation."

"Wrote me?" Charlotte's face was all roses.

"Yes. I believe it was a very nice letter, but Papa doesn't want you to have it until he's thought it over."

"Oh, Chatty, what fun!" Isabel said, excited. Chatty's pretty face was a mask of pleasure and excitement.

"Oh, Mamma, he didn't!" she said. "What did he say?"

"Papa didn't tell me. He didn't seem displeased, but he said he would wait and think it over."

"Mamma, he'll let me have it, won't he?"

"I don't know, dear. I know that he wanted to know if you had encouraged the young man to write, and I said of course you had not. That's all I know."

"Chatty, a man writing to you!" Isabel exulted.

"Now don't go and get your heads full of romantic nonsense," the mother warned them. But it was plain to be seen that she was rather pleased and excited too. "I suppose now the beaus will begin," she said in complacent resignation. "It 'll be Belle and I all over again!"

"Did Aunt Belle have beaus, Mamma?"

"Indeed she did."

"Then why didn't she marry one of them?" Isabel's tone was full of surprise and pity.

"Your grandfather didn't approve of girls having admirers, you know. He always"—his fifty-year-old daughter laughed ruefully—"he always used to treat our young men terribly," she said. "Poor Pa," she added, "he was practically a nervous invalid from the time I first remember. I hate to see your father going that way, but I suppose it's God's will."

"Papa feel bad tonight?"

"He came home feeling chilly, so I had Belle make him a cup of chocolate and he got into bed. I think one of his headaches is coming on; he seems real upset. There's the bell now; come on, girls, or we'll all be late!"

Their father was limping down the long flight of stairs to the lower hall, just ahead of them, as they descended. He was in his handsome claret-colored smoking jacket, his gray hair scraped over the bald place on the shiny dome of his head. The gas had been lighted in the lower hallway now; low beads of it burned in the parlor and library. In the dining room ten jets flared with the soft sound of flowing air, above the long table.

"How's your head, Papa?"

"I've no headache. Who said I had a headache?" He looked sharply out under beetling brows. "Carrie, did you say I had a headache?" he asked his wife suspiciously.

"I said I was afraid one was coming on, Papa," his wife answered, fluttered.

"How late were you girls running the streets?" the old man demanded. "Nice thing if my friends at the club asked me why my girls are running the streets at all hours!"

But his favorite, Isabel, was beside him, and now he asked her, with a semihumorous pettishness, to pour him out a glass of sherry. The girl's hand was white against the dark ruby color of the decanter as she lifted it.

There were sixteen persons at the table now, unrolling

their napkins from the silver rings, turning up the big tumblers that were turned down at every place. Most of them had entered with that effect of silence that indicates an unwillingness to attract attention on any terms. Besides Isabel and Charlotte there were six girls; Fannie, Lucy, Olive, Dorothy, Mabel and Bess, whose ages ranged from seventeen to nine. There were two boys, Arnold junior, twenty-four, the first-born, and Johnnie, who was Mabel's twin, ten years old.

Also there was Gramma, a toothless, gentle, mumbling old lady of eighty-four who removed her food from her jaws when she had chewed it a little; there was Uncle Booth, a dipsomaniac brother of Papa's to whom nobody ever spoke and whose room was back of the sewing room on the fourth floor; there was Aunt Belle, forty-one and skittish and unmarried and given to making fun of herself as an old maid; and there was Eliza Buckminster, fifty years old, also unmarried, dependent, delicate, a slave to her brother, his wife and children, his servants and friends.

Everything in the dining room was dark and heavy, draped or polished or shining to perfection; enormous rep curtains looped in chains shut off the two big bays; there were also shutters of fine brown slats, and lace undercurtains. The chairs were solid; on the sideboard silver bowls and flagons were ranged.

The meal was also heavy. With the thick soup Papa drank his sherry; then came fish and cucumbers and boiled potatoes, and the claret was served. Mamma helped both these courses—the soup from the big china tureen, the fish from the enormous platter. A maid and a helper passed the sauces.

But Papa carved the mutton and Isabel put a blob of mashed potato beside each thick cut and dribbled the flour gravy artistically over it. There were also a chicken pie, beans, cabbage, boiled onions, hot biscuits and fried egg-plant. Papa did not care much for vegetables, but he ate heartily of mutton and chicken and mashed potato. He kept the handsome cruets revolving, more salt, more pepper, Worcestershire sauce on the meat, vinegar on the cabbage; reached his big hand continually for another biscuit with which to mop up gravy; washed the whole down with claret and seemed to feel much better. The dessert was hot tapioca-apple pudding and crullers. Aunt Eliza had made the crullers, and when Arnold, who was always full of the old Nick, dropped one and at the same time thumped his foot on the floor, she was so hurt that she left the table in tears.

"She was all upset because Bess said she wasn't named for her," Mabel volunteered. Her pudding was too hot and she bent her head over and let the dessert drop back on her plate.

"Mabel!" said her mother.

"What 'd she do?" The man of the house peered down the long table.

"Nothing, Papa," his wife said. Mabel watched her father fearfully.

"I asked what she did, Carrie."

"She really didn't do anything, Papa. It was just that her pudding was hot."

"Well, I guess she'd better not eat it then. Leave the table, Mabel," her father said. In silence, bitter tears flooding her dropped eyes, Mabel obeyed. A single sob sounded as she closed the big door. There was a somewhat conscious pause after she had gone.

"You didn't ask any whippersnapper lieutenant from Cheyenne to write to you, did you, Chatty?" her father asked suddenly, turning upon his oldest daughter.

"No sir." Chatty's blue eyes were clear.

"Sure you didn't?"

"Absolutely."

"Honest she didn't, Papa," Isabel said eagerly.

"I didn't ask you, Pussy." But he never was very cross with Isabel. He was eating cheese now, smearing it on crackers. He asked Peter, the colored butler, for the decanter of whisky. "You girls going anywhere special tomorrow afternoon, dentist, something like that?" he asked.

"No sir," said Charlotte and Isabel together, expectantly.

"Then you stay at home with your mother all day, and we'll have a little less running the streets," he said quietly. "Remember, now, you're not to leave the house tomorrow. You can get at your sewing or your reading."

"Yes sir," the older girls murmured, their faces crimson.

" 'Was thinkin' today," the old grandmother spoke up suddenly in childish pleasure, "of the day your gran'ther brought me down to the city. They'd filled in Montgomery Street then, where it useter be all watter, and there was stores instead of just walkin' down to the Embarcadero to see what th' ships had brought in! Welsir, he come after me with a pencil and 'Looky here, Betsey,' he says. 'There's a smart trick some Yankee thought up for ye!' It had a little rubber fastened on 't with a brass holder. Well! I took that back to Marysville and I surely thought the world and all of my pencil! They wasn't anyone back there who had one like it, and it was town tok for nine days of Sundays! Your gran'ther . . ."

Her voice mumbled away into silence. Mrs Buckminster, flushed and breathless at the head of the table, after much helping of vegetables, some undertone directions to the younger children and several asides to the maids, finished a mouthful of hot meat, drank generously from her tumbler of claret and water and observed conversationally:

"If things go on we'll see queerer things than pencils with rubbers on them. Did you see that article in the paper today about the telephones? Talking from one town to another as natural as if you were in the same room!"

"They're coming," the man of the house said, wiping gravy from his walrus mustache by lifting its bushy weight carefully. His pink full mouth always showed rather sensually as he did so; from her very babyhood it had always had a queer, repellent fascination for Isabel when she saw it so. "They are certainly coming," he said. "Mr Willie Cates asked me yesterday if I would like to invest in some bonds for the company they're forming. I said no. Too much of a speculation. Never can tell how long the American people will be interested in that sort of thing!"

"There 'll be hotels someday with telephones on every floor, you mark my words, Papa," the oldest son said, passing his big pink plate for more pudding.

"Foolish talk, my boy," the father said briefly.

"You don't agree with me, Papa?"

"It isn't a question of agreeing with you or not agreeing with you. You are wrong!" Arnold senior said heavily.

His son laughed cheerfully. Little Bess, the baby, had straggled about to the foot of the table and was standing crying and complaining at her mother's ear.

"She says she's got that stomach-ache again, Papa. She hardly ate any dinner at all. I guess you spoiled your good dinner with all that candy this afternoon, baby," the mother said fondly. "Don't you want part of Dorothy's cruller?"

"Mamma, she gave us ten examples," Olive said aggrievedly. A stout little girl of twelve, she leaned her stocky form and ruffled school apron against the table. Her straight dark hair was held from her forehead by a round comb and hung in a mane on her neck; she wore a silver locket with a blue stone in it.

"Lissen, Mamma, looky, she gave us five, and they're terribly hard," Dorothy added eagerly. "And then Jessie Arkwright—listen, looky, all she did was sort of look surprised, and she says—Miss Cutts says, 'Very well, for that you girls can take the other page, too, and do all of them!' And, Mamma!" Dorothy, who had gotten home from school at quarter past three and who had been playing paper dolls and buttons quite happily for several hours thereafter, began to weep bitterly at this point. "We can't do them!" she sobbed. "They're *terribly* hard!"

"Mamma, honestly we can't!" Olive added, crying too. Both girls were stout. It was Mrs Buckminster's steady grievance that her girls were either too fat or little skeletons.

Half the Buckminster children were overweight and the other half bilious; it seemed hard luck for a woman with eight daughters to marry off. Olive and Dorothy were of the stout type; they had been eating candy in the afternoon and had now finished double helpings of everything, including the pudding, and had topped the dinner with a banana apiece from the fruit display on the revolving silver stand in the center of the table. Their faces looked hot and wretched, their pudgy little hands continually removed their back combs and pushed their thick hair freshly away from tickled foreheads and burning ears.

"But of course you'll have to do your homework; I'm sure Miss Cutts knows what she's about!" Mrs Buckminster said, not unsympathetically but firmly in a low, monitory tone as she peeled a banana for Bess.

"But, Mamma, we have our compositions, too, and our jography!" Dorothy protested. Their mother had pushed back her chair now and had Bess in her lap.

"Isabel will help you with your examples. Isabel, can you help the children with their homework tonight?" Mrs Buckminster asked. Isabel was twisted about talking to her father. She turned her bright face about.

"Tuesday night, Mamma, and all the wash 'll be upstairs. I usually help Elsa."

"You help the girls then, Fannie," Mrs Buckminster, addressing a thin girl of seventeen, said decidedly, "until Isabel gets the wash put away."

Fannie's eyes met Lucy's. Lucy, uncomfortable in her first corsets, was two years younger; the two girls were always in league against Isabel and Chatty, as privileged, graduated and older.

"Couldn't Charlotte do it, Mamma? We've our own schoolwork to do," Fannie said primly.

"Fannie," said her mother quietly. Olive looked up eagerly, but Fannie was too old to be sent upstairs to wait for a whipping. But Olive saw Fannie's ears grow red as

Fannie looked through a glaze of tears at her plate. Lucy tossed her head as one sulky and defiant, but she said nothing and took care not to meet her mother's eyes. "All go upstairs now and get your work started," Mrs Buckminster said. Bess was almost asleep and stood crying and stiff-legged like a dazed little chicken when her mother set her upon her feet. "I doe want to go to school tomo'w," she wailed.

"She's got another of her colds, Mamma."

"Yes, I thought she had! I guess Bess is a Truslow, all right," the mother said ruefully. "My mother used to say that she'd had a cold for twenty years. Winter or summer, it didn't make any difference!" She got to her feet, walked about the table to her son's chair, laid a plump hand on his shoulder. "Going out tonight, dear?" she asked.

"Yes 'm." Arnold junior got up and kissed her. "I'm meeting Jack; I'm late now!" he said.

"Don't be too late tonight, dear!"

"No ma'am."

"Jack White's a regular dude, isn't he?" Isabel said. "I saw him with his mother at church Sunday. Checked overcoat—oh, my! Just my style!"

"I don't think that's a message a boy cares to deliver for his sister," Mrs Buckminster said monitorially.

"I think I'll fool her and deliver it," Arnold said. Isabel and Chatty immediately chased him about the table, emitting horrified shrieks at the thought. Isabel even ejaculated, "You holy terror!" and as she said it caught her mother's eye and knew that she would be reproved later. Mamma did not like that expression. Arnold presently stopped, both sisters hanging on him, at his father's chair.

"How about a little spondulix, Papa?" he asked with studied casualness, laughing and panting still. His father glanced at him over his glasses, took out a wallet. Aunt Belle was also lingering near.

"I think I'll ask you for a little pocket money, too, Arnold," she said. "I'll probably be gone before you're down in the morning."

The man of the house gave his son a small five-dollar gold piece; his sister-in-law a round big silver dollar.

"What's happened to the strong-minded lady that had music pupils?" Arnold senior asked sarcastically. Miss Truslow laughed, reddening a little.

"They come to lessons, but they won't pay!" she confessed, putting the money in a pocket in her skirt. "I guess you're right, Arnold: ladies don't belong in business!"

The children were now straggling upstairs, hopping or crawling from carpeted step to step; Johnnie found the particular knobbed brass rod that was loose on a certain tread and rattled it as he always did going upstairs. Dorothy had hidden a pencil behind one tight stretch of the runner; she groped here and there but could not find it again. When Fannie finally called her sharply to come upstairs and start on her examples she began to cry and said that her head ached.

Aunt Belle was getting Gramma to bed in the little back room; they could hear the old lady protesting: "I b'lieve my water-brash is comin' back on me, Belle!" Elsa, the upstairs girl, and Alma, the waitress, were putting away the wash, and tonight the cook, Annie, had come up, sweating, stout and faintly mustached, to assist. It appeared that Mrs Hicks, the laundress, had been summoned home at noon because her grandson Frankie had been hurt by a runaway horse in the street that morning, so the other girls had finished the ironing. All afternoon a fire had raged in the little laundry stove, and the flat-bottomed irons with the big 7s stamped into their sides had been clamped on the stove, thudded on the linens, clamped back on the stove again. The Buckminsters had ten irons, a number of which to be proud; ten irons meant that as many as three persons could be ironing at once without undue waiting.

Now Cook and Alma and Elsa were tired. Indeed, they

were aching with fatigue. The younger maids had merely piled the mountain of dinner dishes in the pantry, as Cook had piled pots and pans belowstairs. They would dispose of them when this weekly wash business was done. Almost in silence they carried the flat heavy piles of big sheets to the big linen closet, went into the girls' rooms, laid great heaps of frilled nightgowns and tucked and embroidered undergarments on the bed. Each of the eight Buckminster girls wore at least two white petticoats a week; in summer their muslins and dimities counted up to perhaps forty garments more. But as this was March, no light frocks were worn now, and the curtains from the various big rooms were substituted in weekly batches. Mrs Buckminster liked to call herself the old-fashioned kind of housekeeper who did her housecleaning all year long.

Isabel helped the maids untangle the bewildering puzzle of handkerchiefs, stockings, towels. Gramma had a pair of warm red flannels in the wash every week; this week Aunt Belle had a scalloped crocheted underpetticoat of brown, with red arrow stripes. There were more arrows on Johnnie's little school shirts; Papa's and Arnold's shirts were handmade with many fine parallel tucks.

All over the spacious bedroom floor there was activity in the close spring evening. Johnnie had opened the hall window, a thing forbidden on account of the danger of night air, and dropped a pencil on the front steps. Then he and Mabel had had to charge downstairs and rush out on the stoop to recover it. Isabel heard Papa shout, "Who opened that door?" and Johnnie's explanation. Meanwhile a steady discontented murmur about her aching back and her waterbrash came from Gramma's room. Fannie, in the old nursery, where the naked gas jets were shrieking and where the air was hot, was sulkily superintending the homework of the younger girls. Dorothy felt so wretched that Cook puffed down to the kitchen and brought her up some hot water with soda bicarbonate in it. In all the rooms low beads of gas had been lighted. When Charlotte went into her own room she drew the jointed bracket toward the bureau mirror and turned up the gas, and wondered if Lieutenant Browne thought she was pretty. Isabel was presently replacing Fannie as schoolmistress, was being consulted as to compositions and examples, was begging Olive to keep her hot hair from falling all over her, Isabel's, neck, as she demonstrated the position of Hugh and his quarts and pints of milk, and was meanwhile writing a letter to Josie. Josie was her adored best friend whose Papa had died and whose Mamma had remarried and taken Josie to Sacramento. Josie and Isabel wrote to each other three or four times a week; a letter from Josie would keep Isabel excited and happy for a whole day.

Aunt Eliza came in and apathetically took Bess off to bed. As usual Bess cried and whined and clung to Isabel, and as usual Aunt Eliza never seemed to hear her. She merely waited, and finally the tired, tearful little girl went away. Mrs Buckminster came upstairs to see why the children were so late and was in time to defend Johnnie against Isabel's scolding.

"Mamma, he doesn't do one thing! He waits and copies Mabel."

"Oh, I don't think so, Isabel," her mother said mildly.

"I do not!" said Johnnie eleven times in rapid succession.

"He writes his name at the top of the paper and then he just doesn't do another thing!"

"Looky, Mamma," said Dorothy. "I drew two little flowerpots on my composition. D'you think Miss Brewer will like them, Mamma? Do you think Miss Brewer will like them, Mamma? Mamma, looky——"

"Mamma, where's the old map? I and Olive have to bound eight states——"

"Mamma, Jocko came upstairs, and he couldn't get out—it wasn't his fault——"

"Help Johnnie just ten minutes more, Isabel. It 'll be nine o'clock then, and they'll all have to go to bed. Did Bess go to bed? Was Elsa up here? Papa has to send her with a message to Mr Porter's house."

"Oh, Mamma, that's way across town!"

"I know, but Peter's gone, and Papa has nobody else to send."

"Couldn't Arnold? He could take the trolley."

"He's gone downtown," his mother said and sighed. "Elsa," she went on, "can get the nine o'clock trolley. She may have to walk back. Well, it won't kill her if she does. She's young and healthy. I'm sure I used to love to walk when I was young."

"Elsa has a sweetheart; he's a carpenter. He'd walk with her if he only knew," Fannie said daringly.

"Who told you about it, miss?" Isabel asked.

"I don't like you to talk about such things, Fannie," the mother said, "and I don't allow the maids, as you know very well, to have followers. I've told all of them that before engaging them. Elsa gets her twelve dollars a month——"

"Mamma, does she get as much as that?" Isabel asked, struck.

"Indeed she does. I don't know what the girls do with it! She says she gives it to her mother; there are seven or eight children. I hope she does. Now hurry up, all of you. You know Chatty and Isabel have to go to bed at ten, and you're wasting their whole evening. Get started on that, Johnnie. Let me see that, dear." She stretched out her hand for Isabel's letter.

"It isn't quite finished, Mamma, and there's one page I have to copy. I'll bring it down when I come."

"What do you have to copy it for?"

"Blot. Johnnie bumped into my elbow."

"Oh, that's all right then. I thought you might have written something to Josie that you were ashamed of."

"Oh, Mamma, no!"

"How's Papa feeling now?" asked Chatty.

"Not very well. He says he doesn't think that fish was very

good. Poor Papa, he has his father's headaches. I'm going to beat him up a sherry-and-egg before he goes to bed. Come down soon, girls; he likes to have a little time with you."

Ten minutes later, leaving a disorderly darkness on the bedroom floor for Alma to wrestle with in the early morning, Chatty and Isabel descended to the sitting room. This apartment was not so elegant as the parlor, not so stately as the drawing room, not masculine and scented with leather and cigar smoke like the den. It was comfortable and homelike, filled with easy chairs, furnished with a coal fire and bookcases and a big center table. Beside Papa's deep leather chair a droplight with a Welsbach burner cast a cone of mellow illumination; from the center of the ceiling sprang a cluster of lights, flaring away noisily in peach-pink skirts of opaque fluted glass. There was a shiny black hod for the coal and a blower for the fire; a handsome brass spittoon was placed conveniently near Papa. His chair was close to the window, a few feet from the fireplace. On close nights, as tonight, he liked to have the window opened a few inches, so that he could hang a hot hand out in the cool night air. But in the main he agreed with Gramma and Mamma and all other authorities that dangerous miasmas were abroad at night, and the big house was accordingly hermetically sealed from sunset to sunrise.

When Isabel and Charlotte came down he was sleeping lightly, his full bearded face flushed and his big chest moving uncomfortably. Isabel took a hassock at her mother's knee; Charlotte, noiselessly turning the pages of Louisa M. Alcott's *Work,* chose a seat with a better light. Both girls were as conscious at the moment of Ouida's *Moths,* hidden in the bookcases behind the set of Great American Statesmen, as if it were a presence in the room. They had never asked Mamma about it, but they knew her opinion of Ouida. Mamma was extremely careful about their reading. She had caught Isabel and Charlotte reading the story of *Faust,* in the front pages of the libretto score, some weeks ago, and had been deeply displeased.

Pauline White had slipped *Moths* into Chatty's frightened hand two days ago, and Chatty, coming into the house with it, and hearing Mamma scolding Alma in the upper hall, had carried it into the sitting room and hidden it behind the long untouched books. Just how soon or under what circumstances she and Isabel could dare take it out again, and how they could possibly manage to read it, was all undecided now. But they thought of it whenever they were in this room, and often when they were not, and their hearts beat faster when they whispered to each other in bed at night, how awful it would be if Papa took it into his head to look at those old sets of books someday and found it! The Great American Statesmen, however, had been crowded out of the real library as not handsome enough for it; no one had ever opened them. Papa had bought them years ago to help fill shelves; long years from now they would find themselves in a secondhand bookstore somewhere, still uncut and unread.

No, *Moths* was safe enough at the moment. It would be quite different when they were reading it, but despite all risks, read it they would. The girls had read two of Ouida's earlier books and had thrilled to the manly charms of the most fascinating heroes that ever had come their way. To Chatty, David Copperfield, after Dora's death, riding to Canterbury on a winter afternoon to ask Agnes to marry him, had always been an almost unbearably romantic spectacle; she could hardly read of it without a shortening of the breath and a quickened heartbeat. But Ouida's men, with their sophistication and their devilish ways and sureness of charm, outdistanced even David.

Isabel had been secretly in love with Byron. She had his picture in her handkerchief drawer. *Don Juan* her mother had cut out of the big illustrated gift book and burned, page by page, but there were shorter poems of his in the *Household Book of Verse* and Isabel had read them over and over, had thought of him dashing them off, and loved him unashamedly if unadmittedly. But that was over now. Now Strathmore had wiped him from her heart. To read a new Ouida—oh, the thrills of it!

Tonight when she entered the sitting room she gave Mamma the eleven pages of her letter to Josie, three of them lightly crossed with postscripts. Both sides of the paper were covered with her sprawling girlish hand; Mamma put on her glasses and read them all patiently, a look of indulgent protest and of puzzlement in her eyes. Now and then she laughed a little and shook her head; Isabel watched her eagerly. Sometimes she helped her mother find the right place to read.

"Isabel, I cannot understand how you and Josie can find so much to write to each other!" Mrs Buckminster said when the pages were all read and back in the envelope.

"But you don't mind, Mamma?"

"No, dear, I don't mind. But it seems such a waste of time. Two silly girls, scribbling nonsense like that to each other. It does seem as if you could find something better to do."

"Ah well . . ." Isabel smiled pleadingly. "Mamma," she began again with sudden animation, "may Chatty and I run to the corner and mail it?"

"Oh, please, Mamma?" Chatty added eagerly, looking up from her book.

Mrs Buckminster laughed indulgently.

"Why, I think you two have lost your silly little noodles!" she said. "Go out at night without your father or brother? What would Papa say?"

"But, Mamma, it's *only* to the corner."

"I know, dear. But it's out of the question. Now don't be silly about it, Isabel. You knew very well when you asked me that I wouldn't consider it."

Isabel looked through disappointed tears at the fire.

"I think Josie can wait for this very important information until Monday," the mother said, playful and placating.

Chatty took a low chair beside her mother's; the heads of the three women were close together. As they murmured they glanced cautiously from time to time at the sleeping man.

"Mamma, why does a boy have to sow wild oats?" Chatty asked in a low voice.

"Who told you anything about wild oats, Chatty?"

"Well, Papa always says that. Don't you know, Monday night he said to you, 'I suppose the boy has to sow his wild oats like all the rest of 'em!' "

Mrs Buckminster sighed heavily.

"I've never questioned Papa about that, Chatty. I've always felt it was something men would rather ladies didn't discuss."

"But was Arnold riding with Bob Sessions in his buckboard the night he was arrested?" Isabel asked interestedly.

"I tell you I don't think we ought to discuss it, dear."

"Nell Aldrich says her cousin knows Bob Sessions well, and he's *fast,*" Chatty said daringly.

"Chatty, I don't like you to talk that way."

"He took a bad woman to the Poodle Dog to dinner. Nell Aldrich's cousin said that his father was there with some men from the club——"

"Charlotte!"

Charlotte was silent. Isabel said, gallantly filling the awful silence:

"He scorches all the time. Little Pansy Frost takes dancing from Mam'selle Richter, and her rooms are right out on the park, and she says every time Bob Sessions takes his bicycle out, practically, he scorches."

Mrs Buckminster was not listening. In a low, pained voice she said:

"Chatty, we have to go back to this. What do you know about bad women? Who has been talking to you and Isabel?"

"Nobody, Mamma," said Chatty, very uncomfortable.

"But somebody must have. Tell me, Chatty, or I'll have to report it to your father, and you know what he's likely to do."

"Arnold told me," said Chatty. It was the sure way out. Her mother's face altered. Her first-born son could do no wrong.

"Arnold certainly would not talk to his own sisters about . . ." she began and hesitated, frowning.

"Oh no, Mamma, he didn't *talk* to me about them! I was speaking about the Poodle Dog Restaurant, and that Papa said he would take Isabel and me there some family night, and he said not to go there, that fellows like Bob Sessions took some pretty queer friends there, and then Nell Aldrich said that her cousin——"

"I don't want you to encourage Arnold to tell you such things, even in the kindest brotherly way, dear, and I don't want you to discuss them, and I don't want you to think about them," Mrs Buckminster said, laying an admonitory finger tip on the lip of her oldest daughter and speaking with steady kindness.

"No, Mamma."

"You and Isabel must promise me that you will put all such things out of your heads."

"Yes, Mamma."

"Mamma," said Isabel, "listen, this is something Chatty and I really want to talk to you about. It's about Santa Cruz, in June."

Mrs Buckminster, knitting now, glanced at her daughters over her glasses.

"Well, Papa said he would give you the twenty dollars each, and you could each have your two weeks with the girls," she said. "Aren't all the girls going? I thought there were to be twenty of you."

"Yes, I know, that's right, Mamma. But Papa said we

couldn't go unless Fräulein Stimml went as a chaperon and was with us every minute. When we're swimming and everything!"

"But, girls," said their mother with a genuinely astonished look, "you didn't expect to go without a chaperon!"

"No, Mamma, of course not. But Josie's married sister will be there, and Betty Payne, and the Monteagles' mother."

"Betty Payne's younger than you are, Chatty."

"But she's married, Mamma!"

"She's a very giddy little thing. And I don't know Josie's sister. Mrs Monteagle I do know slightly, but not enough to impose on her the responsibility—oh no, darlings, Papa wants to send Fräulein, and that's settled."

"She's so frightfully nervous about us that we never have any *fun,*" Isabel said with a break in her voice as childish as Dorothy's had been a little while earlier. "She just follows us round saying, 'Your mamma von't let you do dat!' until we're nearly *crazy.*"

Mrs Buckminster touched Isabel's pretty tiptilted little nose with the end of a knitting needle.

"Then you will simply have to go crazy," she said good-humoredly. "Poor me, with two crazy daughters!"

The girls laughed sulkily. Isabel muttered under her breath.

"What did you say, Isabel?"

"Nothing, Mamma."

"If you feel that you'd really rather not go," the mother said smoothly, in a tone whose every self-confident cadence they knew by heart, "you may come with the other children and me to Cloverdale. Papa, you may be very sure, isn't going to insist upon your going to Santa Cruz. Chatty," she went on reproachfully, "how could you be so silly as to suppose that you could go unchaperoned?"

"We didn't, Mamma. Here's what we were thinking." Hope revived in Chatty's voice. "Why couldn't Aunt Belle come, Mamma? All the girls adore her, and she'd love it, and it 'd be a wonderful vacation for her, too, and we'd be angels for her, Mamma, *honest* we would!"

"But Aunt Belle isn't married, darling."

"I know, but she's old. She says she's nearly forty."

"But she isn't *married,* dear."

"Well, but neither is Fräulein, Mamma!"

"That's quite different, Chatty. Fräulein is a governess—a teacher. She gets paid. Now don't be little silly-billies about this, girls. There's no use discussing it. I'd be delighted to have Belle have such an outing, and of course Papa wouldn't have to pay her. But I have to think of you girls first."

"Mamma, you don't know how awful Fräulein is! You can't start dancing with anyone but what she's watching and asking everyone around the most embarrassing questions, if he's married, or anything!"

"Well, I know, dear, but that's the way it has to be. I don't suppose poor Fräulein has a very good time, sleeping in the same room with you two chatterboxes. I want you to be very considerate of her and not be up too late if there's a beach party or a dance. She gets cold very easily."

"But, Mamma, honestly——"

"Why, what a tragic face! This is only March, darling, and the party isn't until July. You're not going to cry now about something that isn't going to happen until July? It's ten o'clock, girls; I believe I'll take Papa upstairs; he might as well sleep in his bed as here. When Elsa gets back with a message from Mr Porter she can bring it up to my door and I'll wake him if I think it's necessary. I think it's about that Japanese tea shipment; he had a dispatch about it in the office this morning from New York. Willy Cutter wrote it in New York yesterday and Papa gets it this morning by telegraph! It seems too wonderful! Come, Papa. Come, Papa. Time to go to bed."

The man rose up bewildered and fuzzy. His big mouth was torn open in two or three devastating yawns.

"Bedtime, hey, Mamma?" he asked. "I've got that fish

taste in my mouth yet. Annie did something to it that spoiled it. What have you women been gossiping about here?"

"No gossip." Isabel went to the wall and twisted a rotary bell. They could hear its hysterical jangle faintly, far below, in the big kitchen. "When's Peter going to sleep in the house again?" the girl asked. "Alma's been on the go all day."

"As soon as his leg is well. He goes to the hospital and has the doctor see it every night and then goes home and stays with his wife. She fixes the dressings. Alma hasn't very much to do," Mrs Buckminster said.

Alma appeared, very pale, with beads on her forehead. She was tying on her apron as she came in.

"Will you put out the lights, please, Alma, and lock up? Peter won't be here this week. And, Alma," said the mistress in a low voice, "another time put your apron on in the pantry. Don't dress on the way upstairs. You haven't company in the kitchen, have you?"

"No ma'am. We were puttin' the dishes away, becuz Cook helped us with the ironin' becuz of Mrs Hicks's little boy bein' hurt in the street."

Papa was locking windows. Now and then he stopped for a great yawn. The four Buckminsters trooped sleepily upstairs; there was silence everywhere now, and darkness except for beads of gas here and there. The girls went into their own room and began to undress. They took off dresses, petticoats, underpetticoats, corsets, tucked and embroidered nether garments of fine linen, corset covers, long ribbed shirts and long ribbed lower garments that had to be folded and smoothed every morning around their legs under the black lisle stockings. They set this clothing on chairs, washed their faces with hot water and soap, brushed their hair, put on their long white nightgowns with the pleated, buttoned yokes, and knelt, their four hands locked, to say their prayers.

"Oh, Isa," said Chatty then, in a whisper, "do pray that Papa gives me Frank's letter!"

"Frank's?" Isabel whispered back. "Oh, Lieutenant Browne?" she said. "Well, he wrote you anyway."

"Isa, he's so wonderful! And he—well, I told you what he said. He asked me to call him Frank and he called me Charlotte."

"Well, let's say our prayers and think about it," Isabel suggested.

They had only reached this point when an uproar broke out in the house. The girls jumped to their feet, excited and expectant eyes meeting. For weeks they would discuss this delectable moment with insatiable appetite. Something was happening!

Aunt Belle's voice, crying, or was it laughing? Papa's voice shouting; Mamma's voice soothing and frightened. Then a closing door, and Fannie and Lucy creeping in from the adjoining bedroom, wide-eyed, to tell what they knew and speculate as to what was going on.

They crouched together on the wide bed, four night-gowned sisters. Now and then Isabel or Fannie, the more daring spirits, crept to the door, opened it a crack, listened. Nothing more to be heard or seen, except that the stairway gas and the gas in the lower hall were lighted; sure signs of something extraordinary. Was Aunt Belle in Mamma's room, and were they all talking?

"Maybe someone's shot President Arthur, like they did Lincoln?" Lucy suggested.

"You said Aunt Belle didn't come to bed, Fannie?" Isabel asked for the fifth time. Belle slept in the room with the younger girls.

"No, she didn't."

"Maybe she was helping Annie in the kitchen."

"No, she wasn't. She had her coat."

The door opened; their mother came in. She looked hard at Fannie and Lucy; it was the old spanking look, one of love and duty and sorrow, and Lucy had to reassure herself that she was too big for the old form of nursery punishment, as she and Fannie melted from view.

When alone with her older daughters Mrs Buckminster said:

"Something has happened, girls, and I don't want any comment on it, and I want you to go *straight* to sleep. Aunt Belle just came in. . . . Yes, she had been out. She has just told Papa and me that she and Captain Runyon of the Merchant Marine were married three months ago."

The girls sat straight up in bed, paling with the shock. Comment? They could not have spoken to save their lives. Their mouths fell open; their eyes blazed.

"Yes. You'll hear some of the details tomorrow. We don't want a word to the other girls or to Gramma. Aunt Belle's been crying, of course, but Papa's been very nice and gentle with her, and you're not to make her feel that it's ridiculous or anything like that. Now don't talk about it; go to sleep. Turn your pillow over, dear; you've got the daytime side up. I'm going to put out this light now, and I don't want to hear any talking."

For five full minutes they did not speak; they lay panting, their fingers gripped. Then they began to whisper. They whispered for almost an hour, the talk ending on smothered joyous laughter when Isabel, sleepy at last, laid the capsheaf upon the new excitement with her:

"Oh, and, Chatty, lissen! She can chaperon us now to Santa Cruz! Oh, and Geraldine's party Saturday! Everything at once!"

Caroline Buckminster, meanwhile, forty-eight years old, mother of ten and manager of a household of twenty-one souls, had descended to the kitchen to mix an eggnog and to question Cook as to the propriety of the help drinking coffee at this time of night. Cook and Alma and Elsa stood respectfully while she spoke to them; tired, sweat-soaked, pale. They made no answer. Cook had had her shoe off and had been treating a bunion when the mistress unexpectedly appeared. "Put your shoe on, Cook," said Caroline sharply, departing. "Bring the silver upstairs now, girls, and let Annie finish down here."

Elsa and Alma carried the three heavy baskets of silver up to their rooms on the third floor. Olive was out in the hall in her nightgown when her mother mounted the stairs, to report that Mabel was throwing up.

"Get Aunt Eliza," Caroline said. "I have to take this in to Papa. He doesn't feel well."

Aunt Eliza was awake. She went to the sufferer at once, was active with basin and towel and final drink of nice cold water. Then there was darkness and peace everywhere again, except for the gas burning low in Aunt Eliza's room. She lay on her bed, slippered and in her old blue wrapper, waiting, waiting.

After a while her sharp ears heard footsteps on the sidewalk far below. She was up like a flash then, and down the long flights of the stairs; she had the front door open before Arnold could even fumble for his keys; she stood gaunt and gray in the hallway, with her lighted candle in her hand.

Neither she nor Arnold spoke as his eyes, feverish in a flushed face, met hers. He went upstairs, and she noiselessly closed and locked the big door and followed him. No matter how bad he was, he always knew enough not to make a noise. Aunt Eliza helped him undress, pulled the nightshirt with the red stitching over his head, flung open his bed.

He stumbled into it, caught at her hand and drew her elderly, liver-mottled, faded face down against his.

"Those were dandy crullers!" he said mumblingly. He plunged into blankets; he was asleep and snoring within the space of five seconds.

She had had him to herself when he had had scarlet fever, fifteen years ago. She had him to herself in these moments now. She stooped and laid her cheek against the rich waves of his hair; her lips touched it.

Then she and her candle went away through the big handsome halls with their stained-glass windows and up the wide stairs with the brass Niobe holding three gas jets on the newel post, and so to her own room, next to Uncle Booth's. Eliza could remember when her handsome brother Booth had been a boy like Arnold. Well, that was the way men were. Some of 'em turned out hard like Arnold, and some of 'em was weak like Boothie. And she was tired.

She got into bed. On the floor below and on the parlor floor and far down in Cook's kitchen the clocks rang out a single note.

A Break for Eve

WHEN A FLOCK OF SHEEP went by the ranch house clouds of fine choking hot dust arose and fumed among the dry garden shrubs like smoke and settled slowly on anything and everything—the weather-beaten unpainted steps of the side porch, the clothes that were hanging, stiff and dry, on the line, the kitchen window sills.

Evangeline Wiggin, nineteen years old, always sighed when the sheep went by in the hot dry summer weather. She could stand anything but the sheep. She could bear the burning hot dawn after the scanty, grudged hours of hot darkness; she could bear the smell of lukewarm dishwater and of cold coffee grounds, tumbled from the old black pot into the pig trough; she could bear stringing beans, shelling peas, stripping the clothy skins from the big freestones, boiling currants for jelly. All that was just a part of being Evangeline Wiggin and having to live with Gram and Gramp Wiggin on the ranch.

But from the bottom of a fiery heart she resented the sheep. They bleated, as they trotted anxiously by, being driven from river-bottom pasture up into the blue gauze mountains that shut off the east, and their nervous muffled cries, and the strong, hot, oily smell of their heavy coats, and the sight of them, dirty thick rounded backs crowded against dirty thick rounded backs, bulletheads protruding here and there, seemed to Evangeline the most repellent sight in the world.

"I sure hate those sheep!" she would say to her dishpan.

Outside the kitchen window was a wide bare yard, under cottonwoods. There were also a few peppers and eucalyptus trees, but these had been planted for shade. The long, dry, blowing cottonwoods were native; they belonged to the burned dry hills and the brown grass and the arroyos—the empty gullies where water had once run swift and deep, but that were dry now, like all the rest of the world.

The yard was bounded by old unpainted sheds and barns and by stretches of split-rail fence. Hay barn, cow barn, chicken sheds, their outlines were lost in a tangle of lesser buildings that housed tools, old and new, the grindstone, the pump machinery, the fruit trays—all the accumulated litter of a century-old California ranch house. The oldest building of all, where baby calves and sheep were sometimes sheltered in winter, and where half-wild cats glared and mated and brought forth their young in dim recesses of piled potato sacks and old camp gear, was a genuine " 'dobe," built by Spanish ranchers long before the wagons came.

Janesville, the nearest town, where there were some sixty wooden cottages with bay windows and hollyhocks, and a movie theater that was open twice a week, and a post office and general store, and where there were a doctor and an undertaker—the last named also handling life insurance and mail-order furniture agencies—Janesville was seven miles away. Seven hot steep miles downhill on a dirt road; Evangeline didn't take that walk very often. For even if the insurance man or some buyer of wool or mutton offered her a lift, she had to think of the two hours pull home. And she was generally too tired for that.

But Mott and Mex, who helped Gramp on the ranch, both had rickety cars, and sometimes she went in, on a quiet winter afternoon, with Mott's wife Susie and sometimes with Mex's mother, if she had to go down and have the doctor change her medicine.

Mott and Mex lived half a mile from the ranch house,

down by the sheep sheds, in two rambling shacks completely surrounded by rubbish, rusty tins, bottles, ropes, old clothes, papers. Whenever they were finished with anything they threw it out into the yard, and flies, babies, chickens, puppies, kittens, all played about in the mess happily. The place smelled and seethed and sweated in hot weather, and weather was hot on the ranch from June to November. In winter the Motts and the Mex family withdrew into the dark, grease-soaked little cabins and sealed the windows and doors hermetically. They then began a diet of beans and pork and coffee, and the children went from whooping cough to diphtheria, and frequently from diphtheria to the Cemetery of All Saints, down below Janesville.

Even in summer the hands liked pork and fruit pies better than what Eve anxiously thought they should eat. Eve read in magazines of salads, fruits, jellies, cool things like junket and cornstarch, custard and sherbets, for summer eating. But after a few attempts she abandoned all efforts to convert the hands to her ideas. They not only despised such food; they rebelled, and the peach crop stood in peril of not being gathered for a week. Then Eve began on pork chops and flat berry pies again, and peace was restored.

Gram—a lean, oily-haired, sparse, clean old woman at sixty—baked and put up jelly; Gram never tired and never shirked. Gramp killed pigs and roosters and got them ready for the table. Eve did pretty much everything that her grandparents did not do; she went out into the blazing vegetable garden to gather tomatoes and corn, she shelled peas through whole afternoons, she gathered blackberries until her fingers were soaked in to the bone with the red juice. She washed mountains of thick white dishes and knives slippery with grease; she rubbed dish towels on an old washboard whose broken corrugations caught at her knuckles and made them bleed.

She had little leisure, and when she had, was too tired to use it. It was luxury enough in quiet intervals simply to sit still, panting, resting, thinking luxuriously that she need not move for twenty blessed minutes.

"Don't let that fire go out!" her grandmother would say, hurrying by her with dustpan and brush.

"No ma'am, I won't."

"Git that nettin' over the milk?" her grandfather might ask, a moment later, from the porch corner where he was mending the churn dasher.

"Yes sir."

The Wiggins had only three cows; they had no dairy. The milk was poured into shallow pans when Mex brought it in, and the pans carried carefully into the shady dark parlor, whose windows were shut in by close-growing, thick, dusty garden shrubs outside. There was a melodeon in there, and a whatnot on which were ranged shells and a glass tube of sand from the river Jordan and two pink china jars of trembling grass. In the center of the room was a round marble-topped table, where the milk pans stood. Over them a piece of clean white net was stretched, and beside them, in a saucer, lay the little pine stick with which Eve loosened the thick leathery cream, when it was set, and pushed it off into the churn pitcher. The dark parlor smelled faintly of sweet milk and clean tin; Eve liked the smell.

She had been on the ranch eleven years; she hated to count them up, to realize that eleven whole years—her eighth birthday to her nineteenth—had been spent here. Here, where nothing ever happened, where there were neither youth nor fun nor companionship nor friends. Sixteen, seventeen, eighteen, nineteen—and long summers of dishwater and melted butter, and the sheep going by in the stifling dust, and winters of wood smoke, and Dickens and Thackeray, and mud on the kitchen floor.

And meanwhile other girls of her age were swimming and dreaming on beaches and laughing and dancing in white moonlight and being paid unthinkable sums for acting in moving pictures. . . .

But she must not think about them. It was no use, and it only made her bitter. Gram and Gramp gave her a home and were kind to her, and she was a lucky girl. All the apricots and cherries she wanted, in the spring, and figs, and a nice room . . .

And all the time her heart beating like a caged bird: "I want to live, to be lovely, to have someone admire me, like those other girls!"

"What some of those New Yorkers would give for a pitcher of cream like that!" Gramp sometimes said as he poured the thick brown richness over his strawberries. Eve always said, "Imagine!" dutifully enough. But in her soul she felt that there were in the world more important things than Jersey cream.

Gramp liked being manager of the ranch, naturally. It meant that in those elderly years that for some men were so empty he had a thousand interests. He walked about the paths and among the barns contentedly, talking to Mex of harness and to Mott of corn and prunes. He picked up a bit of iron, glanced at it; fastened a gate more securely; scratched the head of Lessy, the shapeless baggy hound who followed him to and fro.

And Gram liked the farm. She was restless, strong, energetic. Cards, beauty parlors, movies, clubs meant nothing in her brisk days. But churns and pies and quilts and tomato pickle were important; her quick-rising biscuit were important, her handling of lampwicks and lard and bay chickens and brooms filled her mind. She broke out halfway through a silent dinner with a sudden plan for using up the goose grease or mending the old roaster. She got herself too thoroughly tired every day to do anything but tumble thankfully into bed at night. Her reading was confined to the "Home Circle" page of the local paper, and her entertainment to the radio.

But even these innocent sources contributed to the agony of ambition that burned day and night in her granddaughter's heart, and when some young movie star was photographed for the paper, or when some successful young actress was introduced to the audience of the air, Eve writhed with jealousy that seemed to affect her physically as well as mentally, and would slip upstairs to her airy, clean, empty bedroom and sink on her knees and bury her despairing head in her hands. Hollywood, with its bathing pools and its silken frocks, its clinking glasses and laughing young voices, its success, its power, its superb insolence and confidence, was but five hundred miles away down the white highway, but sometimes it seemed to Eve that the distance between that life and hers was the distance between two stars.

One burning, merciless August morning, when the dust and the smell and the noise of the passing flocks of sheep, the heat of the greasy kitchen and the glare of the sun were all contributing to make Eve's head feel dull and heavy, Sandy came to the ranch.

Eve looked out of the kitchen window and saw him talking to Gramp; just one more fellow looking for a job. She heard Gramp ask him what his stake was; Gramp didn't like to take on a new hand unless he was going to stay for a while.

Eve made an excuse to go out with a pan of scraps for the chickens and got a good look at a lean, tall, discouraged-looking young man with a smart face.

"A hundred," the man said. Gramp looked at him shrewdly. It was a big stake. Most of these drifting fellows only worked until they had twenty or thirty.

"We ain't payin' what we was," said Gramp. "It 'll take ye right through September."

"That's all right," the man said with a glance that invited Eve's sympathy and a sudden grin that made his brown face attractive.

He worked picking prunes that day. Later Eve saw him

watering the horses at sundown, and he brought in the milk. She was cooking for four hands then; this man made five. With Gramp and Gram that made eight at the table; well, eight was all right. It was only when she was cooking for ten or twelve that Eve felt she had too much to do. She made cottage pudding for dinner. There were figs, peaches, prunes, blackberries, pears in abundance on the ranch, but the men liked hot cake, strongly flavored with vanilla, and covered with clear, slippery sauce, for dessert. No hand ever bothered to eat fruit.

Sandy liked her cottage pudding, and after dinner he and she sat on the side steps in the hot dark and watched the big moon rise over a brown bare meadow dotted sparsely with enormous oaks. Presently each oak was drenched in silver-white light, and a lacy shadow lay on the stubble beneath it.

The night thrilled with sound: the steady hum of crickets, the intermittent cry of an owl in the wood. Cowbells clanked in the pasture lot, were still and clanked again.

"What you going to do when you make your stake, Sandy?"

"What do you know about my stake?"

"I heard you tell Gramp that it was a hundred."

"Well, when I make it," the man said after a pause, "I'm going back south, that's where I'm going."

"Anywhere near Hollywood? You've been there?"

"Sure I've been to Hollywood!"

It took her breath away. Shyly, eagerly, she led him to talk about it, that night, every night. Sandy was laconic; he answered her briefly, unenthusiastically, and Eve was woman enough to suspect that somehow Hollywood had hurt his pride, had disenchanted him. But for all that she hungered to hear more—more; she fed her thirsting soul on whatever drops he would let fall.

Sandy stayed on at the ranch; he was a good worker. And he and Eve met as naturally as rivers meet on their way to the sea. The tall slender girl in the thin shabby ginghams, with her quick red smile and her wistful eyes, had never known anyone like Sandy. He wasn't like the village boys, the big clumsy farm boys who thought that to obtain a job in the hardware store or grocery was to be well started in life. Sandy was cultivated, clever, urban—he was a thousand things of which she had never even dreamed and for which even now she could find no name. He charmed her, touched her, thrilled her into unsuspected emotions and excitements; he enhanced all her values of life breathlessly, incalculably.

Every hour was a rounded globe of beauty and glory now; every minute was like a delicious taste in her mouth. She put Sandy's bacon and eggs before him at breakfast, and his quick fingers touched her thin brown wrist as he took them. She went out to the prune orchard to hunt down the turkey's nest, and Sandy looked up from the pail he was filling with purple fruit and nodded at her. Perhaps he did no more, going on soberly with the dull work; somehow she liked it when he did that, even more than when he came over to talk to her. It made him important, not to let a girl distract him.

He could do anything, and with complete nonchalance and ease. Harnessing horses, handling bees, driving the truck; and he did not care what Janesville thought of him! He would take Eve into town on the truck when he wanted to, and she was always proud to be up there on the front seat beside him; Sandy did not care, and so she did not, either. He wore his clothes with the same fine indifference to onlookers, too, his shirts open at his brown throat, his thick tawny hair uncovered.

Eve loved him so desperately, so immediately, so openly that he saw it before she did.

"Listen here—listen here, kid," he said in his kind, big-brotherly voice, "cut it out. You'll get your little self into trouble if you take things so hard."

They were having pineapple sundaes at Mullet's, among the cigars and cameras and bathing caps and trays of soap.

The drugstore smelled of soap and rubber and cigars; it was to Eve a celestial smell. She was in heaven.

"Oh, Sandy," she said in a whisper.

"Cut it out."

"But I can't cut it out!" Like every ecstatically happy woman, she was shameless; she cupped her pale face, with its beautiful dark eyes and the thin line of red mouth, in her hands.

"You'd go the limit for me, wouldn't you?" he asked her wonderingly, a day or two later.

"Fifty limits!"

"Well then, that only shows that you're a fool and that you don't know what happens to girls like you!"

His arm was about her; it was starlight again. Eve laughed, unalarmed, and rubbed her cheek against his brown hard cheek.

"So you see, I've got to have sense for us both," he complained.

"Oh, Sandy, it's sense to love each other."

"Yes, it is," he drawled. "You'd have a swell chance in life, marrying me. You know what my stake is, and for all you know that's all I've got."

"Listen, you're always buying me sodas and taking me to movies. And movies are twenty, aren't they?"

"Oh well," he conceded, a little shocked at the extreme modesty of her ideas. "That isn't money. I've got enough for that."

"I wanted to get away before you came, Sandy."

"And don't you now?"

"Oh no, not now."

"You haven't," he said kindly, pityingly, "you haven't got much of a life here."

"But I like here better than anywhere now," she asserted.

"You poor sap!"

"Suppose I had run away, awhile back, Sandy, and had got to Hollywood, could I have gotten a break?"

"You mean in the movies?" He felt her head nod, against his shoulder.

"But I don't mean as a—as a *star,* of course. But just in a mob scene, or doing anything, washing windows or running errands for them?"

"Why, you're cockeyed about the whole thing, aren't you?" he asked.

"Well, I guess I am."

The man fell silent, and when he answered her it was in a low, absent-minded voice.

"No, without influence and money and friends you wouldn't have a break—you wouldn't have a Chinaman's chance!"

"I didn't think I would," Eve said bravely, breathing deep.

"Not in that madhouse!" Sandy said.

"Well, anyway, I don't want to go now," Eve ended contentedly.

She was working hard these days; only it did not seem like work any more. She stood slender and young and shabby at the dishpan; she came and went with pans of milk; she went out under the apple trees and picked up the big bellflowers and brought them into the kitchen in her apron. Now and then she saw a reflection of herself in the mirrors of the movie theater or the drugstore, or in the glass over Gramp's certificate as a dentist, in the dark parlor, and it was the reflection of a happy, pretty creature, with soft dark hair tumbled on an erect head, and dark eyes very big in a heart-shaped face.

It was not like living, the feel of these days, or like walking or eating or sleeping. It was like flying and dancing; needing neither food nor sleep. Eve loved the nights, because she could lie awake, slim and straight and bare, under one thin sheet, in the hot dark, and think of Sandy, and she loved the daytimes because he was always somewhere in the scene, or just out of it, or just coming into it.

"What 'll you do when I go away, Eve?"

"You won't go away."

"Your grandfather told me this morning he's got to cut down."

"Oh," she breathed, a brown thin hand at her heart. "Then—then I'll go too!"

"What on?"

"Sandy . . ." She was very pale. "Don't talk like that. Don't do it! You can't—you can't leave me now."

He was not often serious, despairing. She saw despair in his handsome haggard eyes now.

"Honey, suppose I gave you the price of a month in Hollywood?"

"I don't want to go to Hollywood!" She had been a girl, telling him her dreams, a month ago. But now she was a woman, loving, suffering, afraid.

"Look here, Eve. I love you, you know that. But—but we mustn't go any further!"

"Any further!" She was stabbed to the heart. "But why not?"

He turned in the starlight to kiss her restlessly, in the center of her forehead, laughed, put her gently aside.

"I've never done anything but kiss you, have I, darling?" he said in a quick, feverish voice. "I shouldn't have done that. But at least I didn't—didn't take all you would have given me."

"Sandy, I don't understand you!"

"No, of course you don't." He had his arm about her again, but she did not put her head back on his shoulder. Instead she sat erect, troubled, her eyes searching his face anxiously in the gloom.

"But what is it?"

"It's only—— Why," he interrupted himself, in a lighter, more usual tone, "it only means that I haven't anything in the world to offer you and that I'm going away in a week or two—your grandfather said about the twenty-eighth—and that I—well, isn't that all there is to it?"

And again he framed her puzzled face in his big hands and

kissed her forehead feverishly, restlessly, as if he hardly knew what he was doing, as if he were distracted.

"But I go with you," the girl said firmly.

"What? On a hundred-dollar stake?"

"We could earn more."

"When I do earn more, Eve, I'll send for you, honey."

A silence. Then the girl spoke in a remote, infinitely sad voice.

"Oh no, you won't, oh no, you won't! I know it. I'll wait here, and wait here, and it 'll be winter, and you won't ever write!"

"Eve, I swear I will!" She saw sweat glistening on his forehead, in the weak, early starlight.

"I can't—I couldn't bear it!" she whispered. And then, clinging tight to him in sudden fear and despair: "Oh, take me with you, Sandy, let me live—let me *live!* I'm so lonely here, and the years go by, and nobody helps me to get out! Take me with you. I don't want Hollywood, I don't want success, or to have my picture in the paper—I just want to be with you! I'll cook for you, Sandy, I'll wash your clothes! We'll have a little place somewhere—one room! I'll make it wonderful for you, I'll always be kind to you. I'll not mind not having any money——"

She was crowded against him, her wet cheek against his, her panting body in his arms. The man laughed briefly, mirthlessly, gently catching at her hands, gently holding her away.

"Hush, you—you child!" he said.

"Sandy, I'm not a child! I know what marriage is, and having babies—I've been down at Motts'! I know you're nearly thirty, but I'm nearly twenty—I'll be twenty in May."

"Sh-sh-sh!" he murmured. "Of course—of course I'll take you if you feel that way. We'll plan it tomorrow, we'll tell Gramp and Gram tomorrow. You'll have an awful row to hoe—you'll be sorry. But if you feel that way about it——"

"I *do* feel that way about it!"

"Well then, that's settled."

She laughed an exultant laugh, pressed her cheek against his.

Some hours later, when the ranch and the world had long been locked in the complete darkness and silence of a moonless night, and when Gramp's stertorous snore and Gram's unfailing echo were sounding steadily through the thin walls of the old farmhouse, Sandy came noiselessly down the uncarpeted stairway, and through the deserted dark kitchen and out of the side door.

It was after two o'clock. The hot autumn world was cooled into a wide circle of shadows and drenched with heavy dew. Against the faintly luminous sky the silhouettes of tall cottonwoods were dimly outlined; down the looped road, toward the village, an occasional wakeful household showed a spark of light.

Sandy walked the half mile to Mott's cabin. The hired man's disreputable open car, mud splashed and rusty, was parked there. He put his bundle on the front seat, got in at the wheel.

There was a bad moment when the ignition refused. Sandy fiddled with the choker; wheels moved, he was driving down the road toward Janesville. It was then he heard Eve's voice.

She had been crouching against the back seat; she had drawn sacking, baskets, partially over herself; he had not seen her.

"My God!" he said.

"Sandy, I'm here."

The car slackened pace; the girl was over the back of the seat, was close beside him.

"I had to come!"

"My God!" the man said again, almost as if he prayed.

"I had to, Sandy."

"How'd you know what I was going to do?"

"I followed you—after we talked. And you walked down to Motts'; I was right behind you. And you threw your coat in."

"Now what?"

"Now—ah, but don't stop, Sandy. I'm so afraid they'll follow us, stop us."

"How can they stop you? You're nineteen."

"I know. But does Mott know you have his car?"

Sandy spoke sulkily, childishly, his hand idly playing on the wheel. They had stopped now, beside the road.

"I'm not stealing it, if you mean that."

"I didn't mean that!" the girl said with spirit.

A pause.

"What do you want to do this for, Eve?"

"Because I love you!"

"That's no answer."

"That's all the answer I need. It's all I need, Sandy—my chance to live, my chance to get started! I'm going to have a wonderful life," Eve told him eagerly, her face a dim blur in the shadows, her slender body against him. "I'm going to be one of these women who have adventures, who do everything. I don't care what it is—the stage, or keeping boarders, or going on a ship somewhere, or having a whole pack of children, but I'm going to *do* it—if once, if *once* you'll help me get a start!"

He was listening; she felt rather than saw the gravity with which he was listening.

"Maybe you're right," he said slowly, in a pause.

"You'll take me!"

"We'll drive to Sacramento. Or no, we'll get the up train here in Janesville, and I'll leave fifty cents on the seat to pay Mott. And we'll go to Sacramento and get married tomorrow. And then we'll—we'll go down to Hollywood. I'll see if I can——" He interrupted himself, started the car again. "I'll give you your chance, kid!" he said.

So they left Mott's car outside the post office with a note and got into a train, an enormous and imposing train, and when Sandy paid the conductor Eve was amazed to see how many big bills he had. And at ten o'clock in the morning, having brushed up in the station rest room, and had coffee and rolls, and bought a new hat, they were married.

Shortly afterward, when Eve was still waiting in the rest room, supposing that the next step would be a train to San Francisco, and then another for magic Hollywood, Sandy came in and explained that he had met a friend who wanted his car taken to Los Angeles anyway, and so they were driving down. This was only too exciting! Such a nice car, and such fun to ramble along country roads and go southward—southward—southward, in the pleasant autumn weather.

Eve was ecstatically happy; she was not afraid of anything. Not afraid of roads and roadside meals and heat and fatigue, not afraid even when it was dusk, and they came to the Motel Inn and had dinner in their own shady, luxurious cottage, and sat on their own porch after dinner, talking and weary and happy.

And the next day, going to Santa Barbara, and toward a cool swim in the ocean this time, she said to him, "Sandy, I love being your wife. I was an awful fool to talk about being in movies or on the stage. I just want you, always and forever."

But to this he made no answer.

Later she said, "Look, there's a darling, darling cottage to let, Sandy, near the ocean! You could get a job here, couldn't you? There's a fishery, there are cattle ranches!"

"Not many jobs these days, honey."

"No, but you've lots of money!"

"That wouldn't take us far."

"You—honestly you can do anything!" she said in simple admiration, when they had been swimming, and when, instead of perching on the stools of a sandwich counter, he took her to a shady restaurant, with an attentive waiter and a dazzling menu. "There—was that tipping him?" she breathed excitedly as the bill was paid.

"That's what that was." He was amused, touched by her artlessness, her simplicity, and yet it was a sad sort of amusement, somehow. There was something serious, something troubled in his manner; he was no longer the careless hand who had agreed to work for Gramp for a hundred-dollar stake; he seemed older and graver as every hour went by.

"Don't worry, Sandy, we'll get along!"

"I'm not worrying for me."

"Well, I'm not worrying for Mrs Edward Horace White!"

"You're stuck on your new name."

"You said it. But why'd you tell Gramp your name was Sandy Leonard?"

"Oh well . . ." The idle answer was as casual as the idle query. "A feller does that, sometimes."

"Changes his name?"

"Sometimes."

"But what for, Sandy?"

"Oh well—maybe he doesn't want his mother to get on to what he's doing."

"Is your mother living?"

"Died three years ago. They're all dead—all of them."

"Except your wife."

"Except my wife."

"But is Edward Horace White your real name?"

"Yep. It was about all I had to give you, honey."

They drove on, in a lovers' paradise of autumn haze and beauty; smells of fruit and wheatfields; sharp sweet dew on the sunset dust. Sandy bought Eve figs and grapes to eat as they went along; they stayed two days in Santa Barbara and then loitered south, and once he said that he thought they might go on into Mexico. But later, without her having made any suggestion, for Eve was living in a world of complete content and confidence and wanted nothing more, he decided for Hollywood. To Hollywood accordingly they drove, on a soft morning, seeing the sun rise on the mountains and turn them pink and amethyst, and cattle, dawdling away from milking sheds, leaving long trails of diamonds in the wet grass.

Eve was excited to the point of uneasiness at the magnificence of their hotel; it took her breath completely away to follow Sandy through the great doorway and breathe the luxurious atmosphere of spaciousness and flowers, dim rich rugs, glittering splendid great leather chairs.

Their coming seemed to agitate everyone but Sandy. There was a running about of bellboys, a sense of almost overwhelming welcome, an obsequiousness that made Eve feel shy. But Sandy took it entirely for granted and was his usual superb self under it.

Had they had his telegram? Oh, indeed they had, Mr Moulton, and they had a delightful suite ready for him and Mrs Moulton. And would they—perhaps they wouldn't mind? The press was anxious, just for a moment . . .

Men—six or seven cameras at once—were taking their photographs. Eve smiled obediently, clung bewildered to her companion. Why "Moulton," and why were they doing that? Sandy, smoking a cigarette, looking somehow much the smartest of them all, in his old golf clothes, was telling them that he loved what he had seen of southern California and that he hoped to stay.

They went upstairs, to enormous rooms incredibly beautiful with coolness and space and fruit and flowers. The bathroom was all tiles, fat green-striped towels; the sitting room had a lofty porch. Boys were lighting lights, opening windows, displaying closets.

"Our luggage ought to be here in ten minutes. Look out for it, will you?" said Sandy carelessly. He ordered breakfast, and before the last bellboy left, delicious breakfast was on a little table by a window. Eve was in a dream, she couldn't seem to believe it all, or any of it.

"But, Sandy, your name isn't Moulton!" she smiled when they were alone with the hot coffee and the amazing rolls and the grapefruit and the boiled eggs.

"You're right, it isn't."

"But mightn't they—mightn't they think we were the Garnet Moultons, the very rich Moultons? They're coming to California too. It said so in that paper we had at Santa Maria."

"They might, at that."

"Wouldn't that be funny!" Eve exclaimed with her delicious youthful laugh.

"Wouldn't it, though?"

"What are you putting in your coffee, Sandy?"

"Headache stuff."

She was stricken.

"Oh, but, darling, driving in that hot sun! You didn't say your head ached!"

"It doesn't, really."

"This is all like a wonderful dream, Sandy."

"It is a dream, dear." He put down his empty cup. "And you're due to wake up, Eve," he said. The telephone rang in the pause, and he went to it. "Ask them to come up," he said. He went to the window and stood looking out.

A few minutes later, with an air of hurry, agitation, stress that frightened Eve before she had any idea what it was all about a nice-looking young woman and a white-faced young man came into the room.

"Mack!" the woman said in a frightened voice. She went quickly to Sandy, who smiled at her, putting his arm about her.

"Hello, Alma," he said.

"Mack, what's it all about? Lost your mind?" the man asked roughly, almost angrily. Neither one paid the slightest attention to Eve; they talked together for a minute in low tones. Then Eve heard the man shout angrily, "Then you're crazy!"

"No, it's just that I'm sick of it," Sandy told them briefly.

"Sick of it! But you've stolen a car, Mack, you've registered here as Moulton—you're crazy! What you going to do now?"

Sandy walked over to Eve, faced them with an arm about her. She looked, terrified, from his face to their terrified faces.

"This is Eve, Alma. I wrote you I was married. This is my wife."

The woman paid scant attention; she shook his arm impatiently.

"Mack, for God's sake get out while the getting's good!"

"I want you to see that she gets a break, do you see?"

"That . . . ?" The man, whose name was Kent Younger, repeated the word, stopped abruptly. "That's—that's all right," he went on heavily, "but it's you we're thinking of. You've got to get out. You shouldn't have come!"

He spoke angrily, urgently.

"I let Burke know," Sandy said.

"You fool!" the other man said in a whisper after a pause of stupefaction. The woman began to cry. She went over to Sandy and put her arms about him and her face against his shoulder.

"Listen, Alma," he said, "you see that Eve gets a break, won't you?"

"Oh, sure," the woman said forlornly, drying her eyes. "I'll get her something to do at the studio, if you mean that. It's only in the wardrobe, but it 'll be a start. But, Mack, you . . . *you* . . ." she faltered.

"A break!" the man echoed scornfully. "And you say you were photographed, downstairs here, as Moulton. They'll all want to get hold of her; she'll get a contract, don't worry about *her!* They'll all want to tie her up, and she can stay with Alma until she gets started. But it's you!"

" 'Pete Mack's girl,' " Sandy said. "That ought to get her somewhere. You can tell, looking at her, that she didn't know anything about anything, can't you?"

"I don't know what's got you," Kent Younger exclaimed, brushing the diversion aside, "but for God's sake don't waste time talking here, Mack! You've got yourself in deep, now for God's sake think of something and get yourself out!"

"She got me; that's what got me," Sandy told them.

Eve, whose eyes, growing more and more wild with bewilderment and fear, had moved from one face to the other during the rapid, low-toned conversation, clung to Sandy's arm.

"Sandy, what is it? What's going to happen? What are you going to do?"

"Nothing," he said to her reassuringly. "You're going home with Kent and Alma now; they've got a nice baby, and you can help with him. You'll like that. And I'll come when I've finished some business."

"Oh no, you won't!" Eve exclaimed, very pale. "I'll stay with you. I know what it is—I know what you meant when you said you'd notified Burke. That's the police, isn't it, Mr Younger? Isn't it, Mrs Younger? But I'm your wife, Sandy, they're not going to take you away from me, I'll not let them! I don't care if you aren't Mr Moulton; that doesn't matter! But I have to be where you are!"

His arm about her, he looked down at her amusedly, lovingly, a haggard expression on his young, worn face.

"Oh, my God, she's crazy about him—look at that now," Alma whimpered, beginning to cry.

"Don't make me go away from him, Alma," Eve sobbed, appealing to her suddenly.

"Now look here, Eve," Sandy said, his cheek against her hair as he stooped over her, "this isn't the way you ought to do. I thought you were my big strong out-of-door girl. Don't you know the way I've been telling you, all the way down, that you'd have to be strong, if you got a break, and fight for your place, and work hard and take the bad with the good? Didn't I tell you that?"

"Ye-e-es!" Eve sobbed heartbrokenly, clinging tight to

him, "but—but I want to be with you now! I want to stay here—don't send me away!"

"Look, you're throwing me down," he said steadily, with a tension of pain in his smiling face.

"Oh no, I'm not, Sandy! I wouldn't do that!"

"Yes, but you are."

"But I can't bear it!"

"I get you here to Hollywood, I put you with my best friends, I get your picture in the paper the first thing," Sandy reminded her reproachfully, tenderly. "And then what do you do? You begin to cry, you won't make an effort, you throw the whole thing up—you haven't got guts, that's your trouble, you haven't got any guts!"

"Oh, I *have* got guts," Eve asserted in a wet voice as she raised her chin and blew her nose and wiped her eyes. "And I'll do anything you say. Only—only——"

"Now cut that out! I want you to take this money, honey. Kiss me!"

"If it's money I'll help you pay it, Sandy, and if it's anything else we don't care, do we?"

"Naw, we don't care!" he drawled, smiling at the others a strange smile. "Look what she thinks of me, Kent!" he said proudly.

He went to the table, took from his pocket the little box from which he had taken the headache medicine half an hour earlier, shook two pellets into his palm. Eve did not understand; she saw a stricken look on the faces of the man and woman who watched him. They made no move.

"I thought you'd do that, Mack," the man presently said hoarsely.

"Sure. I'm fixed. Take her along, will you? Good-by, Eve," Sandy said.

He kissed her, his own eyes bright and dry, even though hers were brimming, and her red mouth trembling.

"Ah, my God, I'm sorry, Mack!" Kent Younger said.

Eve went between Alma and Kent down the hotel hall to

the elevators. Eight policemen were coming toward them in orderly file. Kent spoke to one of them; there was a slight delay. Then Eve and Alma and Kent went down in the elevator and through a little side hallway and out into Hollywood.

Masterpiece

He hesitated a little, reaching the drawing room; there was a fire beyond there in the soft gloom, twilight, the top of a polished long table, the rounded backs of hospitably circled chairs. But where was Isabel?

Suddenly, immediately, in one of her old characteristic, laughing rushes, she had come out of shadows, she had hold of him. Her hands, in the old way, vital upon his, her old effect of being taller than she really was—of being, indeed, only a tall girl in her childhood. Nothing was changed.

"Peter!" she said in the old voice.

"My dear, dear girl!" he said, touched, shaken. And quite simply, as old friends in the forties may do nowadays, they kissed.

Then they went over to the fire, and she put him in a big chair and sank into one near, and opposite, so that they could stare delightedly at each other. They were, blessedly, alone at the moment, but there were five or six empty teacups waiting on the tray. Peter Penrhyn had a distinct appreciation that this hour was a precious one, in a short lifetime, and that moments were valuable.

But he sat smiling, unhurried, fingers linked, gray eyes under a copper-burned and graying forehead, keen, savoring every word, as befitted a man who had been globe-trotting, exploring, hunting, fighting animals in jungles, and men in Flanders, for twenty years. A man who had not talked to Isabel Yarrington for twelve—fifteen—good Lord, except for that unsatisfactory cup of tea once, five years ago, it was eighteen of them!

"Isabel, what luck to find you alone!"

"You certainly didn't think I was going to have the neighbors in when you came?"

"My dear, you've such wonderful neighbors now—with everyone interesting in the world only asking to be your neighbor!"

"I see," she said with the old, deliciously rebuking smile—she had been playing mother to everybody since she was six—"I see you think I've become a fine lady since last we met!"

"Nothing in the world could have made you a fine lady since we met," Peter said with a little flush under his copper skin, and a little bow.

She narrowed the fine eyes into laughter.

"Oh, thank you! Somebody has made a polished flatterer of you, at any rate," she returned. "Is it perhaps Paris?"

And she indicated the tall, muffled windows behind her, where an opal September sunset was indeed lighting the gray roofs of the French capital.

"Begin with Paris," Peter directed her hungrily. "Anything will do—let's get started! Why are you in Paris just now?"

"Because Timothy likes Paris, always has," she answered. "Not quite satisfied anywhere, he does have his pleased moments here. Because, in the last ten years, it's been New York, Hawaii, Paris again, Deanery Street, Taormina, France, Brittany that time, Amherst—our boy did a few months work there—Russia, China, San Francisco, Paris again!"

He smiled, musing and shaking his head.

"It's been phenomenal, hasn't it, Isabel?"

"Timothy's success?" she interpreted quickly. "Oh, extraordinary. It isn't only the books; let us suppose, for the sake of family modesty, that he isn't Shakespeare over again," she smiled; "but it's the prices, Peter. Thousands—thousands! For movie rights, for serial rights, for second serial rights. It's a day of enormous magazine circulations, a day of big prices. A critic here and there may scorn him, but Timothy says—and truly, perhaps—that most critics are disappointed and unsuccessful writers. The machine goes on."

"Glorious beyond all the old dreams!" Peter marveled.

The woman, with a swift little shake of her head, rebuked him.

"As if anything could touch the old dreams!"

"Ah, you're quite right—you're quite right, Isabel," Peter agreed. "What dreams they were! When you were cooking Timothy's dinners in the Washington Square rooms, when we used to sing and go off on Sunday walks in Staten Island——"

"With nothing but red apples in our pockets! And the day you rigged me up a water jar on the fire escape, to save ice!"

"You've not forgotten that! And the essay the *Atlantic* took. Isabel, I've wondered sometimes, all these years, what *you've* been doing? All the world knows about Tim. What about you?" Peter broke off to ask. "What happened to the essays—the poems? After all, it was *you* who were going to be the writer, who had the start, indeed! I remember some of us didn't think it much of a match for you," he reminded her, smiling, "to marry Timothy Yarrington, a newspaperman merely on 'space and detail.' "

"Fancy!" she said in a sort of amused, awed whisper. "Not much of a match—Timothy Yarrington!"

"Ah well, after *The Skyrocket,* of course, after *Drums Up the Street*—that was different!" the man conceded. "Everyone rejoiced then, everyone said that your faith in him was justified. But you'd been married four years then."

"Yes, but I had Don, the baby. I was busy. I've always," she said cheerfully, "been busy. A man like Tim, exacting, restless, demanding constant change, and a boy like Don . . ."

She stopped on a note of laughter at her own pride.

"Is he so fine?" the man asked with a little twinge of something like jealousy.

"Donny?" Her eyes shone. "You'll see him; he's here now —he'll be in with Tim directly. Tim said that he'd give you and me half an hour or so to weep upon each other's shoulders, but he'll be in before you go."

"Tim doesn't sound as jealous as he used to be, Isabel. There was a time when men didn't have tea with you alone, my dear."

"Ah, but one grows more sensible!" she said with her old, happy flush. "Besides, it's the boy now—it's Donny. If he could be jealous it would be of Don nowadays. His pride in the boy, his talent, his future, his plans for him—that's his world. Don's everything to Tim. I don't know, I don't know," Isabel Yarrington said in a lowered tone, a tone in which he was astonished and strangely sorry to detect a note of pain, "what Tim would do if Don ever disappointed him!"

"Your boy is—seventeen?"

"Nineteen, and as tall as Dad."

"And will he be a writer?"

"Don!" Her astonishment was almost funny. "But you know," she began and interrupted herself. "Of course you *don't* know," she corrected it, smiling, "that Don's a genius. No, this isn't mother talk; there's been many an hour, Peter, when his mother has wished that he wasn't! The life of a genius isn't all roses, and a genius isn't an easy little boy to bring up properly."

"Writing already, eh?"

"Oh, not writing! *Painting!* Painting ever since he could hold a brush in his fat little fist. Screaming, Peter, even when he was little enough to walk, holding tight to my fingers, screaming that the horses' legs all went in slanting lines together. 'See, Mummy, all in scribbly lines!' And when he got home he would do it, on his slate, flying hoofs and manes in the wind. There!"

Glancing about for proof, she saw beside the fireplace the

framed pencil sketch of a woman's head, severe line of cheek, sweep of cock's feather, ruche of rich fur.

"He didn't do that? Of you, eh?"

"Ah, but indeed he did. In twenty minutes, at that."

"Remembering your struggles for recognition, my struggles, Tim's years of floundering before he found himself, one feels like saying, 'How very simple!' " Peter commented dryly.

"Not so simple," she assured him with a smile. "For Timothy isn't simple by any means, and Don is so extraordinarily simple that there is no anticipating him and no classifying him. He has always been a solitary child, of course, dragged—due to this success of Tim's—all over the world, as the children of professional men usually are. He is serene, friendly, sufficient unto himself, he has three or four languages, he has his gift—and he likes to live in a Breton farmhouse, playing with the neighbors' children and painting the sea! Simplicity is a problem in itself, Peter."

"Nothing marketable yet?" Peter surmised.

"Not yet. Although Berét, in whose classes Don began to work last year, has taken him into his own studio. When Don goes into the classes they say a group forms around him. He's really as artless as a child about it. But you'll see him in a few minutes, you'll see for yourself."

"And all this has kept your own pen idle, Isabel?" the man asked sadly.

"Yes." Her answering nod was a little sad too. "Sometimes, when my men are off together, it makes me feel a little —lonely, Peter," she admitted. "Only the other day—oddly enough, for I had no idea then that you would be coming back to ask about it—only the other day I began at last my short story. You remember that I was always about to write a startling short story?"

"The 'Masterpiece,' we used to call that fabulous short story of yours!"

"Exactly, the 'Masterpiece.' Well, a few days, perhaps a

week ago, I began it—a society story. I got paper, my best pen, settled myself after luncheon to write it. I have really—and Tim says it's all one needs—a plot. And if I can write this story," Isabel said, laughing at him with eyes that were suddenly filled with tears, "all the years of waiting won't seem wasted to me!"

"I suppose another life almost always feeds a life like Tim's," Peter said, deeply interested, in a thoughtful tone.

"Ah, but don't make me a martyr! I've had back a thousand times anything I've sacrificed," she warned him sturdily.

"You can't have had, Isabel!" he said, faintly impatient. "Genius like yours—for it *was* genius! A beginning like yours, for everyone who matters was talking about young Mrs Yarrington's stuff. And now for twenty years packing trunks and answering letters . . . !"

"There's nothing like the loyalty of an old friend, Peter," the woman smiled.

"Now," he went on inexorably, "when we're none of us young, when he's sated himself on glory, he tells you that all you need is a plot!"

"I don't think you ever were quite fair to Tim," she commented judicially. "And I know that you were always far too generous to me. What more—what more could I have? Money, travel, interviewers, reporters, photographers, movie men everywhere we go, fairly haunting . . ."

"Timothy!" he supplied grimly as she paused.

"The best suites, the best servants and food and rooms, the best clothes," she continued.

"Clothes!" Peter echoed. "No, Isabel," he added with a philosophic shrug. "It's been a full life, an interesting life. But of course it hasn't been *yours.*"

"No," she agreed in a low tone as he paused. "Perhaps it hasn't. Perhaps it hasn't. But never mind, Peter," she broke off to say cheerfully, "I shall really get at my story this week—my masterpiece! And I shall take it as a good omen that you are here. by chance, to play godfather! And you'll see, it's going to be wonderful. Tim has promised me a whole free afternoon when I am to read it to him—consult him about it!"

"In the old days," he reminded her good-naturedly, "it was not Tim who gave you ideas. You brimmed with them. You gave them—rivers of them, to him!"

It was dusk in the room. Servants were bringing in the tea. The woman leaned back in her chair, almost as if she were glad to hide her face, as several lamps bloomed softly all at once about her. Peter did not look at her.

Presently he heard her speak in quick, fluent French to a servant, who went out.

"I've just asked him to send Germaine in," she explained. "My little foster daughter. She goes back to Brittany in a few days."

He glanced at her, surprised. She had drawn her breath with a sharp stab, as if she drew a sword out of her heart.

"I didn't know that there *was* such a person," he said.

"No? Well, naturally not. But I lost a baby daughter in Brittany, ten—twelve years ago, and Germaine has been like a daughter ever since. She's seventeen now. Very shy, absolutely what she seems to be, the daughter of a fisherman and his sweet, sad, girlish little wife. Drowned, both of them, and Germaine was Don's playmate, without a relative in the world. So she came to us. She's been at school in Brittany, been with us in Italy and here; she's an unusual child. You know we've spent the last six summers in Brittany."

"And to whom does she go back?"

"To school; to the nuns." Isabel's face revealed nothing, her voice was quiet, but there was sympathy in the man's voice as he asked curiously:

"You'll miss her?"

"Ah-h-h!" She admitted it, sighing sharply. "We've had such a happy summer—so many happy summers, all playing about together, sharing soup and apples on the shore, moonlights and early mornings. Sometimes Tim works there, and sometimes he goes off for visits, to Nice or to London. Ah, here she is!" she broke off, with welcome in her voice.

She half turned, over the back of her chair, and a girl came quickly into the lamplight. A slender girl, not tall, built with a hint of boyish spareness and squareness. A very young girl—seventeen. Curly, rich, rebellious dark hair coiled in a knot on the fresh young neck, wide-set, black-lashed eyes, cheeks healthily white, healthily touched with rose and powdered with golden freckles across the short, straight nose. The mouth crimson, wide, the teeth big and white, the manner just a hint unfriendly, suspicious, truculent.

"Germaine—a dear old friend. Monsieur Penrhyn," Isabel said, her fine, long, white fingers clinging to the girl's square, brown, childish ones. "You're coming in for tea, my little daughter?" she asked in French.

"I think not, Tante," pleaded the other in a tone at once affectionate, shy and stubborn. She flung Peter a glance, and Peter, puzzled, thought it strange that any girl who was under Isabel's wing should wear so obviously troubled a look.

"She's glorious!" he said when she was gone. "A splendid, golden, honest, glorious little—animal!"

"No, but do you think so, Peter?" Isabel said eagerly. "Oh, I'm so glad you do! Everyone does," she added; "not that one gets her—quite at once. She's too utterly real for that. Germaine has no manner except her own simpleness. But when she loves . . . !" She had murmured the last sentence as if half to herself; now she fell silent, perhaps pondering it.

She had not been a particularly handsome young woman, he mused, but Isabel Yarrington was wonderful now. That was the word for her, wonderful. In every way the years had refined her, polished, finished her, who had always been one of the finest of women. Her plain gown, with its medieval touch of deep lace at the throat, her crown of dull, tawny hair, her chiseled mouth, the quick appraising glance of her clear, almond-shaped gray eyes, the cadences of her voice, the easy, yet carefully restricted range of her conversation, all helped to make her extraordinary, fascinating, mysterious; in a word, *wonderful*. He would never fall in love with Isabel again; he was forty-six now, and she only a year or two younger. But suddenly it seemed good to him that she was alive, here, in Paris, enriching and making interesting every phase of life that she touched. It seemed good to find himself still in the very inner circle of her valued friends, able to pick up, at a moment's notice, the relationship that had been so sweet for a while, so unendurably hard for a while, and that now was to be all sweet, all good, again.

It was with a quickened sense of the value, the beauty of life that he rose, a moment later, to greet her husband and son.

Timothy! And part of Timothy's phenomenal insolence, where life was concerned, was that he never changed. He prided himself upon not changing. At fifty-two he was what he had been at thirty-two—opinionated, conceited, eager, fascinating, magnetic. He was easily witty, easily epigrammatical; for forty of those fifty-two aggressive and successful years he had been the center of every group in which he found himself.

Handsome, of course. Handsomer than ever now, with the thick smooth black hair cut sensationally by a bar of pure white. What hair but Timothy Yarrington's ever would age so picturesquely? Pale, his big-featured face ascetically lean, his big figure just romantically stooped, fur on his overcoat collar, an inch more width than was conventional on his hat-brim, a big seal ring on his fine hand. And the unchanged voice, the eager, affectionate greeting, the immediate reversion to what had supposedly been interesting him immensely.

"I can't get over it! The doctor sketches this poor fellow's lung on his chest in red—by Jove, I thought the brute was using a red pen! 'Dead?' I asked him. 'Not yet, sir,' says one of the nurses, just as you'd say 'Two lumps'! 'Pas encore, m'sieu'! Oh, my Gawd!" Peter remembered the marvelous laugh.

That was Timothy. Years and friendships were nothing to him. He found his supporting company wherever he happened to be, and played his dozen leading roles a day, and asked no more of life.

"Where on earth *were* you?" Isabel's lovely hands were busy with the tea things.

The boy, who had kissed his mother and flung himself silently into a chair, spoke for the first time. A man's voice.

"I had a bit of anatomy to do. Dad and I went into the emergency hospital; they told me I could look at any number of 'em. A lad there asked us if we'd like to take a peek into the surgery."

" 'Pas encore, m'sieu,' says the lady politely," Timothy repeated with the deep chest laugh again. "My *Lord* . . ." He frowned, plunged deep in thought.

Peter remembered Timothy's trick of falling into a study when there was company about. The writer, taken by a bit of local color unawares. The depicter of naked human souls, piercing through the commonplaces of a filthy, red-spattered workshop for human bodies, caught by it, unable to forget it.

How magnificent he was! How he gloried, gloated, in being himself! He was stirring his tea, flinging careless questions at Peter, making them all laugh, even the gloomy boy, charming them all once more.

Peter studied the boy. He was remarkable; broad, curly-headed, rosy, square-shouldered, with big, keen, delicately fingered hands. He was hirsute, like a French peasant boy, his lip shadowed, his ears, nostrils, the backs of his hands frothed with fine curly hair. His eyebrows were formidable, his dark eyes quiet and indifferent, like a child's eyes, his mouth and jaw large. Young Donald wore his loose clothing comfortably, indifferently; it was obvious that he did not brush his hair, he merely combed its tight rings. And Peter knew that he saw before him one of the souls that fate marks before birth with a golden star. For good or ill, this was no boy. This was merely the vehicle for the dazzled brain, the trembling, dedicated hands through which Art should be born.

He would eat, drink, sleep, exercise those long legs, perhaps beget children, travel, love and hate—but he was Art's child, through poverty and longing, through striving and failing and succeeding, as this contented, ebullient, super-successful father of his quite as positively was not.

Isabel's baffled genius and the maddeningly marketable success of Isabel's husband had produced this creature, to sit there between them like a kangaroo between two puzzled, plodding ponies, Peter thought whimsically, a kangaroo who knew nothing but how to leap.

Donald having had his tea and departed, the three elders fell into a conversation that was to Peter like the pages of a book turning backward, so completely did he grasp now what Isabel's problem was.

Yet Isabel hardly spoke. She sat watching the men, smiling at them with her deep, almond-shaped gray eyes, quite transparently happy in the pleasant hour.

Timothy spoke incessantly. There was nothing overbearing or insistent in his talk, it was just his old gay, irrelevant chatter, one rapid-fire observation hitching itself to another, everything impromptu, careless, born of itself. He was observant, witty, he had an astonishing command of words; Peter observed that Isabel guided him, sometimes with her wide, amused smile of approval, sometimes with just a hint of contraction in her brow, just a hint of pursing at the corner of her mouth.

The old phrases were there: "Of course, I don't know a damn' thing about writing. . . . One of you fellers will have to interpret this damn' thing for me, Peter. . . . By God, I wished, when I saw it, that I could write it! I wished my stuff wasn't such damn' piffle!" Timothy ruffled the black hair with the effective white band on it in the old troubled, youthful fashion.

Yet he had never been youthful, Peter remembered, and would never be grown. He created his own atmosphere, and it would always be the atmosphere of precocity, a child's pompous interpretation of maturity sitting him as oddly as did the middle-age assumption of boyishness and vigor. Perhaps all men were that at heart, or the majority of them, anyway; perhaps that was life, the bloom forced and the fruit denied. That, it might be, was the real secret of Timothy's great success.

"Isabel tell you that she's picked her pen up again?" the writer asked after a while. Peter merely moved his smiling eyes to where she sat, with a faint nod for his affirmative. "She could have been doing it all these years," Timothy assured him. "Lord knows why she ever stopped. Anyway, now she's beginning again, for we'll be anchored here for a year—until June, anyway, if the boy goes on with his classes."

"I've been waiting a long time for Isabel's 'Masterpiece,'" Peter told her smilingly.

"It may be dreadful," she pleaded, flushed and amused at such serious consideration. "At all events, I think I have a plot—'titanic,'" she added, laughing, "as Timothy some times says! And in a day or two I shall have it in shape enough to read it."

"And then you've got to be here, Peter," Timothy suggested suddenly. "Come on now—you and I. We went over her old essays in the Washington Square apartment, do you remember? She didn't ask us for advice then; we sat at her feet—where," he said in sudden and quite genuine feeling, "one of us sits still!"

"Both of us," Peter amended, liking his host better at this moment than he had done today, remembering affectionately how simple old Tim was after all, how easily touched, for all his joy and satisfaction in himself. He *was* handsome, successful, a faithful husband, a devoted father, a hard, straight-ahead worker—and that was much. It was even pleasant to feel that in a life so well rounded, with two unusual men in husband and son, Isabel might sometimes be glad to find room for a third, a companion with whom to wander some of the old streets of Paris, loiter at a picture show or in a tearoom. He had gathered from Timothy's talk that there was small loitering in his busy day. Chairs and tables were reserved for Timothy now, meetings were arranged, every expedition was important, formal, by mere virtue of having Timothy Yarrington in it at all. Winter might be nice in Paris, Peter mused, content, with Timothy and Isabel in one's life again.

The talk took a definitely hospitable tone when the clock struck seven and mellow church bells, in the neighborhood somewhere, confirmed it. He could go home and dress, but he must dine with them this first night; there would be other guests; no matter, Peter was "family" now.

"Don?" asked Don's father.

"I think he'll have a bite earlier. He loves to walk in these autumn evenings," his mother apologized. "Not a drawing-room exhibit exactly!" she explained to Peter.

"Gerry?" asked the writer.

"Germaine—no. She has a bad headache. She dreads the going back to school, poor youngster," Isabel again interpreted, to Peter. And as they separated she asked, smiling and flushing, "Will you really come and hear my story?"

"If you wouldn't rather"—Timothy was out of hearing—"rather read it just to Tim?" he said.

"No," she said hurriedly, half smiling, half troubled. "If you'll come it 'll make it *sure*. Say you will; be sure to tell him so tonight. Otherwise he may put it off and put it off! It's not important really, and he is always busy. But if you make a little occasion of it . . ."

He glanced at Timothy, big, triumphant, humming softly as he shook out the evening paper, enthroned in luxury and lamplight, and glanced back at his wife, slender, quivering, beautiful, the exquisite harp of a thousand chords.

"Of course," he said briefly. " 'Make an occasion of it,' indeed! To hear the author I've been waiting to hear from for twenty years read her 'Masterpiece'! What do you think *is* an occasion!"

So Peter came to the big gray "hotel" again, and again was sent upstairs by the old concierge, and again found himself in Isabel's lovely drawing room; this time with rain gathering and streaming, and gathering and streaming, down the tall, high, gray windows. All Paris smoked under the first rains, the streets gave back steel reflections, and the little steamers that threaded the gray rivers seemed dissolving in falling water, moving water, enveloping water.

It was the day of days for this sort of thing, Timothy said in satisfaction. He was alone beside a good fire, poking the bed of solid, glowing coals occasionally with the steel prod, smoking contentedly, a prisoner, he said, of the weather, and of one of his easy colds. Curse this half-and-half season anyway, he added good-humoredly.

"And where's the prima donna?"

"Oh, waiting for an entrance, Peter! The stage all has to be set for this performance," Timothy growled indulgently. "She has been as fussy as a high-school girl about it. Wouldn't have the boy in—the little girl went back yesterday, by the way. No, this is a first night for Isabel, all right."

"Now *stop,*" said Isabel herself, coming in with her hands full of papers. She slightly changed the position of a big round comfortable velvet armchair, glanced, with a whimsical smile at the men that admitted her own absurdity, at the dull, quiet afternoon light that was entering the window, lighted a standing lamp on a wrought-iron standard and finally seated herself, with a triumphant rustle of settling, like a busy little girl.

The cone of light encircled her beautiful head, with its

crown of thick tawny hair, and sent deep shadows under her almond eyes. Peter thought no mouth in the world ever showed the restraints, the character, the humor and charm, that Isabel's finely chiseled mouth expressed.

She was wearing some sort of loose embroidered gown; Rumanian, she explained when Peter admired it. It was dove gray, gold, black; it fell about her slender body squarely, in stiff angles, like a priest's robe; there was one immense clear emerald on her white hand.

"Isabel, you're lovelier than ever!"

"That's usual in this generation," she conceded, smiling. "Now this manuscript isn't really ready to be discussed," she began with a delightful catch of sheer shyness in her voice. "The most important part, the big scene," Isabel confessed, "I haven't quite finished. But what I want is your ideas—your verdict whether I have a story here or whether I haven't. Sometimes it seems to me tremendous and sometimes just—*bosh*. It's a society study——"

"Oh, Isabel, for heaven's sake!" her husband interrupted, amused and affectionate and impatient. "Get started! Cut out these airs! Did you ever see anything like it, Peter?"

"Well, my characters," she was beginning, when he interrupted her again.

"Go *on!*"

"I will, I will!" she agreed hurriedly. "But I really have to explain a little, Tim, because Peter was brought up in the Far West, and he doesn't know our home atmosphere. This is written of one of America's oldest and proudest New England families, Peter. Aunt Hannah, Timothy," she added with a glance full of significance.

"Oh no!" Timothy ejaculated simply.

"Rigidly theological, without ever having had a faint flash of true Christianity," Isabel resumed, "critical, proud—proud as Lucifer, Peter—cold, narrow, putting the family tree first and even their own terrible and revengeful God a little bit behind it, moribund, rotting, one of those families that has lost all sight of the plain things that began them, the big families, the expansion into a new country, the handling of pioneer problems, the very things that made them great! Old portraits, old dead silver, old rooms full of old, old furniture, old servants——"

"Old letters, hates and feuds, old offices full of rotting documents," Timothy added with a shudder. "That's one reason," he said to Peter, "that we live abroad. My cousin Jenny—br-r-r!"

"You'll recognize her," Isabel said, delighted with his feeling. "I've set my scene there, in a proud, dark, decaying old family," she went on. "Rich as Croesus, useless, and stupidly set in the ways of righteousness. And I've brought new wine into my old bottles——"

Her husband was interested now, already proud.

"What sort of new wine?" he asked.

"You'll see! The wine of youth," she answered. And while the rain lisped and dripped at the high, opaque window, and the coke fire burned, and the clock ticked and tocked steadily, she began to read.

As she read, Peter, listening with his elbow on the arm of his chair and his cheek resting on his palm, felt himself taken away across the salty north Atlantic into one of those staidly established old American towns that are by their very nature older than anything Europe will ever know. Settled only two hundred years, by cold and granite inhabitants, they seem to be a part of their own mountains, of their own flinty soil. Dark rooms, cold in winter, shaded and gloomy on the most burning summer day, polished floors, polished silver, traditions, heritages, judgments.

Isabel called her family the "Judsons," and the very name came almost instantly to Peter to express their adamant pride and reserve. Their woolen mill. Their wealth. Their heavy, quiet meals in a heavy, quiet dining room. Their bachelors. Their spinsters. Their solid, impregnable rectitude.

Old Madam Judson, sixty, steel eyed, lace shawled, silent.

Sarah and Caroline, unmarried at forty-three and -five. George, Cyrus and William, all unwed. Henry, eighteen years dead, and Henry's little girl, Ellen, eighteen years old and motherless since babyhood. Finally Henry Cyrus, father of the family, spade bearded, righteous, sixty-five.

Books, talk of reviews. Talk of national politics, of ancestors, of women's clubs. Talk of bridge, of golf, of the new factory. All talk merging into the silence that itself seemed something tangible in that old house.

Little Ellen with gold hair and shy brown eyes saying, "Yes, Aunt Sally. No, Uncle Billy." Little Ellen going daily with her grandmother and aunts for a drive with young Dick Sloane, the chauffeur, at the wheel of the big car.

And suddenly for little Ellen—love. Dick Sloane's murmuring voice, warm and trembling, in her ear; Dick's hand, hard and young, over her soft little aristocratic hand; Dick's hot kisses, frightening her, awakening her. Dick's arms——

"My God," Timothy Yarrington whispered at this point. "You make me sick. You make me sick. They're going to crush her?"

Isabel paused, her eyes bright with unshed tears, her cheeks red with excitement.

"That's my story," she said, breathing a little hard with sheer pleasure and pride at the look she saw in the men's eyes. "Life comes at last, after so many barren years, to the Judsons. The girl's body is perfect, the boy's is perfect. Perfect love, in the sweet, soft summertime, brings them together, and they find each other! But the Judsons, for all the elaborate frame they have built for life, for all their treasuring of its mementoes," Isabel, looking off the manuscript now, ruffling the pages with a nervous hand as she spoke, went on, "the Judsons won't have it! The girl is a Judson, the boy is a nobody. They must be parted; young and palpitating with their glorious first passion, they must be torn apart by the dry old empty hands of the Judsons——"

"By God, Isabel, you have a story there!" Timothy said

in a sort of breathless admiration, when she paused. "That's a story, dear—if you can develop it. Fish-eyed, flat-chested old maids, but they can put their narrow old Congress gaiters down on *that,* fast enough!"

"In the story they have her up for one of those family court-martials," Isabel proceeded. "You remember them, Tim?"

"How they love them!" he said bitterly. "A blubbering kid contradicting himself, getting in deeper and deeper. 'Let him speak, Jenny. Let him explain this himself!' "

He shuddered, and Isabel looked back at her written pages.

"It is decided to dismiss the chauffeur," she resumed. "And to take the little girl, Ellen, around the world with Grandma and Aunt Sarah."

"Good!" interpolated Timothy with acid relish. "Show her the Pyramids. Good!"

"The child stands stricken and silent," Isabel continued. "She has always been biddable—always obeyed. She listens, agrees, she has very little to say. Trunks are brought upstairs, and the man, Dick Sloane, sent ignominiously away. There is even a cold letter of recommendation written by Miss Carrie for Dick, so that all appearances shall be in order."

"Good touch!" Timothy said again, grinning appreciatively.

But the story, Isabel said, wasn't finished. More than love had found little Ellen out, it appeared. To the chill, stark consternation of all who loved her, there was worse. The child was no longer a child. The delicate little body was the chalice, now, of more than Ellen's life.

Peter had known that Isabel was a born writer. But in the few iron sentences in which she described the attitude of the Judson family he saw more than a mere piece of stupendous writing. It was the cruel, Christless religion of minds poisoned by jealousy, by worldly pride, by fear, by anger, by deep-rooted and quite unconscious limitations and stupidities, laid bare here before him.

"Is it as bad as that?" he asked when she paused. Isabel looked questioningly at her husband.

"Isn't it, Tim?"

Timothy Yarrington had his affectations, as none knew better than Peter. But he was not acting now. He was restlessly pacing the hearthrug, his hands sunk in the pockets of his velvet coat, his leonine head a little fallen forward, his brow dark.

"Yes, it *is* as bad as that!" he conceded. "The boy banished, the minister, the little girl convulsed with tears, disgraced, heartbroken! The aunts going about, opening and closing doors—everything kept from the servants, of course. Gloom. Gloom. The house full of horror because something *real* has happened in it! Yes, you've a story there, Isabel. How do you end it? They run away. They always do, God bless 'em! Thanks to them, there isn't an old family that hasn't its scandal!"

"No, I don't have them run away," Isabel said, turning back to her papers once more, her eyes sparkling. "They may. But that isn't the way the story ends. The boy has vanished, do you see? The girl is shut up in this mausoleum of a house, frightened, ashamed, overborne. There is to be a hospital experience, arranged with the discreetly horrified, discreetly helpful old family doctor——"

"And they would do it too!" Timothy breathed, now in his chair again, with his locked hands hanging between his knees and his eyes on his wife. "They would do it too!"

"My last scene—and this is the scene that I'm worried about," Isabel confessed, "is on the day when they are going to take the little girl to the hospital. One aunt has packed her bag, another has engaged two fine nurses; the limousine, with an old driver this time, is at the door. Grandma has succumbed under the blow, and the family friends hear that she has had a little return of her nervous breakdown. The uncles are all silent, watchful, determined that the blot on the family scutcheon shall be as quickly, as quietly as possible, wiped out. The old man, like a tiger on a short chain, is breathing through his nostrils while the insufferable details are dispatched; anything to have this thing behind them, to be walking impressively up the church aisle with the collection box again!

"Then the child, Ellen, speaks for almost the first time in the story," Isabel went on. "She sees the car waiting, she sees the stony faces, she doesn't know where her Dick is nor how to find him, and in one last frantic burst she begs for—life. She goes on her knees, she turns from one to another, she catches at her aunts' fingers—those cold, righteous, maidenly fingers.

"She sobs out that she isn't bad, she loves Dick, she loves her baby. Ah, please, please, they aren't to punish her little innocent baby! They've never had a baby in the house; she's always wanted one! He'll be hers—can't they see that? He'll be *theirs!* She doesn't want to go to the hospital and have Aunt Carrie's friends and Aunt Sallie's friends and Grandma's friends come in and see her and talk to her about appendicitis—she wants her little baby! Ah, please—he will be so cute! He will sit up in his high chair and blow those silly bubbles, as the babies do in the parks; he will have curls all over his little head! She's been bad, she knows that now, although she *didn't* know it—she had been so happy about Dick's loving her, until that night—that night was all wrong, they both knew it. They had worried about it, prayed about it, God knew how sorry, sorry, sorry they were! And as she sobs and stammers this out," said Isabel, "her face is soaked with tears. Wouldn't they *please* forgive her—let her go to Dick, let the baby come! Kings—kings had asked God for babies. Everybody couldn't have them! They were—why, babies were the world, after all. In a year or two he'd be in little ankle-strap slippers, he'd be toddling with his little head bobbing over trains and blocks! She *wanted* him so! They had told her that she could never marry now, that no decent man would want her now; she didn't mind that. But she had been dreaming of having her own baby in her arms. . . .

"And the story ends," Isabel said in a dead silence, her voice thick with tears, her cheeks washed by them, "by an aunt lifting her from her knees, and another aunt quietly opening the door, and a butler opening the big street door of the Judson house, and the old chauffeur opening the door of the limousine. And so life, and youth, and love . . . go out."

She stopped. There was absolute stillness in the library. Neither man moved his eyes from her for a long time.

Then Timothy cleared his throat and quite openly wiped his eyes and blew his nose. He stretched a hand for the manuscript, smiling unsteadily.

"Isabel, give it to me. I wouldn't trust you, or anybody, to touch it again. Leave it with me, I want to go over it. You have done it, my dear. It was worth waiting for!"

"Ah, Tim, you're not fooling me, after so many years?" her voice said wistfully. Peter saw that the whole thing had shaken her to the very soul. So potent had been the power of her words, her strangely vibrant, passionate tone, that he himself felt weak. He wondered if the world that would read Isabel's masterpiece would have even a faint shadow of the knowledge of what it was to hear it first in Isabel's voice.

"Peter," Timothy said, his voice still husky and his lashes wet, "is there anybody like her?"

"If you ask me," Peter said simply, "no."

The writer was eagerly handling the crumpled, written and rewritten pages. Isabel stood up. Peter, rising to go with her to the door, found himself invited, with one of her eloquent glances, to accompany her.

"Look at it, Tim," she said. "I'm going to show Peter your etchings." They left Timothy absorbed.

But in the hallways he felt that she had forgotten him. She

stood outside the library door, silent, and constraining him to silence. She was waiting for something perhaps. Her breath came unevenly, she gripped Peter's fingers in a cold hand, tapped the floor with one slipper.

Don came downstairs. Had she been waiting for Don? Peter looked at her expectantly, but she had no eyes for him. Her son came close to her, and she put one hand on his shoulder and raised her lovely face, white with a mother's love and a mother's anxiety, to the boy's grave, affectionate kiss.

"Remember how he's always loved you, always understood you, Don," she said in a whisper. "Go in, now, and talk to your father!"

'Twas the Night Before Christmas

CATHERINE BRUCE BOWDITCH, twenty-four years old, sat at tea in the Whitakers' impressive drawing room and wished from the bottom of her heart that she was dead.

If she could only die here, now, in the great brocaded chair that rose up like a throne behind her too correct new sportswear and her unfashionable knot of flyaway pale hair! If one of these horrible persons might suddenly look at her and exclaim: "Why, she's dead!"

But of course she wouldn't die. And unless she died she would have to go upstairs to dress, presently, and somehow get through dinner, and somehow endure the endless humiliations of the dance. And all the while she would have to pretend she was having a wonderful time.

Why had she come? *Why* had she come at all? But of course she knew why she had come. She had come because Mrs Whitaker, an almost forgotten friend of Aunt Ellen's gay youth in San Francisco, had taken it into her kindly heart to write Aunt Ellen and protest that it was ridiculous to have "Katy's darling girl mewed up" in a "preposterous" place like La Paloma. Catherine must come down to the Whitakers' Christmas dance and meet the children of her mother's old friends and have a "beautiful time." May Bayard's children were coming, and the Billings boys—Ellen remembered dear Sue Sweet, who married Henderson Billings?—and the Cowles and the Everhards—all of them. Ellen was to tell "little Catherine" that her "Aunty Whitaker" simply wouldn't take no for an answer. And if she needed a frock or two she could get them in San Francisco.

Catherine had merely raised the dark eyebrows, that were so odd a note in the general fairness of her hair and skin, upon the reception of this note. She was twenty-four; she had never had the feeling that she was either mewed up or vegetating in La Paloma. To be sure, she did not like dancing and crowds and excitement as much as some of the other girls did. But with Dad and his doctor friends making the dinner table interesting, and with three history classes to teach in high school every day, and with walks and terrace suppers and her garden, with all the books she had to reread, and all the books she had still to discover to amuse her, to say nothing of church and Community Chest and hospital visits and her club to fill her days, somehow she had never had any time to feel herself solitary or handicapped.

"Poetry and dreams," Aunt Ellen had once summarized her days. Which was nonsense, of course. There was small poetry in the problems the glove factory girls presented to the president of the Girls' Mutual Help Club; there was no element of dreams in the tiresome correcting of smudged history papers, week after week! That she liked poetry was undeniable, certainly, but so had her mother, and so did her wonderful father. Certainly she wasn't going to like her own life less because of any three days visit to the Whitakers', she had argued.

But in the end Aunt Ellen's counsel had prevailed. Aunt Ellen had reminded her that she did rightly belong to that Peninsula set that had loved her mother twenty-five years ago. There was a cultured, hospitable, amusing, interesting group down there, whose youngsters had grown up in a happy sort of cousinship, whose members traveled, played golf and polo, entertained the great personalities of the world from time to time. Why should Catherine content herself with the Jamiesons and the Thorntons of La Paloma when she could so easily cultivate more pleasing relationships?

"I adore Mary Jamieson, and Alice Thornton is my best friend," Catherine had protested.

"Yes, but you won't marry either Tod Thornton or Buzzy Jamieson."

"Ah? I perceive I am going after a husband?"

"Not that, of course," Aunt Ellen had said with a little red suddenly in her face. "But—but after all, you're twenty-four, and you've never noticed any of these boys at home."

Catherine had not answered, except presently with a wistful, "Oh, wouldn't it be nice if we could always be children in clean little ruffly white aprons out at the gate under the apple tree?"

A remark which had caused the doctor to look at her a little uneasily over his glasses, and which had the effect of redoubling Aunt Ellen's exertions to get her a new suitcase and a new coat at the "La Mode" and a really lovely gown of primrose yellow crepe at the shop whose smart new windows bore the impressive legend "Wilson Sœurs" above a smaller notice: "Ici on parle Français."

Beside all this there was the blue velvet and the sturdy brown tweed that was not yet a year old, and shining pumps, and transparent stockings, and violet soap, and the Chinese pajamas for such times as "the girls will be lying about on their beds talking over the good times," as Aunt Ellen had said. Catherine's new suitcase contained an outfit that had heartened her in spite of herself. After all, if somewhat small in build and shy with strangers, she *was* nice-looking, and these persons did mean to be kindly, and if she did not set the bay on fire, or rate as a beauty and a belle, still she might have a very nice time. And anyway—anyway she would be home again on Christmas Day, and the placid waters of her quite contented days would close again over the interruption.

So she had presently capitulated, and Buzzy Jamieson, on his way down to the city anyway—or he had said so at least—had brought her down and landed her at the Mark Hopkins Hotel in time for a sort of scrambled luncheon that preceded a general departure of all the Whitaker crowd for the Hillsborough country house.

And from that first moment everything had been awful. To begin with, Mrs Whitaker, rather large and noisy and formidable, had, it appeared, mistaken Buzzy for a chauffeur. Buzzy had been allowed to make a rather hesitating departure before either Catherine or Mrs Whitaker had realized that she was making the mistake.

Afterward, in the jumble of young people in the upstairs hotel dining room, Catherine had been able to identify no one and naturally had had no opportunity to identify herself. Young men and smartly groomed girls had been surging to and fro about a table loaded with cold foods; a great roast turkey was in process of demolishment; there were salads and sandwiches and a great many glasses. No one noticed her at all. Mrs Whitaker had been talking with intense concentration to a small, hard-looking woman whose fingernails, face, lips, hair, eyebrows and lashes were all thickly painted or dyed. They had been discussing some Harold, who had been "atrocious" to Laura.

"But I mean, it was simply unforgivable," said Mrs Whitaker.

"But I mean, it was outrageous," the little woman said.

"But I mean, after all, if you can't depend upon a man like *Harold* . . ."

"Well, *exactly*."

They had said these things and others just like them tensely and quickly to each other, frowning and eating and drinking and smoking as they talked. But after a while Mrs Whitaker had noticed Catherine, deserted with her plate of luncheon in her big chair, and had said brightly and loudly:

"Tell me about my old crush Johnny Bowditch. You know I was madly in love with him once. Does he just die of ennui in that God-forsaken town of yours?"

Catherine, the eyes of all the room turned curiously toward her at this onslaught, had rallied herself bravely. They were just persons like all other persons, these strangers; it was too absurd to let them alarm her right in the beginning!

"Oh, Dad's always busy," she had said, her voice growing more audible as she strained it a little.

"I know he was a perfectly wonderful doctor who buried himself and his books there when your mother died," Mrs Whitaker had said in her heartening loud way. "But what on earth does he *do?* He was on his way to be the best baby doctor in San Francisco when he went away," she explained to the room at large. "And one of the dearest of men, wasn't he, Betty?"

"He's busy night and day," Catherine had said. "You'd be surprised how many babies there have been in La Paloma since Dad got there!"

Oh, if she had bitten her tongue out before she had phrased it that way! But she had indeed been so innocent of any second meaning in the sentence that it had come to her only when some boy's voice gasping "Day and night is right!" and the cruel first burst of laughter, and the ensuing other lesser bursts of laughter, had died away, and when Mrs Whitaker, herself laughing until her fat face shook and the tears had rolled down her cheeks, had protested, "Now stop it, you're all very silly; stop it, I say!"

One or two of the girls had quite obviously tried to be nice to Catherine after that; they had felt sorry for her. But their own affairs were very absorbing, and even the kindest of them had not been unwilling to let her see how intimate, how happy, how diverted they all were.

Nicknames flew to and fro; all the allusions were to times and events of which she naturally knew nothing.

"Dodo, you remember what I told you I thought yesterday? Well, my dear, it's true, and don't breathe it. Lin, how about Monday? I can't, my dear. I'd adore to—I can't. Who's heard any more about Eliza? My darling, don't speak of it. I've got buckets to tell you about it; I can't now. Did you get the hat, Marian? Oh, you lucky! My dear, I met him, and I saw exactly what you saw, and I think exactly what you think, and I lay it entirely to his impossible mother. As to that other thing, I think it's the most awful thing that ever happened in the club, and I think he ought to get out."

There had been much of this, and on the side the murmur of the two middle-aged women about Harold. "No, but, Anna, someone ought to do something about Harold. I know, and I feel dreadfully about it. But I mean, we've got to do something. Well, *exactly.*"

After a while Marie Louise Billings, quite obviously the leader among them, as she was also the most startlingly beautiful and smart, had murmured to a boy, and Catherine had heard the boy say simply: "Oh, help!" Without an intervening pause the boy then had come to Catherine and had said abruptly: "I'm driving you down. When d'you want to go?"

He had hardly spoken on the trip. Not that it mattered. Catherine had not wanted to talk to him.

Then there had been an interlude not too dreadful. The rooms given to Mrs Whitaker's girl guests had adjoined; in fact, a rather sweet girl named Olive Boldt-Smith had shared Catherine's room. All the doors had been left open, and during the long processes of resting and bathing and dressing the girls had wandered to and fro in somewhat the fashion Aunt Ellen had suggested, talking more simply and pleasantly than was their custom when the boys were about, and making Catherine feel herself rather more like one of themselves.

But after that it had been bad again. The cocktail hour had been uncomfortable and self-conscious; dinner had been dreadful; the informal exodus to the country club and casual dancing there had been beyond words humiliating and difficult. There had been a luncheon scheduled at some place called Hollyhill the next day; all the girls had played bridge passionately both before and after it, and all the boys golf. Catherine had played neither. The meal had been very late; the hostess had twice quite audibly asked someone who on earth the little girl with the light hair was, and had twice said thoughtfully: "Oh, I do remember the mother—yes. I do remember John Bowditch—yes. Anna Whitaker asked her. Of course."

And Catherine had said another dreadful thing! Her face burned when she thought of it. She had said it at dinner the first night when a question had arisen of the courage of little Mrs Harrison, who would be left alone in the Harrison bungalow next month when Billy went East. Mrs Harrison had been one of the few persons who had talked kindly to Catherine that day, and Catherine, in the pause at the dinner table, could speak of her plans familiarly.

"I couldn't stay alone in any house at night," some girl had shuddered. "I think Emily Harrison is crazy!"

"She said today that she was having the chauffeur sleep in the house for protection," Catherine had contributed, just to say something, just to get into the conversation and show them all that she was not dead.

There had been a pause; a stare of surprise. Then the superb Marie Louise had demanded arrogantly: "Who said so?"

"She did. She told me so today."

"Well, I don't see where on earth she can put Martin," Ethyl Whitaker had said with that instant detailed concern for the affairs of her own set that was characteristic of the whole group and only matched by its entire ignorance of and indifference to the affairs of any other.

"If I had kept my mouth shut, if I had kept my *mouth shut,*" Catherine writhed, thinking about it. But she had not kept her mouth shut. Instead, remembering that the kind little Mrs Harrison had told her of her plans to turn Billy's study into a bedroom for the chauffeur, she had volunteered further: "Well, she said she wouldn't have room for him until Mr Harrison had gone!"

Then the delighted looks again, and the gales of quite uncontrollable laughter, and the gasping and strangling, and the monosyllabic stammered additions and comments, and the tears of joy, and finally the young man who had said at the hotel lunch, "Day and night is right!" exclaiming sorrowfully: "That nice Emily Harrison!" to set them off into pandemonium again.

Well, it was all very silly, but time was passing. Thank heaven this was Thursday afternoon, and tonight the night of the big dance. Tomorrow, blessedly, would be Christmas Day, and Buzzy would be waiting for Catherine to take her home, at four o'clock. She would be safe in her own bed tomorrow night, and she need never see these people again—no, nor think of them either.

But she was afraid that she would think of them. Shame and pride had been bitten too deep into her to forget. Burned into her soul was anger against the woman who had asked her here to make her wretched, and anger against herself that she had come.

They were having tea in a sort of drawing room; the handsome old country mansion was rich in these social rooms, with lamps and rugs and fireplaces and deep comfortable chairs. Outside the big draped windows showed vistas of bare garden and tossing trees; in here was firelight and warmth and beauty—only there was no light nor warmth nor beauty in Catherine's soul. She felt that somehow she had hurt it, hurt herself. She did not belong here, and if the young arrogance and security of these people were somewhat to blame for her sense of unwelcome, of superfluousness, she herself was to blame too. Well, there was less than another day of it to bear now; it was nearly over! They would presently be dressing upstairs for the late dinner and dance, and then the dance itself must somehow be endured, unless she dared claim sudden illness, and then it would be tomorrow, and time for packing and good-bys!

They were all still in the day's sportswear, stuffing sandwiches and cocktails; she was the only one who really was drinking tea. Marie Louise was more stunning than ever in her rough tweeds with her little hat at just the angle that suggested the covers of all next month's fashion magazines. That nice boy, the boy who had joined the house party sometime after luncheon today, evidently was chained to her side. Well, that was all right. Catherine never expected to see any of them again. . . .

He came over to her with the round brown sandwiches that had cream cheese in them. Oh, he *was* a nice boy, with a pleasant, rather long-featured face! Not exactly handsome, for the coloring was all a monotone of pale brown skin and pale brown hair and pale brown eyes, but his smile was so attractive!

He said: "Have you had one of these?" and Catherine smiled and said: "I don't dare have any more."

Instead of going away then, back to the little group in which he had been talking on the other side of the hearthrug, he sat down and said quite seriously:

"They say everyone is going to be fat next year."

Catherine laughed and, suddenly feeling quite happy, told him that she would have to wear out her new clothes, anyway, before she would dare get fat. The man—his name was Gregory Hull—watched her while they talked of the weather and of the house party and then said:

"If your mother was Katy Bruce, I think my mother knew her."

"Oh, did she!" Catherine said, pleased.

"I think so. I think your mother was my mother's bridesmaid."

"Oh, I would love to meet your mother then!"

"My mother died when I was seven."

"Oh?" Catherine said in a hushed voice. She told him that her own mother had died when she was three. They talked of motherless childhood—it had come to them in the same year—and Catherine went on to tell him something of her father's retirement into his work and his books, and her own life. Suddenly Gregory Hull, lowering his voice, speaking with an odd nervous smile, said:

"Tell me, do you like white kittens?"

It was unexpected. The girl looked at him bewilderedly.

"White kittens?" she asked, puzzled.

"Yes."

"I've never had one. Aunt Ellen has a big gray cat, but Dad has three dogs, and cats don't like a doggy house. I had a brown puppy once. But—but he was killed!"

She stopped abruptly, her strange black brows drawn up into a faint frown.

"I see," the man said quickly, seeming puzzled, even a little disappointed in his turn. "Well . . ." he added vaguely, in the tone that ends a conversation. "It's nearly six. I suppose we'll be starting up to dress pretty soon."

"I suppose so." Her heart sank. He was tired of her all of a sudden. "Do *you* like white kittens?" she asked timidly. It seemed a silly question, but after all he had opened the subject.

"I adore them!" he said under his breath, not looking at her. Instead he was looking at Marie Louise, dramatically beautiful as she stood talking to Van Whitaker before the fire.

"She's lovely, isn't she?" Catherine said.

Gregory gave her a serious look.

"Matts? She's quite extraordinary. She's what they would have called a 'toast' in the old days."

"Men like her so much?"

He laughed briefly. "Too much!"

"You know her very well, don't you, Mr Hull?"

"Judge Billings was my guardian. I lived with them for five years."

Catherine's heart was a little chilled again. But presently, when the girls all trooped upstairs to dress, she found it lighter than she had ever thought to feel it here, and the Whitaker mansion seemed for the first time what it might always have seemed to her—a luxurious country house filled with warmth and fires and lamplight, and the quiet service of maids in gray moiré, and the gay voices of the house party. House parties might be fun, under certain circumstances, the girl thought. If for every girl here there was a man as charming and gentle and cultured as Gregory Hull, then she no longer wondered that they found the occasion thrilling.

Upstairs, in the delightful big bedroom, tubbed and fresh and with still a long hour and a half to wait for dinner, she flung herself and her Chinese pajamas down on the big bed and lay, half musing, half reading, only dimly conscious of the voices and laughter of the other girls, and the rustle of taffeta slips and the running of bath water.

And from the half sleep she went into real sleep, light, deliciously refreshing and made magic by the old familiar dream. Catherine, awakening to find the room empty and the clock still giving her time to spare, lay idly, happily trying to recall it. In this special dream she was always a child again. Sleeping here in the Whitakers' guest room, once more she had been a child. The dream would not quite come back, but the impression of it remained, infinitely sweet, mysteriously bright.

A garden—there was often a certain garden in the dream—with a picket fence against which Shirley poppies crowded in a scarlet-and-pink jumble. She herself was at the gate, small and daring, in a stiff blue apron and flat white shoes. But of course the magic wasn't in the apron or the shoes or the garden; it was in the feeling—the feeling of littleness and daring and safety between the blueness of the sky and the drenching sweetness of the lilacs; it was childhood again. Nothing in her waking life ever had quite that glow, that pulsing thrill.

She and the Brown Puppy always opened the gate, in the dream, sometimes to find themselves close to the sea of which they talked respectfully, for the sea in the dream was really a kind old man. Sometimes they were climbing a hard, shrubby sort of hill over whose peak two cows looked, and then there was uneasiness in the dream, and Catherine would awake trembling and frightened. Now and then the dream went to the big white palace with bags of pearls and emeralds banked up behind the dancing girls, and the Brown Puppy reminded her that this was the *"Raybian-Nice,"* and Sindbad and Morgiana lived here. Lida, Catherine's old colored nurse, was often there, darning. And she sometimes told Catherine to stop thinking about the *"Raybian-Nice"* and do her arithmetic, at which Catherine and the Brown Puppy departed at a wild childish gallop, and got through the Sandy Place to the Attic where the rain was beading the little low dusty windows, and where the Goat was.

Not often, not always alike, yet always with that same feeling of a child's heaven in it, the dream had come and gone through all her days; through her motherless, quiet childhood, through her country girlhood, through these grown years when between her teaching and her gardening, long walks in the woods with her father, long evenings of poetry and talk by the fire, she had been still in her heart the aproned child of the garden of long ago. It was always like a special privilege, a sort of blessing, to find the Garden Gate and the Shirley poppies and the Brown Puppy again, and she always awakened from the dream with a feeling of complete well-being, of something more than mere everyday happiness.

That happiness was upon her now as she lay thinking, watching her bedroom fire; it remained when the girls came flocking in, all agog over dressing; it colored all the house party with a rosier light. They *were* nice girls; they had only been a little strange, as she had been. And probably the boys had meant to be friendly, too, if they had only known quite how to go about it. And especially had Mr Hull—Gregory Hull—been wonderful and kind. Putting on the primrose-yellow crepe, fluffing up her primrose-yellow hair, she listened to the girls' talk about him.

"Greg Hull—isn't he superb? Oh, he's marvelous. I'm mad about him. Marie Louise, isn't he marvelous?"

"He's been away at medical school for two years; he's just

doing his intern work at the City and County," Marie Louise, draping her black-and-ivory beauty in savage gypsy stripes, answered with a modest air of possession. "He only got back yesterday and took Mamma to a movie last night and came down here today."

"Is he staying with you, you lucky thing?"

"Off and on. He hates parties and things. He's studying too."

"You're crazy about him!" some girl said accusingly. The beauty arched her flawless eyebrows, shrugged matchless ivory shoulders.

"I should be crazy about a man who is going to spend all his money on a pellagra germ in Puerto Rico!"

"Is that what he's going to do?"

"Something like that. He's a visionary, Greg."

But the color had come up into Miss Billings' face, Catherine noted, and there was a complacent little drag to the corner of her full red mouth.

"Is he rich, Matts?"

"Well, his mother was Florida Parsons, you know. Oil. Yes, he has enough money."

"My mother was his mother's bridesmaid," Catherine said, powdering her small white nose busily.

"Who said so?" The query came like a pistol shot from them all. They were so entrenched in knowledge of themselves that a new detail was always a sensation.

"He just said so tonight, when we were having tea."

"I saw him making passes at you," said Ethyl.

"And your mother knew his mother?"

"It seems so." She might be going to have a horrible time tonight, but at least, Catherine reflected, she was looking her more than best. The soft rich shade of the new gown was infinitely becoming, and the happy dream had left a glow in her eyes and a tinge of transparent apricot on her cheeks. She felt confident, expectant, as she went downstairs with the others.

The dance was at the club, and the dinner preceded it and got well mixed into it; there was small formality and it was all lots of fun. Boys who had ignored her until now came up and asked Catherine to dance, and girls she hardly knew brought up other boys, and everything went with a happy rush. Even if one had to sit out a dance, one sat at the table, which was quite different from occupying one of the dreadful chairs along the wall, and there was always nice Richard Everhard, with his crutch and his bandaged foot, for a companion. Marie Louise Billings, and apparently Gregory Hull also, had had to go to another dinner, and they and their party were late. But they came in at about eleven; Catherine saw them come in, and her heart did something that it had never in her life done before when she noticed that after a little preliminary laughing and talking with Mrs Whitaker and Ethyl, who still intermittently kept their reception positions at the door, Gregory was making his way to her.

It was like a burst of sunshine in darkness . . . it was floating . . . it was singing and flying and suffocation. . . .

He was beside her; he had sat down in the empty place next to her own. The fine, good, smiling face, with its rather pale tan and its rather light brown eyes and its brushed thick mop of pale brown hair, was close to her own.

"Dancing this?"

"No. I was just telling Mr Everhard that I'm panting it out. I'm not accustomed to much dancing, and I'm—honestly—out of breath."

Gregory Hull picked up the wrap that was lying on a near-by chair.

"May I put this on this girl, Dick, and take her outside to get her breath? I don't know whose it is?"

"It happens to be mine," Catherine said, smiling, getting to her feet. She thought everyone looked at them as they quite openly crossed the floor between two dances, and was not surprised. Mr Hull was a well-groomed figure in his evening wear.

They went through a sort of glassed big porch and out upon a terrace drenched with winter moonlight. The air at Christmas-time was balmy, soft; other couples were standing on the wide, flagged space that was broken with pots of flowers and low wicker chairs; Gregory guided Catherine to a somewhat inconspicuous corner and drew two chairs together invitingly.

"Are you going to be warm enough, Miss Bowditch?"

"I'm smothered in this thing. I was thinking of you."

"Oh, I'm fine." A certain repressed excitement was to be seen in his manner. The girl's thoughts went to her unknown mother, who had been bridesmaid to this man's mother; what was he so anxious to say, and had it to do with these joyous, pretty girls of the long ago?

"You're sure you're not going to be cold, Kit?"

She leaned forward with a sudden motion in the soft gloom, one hand at her heart. He heard her breath come short.

"What's the matter?" he asked, a trembling laugh in his own voice. "People call you Kit, don't they?"

"No," she said, swallowing, her voice almost inaudible. "Nobody . . . nobody . . ." And then, in a whisper: "Who told *you?*"

"The little lady at the other side of the Sandy Place, dear. You know how she calls out, 'Your apron, Kit! Don't get your apron wet!' "

A silence, when his hand was warm over her icy one, and her eyes glittered upon his in the shadows. Beyond them the music pulsed softly, and about them, through the bare trees and the grapevines and down the angle of the roof, dripped the silver moonlight.

"Don't be frightened. It's terribly exciting, but there's nothing to be frightened about. I'm right here, darling. I'll take care of you!" Gregory said.

"But you . . . you . . ." she whispered. "Who are *you?*"

"I'll tell you. But it's all so—— You're not going to faint?"

"No, but—but it was a dream. It's all only a dream. Are we dreaming now?"

"Perhaps we are, a little. And perhaps all that was part real. You're all right, aren't you, dear?"

"I'm—oh yes, I'm fine." He had drawn his chair closer to hers; his arm was almost about her, and her cold hands were tight in his. "Tell me," she breathed.

"I can't tell you much; I'm as puzzled as you are. Only—only I found it out first, do you see, and I've had hours to think about it. It came to me at lunch."

"What did?"

"The—well, everything. I've had time to get used to it—you haven't. I was all shot to pieces, at first, just as you are. But it's all—well, no story out of our *'Raybian-Nice'* compares to it!"

"Our *'Raybian-Nice'!*"

"Remember? Rain, and being in the Attic——"

"Oh, *remember!* Why, it was only this afternoon——" Her gaze broke wonderingly over him. "You—you never were in that Attic?" she asked.

"But of course I was, darling! That was my grandfather's attic in Boston, where I was when I was a small boy."

"It isn't a *real* attic?"

"Of course it is. And you and I'll see it, someday. The Garden Gate was dream——"

"What Garden Gate was dream?"

"The one with the pink and red flowers, and the white pickets, and the chipmunk that had the little store——"

"Oh, the chipmunk! Oh, so there was a chipmunk! Oh, Gregory," Catherine said, clinging to his hand. "I'm a little scared. But that garden is just our garden, and those are the Shirley poppies I plant every year. It's there—you could see it. But—but—but all this can't be happening!"

"*Could* see it? I will see it! I'm going to take you home tomorrow, of course, and eat my Christmas dinner with you. What do you think I'm made of? And of course it's all happening! Our dream has come true, Kit, and all we've ever got to do is just go on dreaming it. It 'll be our secret; we never must tell anyone——"

"Yes, but you never—there never was anyone else in my dream. *You* weren't there!"

Gregory laughed joyously.

"But of course I was! That's where all the delay comes in!"

Her puzzled laugh echoed his.

"Has there been delay?" she asked excitedly. "We only met before lunch today."

"I know. But let me tell you from the beginning. You see, I've been working myself dizzy getting through my medical work; even now I've got to go to Vienna for six months; I'll tell you all that later. But the meaning is that I've not had much time for fun; nor wanted it either. Nor ever been in love, Kit, though I've liked lots of girls well enough.

"Because I've always had this dream; it's come to me off and on ever since I was a little boy crying myself to sleep because Mademoiselle was mean to me."

"Mademoiselle! Then she was that—that—— Wait a minute. . . ."

"Go on, darling, you're close to it!"

"That Voice in the Chicken House! Oh, and that was terrible! I always used to wake up frightened when we came to *that.* I remember trying to drag myself away from it, and having darling Budge say, 'It's Mam'selle; we've *gotter* go——' "

"Budge? Who was Budge?"

"The Puppy. My little sweet Brown Puppy that was killed when I was five. I saw it—saw the butcher cart do it, and they couldn't comfort me. They were afraid I was going to die of grief. But what they never knew, and what I couldn't tell them, you see, was that he came back to me; he was always along, and we talked together in my dreams. I always used to wake up rested and happy, but I never could explain why."

The man was silent, smiling; she could see his face in the dim light from the terrace as she went on hesitantly:

"And you dreamed the same dreams and went the same places? But I knew—I knew today, when we first met, when I heard you laughing and talking with Ethyl, that somehow and somewhere I'd known that voice——"

"And I knew you by your voice. I knew instantly that it was you. And that's what I was trying to get at, at tea this afternoon. Remember?"

"I remember you came over, and we talked of our mothers. But you didn't say anything about *this?"*

"Yes, I did. But you didn't get it. Remember I asked you if you liked white kittens?"

"White *kittens!"*

"Yes. Because—now don't get scared again, and I'll tell you how I think it is. You were a little lonely girl whose whole heart was wrapped up in a Brown Puppy, weren't you? And the Brown Puppy was killed. And I was a little heartbroken motherless boy three thousand miles away whose one comfort, whose only companion was a small, square white cat with a ruff about her neck. Mademoiselle took her away from me; she said cats gave children ringworms and poisoned their breath and I don't know what, and I grieved as only a puzzled, lonely child can grieve for a pet.

"Then came our dreams. My very first one was of a garden filled with bright flowers, and a sense of complete happiness and—and——"

"Oh, safety, being safe!" she supplied eagerly as he paused.

"And running round there among the flowers on a brick path——"

"Yes, yes, a brick path!"

"With bottles beside it, under those flamy flowers, and the little sweet white ones——"

"Nasturtiums and alyssum! Yes! You'll see them!"

"Running round there was my white kitten—my Kit."

"Then you—you——" the girl stammered in a whisper, her hand against his shoulder to hold him off while her eyes found his. "You're *Budge!*"

"I'm Budge. Or I was. I haven't been for a long time, and you haven't been the white kitten either. But that's the way it started, and that's the way of dreams, too, Kit. You never see people in dreams, you just feel them—know that they're there and who they are. You were my white kitten first, and I was the puppy you were breaking your little heart over, and then gradually we were people. Why, I used to take your hand in the Sandy Place, darling. Kittens haven't hands!"

"Oh yes, and we talked—from the beginning. And you buttered my bread—a puppy couldn't butter bread!"

"You weren't the white kitten any longer, and I knew it; you were someone called Kit, my friend, the person who waited for me."

"And you weren't Budge, of course! I suppose I hardly remembered the real Budge. I only had him for a few weeks. You were someone who had started with that feeling—it was something I never thought out; I can hardly think it out now. But it—you—had to have a name, and the name stayed Budge."

"You'd tell me, I know, that you had on your best green velvet gown. But I don't remember really seeing it."

"My green velvet gown! Then you don't see each other in dreams, Gregory? It's knowing—feeling—sensing each other by some other way?"

"It must be. We never really saw each other; we were just together, and knew it, and it made the dreams heaven."

"And it lasted after I wakened, Gregory. For whole days the glory of it would stay with me."

"And it's here now, Catherine. My little white-kitten Catherine. Remember you were talking of Emily's staying alone in her house, at lunch?"

"I remember," her contented voice said from the shoulder where her head rested. "I remember something about it made me feel embarrassed. I can't remember exactly what, now. It doesn't matter."

"Well, the instant I heard your voice something shook me like an earthquake, and my hands got cold, and I couldn't swallow. There was the white kitten's adorable voice, and where was the white kitten? I looked at you and looked at you, a little girl with gold hair and funny kitteny eyes and—well, I tell you I was trembling, darling, and I didn't know what to do.

"Playing golf with Van and Simp later, it began to come to me. I took twelve shots on the ninth. I didn't know what I was doing. I couldn't wait to get home and ask you that question about the white kitten.

"And there you were at tea, still seeming a little strange and shy with them all, but so adorable, and I went over and sprang my question, and you looked completely puzzled.

"I came down to earth with a crash. I tell you it made me feel sick. You didn't know anything about it; it was all blank to you. The voice was there, and every time you spoke it went up and down my spine like a galvanic battery, but you didn't know anything about it! Everything seemed to go to pieces.

"And then, when I was dressing, I remembered your saying that you'd had a little brown puppy—and the funny look in your eyes when you said it—and I realized that though I'd never seen your eyes before today I'd *known* them, known that scrunchy, kitteny look in *somebody's* eyes—*something's* eyes. . . .

"And then everything was clear! 'Why, of course,' I thought, 'she was only a baby and I was only a little boy when those dreams began. No boy meant anything to her then. She dreamed of her puppy, just as I did of my kitten, and in the strange other values of that other world things happened that couldn't happen here: the dream grew up, and the love that was the strongest the little girl and boy could know transferred itself to each other; and they knew it, too, even though things had their old names. Terror was still 'Mademoiselle,' even long after they'd grown away from her, and to get one's apron wet was still naughty, and bread and butter——' "

"With 'razums'!"

"With razums, of course, or brown sugar—bread and butter was still the treat of treats!"

The girl was silent, her eyes not moving from his.

"Did our mothers do this for us, Gregory, do you suppose?"

"I don't know, my darling. Perhaps so. Ah, here come dreadful people toward us, to break us up—Matts and Van, I think."

"They think I'm monopolizing you."

"They think you're stuck with me and getting bored. But I drive you home tomorrow, darling!"

"But how are we to face them, Gregory?"

"They'll not see anything. Remember that they think we met only today!"

"Oh, but I'm all to pieces—I'll laugh like an idiot and burst out crying and not know what I'm saying!"

"You'll have me, right near you most of the time, bucking you up, and scared to death too!"

"And are we 'Miss Bowditch' and 'Mr Hull'?"

"Oh, Lord, no! We can't go back. My darling, say it just once, before they can hear. Because I'm so drunkenly, idiotically happy, and I do love every feather of your yellow hair so desperately!"

She was close beside him; they were both standing now. There was only time for a quick whisper.

"Ah, I do, Greg, with all my heart and soul!"

The moon was high overhead; it turned her hair to pale silver and made her eyes look black. Down in the village suddenly began an uproar of Christmas bells against the warm silence and darkness of the night.

High Holiday

THEY STOPPED THE CAR half a mile below Bellamy Beach, and the woman looked thoughtfully at the man who was driving.

"This," she said thoughtfully, "was an idea."

"It occurred to me," the man responded modestly, "that nobody would ever see anybody, at Bellamy Beach."

Sally Pinckney, who was exquisite, cool, fresh, even on this terrible day, regarded the swarming crowds, the flags, the peppered beaches half a mile away, with a faint, puzzled frown.

"Ugh!" she said. And presently, "Why do they come here, Bob?"

"The people?"

"The people. These fat women, panting and perspiring, and these men in thick clothes, and these frightful children."

"They like it," he stated simply.

"What can they *like* about it?"

"Oh, noise, excitement, company . . ." he offered vaguely.

"It is my idea of hell," Sally mused. "Bob," she said after a pause, "I am very unhappy. My heart is breaking."

"I know!" he said quickly.

"And yet I have everything," Sally continued in a puzzled voice. "I have—oh, looks, position, money, a nice child . . ."

"Conceded. You have everything, Sally," the man said briefly as she fell silent.

"We have our basket, with caviar and chicken and iced drinks and peaches," Sally pursued, "and we go back to Pleasantways—servants, coolness, fresh rooms. We could start to Canada or to Hawaii tonight, if we wanted to. . . .

"And yet," she persisted, sudden tears in her beautiful eyes, "yet we are *wretched*. I've always been wretched. I always will be.

"It's all such a farce! 'The beautiful Mrs Pinckney!' Oh, bah!"

"You wouldn't be unhappy—with me," the young man said steadily.

"Oh yes, I would, Bob!" she said, with a stabbing sigh, after a long appraising look. "I know, we like each other now," she resumed feverishly, "we talk as if—oh well, we talk the usual thing now! But we wouldn't be happy. The women who do it, even if they get divorces and make everything legitimate—they're wretched too. We're all wretched!

"What I'm saying this for," she added in a silence, "is because *we're* supposed to have everything. But look at them—those horrible creatures swarming over there at Bellamy Beach. What of *them?* They have nothing! They haven't wealth nor youth nor beauty nor position; they're all poor, greasy, crowded, ugly, they have on filthy, cheap clothes, they live in filthy, cheap neighborhoods! Do you suppose," she asked, turning to her companion her dangerous, sad, wild amber eyes, "that any human being ever had a moment of happiness of any sort in a hell like Bellamy Beach?"

Robert Lippincot, instead of answering, looked deeply into her eyes for a long, long minute. Then he said huskily:

"I neither know nor care. I know that I adore you!"

Her soft, boneless little white hand fluttered to meet his; her whiteness, her sweetness, her fragrant youth, leaned against his shoulder.

"Oh, how I hate—living!" she said.

The day—this same broiling August day—had broken for another woman some hours earlier "like a boil," as she herself simply expressed it.

It was the nineteenth of August, always a bad day in

Martha's annals. Tearful and bewildered and ashamed, she had married her good man on this day, twelve years earlier.

Martha had been working for Mrs Percy Patterson then —working hard, like the nice, clean, straight, honest Irish girl she was. And she had been going with Thaddeus O'Day.

Thad had brought her home from an all-night dancing contest, in the summer dawn, and Mrs Patterson, jaded and icy-tongued and fish-eyed, had been awaiting them. Besides Mrs Patterson, on the porch, had been Martha's gorged suit-case of cardboard painted not very successfully to look like alligator skin. Mrs Patterson had already packed Martha's bag for her.

Mrs Patterson had sassed Martha, and Thad had sassed Mrs Patterson, and Martha had cried. Then Mr Patterson had come downstairs, tousled and red-faced, to reinforce his wife, and Martha—well, the upshot of it was that whether Martha was really as innocent as a lily or whether she wasn't, she was fired.

She and Thad had been married that day, hurried and shamed and bewildered by the dirtiness of life. Thad had had a few debts. Martha had had half a month's pay at the rate of fifty-five dollars a month, and the ten-dollar gold piece that she had won the night before for dancing down all the other girls.

A year from that day, in the little annex to hell that was called "Ward III. Obs. No children," young William had been born. And two years later, to the minute, little Sarah. It had been on the portentous nineteenth of August that Thad had been brought home dying, too, although he had lived for months.

And now Thad was two long years dead, and here was the nineteenth of August again, finding Martha, who had been such a scared little innocent rose on that first nineteenth, a lean, colorless, sad-eyed woman of thirty-three, and finding William eleven, and little Sarah nine.

Martha, awakening in the decent cramped servant's room

in an apartment in the East Sixties, thought first of the heat, and then of the day, and then of the children. William, eleven. Little Sarah, nine. God help the kids!

Then her musing reached money, and here her thoughts lingered for a long, long while. Her clock went around to six-thirty; she stretched out her hand and silenced the alarm. She had nine dollars and seventeen cents; it was visible, piled on her decent, ugly bureau. She had counted it last night. She also had a faint suggestion of toothache.

Under ordinary circumstances she would have taken some of the dollars to a dentist and traded them to him, with the toothache, for peace. But these were not ordinary circumstances. This was the Birthday. The children would be looking for her already, although they well knew she never got old Mrs Canning started for the day until after ten, at the earliest.

"My God, what a day!" Martha said half aloud. It was a prayer. She did not feel equal to the demands of this day. She hated it already, sending its puffs of warm, lifeless air into her room at six o'clock. What would it be at eleven? What would it be at three?

A desperate unwillingness to carry out her prearranged program with the children beset her. Its details smote upon her mind appallingly and crushed her spirit with utter weariness. Left to herself, waiting on the stupid old lady, in the quiet airy apartment, she might have gotten through the day, even in the burning heat, even with the toothache.

But to face the Birthday—today!

She got up, sick with heat already. The William Ayers Pinckneys were down on Long Island; only "her mother" and Martha were in the apartment. The old lady slept late. Martha could take her bath in leisure and repair, already perspiring and wilted, to the blazing kitchen. August battened at the shaded windows like a besieging army.

The clean icebox smelled vacantly; the clean milk bottle smelled. The breadbox smelled; the spotless sink had its own odor. And from outside came the frightful city smell—pavements, walls, garbage carts, tar melting in sunlight, wood rotting in it.

Thunder had been muttering in the southwest yesterday afternoon; it had growled all through the short, airless night. But there was no sound of thunder now; there was not a shred of cloud in the white, merciless sky.

Martha aired the apartment cautiously, darkening it immediately again. She took the old lady her milk, her morning newspaper and the dutiful daily letter from Mrs Pinckney. There was a letter in Doris' nice little block lettering, too—a letter Martha would hear later, many, many times. It would tell of "swiming" and "divving," and that Doris "gessed" Granny could hardly "beleive" that they had to wear their "swetters" as soon as the sun went down. Doris' governess didn't believe in spelling; she liked Doris to spell all wrong because it freed Doris' psyche.

Doris was just little Sarah's age—nine.

The substitute nurse came at ten, and at three minutes past Martha was hurrying down the hot street to the stifling subway. It was almost insufferable today; on the seat opposite Martha the young woman with the heavy baby, and the new baby so near, looked faint and sick.

She went to St Margaret's first, for William, a lean, nice, quiet, shabby little boy, and then three blocks walk in the heat, asking questions about arithmetic and about the other boys, and a car ride to Holy Angels, to get Sarah. And then they three were together, as they so loved to be, bumping along in the subway. It was a terrible day for the subway, but time was precious, and since the expedition was irrevocably and unchangably to be to Bellamy Beach, Martha's timid suggestions of some cooler plan had met with no encouragement; since it was positively to be Bellamy, the sooner they got to the sea the better!

Willie was like Thad, quiet, affectionate, uncomplaining. Sarah was bolder, articulate and eager. Willie looked rather peaked, his mother thought; he was not half so happy at St Margaret's as Sarah was at Holy Angels.

"Are you all right, Mamma?"

"Well, I woke up with a sort of a little toothache, dear."

"I'll say a prayer for it!" Sarah promised loudly, instantly withdrawing into her own soul, her lean little stubby hands tight on her eyes.

"Oh, Mamma, can't they fix it?"

"Well, I knew it 'd go away immediately, so I didn't bother. I didn't"—all gallant motherhood was in her smile —"I didn't want to lose a minute of today!" she reminded him.

But the boy's blue, tender eyes were unsatisfied.

"If it gets worse will you go to the dentist, Mother?"

"Oh, sure I will!"

"You said last Sunday it would soon be the day, and it *is* the day!" Sarah exulted. Her small face clouded, she leaned against her mother. "But when it comes night I won't want to go back," she muttered sullenly.

The sword turned and twisted in Martha's heart, and she wished they were all dead and safe with God.

"Well, now let's not think about that till we have to!" she said cheerfully, beating lightly on the little hand that clung so tightly to her own.

"The fun won't really begin till we get to the beach, will it, Mother?" Willie said in his brooding, strange little voice.

"Was any little feller in trouble this week, Willie?"

"How'd you mean, in trouble?"

Willie had found a discarded page of comics from the morning paper. He was devouring it eagerly; his sister crammed against him for her share.

"Like you told me that little boy cried all night, that's mother went to the incurable cancer," Martha said obscurely. But Willie understood.

"A feller got whipped!" he remembered. Martha winced.

"One of the big boys?"

"No, he was a little kid that sassed them," Willie answered absently, studying his comics.

She shut her eyes. The subway buzzed and roared and shook and hammered hotly upon its way. The underworld smelled of earth, of dust. They crashed into stations, crashed out again.

"Did the little feller they whipped cry?"

"No ma'am," Willie said. Presently he added, "He sort of sniveled at night. His mother's dead. He said his mother used to make him little tiny pancakes, no bigger than a quarter."

Her heart was sick again. Her tooth drummed, drummed, tirelessly.

"I used to make you pancakes before Papa died," she said wistfully. Willie did not hear. But Sarah fawned lovingly upon her and said tenderly, "'Member that I useter drink your tea, Mother? Evvy Sunday night you'd let me have a little cup of tea all to myself? That said 'Baby' on it?"

"I have your little cup," Martha told her in a dreaming, dispassionate tone.

"Have you my blackboard Papa bought me?" Willie demanded with interest. He never forgot to ask about the blackboard.

"Stored with the other things."

She was in despair when they reached the end of the line. It was some way from the beach, and the world was blazing in noontide. Dust, sand, heat, glare; their feet chipped hopelessly along the endless cement walk. A blur of pink and blue and white, ahead, was the concessions and the boardwalk, the flags and the ocean.

Very few pleasure makers were astir. Awnings were motionless in the heat; the very shade they threw throbbed with hotness. Willie's pale little face was moist with sweat; Sarah's cheap voile dress stuck to her arms. Martha carried their brief, thick coats. Her tooth settled down to a racking ache; her temples were sore.

"We're at Bellamy!" Sarah shrilled, undaunted.

"But ain't there usually crowds here, Mother?"

"The crowd 'll be here this afternoon, all right."

They began to smell popcorn and the oily grease from sausages popping on sheets of hot metal. Flags hung weak and weary. Passing restaurants, they caught sickening whiffs of decaying shellfish.

The little shops and concessions and counters were packed closely together. Every inch of the shore was occupied. The ocean looked pale and dispirited, it looked low; the surf came in in little sluggish slaps. Martha was conscious of throbbing tooth, throbbing temples, hunger.

"Can we have hot dogs, Mother?"

"You can, then, unless you'd like the little meat cakes better."

The thought of either was forbidden her, for the tooth was a biting tooth. She had some buttermilk. The children had frankfurters in rolls, ice-cream bricks, potato chips and heavy oblong cakes of cream-filled chocolates wrapped in silver paper.

"Gee, Mother, you're kind to us!" Willie said, rubbing his lean little cheek against her shoulder.

"Well, it's your birthday!" she reminded him. "Oh, my son, my son," said the heart of Rachel within her, "how kind I could be to you if I might!"

"Mother, could we wave? A girl at Holy Angels mother lets her wave."

"Well, here's what I was thinking, darlin'." She must pull herself together; the heat was nothing, the toothache was nothing, and as for the constant aching loss of her children, why, there were women in the old country who knew that the creatures, winter after winter, wouldn't get enough to eat! "Here's what I was thinkin', dear," she said, "that we'd do a few of the things now, whatever you'd chose—the railroads or the caterpillar or the swings or whatever—and then we'd go down and sit under the pier, on the beach, and you could wade then if you wanted to!"

Willie had always been an affectionate, appreciative little fellow. But she never remembered him quite like today, when he looked up at her again, all tenderness, and said:

"Gee, you are kind, Mother!"

She smiled, taking a neatly ironed handkerchief from her bag and wiping her wet face. The heat, the throbbing toothache, the consciousness of parting coming so fast. And above all, money.

Her thoughts wove money like threads on a loom. Seven dollars—and the cheapest concessions ten cents each, and some of them fifteen cents.

"Are we going to have our pitchers taken, Mother, like we did last year?"

"Maybe we will, when we come back, if he's open."

"He's open now!" Sarah exclaimed. Martha pretended not to hear.

Willie dared to ride on the Big Dipper; Sarah wept because she did not dare. Martha stood outside the painted gay pickets that fenced the entrance and tried to comfort Sarah. They all walked on, and Martha let them divide an enormous popcorn ball. But Sarah would not stop crying, and the crushed particles of the corn stuck to her wet cheeks.

"Gee, I could ride round that thing fifty times!" said Willie. "Would that cost seven dollars and a half, Mother?"

"It would cost a terrible lot," Martha answered, pressing one work-worn, thin hand tightly against her cheek.

She looked at her wrist watch; it was ten minutes past two. The day was merciless, blazing; the heat had not even now reached its height. The boardwalk was insufferable, even the sea looked hot.

Under the pier a few nurses and children were spread out in the hot stripes of shade. Martha and Willie and Sarah sat down near them and looked at them interestedly; their fretful voices pierced the sticky, endless afternoon.

"Don't do that, Lloyd. Don't do that. Lloyd!"

The littlest girl was lying on her back with a pail inverted over her face. Occasionally she stuck a long bare leg straight up in the air.

"Don't keep that nasty tin thing over your face," the nurse kept saying. "Take that nasty tin thing off from over your face!"

"I like it, it keeps me cool," the little girl kept answering fretfully, annoyingly.

"It's half my bucket! It's half hers and it's half mine!" the older child stated jealously from time to time.

"Whew!" the nurses said. "Isn't it hot? Isn't it *awful!*"

"I don't know that I ever remember a day as hot as this one," Martha said in an undertone.

Willie was digging; just the sand he could scoop without moving, but beside him was growing a formidable holc. The scenic cars roared and crashed, and the faint ecstatic screams of women passengers smote the lifeless air.

"What would they give you, at St Margaret's, for supper, on a night like this, Willie?"

"Oh—I don't know." His thin little hand graded a terrace carefully. "Beans, I guess," he said indifferently. "Or maybe spuds. Bread—you can have all the bread you want, and sometimes you get another guy's butter. And puddin'."

"You wouldn't get any fruit, deary?"

"You might get apple sauce," Willie conceded after thought.

"Nor corn on the cob?"

"Oh gee, no."

"What would the puddin' be, Willie?"

"Oh, tapioca or rice, I guess. Sometimes they have a sort of jelly; it's keen." He was paying no attention to his words.

"Mother, when can I wave?"

"But, darlin', the other children are waitin' to wade until it's a little cooler, can't you see?"

"But it's my birthday!" Sarah protested jealously.

She began stubbornly to wade, but there was small pleasure in it, with the sun beating down upon her head, and she came back, to sit with wet sandy legs beside her mother. The conversation took its usual turn.

"Tell about the house we're going to have, Mother!"

Willie deserted his sand castle to crawl close to her and listen. Martha's thoughts had been traveling during the past half-hour; traveling back to the city, crossing town, rising up through a great city building in an elevator.

"Doctor Graham, I'm the practical nurse that brought Mrs William Pinckney's little girl in to see you, if you remember? I'm in a great deal of pain, Doctor. . . ."

But it was the Birthday. And the children knew that they did not have to be returned to their respective institutions until seven o'clock. Martha abandoned her dream of flight, of God-given relief. If the toothache might stop, and if the thunder and the blessed rain would come nearer and nearer and nearer, and soak and splash and stream over the baked city, and if the children would go back with reasonable cheerfulness . . .

She roused herself.

"Well, you see, the first thing to it would be that we'd house-hunt."

"No, first you'd tell us, Mother!"

"Oh, sure I would. Well, I'd come up some Sunda' afternoon and say to you, very quiet, 'Oh, by the way, Willie, I've got a different kind of job, and I can get a few rooms together.' "

"And you'd tell Sister——"

"I would. I'd say, 'Sister, you've been very kind to the child all these seven months, but I believe with a little state help——' "

"And I'd sleep with you!" Sarah said hungrily.

"Indeed you would, like you used to when Papa worked nights in the subway. When I'd come in to bed wouldn't I see you layin' there, all curled up over me pillow——"

"And, Mother, Sundays!" This was Willie again, his thin little face aglow. "Sundays—not having to go back to St Margaret's, oh boy! We'd all walk home from Mass——"

"I would too!"

"I said we all would, didn't I, Mother? And then we'd have breakfast in the kitchen."

Her heart was wrung. Her heart was breaking. If once—once!—they would spare her. But when they knew enough to spare her they would be no longer children!

"And would you tuck us in, Mother, and say your decade on us?"

"I would that, Sarah, baby."

"Evvy night?"

"Every single night. I'd never leave you!" Martha said, half to herself.

"Mother, you know when we first went to St Margaret's and Holy Angels, you told Sister it might be only for a month?"

"I know, dear."

"If old Mrs Canning died, could we, Mother?"

"Well, maybe. I'd have to get other work, but maybe . . ." She fell silent. "D'ye mind it so much at St Margaret's, dear?" she had to ask.

He hesitated. And it stabbed her to see that he was trying to be brave.

"No, I don't mind it—always," he said. "I kind of hate—well, days like this, when I go in again, and—sorter smell it again. And when my head ached, I—sorter—felt badly."

"That was when the boy kicked you, in the football game?"

"He di'n' meanter."

"No, of course not."

"Mother," Willie began again, out of a silence, during which she continued to hold his hand. "Could I work?"

"Not when you're only eleven, deary."

"I could sell magazines—I could bring you home wood?"

he said hopefully. "And I wouldn't eat much, Mother; I'd eat only a little. Sister said I didn't eat much!"

Martha did not look at him. She stared out at the level, tired sea and patted his hand.

"I don't want to go back to Holy Angels!" Sarah said suddenly, on a burst of bitter crying. "I want my own mother! I don't want to go back!"

It was quarter past three. At six they would have chowder, or more hot sausages, ice cream, sandwiches—they would have all they wanted to eat, perhaps along the boardwalk, perhaps in the cafeteria. If they passed a drugstore Martha thought that she would take a tablet of anything the druggist recommended as being good for toothache.

Three hours to spend somehow, before they could start back, unless they were to admit the whole day a failure. Martha led them all the hot length of Surf Avenue, and they looked at everything—sad little draggled monkeys, blinking doubtfully, scratching themselves, prizes in the Japanese rolling games, painted plaster kewpies dressed in flues of colored ostrich feathers.

"I wouldn't want to win one of *them!*" Martha said fervently.

Sarah wanted to win the little baby ice-cream freezer.

"Wait until we have our little place, dear, and I'll get you one like it. And you can freeze yourself your own dessert——"

" 'Member how you used to help me with my lessons, Mother? I never was kept in then."

"And are you kep' in now, Willie?"

"Oh, sure, nearly every day. Sister thinks I'm awful dumb!"

"But it's only because you were sick at Christmas; you skipped a lot of the lessons, deary," she said anxiously.

They came to a playground with slides and sandboxes, and the children joined a score of other children and were happy. Martha could sit in the shade, watching the bathers who were gathering in greater numbers now, and pressing her hand to her tooth. She reflected that she could not get in to Dr Graham now, anyway. It seemed impossible that she would presently, after hours or days or weeks, be back in the Pinckney house, in her own orderly, impersonal room—without the toothache. And with the memory of her shabby, wistful children, who had been awaiting this day for months—this hot, sticky, shabby, sordid, cheap day!

They would go meekly into the institution doors, she knew; Sarah crying but obedient, Willie pale and tearless and patient. "Thank you for our lovely birthday, Mother," Willie would say.

It would be lovely, she thought, to have some place to take them now. A room somewhere, with a bath and a bed. Willie could have a cool, full bath, with plenty of splashing and soap, and Sarah could lie flat on the bed and rest. She, Martha, could rest a little, too, talking to them, getting acquainted with these children who seemed like strangers every time she met them after weeks of parting.

There was no such room. The children had been only once to the Pinckney apartment, and then, sitting quietly, timidly in the kitchen, they had been discovered by Mrs Pinckney herself, who had been manifestly made uneasy by their presence.

"Yes, well—how do you do, Sarah; how do you do, William," she had said nervously. "I think perhaps . . . another time, Martha . . ."

There was always, of course, the danger of infection of some sort for Doris. And then there was the danger of letting people like Martha feel that they could take liberties; visits led to meals, meals led to smuggled overnight visits; the whole principle was wrong. . . .

Martha had read Mrs Pinckney's confused thoughts as well as heard her confused words. There were seven unused, spacious cool rooms in the Pinckney apartment, on this stifling day, and two baths that were not used, to say nothing of the compact little bath connected with Martha's room. But she couldn't take the children there.

They were all three sandy, hot, tired, sunburned. Willie kept jerking his little pipestem of a neck as if sand tickled him. Sarah's eyes were bloodshot from salt air and hot dry wind. The sky continued high and white and cloudless; an unrefreshing afternoon wind was beginning to blow the dry sand along the boardwalk.

"Would you like to try to raise the heavy weight, Willie?"

There was no charge for that. But the child glanced about with an embarrassed laugh.

"Gee, Mother, it takes a great big heavy guy to do that!"

They were all thirsty. Sarah wanted orange nip and Willie "Hoo-hoo Henry." Martha rather timidly asked the girl at the fountain counter for a glass of water.

"Green Rock or Petropolis?" the girl demanded indifferently.

"Well—just plain water."

The girl elevated her eyebrows and looked even less interested than before. But with a shrug she placed a very small glass of icy water before Martha. The children luxuriated in bright green and strangely pink drinks sucked through straws from bottles.

"Well now, what 'll we do next? Let's do one more real good concession!" Martha suggested brightly, out in Surf Avenue once more. Twenty-five minutes past four; it would soon be something to five. And after five came six!

"*One* more!" Willie echoed blankly.

"Well, I mean, let's pick a real good one."

"For fifty cents each we could go into Saturnalia," Willie suggested. "You can do everything in there free!"

She laughed.

"Well, do you know, I think I lost a dollar! I must of left it on the counter back there, when we got the drinks."

"No, you di'n'," Sarah said interestedly. " 'Cuz you gave her two dimes and a nickel, don't you 'member, Mother?"

"That's right, I did." She looked about for a place to sit down, dragged onto a green bench. "Let me think it out," she began. "Hot dogs was twenty, ice cream twenty, chocolates ten—no, I guess that's right. You don't realize how it's goin'."

"How much have we?" Willie asked anxiously.

"Well, we have plenty. We can do two more things and then have plenty for supper."

"And did you pay your insurance, Mother?"

"I did, deary. That was what made me a little short this week."

"Is it—twenty-two thousand, Mother?"

"Twenty-two hundred, dear."

"And when 'll you get it?"

"Oh, in no time now! In—well, it's not six years."

"I'll be fifteen," Sarah computed. And again a dagger went through the mother's heart.

"Oh, my God, my God, my God," she said conversationally in her secret soul, "may Thy holy will be done now and forever. But it seems like they need me so, and they will not be little very much longer. If I could have them with me!

"It seems sometimes like it was very hard to bear," her prayer finished simply.

Sarah and Willie went down the chutes, and this time Sarah was so excited that she wanted to try it again, she wanted to do it a thousand times. Everyone in her neighborhood could hear Sarah's enthusiastic description of how she held tightly to Willie and was not scared at all. She wasn't scared at all!

They both wanted to try the chutes again; but their mother suggested that they wait and see some other things first and then come back to the chutes. Sarah had not much faith in this promise, and she began to cry silently as she walked along in the late afternoon glare, between Martha and Willie.

Martha felt half mad with irritation and sympathy as she leaned down close to her.

"What is it, darlin'?"

"I don't want to go back to Holy Angels!" Sarah whispered, weeping faster, turning to screw her face into her mother's shoulder and putting a thin little arm about Martha's neck.

"I know, dear. I know, dear. But don't cry, dear. Don't, dear, it makes Mamma feel so badly!"

Suddenly, unobtrusively, yet in the center of the sidewalk, Sarah was violently ill. The strolling crowd of women in white, the hairy-legged, sandy men in dressing gowns, with towels, parted swiftly. Martha drew Sarah aside, wiping the patient little pale mouth. Sarah looked scared, apologetic; her face was a whitish green; she said nothing. Her eyes were fixed faithfully on her mother's face as Martha wiped her mouth.

"You poor little thing!" Martha said quietly after a moment. "Never mind, dear. It happens to everybody! Nobody cares a bit, dear."

She looked desperately about. The child must have a drink of cool water and ought to rest if the little stomach were to right itself. Little shabby Sarah ought not to have to stagger on, somehow, in this crowd. . . .

Martha kept her arm about the child's shoulders; she guided Sarah along to an obscure corner, behind a great angle of signboard. She kept wiping her mouth and smoothing back Sarah's tawny, neglected hair, with an occasional dab at shoes or dress. Willie, carrying Sarah's hat, ran sympathetically alongside.

"Now we're all right," said Martha, panting. Her toothache, forgotten for a moment, began again to throb and pulse. "I think maybe we were doing a little too much," Martha added sensibly. "The hot dogs and that green drink —well, anyway, that's over, and there's no harm done. We'll just rest a little while and look at the ocean and all the people swimming."

They sat down against the great piles that supported a pleasure pier; this part of the beach was all in shade now; across the face of the still high sun warm smothering veils had been imperceptibly drawn. The world dripped heat; the sand, in which Martha's shabby shoes and the children's shabby shoes dug deep holes, was littered with newspapers, fruit skins, cigarette and cigar stubs, paper bags, peanut shells.

"I let you do too much, dear," Martha said repentantly. "You never should have gone down the chutes so soon after that drink."

"It wasn't your fault, Mother!" Sarah assured her gallantly.

"Is your tooth better?" Willie asked.

"Well, it was for a little while, and then . . . just now . . . However, it 'll die down again!"

The crowds went by them; there were hundreds of persons in the shallow fringes of the warm sea now, and Sarah might have waded if she would. But she preferred to stay close to her mother, and Willie wedged himself tightly on the other side, and they sat so, resting and talking.

Long shadows followed the bathers, walking on the beach. The air was hot and seemed to come in puffs, like the breath from a chimney.

A sort of heavy relaxation came over Martha, and over the children too. They sank into a lethargy, and the time that had dragged so heavily on the mother's hands all day flew all too swiftly now. It was five o'clock, and before six they must move. Martha felt as if she never would want to move again.

Just to sit here and talk, with her little boy and girl, was luxury. No one was disturbing them, no one knew that they were here. She ached from head to foot with fatigue; she felt weak with love for this hapless little couple: Willie, affectionate, patient, needful of his mother; Sarah, pallid and quiet, still shaken from her recent moment of sickness.

"We couldn't stay down here all night, could we, Mother? Just sitting on the beach?"

"Oh, Willie dear, I'm afraid not."

"There's hotels down here, Mother?" Sarah whispered hopefully.

"I know, darlin'. But all Mamma's got is a dollar and fifteen cents, and we have to get our supper out of that and get back to town."

"I'd go without supper, Mother!" Willie promised eagerly.

"Oh, I know, dear, but it isn't that. What would Sister say if neither of you came back? And old Mrs Canning, if I didn't come?"

"The Thursday nurse could stay," Willie pleaded.

"I know. But . . ." Martha's voice was the harder because she was so conscious of their disappointment. "But we couldn't, not tonight," she persisted firmly.

The children were silent for a while, clinging on either side of her.

"Mother, could we stay if there was a miracle?" Willie suddenly demanded.

"We prayed that we never would have to go back!" Sarah added explosively.

"I know. I know," Martha said cheerfully, pressing both her thin palms to the little hands that were clasped across her, so that all their hands were united. "But—you see, Willie, you see, Sister, we oughtn't to pray for what's ridiculous . . ."

She paused, and Willie said respectfully but firmly:

"But you don't know what's ridiculous or what's not ridiculous to God, Mother."

"No, maybe I don't," Martha admitted. "But now, for instance, take my tooth," she argued, seizing upon the subject uppermost in her thoughts. "It's been botherin' me for several days, and I know why. I had Doctor Graham look at it when I took Doris down to him last week, and he said there was an old cap on it that had to come off. And he told me to come in, but I didn't. Surely, surely," Martha finished, looking at the attentive children expressively, "I'd have no right to ask God that He'd let me off this toothache that I brought on myself?"

"But did we—did we bring living at the homes on ourselves?" Willie asked doubtfully.

"Well, no, dear, and if Papa hadn't died you'd never have known there was such things. But that's because Mamma hasn't any money. And Mamma won't have any until she earns it, do you see? And here it is nearly half-past five; how could I, or anyone, earn money now, in time for dinner, and to buy nightgowns and toothbrushes and telephone Sister and get rooms here for the night?"

"God might do a *part* of it," Willie suggested dubiously.

"But it 'd be very silly to ask it, dear. No," Martha said stonily, relentlessly, speaking more to herself than the children now. "No. We're not goin' to find a thousand dollars in an envelope, and we're not going to have a miracle."

"But, Mother," Willie pursued. "If God is going to do a miracle at *all,* why couldn't He—He has all the money there *is.*"

"Because it's silly to talk that way, Willie! There's things you can pray for, and things you can't. . . ." She paused, shaken.

"God can do anything!" Sarah asserted boldly.

"He couldn't make a sin right!" Willie countered, dredging up with the freshness of the rising generation the quibble that is as old as Augustine.

"He could!" said Sarah.

"Could He, Mother?" Willie asked triumphantly.

"God couldn't approve of what was wrong," Martha said absently, sententiously. She felt quite stupid.

"The toothache, the money," Willie summarized it, "the

nightgowns, Mrs Canning, St Margaret's and Holy Angels. It would be a good deal," he mused, "for Him to *do*."

"And if we asked Him things like that, we need not be surprised that He'd not hear us," Martha added severely.

"If I was a nigger I'd ask to be white!" Sarah said unexpectedly.

"It 'd be much better to ask Him to make you good, even if you were black," Willie told his sister morally.

Sarah scowled at him.

"You could say, 'Do it if You can, and if You can't, don't bother,' " the boy suggested.

"We know this, that if we do what He wants us to, He'll protect us," Martha said loyally, but in an unconvinced and unconvincing tone. She pressed the fingers of one hand tightly against her cheek.

"I wish tomorrow was our birthday!" Willie murmured wistfully.

Martha stirred wearily.

"Maybe we ought to be goin'; it's a long way to the train, and we have to stop for somethin' to eat," she said reluctantly. Immediately she became motionless again, her head resting back against a pile, her feet driven into the sand, her eyes closed. "Oh my," she sighed on a long yawn, "I'd like to rest here all night!"

"I'll tell you what time it is," Willie said officiously, twisting her wrist. "It's ten to five," he said.

"It's much later than that, dear! Maybe that's ten minutes of six."

"No, Mother, five." She had opened her eyes; she looked at her watch.

"It's stopped. No matter. We ought to be goin'!"

The weary walk, the stifling restaurant, the subway, the furnace of a city lay ahead. And then a wakeful night with toothache. But never mind! She would see Dr Graham tomorrow, and see the children next Thursday afternoon, and somehow life would go on. . . .

"Shake the coats, dear! And lend me your hand, Willie, my leg's asleep on me."

She staggered, laughed, caught at her balance. Sarah was half asleep, crying, weary. They stood up stiffly, yawning.

A stout, rather baggy man came by. Martha addressed him.

"Would you tell me the time, please?"

He looked surprised; pulled out his big silver watch without moving his eyes from her face.

"Martha Oliver," he said simply.

"The dear Lord love us," Martha said. "Joe Cahill."

"Well," the man said. "I didn't know ye were down here."

"I just come with the children for the day. It's their birthday."

"Twins, is it?"

"No, the boy's the better by two years."

They stood staring, smiling at each other.

"You're here only the day?"

"That's all. I've to get them back now."

"To the city?"

"To the city."

"It's goin' to be hot tonight in the city. You'd have Thad crazy did you stay down, I suppose?"

Martha hesitated; her voice was lower.

"I burrid Thad two years come February, Joe."

"Do you say so!" the man exclaimed, sympathetic and shocked. "Well, you've got a good man here," he observed kindly.

"Willie?" Her tone assumed the peculiar apathy of the adoring Irish mother. "He's a good boy," she said unenthusiastically.

"And you've a girl too?"

"Sarah."

"She's the cut of the one we had," he said thoughtfully. "We lost her, it's all of ten years."

"It must be hard to lose them."

"Walk up the steps here, and I'll run ye to the cars," Joe Cahill said thoughtfully, by way of answer.

"How's Nelly?"

The stout, baggy man had suddenly shouldered Sarah.

"Here, my lady," he said, "I'll give you a lift. I used to carry me own little girl this way, do you see? And then I'd tell her, 'Now, when I get tired it 'll be you that 'll carry me!' "

Sarah was too tired to do more than smile. She had linked her thin little arms about his neck.

"What brings you here, Joe?"

"I live here," he said.

They crossed the boardwalk, crossed Surf Avenue, sweltering in sunset and buzzing with flies, and walked past broad, cheap seaside cottages with painted name boards, where languishing boarders sat on narrow, blasted grass plats.

"Is this you?" Martha said surprisedly when they came to a quieter region and to a square white cottage with the fresh net curtains of the dentist's office in the lower windows and a sign reinforcing them: "J. P. Cahill, D.D.S."

"This is me."

"Where's your boy now, Joe?"

"He's finishing college. He'll be here with me someday."

"Well, isn't this nice?" Martha said appreciatively. "Is Nelly out?" she asked as the dentist took a key from his pocket and opened the front door on a spotless hall.

He carried Sarah into the office, deposited her in a chair. All about were the tubes, the trays, the aligned instruments, the shining cases of his profession.

"I wish I'd known you were here before!" Martha said, smiling ruefully. "I've a tooth has been driving me mad all day."

"Hurt ye now?" He was shrewdly interested. "Let's see it!" he commanded, looking over his shoulder as he washed his hands.

Martha took her hat from her flattened, colorless hair, sat down in the balanced chair. She laughed as she opened her mouth. The children looked on in fearful expectation.

"That one, hay?"

"Oh, Joe, don't touch it!"

He selected an instrument, was busy for a moment, humming.

"Whew!" the woman said. She rose up on a spur of pain, collapsed with a sigh of relief.

"Better, is it?"

"Joe, what was it?"

"Well, let me fix it up for ye, and I'll tell ye. Now," he said, packing and punching, "that 'll last ye for a while!"

"Oh my!" she said, broken.

"Stopped aching?"

"Joe, if you knew the relief!"

"The pain may hang on for a minute."

"It's gone!" she insisted weakly.

"You asked me," the doctor said, washing and replacing his implements, "you asked me where was Nelly. I lost her a year ago, Martha."

"No, Joe!"

"Yes," he said seriously. He took a framed photograph from his desk. "She had that taken for the boy," he said, looking at it appraisingly.

"She'd got quite heavy."

"Nelly."

"Tut-tut-tut-tut!" Martha, studying the picture, said regretfully.

"Well," said the doctor, "let's have a look at the house. These kids want to see the house, don't you, kids?"

He pinched Sarah's pallid little face with kind fat fingers.

"She don't look any too strong, Martha."

"She was just kinder upset," the mother explained. "Usually they eat very careful. But today we sorter . . .

"My God, Joe," she said, following him through the neat, darkened rooms. "If you knew what it was to be rid of that toothache!"

"I have a Japanese boy—Nelly got him—who comes in here every day, but since she died we don't do no cooking in the house," the doctor explained in the kitchen doorway.

"It seems a shame," Martha observed. "She had her kitchen cabinet and electric refrigerator and everythin'," she mused aloud. "Ain't that a shame!"

"If you folks can stay there's Nelly's things and the little girl's things here," Joe Cahill suggested.

The children looked frantic hope at their mother.

"Oh, Joe, I couldn't!" Martha said. "The nuns expect them back."

"You could phone the nuns. After all, they're your kids," Joe reminded her.

"I know it." She laughed helplessly. "But sometimes it don't seem like they were!" she explained a little sadly.

They went out into the little back yard and found the storm low and close; black clouds were piled over the darkened ocean, the beach was deserted, and the quiet upper selvages of Surf Avenue were busy with a hurried furling of flags and slamming of shutters.

The first hot, leisurely drops fell through the heavy air. They pattered in the unearthly sulphurous gloom of the doctor's oceanside back yard, with its empty chicken house and its deserted clothesline. A heavy, salty wind, shocking with a first breath of coolness, swept over the world.

"You can't take them back to the city in this. Better stay!" the man said.

"Joe, if I stay I burn my bridges behind me."

"Well, they're good things to burn!" he reminded her comfortably. "I've been waitin' a long time for you, Martha."

"It 'd mean trouble, maybe, with the authorities," Martha mused aloud, doubtful eyes moving from the children's tense, excited faces to the man's kind eyes.

"Mother, you mean we could stay here all night?" Willie asked.

"Oh, Mummy—Mummy," Sarah whispered.

"You mean you'd like to, Ladybird?" the doctor asked.

Sarah's answer, disgusting to Willie, was to burst out crying and bury her wet face, her silky tangle of neglected hair, her hot little whisper, against the doctor's ear. The man had half knelt to receive her tearful confidences, and when he stood up Sarah was in his arms.

"I love you," little proud, cold Sarah was whispering to him fiercely. "I want to stay with you!"

"You're goin' to stay with me always," the doctor whispered back. "You're goin' to be my little girl. Do you know that I used to love your mamma when she wasn't much bigger than you?"

They had supper in the kitchen; fresh, spongy rolls and iced tea and pears and cold ham. The rain had not yet come, the sea looked sulphurous, dark; there was a strange unnatural twilight over the world which smelled unhealthily, like a hothouse.

Afterward Martha sat on the steps with the children and Joe. She said:

"I never knew anyone could feel as thankful, as happy, as I feel tonight, Joe."

"It's a good way to feel," he said. Sarah was going slowly to sleep against his shoulder, and he had let his pipe go out rather than jar the child.

"It seems as if my heart was burstin'," said Martha. "It seems as if life couldn't be as wonderful as this!"

"If you ask me, it's God's hand," said Joe.

Faint echoes of excitement came to them from the crowds on the beach. Raindrops fell again, stopped.

A beautiful shining black car, striped with thin lines of yellow, slipped by like a snake in the deepening dusk.

"Look at that," said the woman inside the car. "A dentist's office at Bellamy Beach! I ask you, Bob, I ask you if there is a God when somebody has to be a dentist at Bellamy Beach!"

"It seems about the limit," the young man agreed.

"It's cruelty!" Sally said with fire. "It's cruelty to create all these helpless fools and then torture them!"

"Better forget 'em!" he said soothingly.

"I'd gas them all!" she persisted fretfully. "I'd put them out of their misery!"

But fortunately for them, Joe and Martha, Sarah and Willie, drowsy on the top step, waiting for the rain, were sharing a foretaste of the Kingdom and could not hear her.

The Shortest Way Home

AFTER A LONG WHILE she said in a musing, quiet voice:

"Alice, I was too proud."

Alice's heart gave a mad leap of fright. The moment she, and they all, had dreaded, the moment for which she, and they all, had hoped, had come.

Jacquetta was looking at her thoughtfully, her eyes infinitely tired, infinitely sad, but sane.

"That was it, Alice," she said again as Alice did not speak. "I was too proud."

"No—no prouder than the rest of us, dear," Alice, trembling, hoping, fearing, said lovingly.

The other woman did not answer. But she did not lapse into her usual remote mood of brooding and introspection either. She remained motionless among the heaped pillows and delicate rich coverings of her garden chair, one elbow resting on its wicker arm, fine bloodless fingers pressed into her white and sunken cheek.

All about them the orchard swam and pulsed in the glory of a perfect April afternoon. The young grass was emerald green, against it the blossoming cherry and apple trees swept branches of dazzling whiteness. Flawless green grass, flawless white and flecked pink of the blooms, and over and beyond and above their riot of color and perfume, the dim, soft arch of the dove-blue sky.

There were birds in the orchard, lacing it with the flash of busy wings; about one certain cherry tree's glorious spread of popcorn blossoms bees filled the sweet warm afternoon air with steady buzzing.

Behind the orchard, on a little rise where there were mighty oaks and maples whose tips were already showing tightly folded curls of red, was a gracious old farmhouse, clapboarded, sloping-roofed, dormered, green blinds folded back against the prim white angles of its walls. All about it, on the descending grassy slopes, were mighty barns, sheds, fences and paddocks and outhouses, all mellowed into harmony and beauty by the service of a hundred—almost two hundred, kindly years.

The trees scattered gracious dappled shadows upon the roof; long slanting bars of westering sunlight struck fire from the small-paned windows.

"Alice," said the woman in the garden chair wearily, bringing her eyes back from a faintly frowning study of blossoms and roofs, "I've known, all along, how hard I am making it for you—for all of you! But I haven't seemed able—haven't seemed *able*——"

She stopped short, abandoning the too painful effort, and the other woman spoke quickly, reproachfully, fondly.

"Jacquetta dearest—as if that mattered! What matters is that you are going to get well."

Silence again, and then Jacquetta Pomeroy said indifferently:

"I suppose I am."

"It takes so long to get the whole thing straightened out in my mind, Alice," she said slowly after a while.

Alice, apparently going on with her needle point, watched her anxiously.

"I wouldn't try to hurry it, dearest. Just take it easily, day by day!"

To this Jacquetta answered with a brief, light, bitter laugh.

"*Haven't* I?" she presently asked. "Days—weeks—how long is it, Alice?"

"Why, we only got you out of doors a week ago," Alice said cheerfully, in a matter-of-fact tone.

"That . . ." Jacquetta sighed and closed her eyes. "That wasn't what I meant," she said mildly. "Am I—don't be afraid to say so if I am, but am I too sick to talk?" she went on.

"I don't think so," Alice assured her promptly and soothingly. But her eyes were uneasy.

"You know, nothing can stop my thinking," the convalescent said with a delicate, significant emphasis on the last word.

"I suppose not, dear!"

"How long is it since the accident then?"

"Let me see." Alice pretended to consider, head slightly on one side, lips slightly bitten. "It was the nineteenth of March, and this is the twenty-sixth—seventh—the twenty-sixth or twenty-seventh of April."

"Five weeks."

"About."

"And what do you do about your doctor and your boys, Alice? For you're living here, aren't you? It seems to me"—Jacquetta mused, smiling a little sadly, her beautiful deep eyes fixed on her companion's charming and concerned face—"it seems to me that in the conscious spaces between agony and sleep and narcotics and unconsciousness and fever——"

"Ah, don't, dear!"

"I was only going to say," she finished the interrupted sentence mildly, "that through it all I seem to remember you, Alice, helping, crying, sometimes kneeling beside the bed with your face against my hand. . . ."

She was still very weak. The water brimmed her smiling eyes, and her lips trembled.

"I come and go!" Alice said in the silence, wiping her own wet eyes, clearing her throat but speaking with resolute sweet steadiness. "My doctor and my boys get on very well indeed.

I see them every day. When you were sickest Frank came up every night and sat with me, reading or working over his mail. . . . Look, Jacquetta, look at the darling with that long thread of my yarn! She's been coquetting with it here for ten minutes, afraid to take it!"

The somber, heavy eyes followed the flight of the little, overbalanced bird through the blue air.

"Alice, before my poor little baby came—and died," Jacquetta presently said heavily, "I used to lie in the upstairs living room, in the wet spring afternoons, and Hugh would read to me until I fell asleep. I used often to have strangely realistic dreams, and I'd wake up fuzzy and headachy and frightened and find him sitting there, with his fingers tight on mine—dusk, you know, and firelight and—and Hugh. No, let me talk! I'd tell him my dreams—such queer twisted visions of the baby being born strange—something queer about it! Once I thought the baby was quite a grown boy, and once it seemed to me that Hugh and I and quite a lot of babies—ten or a dozen of them . . ."

Her voice faded, died. She lay still. Alice, her heart beating thickly and heavily, her brain an apparent blank, no words of any safe description available, went on sewing with shaking fingers.

"Is this bad for me, Alice? Has the doctor said so?"

"No—he said we must—he said," Alice floundered, "that if you wanted to talk, one of these days, it would relieve you—it would be a good thing. But I wish Frank was here!" Alice added fervently in her secret heart.

"Lying in the garden here," Jacquetta resumed, "dozing and waking, having you all such angels of goodness to me, I've thought—so many times, that—that all this was just another dream.

"And that presently I'd wake up, sticky and fuzzy and uncomfortable, and see the firelight, and Hugh silhouetted against it, holding my hand—ready to comfort me. . . .

"And that my baby wasn't born at all yet, Alice, but coming still, still mine to think about—and love—and plan for. . . .

"Not killed, as his father was killed—Hugh and the baby both—because I was so proud!"

"Jacquetta," Alice said in sharp reproof, "you may talk, of course. But this kind of morbid stuff isn't good for anyone! I'm—I'm *surprised* at you!"

Jacquetta obediently fell silent, closing her eyes. Presently she opened them, to smile in tired, childish repentance.

"Alice, I know. But it goes on and on in my head."

"Well, you mustn't let it! My *gracious,* if everybody brooded and dwelt on—on everything . . ."

"You're quite right. But, Alice," the other woman said meekly, "will you answer me one question—two questions?"

"Certainly," Alice said. But she felt sick.

"If—if the poor little baby had been born, as it was, too soon, and with me all smashed to pieces, but if instead of being home here I had been in a hospital, where they had everything, surgeons and oxygen and all, *might* it have lived? Would it have made any difference?"

"It wouldn't have made any difference, dear. I'm positive of that."

A long silence. Jacquetta lay still, with closed eyes.

"Did Hugh speak, Alice?"

"No. It was instantaneous. My dear," said Alice, "it was exactly what Hugh would have chosen. No dragging or sickness or pain—just one final flash."

"Yes, of course." Jacquetta, always pale, was ghastly now, and yet struggling, as Alice could see, to save Alice, not to make a scene. "Yes, Hugh would have chosen that. He hated growing old—he hated anything dull and crippled—anything less than perfect health!" she added in a low, tender voice. "He was only forty-four, Hugh—he was eight years older than I, and yet already he had talked of it, he had said, 'Let's never grow old, Jack! Let's be the rosy, eager, healthy sort, winning tennis cups and gold tournaments and polo trophies right to the end!'

"And he used to say, 'We'll make an Indian of the boy.' Poor little boy, who wasn't even going to be born! Hugh and I saw him in leather gaiters, striding along beside us, his little cheeks hot and red, and his hair being blown about—that tawny soft hair, like Hugh's. He was going to have his little sleeping cot on Hugh's porch. Hugh was going to teach him to fish and shoot and sail. Poor Hugh, who never was to have his baby! And poor baby . . .

"And poor me," she finished simply.

"Poor you!" Alice smiled whimsically, pitifully, and laid a quick, impulsive hand upon Jacquetta's knee.

"Pride," Jacquetta said, covering the hand with her own. "I was proud even of my unborn baby! Do you remember how I used to write you, before you came back, that he would be perfect, that I couldn't have loved a baby who wasn't straight and strong and perfect? I even told old Doctor Jim that I wouldn't have an anesthetic when my boy was born, because I wanted to ask him instantly if he was complete—worthy of Hugh, worthy of me, worthy of what our boy was to be!

"Alice, what *fools* we are. If we could go back! If I could go back to that last day!

"Hugh had been playing indoor tennis until he was simply dripping, you know, and I'd been having tea with Maggie Courtnedge and some of the others, at the club, and I went down and got into the car to wait for Hugh. When he came along, he had a thick white sweater, its arms twisted about his throat, and he said instantly: 'You mustn't drive. It's muddy and skiddy, and you'll give yourself some sort of a wrench!'

"And I said, 'Oh, jump in, dearest, and don't argue! The sooner you get home and get into dry clothes the better!'

"My dear, if I'd moved over in the front seat, let him take the wheel—I'd never driven the new car, you know—if I'd given him my place we would have come home, home to the fire and the usual before-dinner rest—myself on the couch, Hugh sitting beside me, and blue, blue twilight on the snow outside, and everyone in the house warm, and happy, and safe.

"And about this time, Alice—no, not even yet! But in two or three weeks more, just as all the trees and flowers were out in full glory, we'd have had our child."

"Darling, you can't be sure. Life is full of accidents," Alice said sensibly, bracingly. "You've always been wonderful, Jacquetta," she went on. "You've always been equal, more than equal, to everything life ever asked of you! You're weak now, and sick, and all shaken to pieces, and no wonder! But when your strength comes back, as it will come—as it is coming, indeed—you'll face things again, you'll—you'll get through!" said Alice in rather shaky encouragement. "Everyone's amazed at the way you've recovered," she added. "We thought it might be actual months. And here you are, walking, eating, almost back to normal, in five weeks!"

"Oh, I am a healthy enough animal!" Jacquetta agreed indifferently. And that day she talked no more.

But a few days later, in the late, warm morning, again established under the orchard trees, and again with Alice for her companion, she said suddenly, out of a silence:

"The reason I spoke about pride, Alice, was that this smashup—this physical change in my whole life—really represents an inner—a spiritual, mental smashup, that is far worse!

"All my life long I've been—*superior*. I've felt sure, somehow, that, whatever went right or went wrong, I could see the pattern, the reason. I could work out the justice of it all, and accept it.

"I was eight years younger than Hugh. We were fourth cousins, you know, both Pomeroys, and I adored him from the time I was an actual baby. That wasn't so astonishing; all women adored Hugh, racing round here in his white flannels, with his horse and his roadster and his tennis racket. I was only little Jack Pomeroy to him, the child of a family that had been here as long as his own, whose grandmother and his had been cousins—that was all. But Hugh Pomeroy was a sort of god—to me.

"When he was twenty-four, and I sixteen, he married Gertrude—and I cried myself into a fever. Nobody knew why. But I had to face it, and I *did* face it. I lived on here, studying languages, reading Homer to my father, giving dinners to scientists and interviewing reporters, keeping up tennis and golf—nobody knew, nobody knew! Hugh least of all. After my father died I went abroad with Aunt Sally. I had chances at other societies, other opportunities of marriage—they simply didn't register. What counted was this little Massachusetts town, with the Roger Pomeroy house up on State Street, and the John Pomeroy house round the corner on Washington Avenue. I was twenty-eight when I came home, and they told me Gertrude Pomeroy was dying. She'd never been anything but a dead weight on Hugh, never given him a child. I wasn't surprised. I knew in my secret heart who was going to give him his son; the little boy on pony-back, galloping along in the autumn leaves, carrying on the Pomeroy name, wasn't going to be Gertrude's child!

"I was with Gertrude every day—posing still, Alice, still seeing the scheme, still in control! I would sit there beside her, reading, talking; Hugh would come in, handsomer, graver, more wonderful than ever. I knew just exactly how I looked to him—bright color, tumbled hair, the broad white collars he was always so mad about, contrasted to Gertrude's thinness and paleness.

"When she was gone, still everything was exactly according to the pattern I had made. There was no hurry, nothing indecorous or undignified. Hugh went away for awhile, and I went on just as before.

"And then one autumn day, standing at the upstairs sitting-room window and looking down the drive, and wondering if I'd have supper upstairs with a book, I saw a man on horseback turn in at the gate—I knew that cap, the set of those shoulders!

"It was one of those clear, delicious days, red leaves, smoke fires, a sort of silky mist rising as the sun went down. . . .

"I called out to Hannah, 'Light my fire upstairs, will you, Hannah? And could you bring up some tea for Mr Pomeroy and myself?' I *knew,* you see, Alice, as if it had been a story I was writing.

"He said, afterward, when we were having the tea before the fire and were talking wedding plans, 'Jack, strange that you should have on one of the gold-brown dresses I love so!'

"I didn't tell him, then or ever, that for weeks I'd been dressed for my part, for weeks I'd been thinking, 'Perhaps this is the lucky dress, perhaps this is the golden day!'

"And the—the gravity and beauty—the *decorum* of our marriage, Alice, with everyone's approval and blessing, the first dinners, the wet Sunday afternoons settling our books in the bookcases, sharing tea, talking about books and tennis—everything, everything! I used to look at him, so handsome, so grave, and say to myself, 'Hugh, are you *mine?* Is this real?'

"It was all part of the plan, part of the story I was telling myself, presently to go to him—we'd been married a year then!—and say, 'Hugh, what would you think of a person you'd never seen, who sent you a wireless that he would like to come and live with you forever?'

"I remember his bewildered, good-natured look as he glanced up, Alice—and then the light in his eyes, and his 'Jack—not really! Jack, not really!'

"Ah well, I can say that I have lived in Arcady, anyway, that's more than some women ever can say! But life won't ever have a reason, a pattern, again. It 'll just be days—days, one after another, summer and winter, forties and fifties.

"And every little while I'll see our gate—we were practically home, Alice!—with snow banked each side and tufted on the dark red bricks, and the black trees, and the sun setting like a fire behind the woods—and everything suddenly slipping and tipping—with that horrible grinding of glass and shattering of wood . . ."

"You'll see it less and less," Alice said practically and placidly, as Jacquetta paused and covered her eyes tightly with her thin, white hand.

"Alice," the convalescent presently said with a surprising touch of her old animation, after a silence. "Do you know what I've been thinking? I've been thinking that someday—if I could find a gorgeous, straight, splendid child, one of those hard, rosy, clear-eyed little boys—about three, perhaps, or perhaps younger—I would adopt him and give him Hugh's name!"

Alice looked interested just to the line of polite sympathy, looked more than a little doubtful.

"You wouldn't?" Jacquetta asked quickly, sensitively.

"Well . . . I wouldn't be in any hurry," Alice hesitated.

"I'm not in any hurry!" Jacquetta said proudly and was still. "To have a Hugh Pomeroy playing tennis again," she went on musingly, after a pause, as if thinking aloud, "racing in the gate, slamming doors, shouting out to me as Hugh used to do! He would lie on the rug before the fire—and I'd tell him of Hugh, tell him he must ride straight and shoot straight and play hard, as Hugh did.

"He'd have dogs, Alice, up here at the stables, as Hugh did, and after a while everyone would forget that he wasn't Hugh's own son, and the world would be richer for having another Hugh Pomeroy in it!

"Alice, come back, you're a million miles away! Do you know anything about this orphanage up in the hills here, the Beulah Something-or-other Memorial Home, where they have babies? That place where they had the incubator experiments, and all that. You know the place I mean. Do they have babies for adoption there? Might they have a really fine baby boy, do you suppose? I mean one whose parentage we could find out about—one with good blood in his veins."

She laughed ruefully, shamefacedly. But to Alice any laugh at all, from Jacquetta, was a miracle in these days.

"There is my pride again!" Jacquetta said under her breath, with a little impatient jerk of her head. "As if his blood mattered. But it *would* matter, to me, if he were to have Hugh's name. Alice, could you investigate, do you suppose? Very cautiously, very carefully—we wouldn't want anyone to know! And he must be—unusual. Something out of the ordinary."

"Wait," Alice advised lightly, as Jacquetta fell to musing. "Frank and I are coming up to have dinner with you tomorrow night, and Doctor Jim says he will come in for bridge afterward. And next Sunday you're coming to us! Wait awhile, Jack, wait until life gets back to normal. Your nurses only went yesterday, you aren't quite on your feet yet. And more than that, dear," Alice pursued, "these things take time —there are legalities, I don't know myself exactly how complicated the process is. You're only thirty-six, anyway, you know. You might even——"

Jacquetta silenced her with suddenly opened eyes, with a hand quickly spread and raised as if she warded off some danger.

"Please, Alice dear! Not yet, and not ever. My bubble of life has burst, once and for all. I'm gray—I made Hannah give me a mirror the instant the nurses were gone. And I'll always walk with that!" She glanced at the stout cane that lay on the grass near her. "It's all gone, youth and tennis and golf, Hugh, and morning rides, and tramps in the snow, gone with the dream of my son—my rosy, eager, noisy boy! I've got to begin life on new terms, Alice, and it has seemed to me that to have someone—some child the better and stronger and happier, because of that little empty place beside me . . ."

She brooded, her eyes far away.

"But you're quite right! Time enough for that," she said presently in a firmer tone.

Alice left her on that note. They went into the house for

luncheon, Jacquetta walking strongly enough, steadily enough, if with that new slight limp that became her so strangely in this new, sobered role, and over the salad and the chops she was charmingly reasonable. Time enough for everything. The duty now was to get well, wholly well, to sleep and eat, to read books that drove away too serious thought, and pay the little circle that loved her for its agonies of care and anxiety by a complete and generous convalescence.

When Alice went away, a little before three o'clock, Jacquetta was to try for a nap. A little before five Aunt Sally would come in to have tea and dinner with her. And after dinner, as usual, genial old Doctor Jim, who had played the part of physician, uncle, guardian, friend, confidant, since the hour of her birth, would come in and sit with her for an hour, after Hannah, only too eager to supplant "thim thrained nur'rses," had gotten Jacquetta safely into bed.

"And I'll be here in the morning!" Alice promised, departing.

"Alice, what a bite I've taken out of your life, you angel!"

But Alice only laughed. Jacquetta went out into the delicious warm sunshine, the quivering tree shadows of the terrace, to wave her a good-by and watch Alice's little car whisk out of sight.

Cameron came respectfully toward her, as he had respectfully approached her now for several successive days. Judge Matison's fine old square-built driver, with the closed car. Would Mrs Pomeroy and Mrs Richie like a little drive?

"Oh no, thank you, Cameron, and be sure to thank the judge. But Mrs Richie has just gone——" Suddenly a change came into Jacquetta's face, a change into her voice. "Wait a minute, Cameron!" she said. "I'll ask Hannah for a wrap. It's such a delicious day I believe I *would* like to drive!"

"You'll take a nurse with you, Mrs Pomeroy?"

"My nurses have gone, Cameron. I'm discharged!" She slipped into the thin light coat, her fingers touching the satin lining consciously. Black—all black! How strangely one's arms looked in it. "Don't look so idiotically pleased, Hannah," she said affectionately, secretly a trifle alarmed at the perspiration that this little effort made spring out upon her. "You knew that eventually I'd feel like driving again!"

Oddly awkward, yet surprisingly simple, too, this management of a lame foot and a cane. And it was exquisite to sit back in the car with the balmy, fragrant spring air entering the open windows and fanning her cheeks, and go safely and alone through the familiar—yet so changed!—streets of the town, past the high school, and the square with the mild-faced old church staring down upon it, and the mills, whose brick walls were etched with pea-green vines in new leaf.

"You're sure you know where it is, Cameron?"

"Oh, sure, I've been there manny's the time wit' the judge. He's on the board."

"Of course! And what's the name of it?"

"The Beulah Michelson Memorial Home."

"That's it."

When they reached it she walked quite easily, quite comfortably, through a clean, empty hallway. How exquisitely they kept these forlorn waifs, at least to the outside eye! Sunshiny windows, closed doors, and behind them small high voices and murmurs of more adult tones.

It was all strangely simple. The superintendent? This was Mrs Wallace. Mrs Wallace, accustomed to secrets, made only a perfunctory inquiry as to her caller's name.

"Does the name matter?" Jacquetta was suddenly shy. "I only wanted to inquire . . . I'm not at all sure . . ."

"Not at all." And the superintendent's bright laugh and quick glance. "Not unless we are to do business. In that case we have to have references, of course—that sort of thing."

"But you *do* have babies for adoption?"

"Oh yes—and others with one parent living. We have one splendid child here with both parents living. I could find fifty homes for her, poor baby——"

"I wanted a boy."

"A boy? Well, that's fortunate, for I haven't but one or two girls at the time. We have eighteen—nineteen—we have about twenty-two little girls here, but not many for adoption. Everyone wants girls, curly-headed girls under three."

"Not really?" Jacquetta widened amused eyes. "I wouldn't have thought that! Do you have——" Her heart began to beat hard in sudden excitement, and her bare palms were wet. "Have you a nice boy now?" she faltered.

"How old a boy?"

"Oh—tiny. But a perfect child, strong and healthy."

"Legitimate? Would that matter?"

"Oh, I think so. I—I suppose so. I wanted to give him my husband's name."

"You're . . ." The woman's eyes softened, traveled over the slender blackness of the figure opposite her. "You're . . . ?"

Jacquetta smiled composedly, nodded. Then her throat thickened and her eyes brimmed, and she looked away.

"Well now, I'll tell you what I think would be a good idea," the superintendent said briskly and hospitably. "I've got an appointment I've *got* to keep. We've been trying—I'll tell you about it—we've been trying to get this adjoining piece of property ever since the home was built, and at last—at *last* I've got this old man to talk business. We're going over it with our own agent this afternoon, so it really *is* important. But suppose you just walk about and take a look at the babies we have; there are fifty—forty-nine, I think it is—here now, and I'll have one of my nurses go about with you. It isn't a regular visitors' day, but you look about—just see what you think. You mightn't see a single child you fancied today—these things take time.

"And meanwhile," she added in a sort of cheerful professional patter, "I'll get through my business, and perhaps see you before you go. And if I get hold of an exceptionally fine boy . . ."

She smiled pleasantly, relegating Jacquetta to the shy and

charming escort of a small, friendly, undergraduate nurse, Miss Dobie.

Immediately they were in a long shining room full of babies, toddlers, scamperers, crawlers, imperious occupants of high chairs. One eager enchanting colored baby, other babies almost as swarthy. Curly golden heads, little dark heads scarcely less engaging. Clean, busy babies in faded rompers, banging things, carrying things, eating things.

On the sunshiny porch, other babies, three marvelous babies, all asleep under nettings. The exquisite little bodies were stretched comfortably, the empty bottles lay discarded, against the flat little pillows spread the loose, damp curls.

"Oh, what a sweet one! What a darling! Is he for adoption?"

"I really don't know. Miss Watts, is this one to be placed?"

"Yes, I believe so. Isn't she a duck? We're all mad about her; she's our pet. She's seven months old—everyone who sees her wants her. Have you seen"—the second little nurse was enthusiastic—"have you seen Benny?"

"Benny? I don't think so."

"We're isolating him because he was exposed to measles. Here he is. Isn't he lovely? How do-do-do-do, Mr Benny?"

A penned porch. An enchanting occupant; three years old, gravely suspicious, gravely friendly. Curls, eyelashes, deep dimples.

"Say how do-do-do-do, Ben."

"How joo-joo-joo-joo."

Jacquetta, trembling, half knelt before him.

"How do *you* do, sweetheart?"

"Here's the dearest little fellow in the place," the nurse said in an undertone. "Father and mother d-e-a-d," she spelled, engineering to Jacquetta's side a beautiful boy of four. The hazel eyes were alert, wide apart, the firm little feet touched the linoleum floor squarely, the boy smiled under a blown wave of light brown hair—Hugh's very hair.

"I have a gun," he stated boastfully, "have your boys guns?"

Jacquetta was almost dazed.

"Is he to be adopted?"

"Oh yes, both parents d-e-a-d. And a lucky thing for him, too, wasn't it, Roy? He doesn't understand me, of course."

"And Benny, is he an orphan?"

"I *think* he is. We usually have someone here who knows, or Mrs Wallace goes through with anyone who's interested. But our head nurse is away this afternoon. She knows about them all. Mary, is Roy to be adopted?"

"Oh, I think so. This is Paula—nine months old," Mary, who had picked up a seriously staring armful of pink-and-white beauty, said interestedly. "Isn't she wonderful? She's an incubator baby, think of it! She weighed five pounds when she came in."

"Five pounds! Can they *live*——"

"Oh yes, five pounds isn't so bad. We have one here—Miss Murray practically saved her life. Mary, is Betty in here? Could we see her?" Miss Dobie nodded toward an almost closed white door. "This baby was almost dead when she was born, and for three weeks she was in an incubator," she explained seriously. "The doctor took Miss Murray off all other work, and she took this case on. They thought the baby was blind, and she *is* crippled—they operated on her foot before she was an hour old—imagine! And she weighed—— Mary, what did Betty weigh?"

"Three pounds one ounce," Mary said in an undertone, accompanying them into the small orderly white room whose window shades were drawn to make a sort of golden dusk of the spring afternoon.

They stood beside the little white crib. Jacquetta had thought the pale, motionless little baby, lying on her tiny pillow, asleep. But as she bent, in fearful fascination, over her, the deep, sunken, reproachful eyes met her own, the dark little monkey face was agitated into a scowl. A bandage about the dark lumpy forehead gave the putty-colored features the aspect of a dignified and annoyed old nun.

"Hello, Betty, you're getting to be a regular bruiser!" Miss Dobie said encouragingly.

"Why the bandage?" Jacquetta whispered.

"Stitches—her little head was cut. But that could come off now," the nurse said in a matter-of-fact tone, "only she puts her little hands up and plays with it."

"Plays! She doesn't look as if she would ever play with anything!"

"Betty? Why, you should have seen her a month ago. They couldn't even dress her; she was on a big pillow. She's getting regular bottles now, but for the first three weeks she had nothing but whey. Miss Murray didn't sleep for more than an hour at a time! But she's out taking a constitutional now, and she goes to bed and everything. We consider this baby well! Except," finished Miss Dobie in a lower tone, "the poor little foot—they may have to operate on that again."

"And that eye—will that be all right?"

"Oh yes!" Miss Dobie laughed the cheerful laugh of youth accustomed to tragedy. "It looked like a baked potato at first," she said. "But now it's fine. She weighs—wait a minute—it's here on her chart. 'Baby Betty.' She weighs all but an ounce of seven pounds."

"And is she an orphan?"

"I believe she is. But they don't tell us about the cases," confessed Miss Dobie. "Mary," she said, raising her voice, "is Betty to be adopted?"

"I don't know—I think she is," Mary, about whose knees small heads were surging like a pack of foxhounds, answered from the adjoining nursery.

"Who," Jacquetta asked, out of a moment of musing, "who would adopt this poor little scrap?"

"I was thinking that!" Miss Dobie confessed ingenuously. "Isn't it a shame? Everyone after the pretty ones! And she may grow up real sweet," Miss Dobie suggested kindly, looking down once more at the pitiful little gray face.

Jacquetta had advanced a finger toward the still reproachfully staring baby; the moist little fingers, as soft to the touch as butterfly antennae, had gripped it with amazing force; they clung there, and the sunken eyes reinforced their hold with a look of desperate and drowning appeal.

"Look at that—how's that for a bottle? That's the way she is now," Miss Dobie, displaying a fat, small, drained bottle, said triumphantly.

"She'll never walk?" Jacquetta murmured, almost as if the child might hear and understand.

"Probably not," the nurse said, shaking her head.

"Dear God," the woman said half aloud, in an involuntary prayer, "why save her? Why save her?"

"Isn't that right?" Miss Dobie said, sympathizing. "But you don't know—her folks may think the world of her!" she added comfortingly.

"You don't know who they are? She's so dark she might almost have Latin blood," Jacquetta suggested, her finger still caught tight in that strangely touching, strangely determined little grip.

"Oh no, she'll whiten out! But you know," said Miss Dobie sensibly, "what fun can that kid have in life?"

Jacquetta spoke rather to the baby than to the girl beside her.

"And she may live seventy years—in some slum, handicapped, bitter. . . ."

"You bet it 'd make *me* bitter!" the nurse agreed brightly.

"Baby, I have to take my finger away," breathed Jacquetta. Suddenly she laid both her thin warm vital hands under the microscopic shoulders, braced them as only mothers know how; murmured, in so ghostly a shadow of a whisper that Miss Dobie heard nothing at all, "But I'm coming back for you, dear! I rather think—I rather think you are my perfect, glorious, sturdy, beautiful little specimen of a boy!"

And suddenly it seemed to her that color came back into life again, into the shaded room, and the nurse's face and uniform and hair. Her feet, cane and all, felt an impulse toward leaping—springing into the future that held such miracles for this lump of unresponsive baby clay.

Cameron, alarmed at the extension of the convalescent's first outing, came anxiously seeking her; she could only scribble her name, her address on a piece of paper, and leave them for Mrs Wallace, with the underscored postscript: "I will telephone. But I so much want dear little Betty that I am almost afraid to ask for her."

Then she drove home slowly, smiling, and went, still smiling, upstairs to the sitting room in which she and Hugh had talked of their boy only a few weeks ago.

Jacquetta stretched herself on the deep couch, pillows piled about her. The spring day was still warm and gracious, latticed windows still were opened into the awakening garden and the new yellow-green of the trees.

Hugh's picture looked down at her understandingly; she could look back at Hugh tonight.

"That shall be my service, dear. Not a well, whole, happy child, whose life would be smooth and serene anyway. But this poor broken little wreck, this little drowned rat—she shall be given her life, from me, as much as any child is ever given life by its own mother!

"She'll have the garden, Hugh—our garden, and birds and puppies and kittens. She'll have music; perhaps someday she'll play my old violin. She'll hang up her stockings and have the other children come in for her Christmas tree. And I'll read her stories, 'Goblin Market' and the 'Would-Be-Goods'!

"Betty. Betty Pomeroy. Elizabeth was my mother's name —I love it. 'Hannah, Betty wants her Teddy bear before she goes to sleep. . . .' "

Jacquetta, sipping her tea, rallied her arguments. Alice would protest, the old doctor would object. This project of adoption was all too rash, too unadvised, too sudden. But Jacquetta would override them. Once again, with that certainty that had given her the serene completeness of her daughterhood, of her wifehood, she felt herself sure. This child, this crippled, sunken-eyed scrap of derelict babyhood, must be hers to save and spoil and make good and wise and happy—and none other, none other, none other!

This beautiful old colonial room, in the beautiful old colonial house, the mellowed garden shut away by faded old bricks from the mellowed street; in this spring dusk they came again into their own, ready to be the scene of one more phase of beautiful and ordered living, the setting for one more sheltered childhood, under hollyhocks and tree shadows, one more happy girlhood spent on a green lawn or with books beside a drowsing wood fire.

Aunt Sally had sent a message that she would be late: it was delightful to have Alice suddenly appear in the living-room doorway, Alice with somebody behind her—who was it? Oh, Dr Jim.

"Ah, what luck! You're just the very two persons I had to see. Sit there, Doctor darling. Alice, sit on my feet."

"Jacquetta—you imbecile!" Alice, her face all concern, was kneeling beside her, feeling her hands. "Did you half kill yourself going out this afternoon? Why didn't you *tell* me?"

"I didn't think of it until after you left, truly, Alice. I had no intention—I give you my word——"

"And you went up to the Memorial Home!"

Jacquetta's eyes crinkled.

"Who told tales on me?"

"Mrs—what's-her-name—Wallace, the matron. She telephoned the doctor, and he telephoned me."

"Did she tell you what I'm going to do?" Jacquetta said. "I gave your name as a reference, Doctor Jim. Darlings, it's all come to me—this is my way out. It's my way round. You'll sympathize if you can't understand, I know. I've found the weariest, sickest, saddest little scrap of babyness you ever saw. And there's the Pomeroy pride, in the dust at last. I want her! She needs me, and I need her. *If* I can have her—and you'll say a good word for me, Doctor?—if I can have her——"

"My dear child," the doctor said, seated in the chair he had drawn close to her couch, and patting her hands, father-fashion, between both his fine, wise old hands, "you can have her just as soon as you're strong enough. You can have her tomorrow if you'll only calm yourself—*calm* yourself."

She sank back, actually pale, her eyes traveling from one face to the other. Her companions both were smiling: there were tears in Alice's eyes.

"She's for adoption, then? It's all right?"

"It's all right."

"Oh . . ." Jacquetta's smiling face wrinkled into tears. "I'm so glad!" she said. "Hannah . . ." she faltered, as the big middle-aged serving-woman came in with fresh hot water for the tea, "you know you said they'd let me have her. Hannah," explained Jacquetta, "when I was telling her about it, said, 'The ways of God are not our ways! That baby 'll be in this house tomorrow night!' Didn't you, Hannah?"

"I did," said Hannah shortly. "And I was all for lettin' you have her from the very first," Hannah continued, straightening cups. "I've two grown ones of me own, an' there never was a mother yet didn't think her own child handsome if both its eyes were out an' *both* its legs broke! But no, it was 'off to the inkybator with her, an' off to the thrained nur'rses' as if Miss Betty was a chicken itself!"

"Look sharp there!" the doctor's tense voice said. Alice was at the couch, had her arm about Jacquetta.

"May God preserve us all, I thought you'd told her!" gasped Hannah.

"You're all right," Alice was saying, steadily and tenderly. "You're all right, Jacquetta. Don't you s-s-see, dearest, how *more* than all right it is! We couldn't tell you, dear, you were too frightfully ill—and *she* was too ill. For days it seemed as if she was going to die—and it would only be another sorrow on top of the first!"

Jacquetta gulped obediently the hot tea somebody held at her lips, pushed away the cup and lay staring from one face to another. Her face was pale, tears lay on her cheeks, there was a sort of touching faith, an entreaty in her look. Hannah, aghast, big fingers loosely resting against the hard red of her peasant cheek, stood frozen with remorse. The old doctor, firelight glinting on his glasses, his forehead professionally wrinkled, his bearded mouth professionally smiling, did not move. Alice, tearful, beaming, knelt beside her, holding tight to Jacquetta's hands.

" 'Miss Betty!' " Jacquetta faltered with trembling lips. "It sounds sweet. My little girl—my own little girl!"

And after a moment's silence she said:

"You'll bring my baby home to me tomorrow, Doctor Jim?"

The old man took off his glasses and wiped them.

"In my own car. Carefully. And see that you and Hannah and Alice are ready for her!"

"Oh, we'll be ready for her!" Alice stammered.

"Don't—don't joggle her, will you, Doctor Jim? Go the long way, by the mill. She's so *little*. And she's—all I have."

"I'll take her the longest way round, dear, don't worry."

"For that," said Alice, frankly blowing her nose, and wiping her eyes, and straightening her hat, "that is *sometimes* the shortest way home!"

The Heart of a Mouse

THE OLD PEACOCK PLACE, the housewives of Friends' Landing would have told you, was a disgrace to the village. Fortunately, from their point of view, it was not, strictly speaking, in the village; it stood in a scattering of shabby houses down toward the shore, beyond the sandbanks, only really visible when one looked for it or caught sight of its untidy environs from the waters of the river. It was a wooden house, two-storied, with a wide porch going all around the lower story. It had a crazy windmill which tipsily supervised a tangle of unpainted barns, chicken houses, woodsheds, dovecotes, tool houses and rabbit boxes, and a very maze of rusty and rebellious wire fencing, sagging gates and tottering railings. This region sloped gradually to the sandy shore and the lisping waters of the busy river, where there were further embellishments in the way of a float, a crooked and rotting pier, two small sunburned bathhouses leaning against each other for support, and such barrels, logs, ropes, anchors and crates as the kindly river had brought to the small greedy hands of Tony and Minny Peacock, and Bud and Hume McKay.

In the yard were further treasures. There were more ropes, all sorts of ropes; more planks and barrels and boxes; there were bicycles in every stage of dissection and rust, wheelbarrows and coasters, old skates and coils of wire, hammers and nails and staples. There were the remains of more than one old wagon, old milk cans, farm machinery long past usefulness, chains and odd wheels. Against one side of the woodshed there was a neat arrangement of paint-pots; half-a-dozen variegated swings dangled from the lower branches of the great maples and elms. Everywhere that children's hands could be busy children's hands had been busy, setting up a little enterprise in horse chestnuts with the old fringed buggy top for a stall, constructing harnesses or carving boats, painting, digging, climbing, tying ropes. The earth in the yard had a bare, packed look; whatever green or blossoming thing the children had not trampled and scraped and denuded had fallen to the rabbits, chickens, dogs or cats. Up the trees were platforms, and down in the soil were caves, for such times as Minny, Tony, Hume and Bud elected to be Bandar-log or prehistoric savages.

The Peacock children's mother, the widow of the older Anthony, six years dead, was a lean, vigorous, black-eyed woman, large of bone and deep voiced, perhaps in her middle thirties, though the children thought her extremely old. She was a hot-tempered, despotic, energetic, impulsive person, given far more to deeds than words, and always briskly busy. No one ever loitered, delayed or philandered in the neighborhood of Mollie Peacock; tradespeople gave her their messages in nervous haste, village women stammered stupidly in their anxiety not to anger her. They said that she would almost as soon spank a small child as speak to it, her hands rather led than obeyed her tongue, and there was short shrift for some youngster every time the lamps were not filled, or the woodbox empty, or the porch unswept. Minny and Tony and their cousins leaped through their daily tasks with passionate zeal, and eyed their mother nervously whenever she unexpectedly bore down upon them. Sometimes, said the women of the village, she whipped them terribly.

The women of the village were almost as one in their disapproval of whipping, although they varied a trifle in their ground upon the question. Mrs Hallowell said that her children were too logical to make it necessary, and Mrs Treanor that Pippsy Treanor was always guided quickest by love, but Mrs Leroy went further and stated, even occasionally from platforms, that corporeal punishment caused a malignant reaction in a child's moral tissues and disturbed his norm until Fear had been vanquished by perfect Love again. They talked of these things at the club frequently, but Mrs Peacock did not come to the club and so did not hear them.

She pleaded that she had not time for the club. Beside her children she had Crazy Lucy and Grammar Peacock to care for. The latter was her husband's tremulous, clean, feeble old mother, who sat in the sunshine all day long throughout nine months of the year, and beside the kitchen stove when the weather was chilly, and knitted and darned and peeled apples and shelled peas in a contented dream that enwrapped seventy years of helpful and sad and happy memories. Crazy Lucy was the cook, a pale, silent woman whose husband had deserted her; unrivaled in the making of gingerbread and rice pudding and graham rolls and all the other inexpensive edibles that the Peacocks consumed by the square yard. Once Mrs Hallowell had mildly expostulated with Mrs Peacock on the subject of Lucy.

"Does thee really think it safe to leave thy dear children with that queer girl?" she had asked.

"The children won't hurt her!" Mrs Peacock had hardily returned. Mrs Hallowell had looked a trifle nonplused and had said no more.

One day some sprightly program chairwoman had suggested, as a means of attracting young Mrs Peacock to the Village Improvement Club, that gentle old Quaker Mrs Peacock be asked to read a paper of reminiscences before the members. Grammar Peacock had known Friends' Landing long before the railroad came, when Indian camps were lingering in the western hills, when the mail came through once a week on horseback, and when some of the bearskins that now graced the floors of handsome brown bungalows had been wandering the woods on the backs of their original owners.

So Grammar came to the club and tremblingly launched

into her memories, and for half an hour—even for an hour—feminine Friends' Landing listened with bright respectful interest, with laughter and applause. But when the clock struck five young wives began to slip away, and the maid who was to serve tea at five began to rattle cups in the reception hall, and still Grammar talked pleasantly on and on and on. At half-past five a flushed and harassed hostess of the day asked young Mrs Peacock if she couldn't just, perhaps, give her mother-in-law just a—well, just a gentle hint, but young Mrs Peacock pleaded vivaciously, and in a whisper, that Grammar was having "the time of her life." So Grammar talked on, past six o'clock, and until half-past six, and until ten minutes of seven, and then finished waveringly with a halfhearted fear that perhaps she had tired "the ladies." The diminished audience was by now too much exhausted to rise to a polite lie, but the gallant daughter-in-law said heartily, "Not a second too long!" and led the proud and weary old woman tenderly away, to an evening of praise and hot tea and more reminiscences, in which the subject of time was never even mentioned.

She was always kind enough to the old lady, it was conceded, in her flighty and despotic way. But oh, said the mothers of Friends' Landing, and especially said the women who were not mothers, how frightfully she talked to those children! How she grabbed them and hustled them and jumped them into the shabby car and out of the shabby car, what warnings she hurled at them, and what punishments she threatened! It was dreadful, in this day of analyzed and interpreted childhood, to realize that a well-to-do woman, and an intelligent woman, could possibly be so far behind the times. In their shabby garments the young Peacocks and their cousins brought wood and milked cows and tramped into town for the mail much as did the Italians and Poles of the lower river settlement; they rode on watering carts and hay wagons, did hair-raising things in their catboat, and apparently were free to start a fire and cook a meal where-ever the fancy took them. They did not go to village parties or the dancing school, or even to the Louvre when there was a carefully supervised children's matinee, with a fairy tale and educational films. Altogether they were a neglected lot, and if it had not been for their mother's genuine goodness to their old grandmother, Friends' Landing would have said her to be a decidedly heartless woman.

There was, however, one other person who had never had anything but tenderness and gentleness from Mollie Peacock, and this person, although he was aged only eight and had known her but ten intoxicating days, was deeply convinced that she was the most remarkable woman in the world and had the most endearing manner. Yet little Paul Craig had known a great many women and a great many changes in his hundred months of living, and was perhaps as shrewd a judge of human nature as might be found in all Friends' Landing. In actual years he came between seven-year-old Minny and eight-year-old Hume and considered Anthony and Bud, who were nine and ten, dizzy heights above him, but in experience he was as old as all four of the harum-scarum youngsters put together.

He had been standing listlessly in a corner of the playground one morning, ten days ago, when he first saw her. She had come out across the bare clean porch of the Children's Home Shelter and down the bare, clean steps and into the sharp clean May sunshine, with Mrs Younger, who was the matron. Mrs Younger had been carrying a bowl very steadily—it was filled with Irish Moss custard, which the matron had been sending to old Mrs Peacock.

There had been other children in the yard—clean, quietly playing children, in blue checked blouses and pinafores—but they had retreated from Mrs Younger. Not that the matron was cross, exactly, but she was Authority, and, unlike other children, these little mavericks in the Children's Home Shelter had no refuge from Authority, no spoiling indulgent arms, no sheltering lap, no competent grownup to stand between their tender, lazy little bodies and the inexorable routine of disciplined work and play, washing and eating, sleeping and waking.

Paul had not retreated from Mrs Younger. He had come only two months before from a place that made the Shelter seem safe and happy and secure. They had said, the decent people who had investigated and exposed that other place, that he was fortunately too little to remember much of it. But he remembered it all and would carry the dim memory into manhood and fatherhood, and would think, when he was dying, of the dark room where two infuriated grownups had faced down a helpless little boy who knew his mother was dead and could not hear him, and that these big people were going to hurt him. He had never talked about it, he was afraid to talk about it, but he had been thinking about it as he stood idling in the healing sunshine and had watched Mrs Peacock and the matron come toward him, and, incidentally, toward the gate.

"Here's a nice child, with such a serious little face!" Mollie Peacock had said. "I'll bet you this is a boy that never cries!"

And as she had stooped toward him he had not noticed that her black hair had been slipping untidily under her dowdy hat, nor her brown lean face freckled, nor her hands muddy from driving. He had only seen something that had melted his frozen little heart almost painfully and had made him touch her hand with his stubby, cold little red hand and smile timidly at her.

"Do you, now, Mouse?" she had said cheerfully. Paul had answered her honestly, if shyly:

"I haven't anybody to cry *to!*"

Mrs Younger had not heard him; he had thought perhaps the other lady had not heard him either, for she had not looked at him. But after a moment the visitor had said suddenly:

"Mrs Younger, will you be a darling and lend me this boy? He'll hold that wonderful custard steady in the car," she had added quickly, "and he can play about with my Siwashes, and I'll bring him back tonight or in the morning. Would you like that, Mouse?"

Authority had hesitated. They didn't like to have the children away at night. Perhaps some other day . . .

Paul's emotions had almost nauseated him. He was cold, he was feverish, he prayed.

And so it really had come to pass. He had got into the front seat of the muddy little car, and taken the bowl between his shaking little red hands, and nearly strangled himself because his breath came so spasmodically and so shallow. The women had chatted, perhaps for three minutes, but for Paul it had meant three eternities in which any second might end the dream, might find the matron suddenly unpropitious.

It had been a golden morning, getting warmer toward noon, with shadows of flickering young green across the road, with breezes kissing Paul's face, with perfume pouring into his little lungs. Mollie Peacock had been silent as they drove along, but when they came to the village she told him what she had to buy at the grocery and asked him if he liked chocolate. Paul had told her that he had had chocolate with silver paper around it once, and he had put the silver paper in his mother's prayer book because it was so pretty. He had been deeply interested when the grocer's boy put butter and potatoes into the car, and when they drove on he had said smilingly, out of deep thought, to Mollie:

"He thinks I'm your boy!"

Then they had come to the old Peacock place and had got out, and Minny and Hume had taken charge of him, and they all had played "milkman," a delightful game in which everyone dragged cans about on the cart and slopped water in and out of all kinds of containers. Bud had given him an old strap, and Tony five heavy bolts of differing sizes, and Minny had helped him button his shoes after they had all been wading. And, best of all, Hume had told him that they would be "podners on everything," and have secrets from the big boys.

At lunch his little heart had sunk a degree—just that much of his wonderful day had gone! Lunch had been at a long table at one side of the kitchen; the old lady had moved only a foot or two from her rocker to reach her place; Lucy had commented and advised while she served the hot, delicious food; Mollie Peacock had not removed her hat, had eaten casually while she telephoned to some insistent woman that she could not take part in a rummage sale. The sunshine had streamed in on the blue bowls and the big loaf, the stove had sent forth an appetizing odor of smoking griddle and browned pudding; the children had seized cookies to bear into the yard, to devour there while waiting to be summoned in for dishwiping.

They had been so good to him! He might feed the rabbits, and he might put his eager little hand into hollows in the hay where there were surely eggs. And he needn't wipe dishes, nor sweep the back porch, nor rake the road; indeed, they would not let him do anything, though he really longed to help. And they had clustered about their mother to beg for a gypsy supper on the riverbank, "because Paul is here!"

How fast the radiant afternoon fled! To Paul it had been dreadful to see it go. It had been drawing toward sunset when suddenly the miracle had occurred. Minny, who had been cross before lunch and drowsy after lunch, had been pronounced by Lucy and Grammar to be "sickening for something." When the doctor and Minny's mother had been called in consultation they said, "Possibly mumps."

These magic words had brightened the children's faces as steadily as they had clouded the grown-up sky. From "no more going for mail" and "no school" the older boys' litany of thanks had risen in joyous crescendo to "Paul can't go back!"

Paul, Mrs Peacock had decided, with one hand on the

shoulder of his heaving little checked shirt, certainly couldn't go back. No, even if it wasn't mumps, the doctor had said—and it proved indeed not to be—better not let the child go back into the institution for a week or ten days.

That was ten miraculous days ago now. Ten days of joy were a long time to Paul, even though these days flew in a perfectly new and amazing manner, from the hour when he wakened in the alcove of Anthony's room, to the long warm spring twilight when, dusty and muscle-tired and ecstatically happy, he stumbled to bed again. They all knew that he was happy, but how heavenly happy they could not dream. It was all a matter of course to the Peacock children, dearly as they loved it. But to Paul the kitchen, fragrant with breakfast, his own chair between Grammar and Hume, the laughter that accompanied the emptying of blue bowls, the soft haze of an early summer morning over the river, the muffled sound of whistles from the factories a mile away, the splash of some invisible fisherman's oars, the pink rose that Aunt Mollie stuck into the strap of his new blue overalls, were alike touched with an exquisite enchantment that would never fade from his heart.

He would wander out with the boys into the yard, almost always silent, except when the rich, surprised little chuckle they all loved escaped him, but eagerly and breathlessly helpful with all their daily duties. He ran for a hammer or a broom as if his life depended upon it, he raised logs that were fully half his own weight, and raked rubbish or picked up chips with a passionate ardor that brought unaccustomed red into his pale little cheeks. When Grammar's knitting ball rolled away, or Lucy wanted a needle to sew up the stuffed chickens, it was Paul who leaped down from his Lotto card or his Parchesi board, only anxious to serve. Grammar in return let him help her cut out cookies, a rapturous and breath-taking responsibility, and Lucy showed him how to weave worsted chains through a spool. The two women, in the endless hours they spent together in the kitchen, or on the back porch that grapevines were beginning once more to screen, agreed that he was a dear little fellow.

"The way them little legs of his 'll run, the minute you call him," Lucy might muse, slopping comfortably over the dented dishpan and the cooling suds. "Run to see what you're after, I mean, not make for the shed or the fence like them other Ayrabs!"

"A body could do sompin' with that young one," Grammar, holding her needle and thread between her squinted eyes and the light, would agree comfortably. "He'll talk to ye like he was eighty. And he'll run to do ye a good turn when Tony and Bud 'll set like graven immidges! 'You fellers 'll blue-mould in your tracks,' I says to 'em yesterday. 'You remind me of a feller your grandpa used to tell about. . . .' "

And so on and on into the sweet fragrant morning, while the bread baked, and the cherries simmered, and the lilacs about the door rustled in their clean green foliage. The warm, shining dishes would be stacked away, and the children murmur and scold over their planks and ropes and wheels, and Grammar, still talking, would move her rocker out of the path of Lucy's mop and pail. It was a homely little community, isolated and primitive, yet it knew utter peace and content, and the presence of the wistful little alien somehow was making these days oddly happier for them all. Paul's deep eyes, glowing with joy, and Paul's wide mouth, that somehow could not so quickly lose its betraying lines of unchildlike solemnity, were the salt that seasoned the carefree days that had always been so gaily taken for granted.

As for Mollie Peacock, whose busy comings and goings were apparently so briskly practical, she was experiencing curious and poignant emotions because of the stray little boy that chance had brought into her own group. When he laughed his rare little reluctant laugh, she oddly wanted to cry, she felt her lashes sting with the tears that had come so rarely and so painfully since Anthony, the tender, big, splendid husband who had been so patient with her untrained and impatient beginnings, had died. Anthony had died despite the desperate prayers she had poured out, her black head bowed against his knees, and five days later, the ashen-faced and stony-eyed Mollie had seen her first-born son go into the darkness, too, the Tommy that had brought father and motherhood to Tony and herself in a golden springtime eight years before, the Tommy for whom they had bought, before he was born, the little moose-skin moccasins from the old Indian woman and the silly alphabet plate at the Hollybridge Fair.

After that there was a dazed time, when Grammar was very good, and little Minny always cried when her mother cried, and traced the tears with a fat forefinger down Mollie's thin cheek. And then a busy, brown-skinned, capable widow had taken the place of the laughing, radiant wife, and they had come to this old house of Grammar's by the river, "for a while anyway." When Aunt Sally died Bud and Hume had come too; when Lucy's husband deserted her Lucy had come.

So six years had gone by, and to Mollie, as is the way of widows, it still seemed only half a life. Her soul seemed still straining on toward that fuller life of daily talk, daily laughter, daily confidences that is happy marriage. She still felt that the cloud might somehow break, that Anthony might slip a big hand under her elbow in the old way, carry her off for some happy city visit filled with strange impressions of restaurants and theaters. He was somewhere, and his "girl"—he had always called her that—was blindly and stupidly seeking him. Why, before she knew Grammar, before Minny and Tony were dreamed of, there had been Anthony, there had been fat, bad baby Tom throwing napkin rings and spoons to the floor of the little Wakely cottage down by the bridge. Grammar and Tony and Minny had never seen that cottage; it had burned down one night, and today the old roses and hollyhocks of Mollie's bridal days were smothered in mallow and willows and rank grass. Sometimes she walked by it and wrung her heart with the bitterness that no one could know or share.

She had shut it all into her heart, and there it had been locked, cold and dark and heavy, beyond bearing, for a long, long time. Mollie had treated her grief as she treated Tommy's little old shoes and Anthony's few letters. She took it into her hands sometimes, but she dared not look at it: she could only shut her eyes and bow her face against it in agony of spirit. No, she was not living now, she was stunned and defrauded, she was like some pathetic little sea creature left high on a rock, waiting, shriveling, suffering for the blessed return of the tide.

And now this solemn little orphan from the shelter, this "mouse," with his stubby, willing red hands and his eager dark eyes, was somehow making her want to cry again, and, incidentally, to laugh again, and to do other normal, simple things that are as wholesome for the soul as fresh air and sunshine for the body. Through Paul's eyes she saw for the first time that the kitchen was a pleasant place to be, that the yard was a children's paradise, and that the routine of porridge and pudding, of overalls and swimming suits and small shabby pajamas had a soul of its own.

For the first time it began to dawn upon her, in an undefined yet infinitely healing way, that out of the wreckage of the old perfect life had grown another life, as complete in its way, and, if less radiant, perhaps more useful. She was not all the lone, lorn woman of her wakeful nights and solitary musings; she was, after all, the center of four children's universe, and the means of making a weary old woman and an ill-treated young wife contented, at least. That this was supremely worth while Paul showed her. Paul was healthy, he was decently clothed, his adenoids had been duly removed, and his Catechism pumped in. But no institution could give Paul or any other little boy a back yard, and chips to bring in, cookie cutting and trotting for the mail, a Grammar and an Aunt Mollie. Tony and Minny and Hume and Bud had always had these things.

"Dear Lord, the poor babies that haven't!" thought Mollie on a shuddering breath, when she came to this point in her reflections. And that night—it was Paul's seventh night under her roof—for the first time in six years, she prayed that God would spare her for Grammar and the children, and keep them all safe in their paths of pleasantness and peace.

"Perhaps I am reaching out for something that I never will have again," mused Mollie. "Perhaps Anthony was just himself, and no other—no other husband could ever mean so much!"

And she thought of Lawrence Rossiter. She had been obliged to think about him a great deal of late. He had told her once that he was one of the men who will not take no for an answer, and he had not taken it. Mollie found it difficult to regard Lawrence and his suit seriously; she felt in the matter unexpected impulses toward girlish flippancy and girlish airs. She did not quite like herself when the dashing, handsome, persistent man was beside her. What did he want her for? she would ask in half-petulant surprise. What would her life be, in a strange city, as the wife of an almost strange man? Certainly her modest three hundred a month—for when the young McKays' board was subtracted it was only that—was not a tempting bait for so successful a man? But, Mollie wondered honestly, could a brown-skinned woman of thirty-eight be the real attraction?

She did not love him of course. He did not expect her to feel for him what she could never feel for anyone but Anthony. But she would be a married woman again, there would be companionship, there would be the blessed plural again in life. She had been so lonely, and the years had been so long.

Grammar was the problem. For Lucy, after all, was not Mollie's responsibility, and the three boys were old enough for boarding school. Minny, of course, would stay with her mother. . . .

"But it's too silly, my planning this way!" Mollie would interrupt herself with a smile. "I'm a fool, and he's no more in love with me than—well, than I am with him! He—he hasn't got in his whole body as much love and tenderness—and gentleness—and goodness—as Anthony had in his dear old clever right hand!"

And perhaps she would surprise herself by bursting into tears.

After all, she reasoned half impatiently, what was to be gained by any change? She had a full life and a most interesting one, here. To become a good man's wife might indeed be a promotion for some lonely girl, but she, Mollie, was a woman—why, just to belong to her and to share her children's privileges had seemed heaven itself to the little Mouse.

"Lucy 'n me's been tellin' you all this for two years," Grammar said placidly, when Mollie, in a confidential mood most unusual with her, tried to express herself to the old woman. "There ain't a woman breathin' any luckier than you—be shoo she may. You got Anthony's memory——"

"I know I have!" Mollie said quickly.

"And you got Anthony's children! You got plenty and runnin' over to live on, even payin' ten cents for a cauliflower and raisin' no more than half your greens——"

"I know it, Grammar!" Mollie's face burned. "But—but it is certainly odd, and it makes one feel—feel young again," she stammered, "to have a man—and he is a prosperous man, too—to have him . . . And it isn't as if I was a rich woman. . . ."

"Maybe there's oil in them lands of yours, upriver, as there was in the Widder Wilson's," Grammar suggested at random.

"Oh well, if you're going to be ridiculous!" And Mollie left the kitchen haughtily. But the disquieting doubt persisted—was strengthened, indeed, despite her air of injured assurance.

On the eighth day of his visit Paul, climbing cautiously into a pantry window under Tony's whispered directions from the geranium bed, stepped firmly if gently into a pan of setting milk. The splash that followed the little boy's agitated jump to the floor affected a sheet of hot gingerbread and seven clean dish towels, and a pyramid of tins clattered after him.

The uproar brought everybody on the place to the scene, Mollie leading. They found a Paul with terrified eyes, as white as the plaster wall against which he was backing blindly. Seeing Mollie, he burst into frightened tears. She gave Lucy and Grammar and the gathering children a look full of compunction and knelt down beside Paul.

"Why, Mouse—Mouse—Mouse," she said tenderly, in a voice that the others had never heard before. "You mustn't be so silly! I'm not angry at you, darling. I'm not going to punish you—it was an accident, that was all!"

Paul dug his wet face into her crisp gingham. He was shaking with sobs, choking with fear. For a long time it was impossible to quiet him. Mollie carried him to the shady side porch and sat down with him in her lap. She banished the audience with a glance, and for a while of silence kept her arms about the dusty little body, and felt the heavy droop of the little rough head against her shoulder.

"Listen, Mouse," she said when the heaving heart so close to her own was quiet, and the tear-stained little face had been wiped dry, "you mustn't be afraid of me. You've had too much scolding and punishing in your life, you poor little scrap. I'll *never* punish you, Paul, when you come to visit us. My darling, do you think I could be angry at a poor little scrap of a child that hasn't got any mother, nor any home of his own? You've seen me punish Tony, and I sent all three boys to bed without their supper last night, but that doesn't mean *you*. Don't ever, ever, ever let me see you so frightened again!"

She had told him that she wanted Mrs Younger to let him

come to them soon again, for another visit, and Paul had nodded, even though he had feared in his secret heart that this dream of bliss might not be. The matron had telephoned every day to know when the child was coming back to the Shelter, and Paul knew what the phrases "discipline of the institution" and "upsetting the child's mind" meant to her.

Now Mollie, sitting in the peace and silence of the porch, with the morning sunshine flickering through the leaves and falling gently on the worn old sunken flooring and the big pan of greenings and the benches where the children had most of their summer meals, began to think of something new. She pondered and reasoned it in her quick mind for only a few moments before she said:

"Your mother is dead, Paul?"

"An' my daddy too," Paul said, by heart, contentedly, from his refuge.

"Then somebody *could* adopt you, Mouse?"

"If they wanted to," Paul agreed.

"Mouse," said Mollie, "don't set your little heart on it, but I am going to ask them—mind, they may not, now!—I am going to ask them if you may not come here to me, to be one of my boys."

Paul got down from her lap, and Mollie's heart contracted with pain at the sight of the anxious, incredulous little face that questioned her own. For a full half minute they looked silently at each other. Then the child said, trembling with eagerness:

"I would try to be very good, for you! And I would bring in wood and sweep the yard for the kids—every day I would! And I'd do anything you *ever* ast me to—even if it was sumpthin' nobody else would do!"

Mollie laughed rather shakily as she kissed him.

"But you won't set your heart on it, Mouse? There are rules and regulations about these things."

Bud called him, and, full of his great news, he fled. Mollie, looking after him, felt a sudden qualm of doubt. What about

Lawrence? Wasn't it enough that he was undaunted by the prospect of two children, without her risking the introduction of a third? Well, perhaps what Lawrence thought was of no consequence. Yet sometimes she felt as if a current as firm and resistless as that of the near-by river was bearing her toward this man and all that his coming into her life implied.

Paul prayed that night that he would never risk Aunt Mollie's anger again. But it was only the next day that another unpleasant episode occurred. He could not feel that he was exactly naughty in this connection, but he knew Aunt Mollie was displeased with him, and his heart sank correspondingly.

They were all in the front garden, making one of their spasmodic efforts to beautify it, raking, burning, digging and sweeping busily. It was the first day of June, balmy and green, cool in the shade, but so hot in the sun that the children panted and glowed with the heat and cast shabby sweaters and hats behind them as they worked. Grammar's chair had been brought out beside the lilacs, and Lucy, who was picking chickens, occupied the lowest porch step.

Presently Lawrence Rossiter stopped his phaeton at the gate, and Mollie, unpinning her turned-up skirt, leaned her rake against the fence and went out to talk with him. She invited him to join their labors, since he apparently had nothing else to do, but Lawrence smilingly declined and asked her instead to come and drive with him; he was looking up some securities, and she was only wasting her time with these children.

However, Mollie could not go, and she had come back into the garden, wondering a little just what his business was anyway, and what "looking up securities" meant, when Paul was found to be white and trembling and close to tears. The stern need of discovering who had been "mean" to the Mouse immediately engrossed her.

Paul, recovering his equilibrium rapidly, explained that he

thought maybe Mr Rossiter had come to take him "back there."

Mollie sat down on an upturned hydrangea tub and questioned him in surprise.

"Back *where?*"

"To—to Mrs Smith's," said Paul in a whisper.

"You mean that villainous place where you were before you came to the Shelter?" Mollie questioned. "The place the police closed in Manville? But what—what has this gentleman, Mr Lawrence, to do with that?"

"He was one of the d'rectors," Paul said readily.

Mollie eyed him a moment in silence. He knew, in his sick little heart, that somehow he had displeased his goddess.

"*Who* was?"

"Mr Rossiter was."

"Oh, was he?" Mollie questioned. The Smith scandal had been duly aired in a virtuous press. But she did not remember his name in it, perhaps because she had not known it then. Of course a man might be a director and still not know that they had chanced to place an unscrupulous and half-crazy woman in charge of an orphanage. . . .

Still, the directors should know. Who else could stand between the children and abuse? Of course Lawrence was a bachelor, had perhaps been drawn casually into the directorship. For that particular institution had had several of the prominent people of the neighboring town of Manville upon its directorate, and a man who, like Lawrence, was both socially and politically ambitious, might be glad to be included among them.

Still, the directors should know. Mollie looked beyond Grammar, knitting peacefully under the lilacs, and into the hideous memory of those newspaper revelations. Babyhood crying with fear; little stammered explanations met with a whip; little bodies wet and neglected; little appetites gnawing and fainting and gnawing again in locked rooms. Of course he hadn't known that. . . .

Still, he *should* have known. Mollie turned troubled eyes to the disgraceful yet happy garden, and she shuddered as if the warm sunshine shook her after the passing of a heavy cloud.

"You are sure this was the same man, Mouse?" she asked. Paul was very sure.

"Because Joe Sullivan talked to him," he said.

"And who is Joe Sullivan, dear?"

"He was a big boy that used to go with Mr Rossiter to hold his horse," Paul explained, "when Mr Rossiter was driving up the river. And Joe told him about it—that they were mean to us kids—and asked him if he would tell his aunt. Because Joe couldn't write to his aunt—they wouldn't let him."

"And what was he doin' up the river?" Grammar asked suddenly.

"He was buying a lady's farm, but after, Joe said, they made him give it back to her, because her husband was dead, and she didn't know about oil wells," Paul said in his innocent voice as he leaned against her chair.

"H'm!" Mollie said, facing Grammar bravely, as was her wont, but with reddened cheeks. "And did he come to see you after Joe Sullivan talked to him?" she asked.

"No," said Paul simply.

"Not when Joe told him you were all unhappy?"

"I don't think he said we all were," Paul said scrupulously. "But he told about Rosy Mason and the Butterick baby."

"The Mason Girl!" "The Butterick Infant!" Mollie knew their names by heart. She had seen them many a time, in glaring print. And already she vaguely realized that a shadow had indeed passed over the garden and out of her life forever.

It made her feel oddly shocked and shaken, even a little ill. She put Paul gently aside and went slowly into the house, and all the rest of that day, and for the few moments that they saw her on the next, she was strangely silent; "mad," Paul decided uncomfortably. She went away from the house very early in the car and came home very late, and she spoke to nobody except Grammar.

But on the following morning she called Paul to her and said:

"This is the day you were to go back, Mouse. I'm going over to Manville now to see a lawyer, and this afternoon I shall be at the Shelter, to wait until the directors' meeting is over, and when I come home I shall know—about you. But you mustn't hope too much, dear!"

"No," said little Eight sturdily, looking straight into her eyes. "I'm not!"

"Well, I am," she said with a shaken laugh, "and if they disappoint us this time we will try again, won't we?"

"Yes, please," said Paul. But she knew he did not believe it. "You'll be back around—around four, I should think!" he hazarded.

"Not so early, for I have to go see a very, very sick lady after the meeting," Molly said, wondering what there was about this child that gave everything he said so oddly sweet a flavor. And as she drove away in her mud-splashed car she reflected wonderingly upon a civilization that found scores, and hundreds, of other objects worthier of time and money than the preservation of a Paul.

For a while after she left he was very silent. His little fortunes hung in the balance, and although the warm, silent spring day might proceed placidly in spite of them he could not quite keep pace with it. He sat on the step for a full half-hour, dreaming and hoping, in his little-boy way, and when Lucy came out with a basket and told him that the children were down on the old pier, fishing, he merely followed her silently down to the three twisted cherry trees and helped her gather the first cherries. He helped her set the table, too, and when luncheon was over he swept the porch and filled the salt and pepper shakers.

Two o'clock. Paul looked at the clock; he thought it had

stopped. He asked Lucy if she thought Aunt Mollie would like to have the inkwell cleaned. Grammar immediately put her hand on his forehead and said she thought the boy had a walking fever. She settled him beside her on the shady porch with a box of fascinating double photographs and a stereoscope, and the crackle of her starched and lacy afternoon apron and the sleepy sputtering of hens fluffing in the cool dust of the yard were forever mingled in his memory with the colored views of Yokohama and Benares.

But after a while Minny came in crying, with a nosebleed. The boys had refused to play with her unless she would let them pull her loose tooth, and had pushed her down. She and Paul were immediately given two saucer pies and were amicably looking at pictures when the repentant boys came after them both. They had rigged a square platform to the high branches of the maples, a platform that moved just above the ground, on four long ropes, with a thrilling and rotary motion.

For an hour, or until one of the ropes broke, catapulting Bud violently against the side of the barn, the children enjoyed the swing. During the few moments when they feared that Bud was dead their shrieking and laughing was silenced, but immediately afterward they recovered their gaiety of spirit and made a fire in the mud oven and baked apples and potatoes.

Large quantities of these, half cooked, and eaten with almost equal amounts of salt and cinders, made them all feel ill, and Lucy at four o'clock reported to Grammar that they were all lying on the riverbank, telling stories. Lucy went into the village with the grocer, to be sure of getting her spices for the cherries next week, and Grammar fell peacefully asleep in her chair.

It was some minutes after old man Fleming had made his kindly gift that the children dragged themselves lazily up from the riverside to look at the half barrel of tar.

"What do you s'pose he gave us this for?" Anthony asked suspiciously, looking down into the turbid depths of the heavy mixture.

"His daughter is going to get married, and maybe he doesn't need it any more," Hume offered lucidly, and after a grave exchange of glances the children accepted this as the simplest solution. Minny advanced an exploring finger to the black surface and drew it slowly up with a fascinating little tent of tar drawing after it. The boys began to jump about, dropping lumps of the soft black substance from hand to hand.

"Golly, she sticks!" Anthony laughed excitedly.

"Jiminy, you bet your life she sticks!" Hume shouted.

"Gosh, she certainly is sticky, all right!" Paul echoed, almost fearful of the adhesive black that caught and caught at his stubby little fingers. And for some five minutes the quintette repeated these words delightedly, with infinite variations, as they danced about with the tar.

When Minny first dropped her sagging lump on the weather-whitened boards of old man Fleming's pier there was immediate consternation, and the place was not only scraped with a board, but stamped and rubbed with ten sturdy boots. But later the children became less scrupulous, and a passing hen was deliberately decorated with a saddle of tar, to her own scandalized excitement, and Lucy found tar that night on the back "stoop," and indeed for several days was continually making unwelcome discoveries of the same nature.

The original inspiration, to tar the side path from the gate to the porch, was abandoned almost immediately. The tar might indeed be spooned onto the gravel, but smoothing it, even with the kitchen broom, was out of the question, and the children even thought it wise to remove themselves and their tar barrel far from the scene of the experiment and to appear to have no interest in, nor connection with, the unseemly blotch upon the path.

They went out near the hay barn and sat down in a rough circle and eyed their treasure thoughtfully.

"It's darn lucky," said Bud McKay seriously, "that there isn't anybody in this village who's been stealing something, or murdering somebody, or something!"

"Why, Bud?" piped Minny, who did not have sufficient self-control to pretend, as the boys instantly did, that this sentence was comprehensible.

"Why?" echoed Bud, with a truculent look about, and in a manly tone, "because they'd find themselves in trouble, that's why!"

"If they stole this *tar,* they would," Anthony, who was six months younger than Bud, hazarded warningly, with an uncertain look at his senior.

"If they stole *anything,*" Bud affirmed, enjoying his cryptic utterances to the full. Minny eyed him curiously, like a robin, with her little bobbed head cocked inquisitively, but was only vaguely aware that she was missing the point. The boys exchanged furtive glances for a full minute before Bud said, "They'd get tarred and feathered, that's what *they'd* get!"

This tremendous thought pleased everyone, and the children nodded significantly at one another. Tarring and feathering . . . !

"What would they feather with, Bud?" Anthony asked with a glance at a passing white minorca. The minorca, suspecting the worst, skittered out of sight, and Anthony, picking up a dropped white feather, touched his finger to the tar and stuck the feather thereon, eying it meanwhile in a thoughtful and abstracted manner.

"Feathers!" Bud said. "Like what's in those old pillers up attic," he added thoughtfully.

Then there was a moment of ruminative silence. Paul, who had picked up another feather, stuck and freed it on every finger of his left hand in turn. His small body, gaining in rotundity daily, leaned comfortably against an empty and upturned trough. Minny, her legs dangling, sat on the trough, Hume beside her. The older boys sat on the chopping block, their knees almost as high as their shoulders, the tar barrel between them. A perfect spring afternoon was descending graciously upon the old Peacock place, shadows were lengthening upon the hammered earth, and great shafts of sunlight piercing the thick new green of the maples and willows. Grammar, pausing at the window of her warm bedroom over the kitchen, looked out and thought the children singularly well behaved. Lucy, hustling into supper preparations, with the grocery boy's pleasantries echoing in her ears, also glanced at them and saw nothing irregular in progress. Presently she heard Anthony going up the attic stairs and asked what they were playing.

"Bud says we can play hoss thieves," said Anthony after a pause. Lucy said nothing more, and the conversation closed.

It was a gracious and gentle Mrs Hallowell who picked Mollie up, when the second tire burst, and offered to take her home. Mollie was most appreciative. Six o'clock, and she had been gone all day from Grammar and the children; she had been at the Shelter, and she had seen old Mrs Ebright. . . .

She was chattering cheerfully, if wearily, when the shining Hallowell car turned into her yard, and it was in her hostess's face, to which her own was turned, that she first read the warning of something amiss. She turned, with a familiar sinking of the heart, to identify—who was it? Pitch, had they gotten? Lumps of it in—which child's hair? And their faces! Good heavens, and the porch . . . and the dogs . . . !

"Thee has never heard in thy life such a dressing down as she gave those dear unfortunate children!" said Rachael Hallowell to her husband that night.

Indeed, Mollie completely forgot her and forgot everything else in the world except the five wrongdoers before her.

"Bud McKay! And Anthony Peacock—you great big strapping boys, that certainly ought to know better!" Mollie began with deadly aim, as she slapped and shook and scraped and wiped angrily. "The very idea . . . when your mother is away. Don't touch me with those hands, Hume. You naughty, *naughty* disgraceful children—all over Lucy's porch! Now stop whining, Minny, you're quite old enough. Throw that away, Hume—every bit of it—and, Tony, you go get that pail of kerosene out of the barn. You stay where you are, Bud! Do as I *tell* you, Tony! Give me those hands, Paul. I don't know *what* I'm going to do, Anthony, but you may be very sure that you won't hear the end of *this* business for many and many a day. Now put your dress on, Minny, you naughty girl, and Paul—you're done!—you pick up your shoes, and you two streak it right *straight* upstairs and get right *straight* into bed. . . . Put your foot into this bucket, Hume! Of all the disgusting—— Go along, Paul and Minny, and don't let me hear another word out of you!"

"Thee would have wanted to cry—to see them creep off like little mutes," said Rachael Hallowell, finishing her description. "They were frightened to death, poor children, and no wonder!"

Yet Rachael Hallowell had not seen the radiant face that one of the children wore as he went upstairs, nor the ecstasy that shone in his eyes and swelled in his heart. Her sixty years were not as shrewd as his eight, and she could not know that in the familiar motherly scolding he read aright the news of his acceptance; that, supperless and smelling of kerosene, and in disgrace, Paul Peacock could have sung for very joy as he climbed untimely into bed and lay awaiting the penitential bread and water that marked him no longer a child apart, but one of the dear unfortunate children in the old Peacock house.

The Mother of Angela Hogan

WHEN ANGELA HOGAN left the Hamilton Home School for Girls, on her eighteenth birthday, Miss Schofield and Mrs Allenby told each other that in one case, at least, their careful training had borne good fruit. To Angela, at eighteen, after thirteen years of their supervision, they felt they could point with pride. Angela had gentle manners, she played the piano, she wrote a clean legible hand, she had had domestic science and stenography courses, and she had a nice little nest egg in the bank to tide her over the time of looking foi employment. Altogether Angela was far better equipped than were most of the Hamilton girls for the struggle of life.

And yet their mutual reassurances as to the launching of Angela somehow lacked a genuine ring, even as their quavering good-bys to her lacked spontaneity. Angela, considering what a timid, silent little creature she usually was, had made them uneasy at the very last moment with a very fusillade of interrogation. She had delivered her questions alternately to Mrs Allenby and Miss Schofield; but they could not answer her of course; she had seen that. She had become silent as abruptly as she had turned vocal, her burning thin little face suddenly white again, her manner once more the timid, quiet manner they knew.

This little final scene, however, did not really flaw the fineness of Angela's record at the Hamilton, nor the confidence of her protectors in her future. She was one more girl saved from the unfortunate circumstances of her birth; she would always be a credit to them and to herself.

Angela, a little dazed with freedom and with the strangeness of being alone in the streets just at the hour when the girls were getting ready to file in for lunch, walked along in autumn heat for some time without any consciousness except a feeling of profound relief. Ah, it was good, if a little terrifying, to get out of the Hamilton once and for all, after a long thirteen years! Thirteen winters, summers, autumns, springs in that one atmosphere of polished halls and mutton stew and chowder; those dormitory cubicles scented with girls' rubbers and serge skirts, those lavatories smelling of carbolic acid!

Angela breathed deep of the sweetness of liberty. Hansen had taken her bag to Mrs White's; she was unburdened. The girls were eating beans and stewed dried apricots now; this was Thursday. She was done with beans and stewed dried apricots forever! She went into a Childs restaurant and sat timidly silent for a long time at a long marble-topped slab. After a while she ordered fried soft-shell crabs, hot butter cakes, coffee, ice cream. It was all delicious; nothing tasted in the least as all meals tasted at the Hamilton.

Courage and confidence returned with the food, and Angela planned as she ate. She was not going to live at Mrs White's, she knew that. Girls from the Hamilton always went to Mrs White's; there would be girls she knew there; girls who knew that Angela had been a Hamilton girl. She must get her bag away from Mrs White's at once, without arousing suspicion. Afterward she could find a safe place to live; one could always go to the Sisters and ask their advice. But not Mrs White's, with everyone saying that she had been an orphan, a girl whose "home influences had been unfortunate"; no, she couldn't stand that! Much better to make a fresh start somewhere else, where nobody knew anything.

Not that the girls knew anything specific of Angela's long-dead mother and father; for that matter, Angela knew almost nothing herself. But the girls who were placed by generous patronesses in the Hamilton Home usually had one history. Without the generous patronesses they would have been city foundlings. Owing to the wonderful founder and supporters of the Hamilton, they were given a better chance than that; they were educated in manners and voices as well as in book lessons, they were nicely dressed, they went up to the Hannah Hamilton Camp in the Adirondacks every summer. And at eighteen each girl was given one hundred dollars, found a good position and placed with Mrs White.

It was a wonderful charity, and Angela hoped that she was duly grateful for it. But burning in her heart were resentment and shame; she had been resentful and ashamed for many years now, ever since she had been old enough to know just the type of work the Hamilton did. She could not shake that shame and that resentment fast enough from her skirts. She must cut away the past. And perhaps after years she might forget it, might come to believe that her mother had been only one more good woman in a world of good women, an honored wife, a happy mother.

"Who was my mother? What do you know about her? Why did I come here?" she had passionately demanded of Mrs Allenby and Miss Schofield. They had tried to pacify her, to put her off. They had said, after swift oblique glances at each other, that they did not know. They did not know anything about any of the girls. They never did. No, there were no letters, no documents of any kind, except of course —except of course, in Angela's case, that nice bank account that meant that she could buy herself a lovely home someday.

Angela's face had flushed darkly at the mention of the bank account. Ten thousand dollars! Her mother had never saved that sum, that was clear. Angela was a white-faced, silent little creature, but she was not dull. Even to her unsophistication the neat finish of the amount said something significant; it had been paid by someone to someone. It had originally been written in one check. She hated the thought of it; she never would touch it!

Strolling along after her luncheon, she bought herself a wet pink rose in a spray of asparagus fern, a bag of chocolate caramels and a movie magazine. She sat in the shade in the park and read her magazine and watched the children and the nurses. At four she went in a taxi to Mrs White's.

She stopped the taxi three doors away and looked at the White house. It impressed her unfavorably. Brownstone and shabby and one of a long row, it might have been a child of the Hamilton itself. Angela asked the taxi man to go and ask for Miss Hogan's bag and say that she was not coming tonight but they could telephone Mrs Allenby about it. Eventually she could, of course, escape from Mrs White, but it would be better to escape now, in the very beginning.

The man came back in two minutes with the familiar bulging bag. Angela could hardly believe her eyes. It was as simple as that, once one was eighteen! Mrs White was out, it seemed; she had probably gone up to the Hamilton to see why Angela was delayed. A colored man had delivered up the bag without question or comment.

Angela stopped at a drugstore to telephone; then she got back into the taxi and gave a Bronx address.

She was tired and nervous and whiter than ever when she reached Mrs Loughborough's kitchen. The heat of the day, the excitement of her adventures—lunch in a restaurant, a ride in a taxi, the capture of the bag—had exhausted her spirit. Angela, coming unannounced into the dim, hot, smelly, cluttered place, was conscious of a great need to cry.

But they soon cured that. Mrs Loughborough opened her great arms to the wanderer; Torey, ironing a white linen dress in the center of the kitchen, was instantly friendly, not to say sisterly.

"Look, Ma," said Torey. "Tom's not home. Hook me out a couple of sheets from the wash there and I'll iron the hems and we'll fix up his bed for Angela. Look, Angela, I've got a date for tonight and Saturday and Sunday, see? But I can break 'em off or else ask Jerry to get hold of another fellow. . . ."

Angela sank into this atmosphere with those ecstatic shudders that beset the freezing who are suddenly restored to warmth and shelter. She could not savor it enough; the loving big capable mother, the beautiful clever daughter who had a fine job, the mismatched plates and shabby chairs, so different from the furnishings of the Hamilton!

Torey had a box of collected savings stamps; she and Kane O'Malley were going out to the office to select a premium. Angela went with them. They saw a movie on the way home and bought a watermelon and ate it in the kitchen. Ma had been to church; sure Angela could go wit' her to siven in the mornin' if she'd get up whin the alar'rm wint off, she assured the guest cordially. It was all intoxicatingly free, it was deliriously exciting, the way the Loughboroughs lived, the things they could do, the things they didn't have to do! Angela, a fish that had at last fought its way to a great stream, swam in it ecstatically.

There was one bad minute. It came when Angela, wiping dishes, had to explain to her hostess for the third time how she happened to come to her.

"I remembered Mamma saying that if ever I needed a friend I was to remember you. But that was when I was only a little girl; Mamma died when I was six. I was at the Hamilton then. Mrs Allenby told me Mamma had died, and let me sit in her room all day and look at her travel books. So today I was afraid that you had moved, but I telephoned old Sister Ligouri, that came to see me twice, and she said to look for Thomas Loughborough in the telephone book, and that was how I knew." Angela went this far and, then trembling a little and lowering her voice, asked quickly: "You knew my mother, didn't you, Mrs Loughborough?"

"Oh, Blissed Mother, tell me what to say to the child!" Ellen Loughborough prayed. Aloud she said: "I did that. But not so well. Because she lived down on Eighth—or was it Christopher Street—an' then they wint to Erie to live, an' my childern were little. . . ."

Angela was looking at her keenly. How much does she know? each woman was asking herself.

"Did you know my father, Timothy Hogan?"

"No, that I didn't, dear'r. He died—God rist him—befoor I knew yure mamma." Mrs Loughborough rubbed the bone of her nose. "I knew some of the other Hogans, Joe and Robert," she said. "But that was later."

"Later than what?" Angela demanded.

"After yure mamma died, dear'r." Mrs Loughborough was floundering in deep water, but her quietly reminiscent tone gave no hint of it. "What you've told me today about the place they put ye," she went on, "makes me think I cud well have gone up to see ye once or twice! But the truth is ye wint out of me mind entirely. I knew poor Kitty Hogan was dead, an' I hear'rd they got ye into a very grand place, an' that was the whole of it! Didn't nobody iver go to see ye, or take ye a dolly or whativer?"

"Never!" Angela answered. But the tears that suddenly splashed on the dish she was drying were not self-pitying tears. They were tears of despair. Once again she had crept up to this subject of her mother; once again she had been evaded, put off. "Why did you call her 'poor Kitty'?" she wanted to ask. She did not dare.

For a long time she made no mention of her mother again. She fitted into the Loughborough clan quietly, as a drop sinks into a stream, and within a few weeks they were taking Angela as much for granted as they did themselves; Torey, Tom, Ellen and Paul and their children, Will and Ag and theirs, George and Eileen and their little boy.

To the Loughboroughs, at first, she was merely a homeless little mouse who paid Ma five dollars a week, worked in the Y.L.I. and couldn't get enough of churchgoing. "One of these days she'll joomp off an' be a nun on ye!" Katty Fealey, noisily drinking tea on a Thursday afternoon, predicted, and

Mrs Loughborough agreed to that solution readily enough. No girl could do better than that, if only the creatures had the sense to see it.

But certain odd developments not exactly encouraging to this theory presently took place in the case of Angela Hogan. For one thing, when she got a little weight and color, she quite suddenly turned out to be a beauty, in a quiet way. Her eyes were deep Irish blue, her mouth had an irregular and indeed an irresistible charm, and the rich mahogany of her hair curled against temples that were as white as Carrara marble, and threaded with the same blue veins. There was a faint hoarseness to her voice that was infinitely engaging, and she had a confiding little trick of touching for a second with her own small hand the hand of anyone with whom she was talking that appeared to be entirely free of coquetry and that yet was devastating to the male heart. Before anyone fully appreciated what was going on Con O'Shea was the avowed slave of little Angela Hogan, who lived at Loughboroughs'.

She did not entirely live there now, for Tom had come back to his room, and Angela was lodging two flights upstairs, with Mrs Con Loughborough, Torey and Tom's Aunt Lizzy. But Aunt Lizzy had her meals in the big twin building next door with her married children, so Angela had her breakfast and dinner with the Loughboroughs and went to church in the evenings with Ma. She never wanted to be out of Ma's sight at any second when it was possible to be near her; her starved little heart clung to Ma; the others in the group were only shadows.

Even to Con O'Shea she paid but casual attention. The richest, the most eligible man known to the Loughboroughs, or to anyone else in the neighborhood, Con was handsome too. He was the only son of rich Mrs Connors O'Shea; he had once been a little wild. But it was funny to see him come back into line and get up for early Mass and attend Benediction when he had a chance of seeing Angela. As for escorting her, that was out of the question; she never went anywhere with any man. The mere thought struck her new roses from her ivory-smooth cheeks.

"I don't know what you'd want better than Con," Tom Loughborough told her.

"Oh, don't say his name to me!" Angela begged, the tips of her ears coloring scarlet as she bent over the dishpan.

"Why shouldn't I say his name to you?"

"Oh, because I don't ever want to have anything to do with him!"

"What's the matter with Con O'Shea?"

"Nothing, nothing, nothing! Only, if I ever was to fall in love, but I never will—but if I ever *was* to . . ."

A long pause. Tom dragged comfortably on his pipe; Mrs Loughborough put away hot plates.

"Don't tease her, Tom," his mother said.

"I'm not teasin' her. I was just wonderin' what was the matter with Con O'Shea. And what was the rest of that, Angela? If you ever was to fall in love—what, eh?"

"Nothing! I've forgotten what I was going to say," Angela said hastily.

"Why, you know that's a lie," Tom said in his pleasant brotherly way. "You know that's one big lie. And you in a state of grace—I'm surprised at you!"

"Well, if it was a lie I'm sorry for it, but I'm not going to tell you what I was going to say!" Angela, backed up against the sink, red-cheeked, but game, like a cornered child, said unashamedly.

"She's goin' to be a little nun, this one is," Mrs Loughborough said affectionately.

It worried her somewhat to discover, as the weeks went by, that Angela had no intention of becoming a nun. Virginal and shy and holy she might be, but on the only occasion when Mrs Loughborough dared question her about it she was quite definite.

"You that don't like the men at all and 'll niver raise yure eyes to thim, is it wit' the Sisthers ye'll be goin'?" Ellen ventured one night when she and Angela were walking home from Benediction. "Sure, ye're niver happy but ye're in chur'rch, or doin' somethin' for someone——"

"Oh no, I'd never do that!" Angela's soft, hoarse little voice said quickly in the dark street.

"Ye might have a vocation?"

"I haven't. I know it full well. I'd no sooner take my vows than I'd be thinking of men," Angela answered astonishingly. "I'd be longing that somebody 'd kiss me or that I'd have the feel of a child in my arms. It 'd come over me like a tiger tearing at me," the girl went on simply. "And I'd go the way my mother went!"

Sheer amazement robbed Mrs Loughborough of the power of speech for a full minute. Presently she asked:

"How d'ye mane, the way yure mother wint? D'ye mane ye'd come out of the convent? Yure mother niver was a nun, Angela."

They were going in the house door now; they were climbing the stairs. Angela made no answer.

But when they were in the kitchen, and Mrs Loughborough was sitting panting in a chair at the table, and Angela had given her a cup of water, the girl pursued the subject.

"I'm like that," she said.

"Like what?" the other woman asked uneasily.

"I act the way I do with men because I'm afraid," Angela persisted. "I'm afraid. I'm afraid of myself."

"A good little angel of a ger'rl like you has no call to be that," Mrs Loughborough muttered, distressed.

"So that's why I'll never marry anyone," Angela said.

"Con O'Shea is turnin' into a fine feller," the older woman offered hesitatingly.

"Oh, him!" Angela said scornfully. "There's others I'd have before ever I'd look at him. But I'll never marry a one of them!"

"You were tellin' me you'd like to have a child in yure ar'rms."

Sudden tears were in Angela's eyes.

"Not for me," she said in a whisper. And, turning toward the sink, she had for a moment her back to the room. Suddenly she wheeled and faced her companion.

"D'you know what's almost the last thing I remember of my mother?" she demanded. "It was Easter, and she was working in the candy factory all night on big rush orders, and she came for me to the Hamilton early in the morning and took me to church. And on the way home she said, 'We'll stop and say "Happy Easter" to your father's mother; she doesn't like me, but she'll want to see my little girl in her white dress and her pink hat.' So we went to some place out toward the Concourse, and up in an elevator, and into a room. There were two women there; one was my grandmother—she's dead now, and the Lord has dealt with her—and the other was an aunt or cousin of mine, I think.

"Well, I forget how it started," Angela said, pale and tragic as she recalled it, "but in a minute Mamma was answering back, and the other woman, the younger one, was shoving her toward the door. And Mamma called out something about my father, that he had left his mother and that he hated her. It was then——"

The girl was no longer thinking of her listener. Her voice had sunk to a whisper, her eyes were gazing into space.

"It was then she called Mamma—terrible names," she said. "My grandmother did. She said that my mother was—bad. She said things—about me. She sat in her chair, hammering on the floor with her crutch and shouting, and the other woman went on shoving Mamma out and locked the door.

"We went downstairs, and Mamma showed me Easter eggs in windows, but I was crying, and she was shaking all over. She took me to a movie, and afterward we had ice cream, and then she took me back to the Hamilton. We never talked about it. I never saw her again.

"But I've remembered that. And it makes me feel that I'll never be like the other girls—like Torey and Ag and Eileen. It's inside me, like a curse!"

Her tone rose wildly. She stopped, and was silent. Mrs Loughborough cleared her throat before she said mildly:

"Yure grandmother Hogan was a very violent woman, God rist her. It's thrue that she drove Tim Hogan forth from the house an' there was bad blood betune thim. But what a child rimimbers, Angela, wudden't mane annythin' at all had yure mother but lived to laugh at it wit' ye. If ye brood over it, sure we're doin' the very thing yure mamma wud want ye to stop. There's none of us dares look back at the past an' do that. All we can do is shut the dure on it, an' go on, askin' the Blissed Mother that she'd kape us from makin' the same mistakes over again. Now you say yure prayers," Mrs Loughborough concluded, encouraged to see that her words were having some effect, "an', if ye don't want Con, ask St Joseph to send ye some other good man, an' go yure way like the rist of us, doin' yure bist, an' raisin' the childern. . . ."

Angela's mood seemed softened. She came over to Mrs Loughborough and got into her lap as a child might have done, and cried a little on her shoulder.

But after that the days went on and were weeks, and Christmas came, and there was no change in her. She still trembled away from anything like serious attention from any man; she still liked best to go to church in the evenings or to disappear early with a book. Con O'Shea took his dismissal hard; after all, girls did not refuse men as rich as Con O'Shea lightly, but Angela never weakened. There were other nibbles, one or two from highly eligible young men; none seemed to make the slightest impression.

Angela moved about the Loughborough kitchen like a transforming genie. The sink boards shone white; the dish towels twisted in ivory purity on the pulley line outside the window. Tom formed a habit of smoking his evening pipe there instead of going around the corner to Pete's, and he and Angela had long talks.

"I've known girls like you before, afraid to get married," Tom told her. "They think it 'll scare them to have a man always about. But take a chance—take a *chance!* Marry the next guy that asks you, and you'll be so busy keeping his shirts clean and rinsing bottles that you'll forget it."

"Maybe someday I'll try it," Angela said lightly, but trembling, as she filled the salt shaker from the red box.

"No, but what are you afraid of? Don't you want him to kiss you? Don't you want your husband to love you? You're a queer one!"

"I'm happy as I am," Angela said.

"Yes, you are! No girl's happy without a man running her!"

"That's not true."

"You'll never have that nice family of little boys and girls the way you're goin' on," Tom said. "Oh, you make me tired!" he added under his breath as Angela walked into the bedroom without replying. When she came out she had on her small brown hat and the big brown coat with the fur collar. "What is it tonight?" he asked half impatiently.

"Vespers. Advent," his mother, following Angela, answered briefly.

"Oh, for the Lord's sake!"

"Exactly. For nothing else," Torey said neatly. Torey had been getting dressed to go to a movie with Lew McGill. She now telephoned the long-suffering Jerry Whalen that she wouldn't go out with him tonight after all, as she had forgotten a most important engagement that she couldn't possibly get out of.

"How about you and me goin' to the flicks with Lew and Torey?" Tom said unwillingly, and almost ungraciously, to Angela.

"Oh, I'm going to church with Ma, Tom."

"I know you are, I know you are!" he said gruffly. "But I said, how about goin' to the flicks?"

"Instead, you mean?"

"Well, what d'you think? You can't take the flicks to church."

Angela, looking somewhat frightened at his tone, slipped out of the kitchen with no answer. Torey narrowed her mischievous blue eyes at her brother's gloomy and preoccupied face, and laughed.

Two weeks later, when the New Year was proceeding upon its icebound, gray-shadowed way, Mrs Loughborough discussed the matter of Angela with Mrs Whalen over a cup of tea. The day was overcast and bitter cold; occasional flakes of snow fluttered down the gloom of the airshaft outside the bedrooms; through the kitchen windows the backs of tenements could be seen lightly powdered with it. The lights of the theater were lighted early; for eight hours the great signs would fluctuate punctually up and down, up and down, against the dreary shadows of the night.

"I wint to see thim at the Hamilton," Mrs Loughborough confessed suddenly. Mrs Whalen's little monkey face wrinkled into dubiousness.

"About Angela," she stated simply.

"I can't make her out," the other woman said in affirmation. "I thought likely they'd give me a tip."

She filled her guest's cup; her own cup. Their worn hands reached automatically for the cream, the sugar. Mrs Loughborough held the blue bowl comfortably in the palm of her left hand while she spooned forth the white sweetness. Mrs Whalen dipped her teaspoon into the cream and tasted it critically. Cream had a way of souring in these hot kitchens.

All up and down the big tenement, and in the twin house next door, and in all the houses round about for blocks and blocks, kitchens were warm and hospitable in the late afternoon. Even the children, coming in with wet, frozen, red hands and apple-red cheeks, had their heartening mugs of milk and sugar and weak tea. Lights shone out on clotheslines and fire escapes and vegetable boxes powdered with snow; the outer world was at its coldest and most forbidding season. But in the kitchens there was warmth and noise and the odors of tea and bread and butter.

"What 'd they tell ye about her?" Mrs Whalen presently asked.

"Oh, they talked a lot," the other woman said with a sigh.

"They wud."

"They had char'rts an' lists on her in a box."

"They'd not get far wit'out their catalogues, whativer *thim* are," opined Mrs Whalen.

"I tolt thim she'd been here six mont's—but sure they knew that annyways; she'd wrote thim that. An' I tolt thim that she was a fine ger'rl wit' a good hear'rt on her, an' that she was grand wit' the childern. But I ast thim did they know why she'd be so agin the boys that she'd niver look at a good lad like Con O'Shea, that cud dress her in silk the longest day she'd live!"

"The dear'r knows!" Mrs Whalen muttered, shaking her head.

"An' I wanted to know did she know about her own mother," Mrs Loughborough added with a cautious look about the kitchen. The other woman also lowered her tone.

"Kitty," she said simply.

"Kitty. I didn't know did she know about her or didn't she."

"Did they tell ye?"

"They tolt me nothin'. They tolt me no more than that they cudden't tell me annything. 'Tis a rule of the home. They know nothin' of anny of the ger'rls, they've no records; they'll give ye no satisfaction. ' 'Tis a protection for thim,' she told me. 'Does the ger'rl know what her mamma done?' I ast her. 'I cudden't tell ye annythin', I don't know meself,' this Mrs Allenby said. She's a big fleshy woman wit' eyeglasses that hooks up against her on a spring. 'I cudden't tell ye meself,' she says. 'I don't know.' 'Does the ger'rl know?' I ast her again. 'Well, that I cudden't tell ye,' she says. 'But I'll show ye the new liberry wing we've built on,' she says. 'I've come to see no liberries,' I says. Wit' that she tolt me that she thought the ger'rl was conditioned."

Mrs Whalen's eyes came up with a startled look.

"Angela!" she exclaimed. "Ye'd wondher," she added after a moment's stupefaction, and in rising indignation, "that they'd say that sort of thing agin a decent ger'rl that never done a thing wrong, but runs off to church the minute she gets the dishes done!"

"They don't mane that," Mrs Loughborough said, not very sure herself what they did mean.

"What else wud it be?"

"They said it meant that the child had been—well, ye cud call it scared-like, whin she was yoong," Mrs Loughborough explained.

"Ye don't scare thim into that condition," Mrs Whalen objected firmly. "An', if they'd ask me, it's a mane thing to say of anny ger'rl, much less this wan!"

"All they mane is that she don't like men because whin she was a baby someone said somethin' or done somethin' that put her off thim," Mrs Loughborough persisted.

"Is that all it is?" Mrs Whalen's little walnut of a face wrinkled in concentrated thought. "Well, that's nothin'," she said dubiously.

"They tuk it very serious. 'Angela,' she says to me, 'may have her'rd somethin' whin she was on'y a baby. But it's there in her hear'rt, an' it 'll niver come out,' she says."

"Thin you mark my wor'rds, woman dear'r, she knows about Kitty," Mrs Whalen said with a nod of conviction.

Mrs Loughborough's great bosom moved on a deep sigh.

"It's that," she said; "but who'd tell her, Jule?"

"She'd guess it."

"She cudden't guess all Kitty done. There was no one knew it but you an' me an' a few that's dead. Poor Kitty!

"L'avin' Tim for a merrid man, runnin' out in the night, an' after he threw her off goin' into consumption," Mrs Loughborough mused, scarcely above a murmur. "D'ye mind how sad she looked wit' her hair in braids on the piller whin me an' you wint down to see her in Bellevue? There was always good in Kitty; she had a kind little hear'rt on her. Poor ger'rl!"

"It was bad look for her that the divil she run off wit' had money," Mrs Whalen said thoughtfully. "If he'd been a poor man there 'd have been no bank account for the child, an' she'd have gone to the Sisthers, where they wudden't have talked about 'conditions' for a fine clean ger'rl who niver looks twice at anny boy, be he rich or poor!"

"It's that tin thousand in the bank worries her," Mrs Loughborough said. "She don't know where it come from, an' it frets her. An' then there was her father's mother, old Mrs Hogan, that was very cross-grained an' crabbed. Angela don't talk to me or to annyone," she went on. "But this she did say whin we were talkin' the other day. 'Ma,' she says, 'me father's mother cur'rst me mother an' me an' drove us out of the house, an',' she says, 'I'll niver take that cur'rse on to anny child of mine!' "

"The dear'r Lor'rd bliss us!" Mrs Whalen said on a tut-tutting whisper. "An' Tom wants her too. Well, she'd bring ye some more fine grandchildren, Ellen. She's a good ger'rl."

"Tom!" Mrs Loughborough said from the stove in the tone of one awakening. She stood still, feeling the sword in her heart. Tom!

After a while Mrs Whalen bundled herself into an old coat trimmed with mangy bands of black fur, settled her widow's bonnet, pulled on cotton gloves neatly darned at the finger tips, and went her way. She left Mrs Loughborough apparently quite the same as usual, beginning preparations for the children's dinner.

But Mrs Loughborough moved as one in a haze. The solid earth was rocking under her feet. It was all clear to her now. Tom, her magnificent, tumble-headed, steady, wonderful boy was in love with Angela Hogan.

He had liked girls before; he had been dashing and confident and teasing and witty and dominant with girls before. But this time it was all different. Fool, fool that she had been not to see it! Tom. Tom in love, and perhaps going to be married, and give that great heart of his to another woman. It made his mother feel strange and chilled and old; she was trembling a little when Tom came in and touched her warm soft cheek with his hard cold one and went on into the bedroom to wash his hands and comb his hair.

She studied him furtively when he came back. Tom had only been cleaning up in this scrupulous way for a few weeks. He had never done that sort of thing before; that was a sign of course. His hair wet and brushed, his big hands scrubbed; he even went so far as to clean his nails. Very handsome he looked when he came out and sat down with the evening paper to wait for the girls and for his supper. Her heart yearned over him; she wanted him to be small, mischievous Tom in the ragged cords and the red sweater again, begging to go down into the dangerous street for play in the late afternoon.

"Aw, lemme go down, Ma, will you, Ma, will you? Go on, Ma. Lemme go down with Ray and Johnny, will you, Ma?"

"What are you thinkin' about, Ma? You look queer," Tom said. She came back to the kitchen with a start, back to realities. He was a man now; he was twenty-four years old. And he was in love.

Torey came in, jaded and pale; Torey dropped into the nearest chair, piled overshoes, coat, gloves, hat, bag together on the floor under the kitchen table, rested her elbows on the cloth and covered her face with her hands.

"I'm dead!" she said briefly as she did nearly every night.

"Go to bed right after supper," her mother said, also for the thousandth time.

"I've got a date," Torey, completing the usual exchange, answered wearily. She seized a part of the paper; the meal was all ready to be served fifteen minutes later, when Angela came in.

Ellen Loughborough watched Angela, watched Tom. The girl was her usual eager, cheerful little self; mildly amused at the events of the office day, quick to spring to the stove or the sink in service, lovely in her quiet content at being here with these friends she so loved.

But the man was changed. He was clumsy, he was silly in sudden spurts of words, he was almost savage in silences. He annoyed her with contemptuous teasing and was violent with Torey when she joined in on it. Finally, crossly and indifferently, he asked Angela if she would like to go to a movie, and upon her accepting, for there was no church service that evening, he became his sunniest, his dearest self, affectionate and amusing and natural again. In short Tom acted like a man in love, and his mother could only marvel that she had not seen long before this what was the matter with him.

"Tom likes Angela, I wudden't wondther," she observed tentatively to Torey when they were alone.

"You're a born detective, Ma, with a nose for news!" Torey jeered good-naturedly. It was as obvious as all that then.

"I doubt does she like him."

"She's crazy about him," said Torey. "But she'll never marry him. Tom's going away—he can't stand it."

Mrs Loughborough, dazed that matters had progressed thus far under her very nose, stood at the sink regarding her daughter bewilderedly.

"Tom's goin' away?" she breathed.

"Well, can't you see that she's driving him crazy, Ma?"

"Tom," his mother murmured, thinking.

"She's got him jumping sideways," Torey observed simply.

"There's no ger'rl alive 'd say no to Tom."

"Mamma, wake up. It's 1938, darling. She's told him so."

"She hasn't!"

"Don't you fool yourself. Tom's been crazy about her since the moment she set foot in this house. But Angela's afraid," Torey explained.

"Afraid?"

"Yip. She's afraid her mother—marked her," Torey said mysteriously.

"Mar'rked her!"

"Yip."

"What way wud she mar'rk her?"

"Well, some of those girls from the Hamilton Home come from queer families, you know. And then there's that ten grand she has in the bank. She went up to the bank and tried to find out who put it in there for her. Of course they said they didn't know."

"She wint to the bank? Angela did?"

"Indeed she did."

"An' she tolt you all this?"

"No, she never told me a word of it. But she happened to say she'd been up in the neighborhood of the bank, and I guessed the rest. And of course that's why she won't marry Tom."

"She likes him?"

"Oh, Ma, she's crazy about him! Now, not the petting kind of crazy, but just a deep-down kind of—well, *fire,* burning inside her," Torey said. "It's as if she was his mother and his sister and his grandmother and all his aunts rolled into one. Can't you see how uncomfortable she is when he acts like a fool, the way he did at dinner? Can't you see the way she always asks for what *he* wants when you're talking about dinner? It's just that she's afraid to let herself go—she's afraid of married love——"

"We'll go no further than that, if you please, Torey."

"I know. But that's the situation, Ma. Lissen, Ma, did you know her mother? She was all right, wasn't she?"

"Kitty Hogan—she was Kitty McQuaide—merrid Tim Hogan whin she give up her job in the box fact'ry," Mrs Loughborough, busy with the dishpan, answered readily. "Tim was a fine boy; he'd a job up in Erie, an' I niver seen much of thim afther they was merrid. They'd only the one child, an' afther Tim died Kitty come back here an' wor'rked in a candy factory. I'd ought to of looked her up, but me childern was small an' I'd me hands full. The next was that Kitty was dead, an' the child put in this place—God hilp the poor little thing!"

"Then where 'd the money come from, Ma?"

"Well, I don't know why Kitty wouldn't have a friend—some kind old woman who'd pay the thousand to get the child into the home an' give her a nest egg aftherward! There's people doin' that all the time, an' no scandal attached to it. The wor'rld is too aisy to take the bad of it," Mrs Loughborough said.

"It isn't the world now, Ma, it's Angela. If you get talking to her someday you tell her you knew her mother and that she was all right," Torey said. "She and Tom love each other—at least I imagine that Angela calls it love, and Tom's got it all right. But she'll go away and give us all up before she marries anyone, the way she feels now. She thinks that with her blood she might go crazy after she was married."

"With her blood!" Mrs Loughborough echoed scornfully.

"Well, you talk to her, Ma."

"I will," the older woman said decidedly. But she took her time about it, meanwhile watching Tom with a heavy heart. He was so desperately, so pathetically in love. He was so wretched. He was vouchsafed by Angela so few crumbs with which to comfort his misery of hunger.

Angela was his whole world; of the mother who had borne

him, who would have had her hand cut off, and gladly, to give him his heart's desire, he was only vaguely aware.

"Thanks, Ma; gee, you're kind, Ma," he said to her sometimes in a quick, dry voice, like a person talking in a fever. It was a fever, his feeling for this deep-eyed, low-voiced girl. Tom had to be near her, had to hear her voice, had to watch her moving about his mother's kitchen, or hold her cool little unresponsive hand while they sat through hours of movies; but being near her was torture only a trifle less acute than the torture of being away. Angela's mood was his barometer; if she was at all kind to him he went into a sort of drunken ecstasy of happiness; if she were anxious and burdened and cold he snarled and jerked himself about like a wounded animal.

One night his mother heard him crying and came padding out to the kitchen in her bare feet to find him at the table, his head dropped on his outflung arms. She touched his shoulder and he raised his face unashamedly, and she saw the tears wet on his face and on his black eyelashes, and heard the break in his gruff whispered voice.

"I've got to get out, Ma," he said.

She sat down, whispering back:

"Why d'ye say that?"

"Becuz she won't look at me," Tom said briefly. "No, nor at any man," he presently added darkly, as his mother made no answer but stretched out her hard scarred hand and laid it on his. "She, that's dyin' to be in my arms, where she belongs, that's dyin' to have a child of her own, while she's kissin' Ag's children, an' Ellie's children!"

"Why won't she, thin, Tom?"

"Oh, becuz of some nonsense!" he said impatiently. "Becuz her mother was this or that! What do I care what her mother was? It's Angela I'm after, not her mother, nor her grandmother either! I've got so I can't work, Ma," Tom went on, looking down at his big knotted hands, a shadow in his eyes. "She comes between me an' everything I try to do.

I keep seein' her hands, the way she cuts bread for you, and her quick look up when anyone speaks to her."

"Where 'd ye go, Tom?"

"Pittsburgh, maybe. Vic Connors is there. He'd get me in."

"I cudden't have ye l'ave me, Tom."

"I'd come back to you someday, Ma," he muttered, his eyes evasive.

"I cud tell ye the whole story of her mother, Tom. She was a good sweet ger'rl, to begin wit'. But afther Tim Hogan died on her——"

"I don't want to hear it," he interrupted grimly. "It hasn't anything to do with me and Angela. If I could once get her into my arms I'd make her forget that a lot of old biddies gossiped about her mother. Suppose her mother *was* a fool? That used to count in the old days. But now—why, Ma, half the girls——"

"Don't tell me about it, Tom!"

"I know what kind of a girl *she* is," the man went on moodily. "She's the kind that if once she let herself go—my God, Ma, the man she married would be in heaven! Ah, but it's no use," Tom interrupted himself impatiently. "She's afraid. 'I'd be too happy with my man and my children and my little home,' she told me yesterday. She didn't want to go see Gemma Walsh on Sunday. 'No,' she says, 'they're just married, an' she has everything the way I'd like to have it, little dotted curtains in her kitchen, an' a baby comin', an' all!' An' she begun to cry, the poor little thing!"

His tone was one of infinite pity; tears stood in his own eyes.

"Tom . . ." his mother began and fell silent. He looked at her expectantly, tumbling his rich hair with his hands.

"I wondther," she began again, after thought, "I wondther cud I talk to her? I wondther if I tolt her that her mother was fine and good wud it change her?"

"She wouldn't believe you."

"I'd make her believe me. There was nothin' vicious in Kitty," Mrs Loughborough went on musingly, "there was nothin' tough about her. All was, she—but I belave I'll not tell ye annythin', Tom, an' thin ye niver can throw it up at her. Whativer it was, it's long ago, an' all that knows it now is me an' Jule Whalen, an' she's got the charity of God in her, that one. She'd niver bethray ye."

"Ma," he said, hope lighting his honest blue Irish eyes, "could you do that?"

"I cud, an' not lie neither," Mrs Loughborough said thoughtfully.

"Lie if you have to," said Tom.

"I'll not. I'd not do that for annyone. But I'll talk to her." There was determination in Mrs Loughborough's tone. She sent Tom off to bed immediately, new confidence in his heart, and presently went to scramble down in her own untidy lair of blankets and coverlets. But until she heard his strong familiar snore she did not sleep.

Three days later her chance with Angela came. It was evening. Tom was working late at the foundry; Torey had gone out with a beau. Angela, very tired after the dinner dishes were done, was at the kitchen table, undecided as to whether she would go around the corner with Mrs Loughborough to Confession for First Friday the next day or go upstairs to bed.

"I always hate to miss a visit to church," she said, trying to keep her eyes open.

"Ye niver got that off the neighbors," Mrs Loughborough, putting broken bread to soak in milk for hot cakes the next morning, answered casually. "Your dear mother was one you'd always find in chur'rch."

"Mother," Angela said softly, half aloud.

"She was very good, Kitty was," the older woman added. "Whin I go on I hope she'll be the one to meet me in heaven an' get me in."

"I guess you don't have to worry, Ma. I wish," Angela said in a little courageous rush, "you'd tell me about her. If she was good, what did she do that made my grandmother hate her?"

"Yure grandmother Hogan was a reckless one wit' her tongue, Angela. There was manny she hated besides yure poor mother."

Angela was silent a few minutes, looking into space. Presently she said:

"Leave that and I'll wash it."

"It's done. It was just a rinse."

"Did my mother ever do anything wrong, Ma?" The girl's voice was sick with fear and pain, but the words came steady and clear.

"Niver, in the course of her whole life!"

"Ah, but you mightn't have known!"

"I knew that. Her hear'rt," Mrs Loughborough said, "was as pure as that of anny saint you'd be readin' about in a book. I niver knew annything but good of her. There's manny thinks of her and says prayers to her to this day."

Angela's usually pale cheeks blazed scarlet. Her stupefied eyes were upon the older woman's face.

"My mother!" she gasped in a whisper.

"Yure dear mother. Where you iver got the notion that it wasn't that way, Angela, I'll niver know. Good she was, protectin' you . . . guidin' you . . ."

"Oh, I knew she loved me!" Angela said breathlessly. "But I thought . . . I used to worry . . . nobody told me . . .

"And then, being at the Hamilton, where so many of the girls had funny histories," she went on, speaking in an almost apologetic tone now, "and they never told us anything —they always said they didn't know anything of our people——"

She stopped short, spreading her hands in a gesture of appeal.

"They'd do that to protect the poor ger'rls that had nothin' but bad news to lear'rn, Angela."

"Well, they might." The exquisite colors of April were in Angela's face; her eyes were shining through wet lashes. "But you never told me that Mother—that Mother—was so good," she stammered.

"Ye niver ast me, dear'r!"

"Oh, but you knew—you knew how it was worrying me to think that she—that perhaps I might someday go that way—that it was in my blood too!" Angela said confusedly.

"How wud I know that?"

"But my being in the Hamilton—someone paid for that."

"Yure mother had manny friends you niver knew nothin' about, Angela. She's done favors for tins and dozens of thim that I know of. There's manny a kindness she's done me. There niver was a betther human woman that iver lived than she, no, nor more beloved either!"

"But if—if they loved her so, then why wouldn't they come see me in the Hamilton? I grew up feeling shut out—different from girls who had homes and friends, out in the world——" Angela stopped again.

"Well, Angela, it's har'rd to say," Mrs Loughborough said after a moment. "But people's as quick to forget favors as to ask thim, we all know that. Here's me, that owed yure dear mother so much, an' I niver tuk the throuble to look ye up. The wor'rld is like that, dear'r. Look, somewan put all that money into the bank for ye; that looks like ye had a friend."

"You don't know who that was?"

"I'd lost sight of her for years, d'ye see, while ye lived up in Erie. I don't know what friends she had or whativer it all was. But this I know, that it was yure good mother guidin' ye from heaven that brought ye here to me an' found ye friends an' a home—yes, an' a good man to love ye, too, an' you puttin' up yure hands to hide yure red face while I say it! If yure as good as yure mother, ye'll be one of the bist of God's creatures, an' me oath on that."

"You mean it!" Angela whispered, her eyes stars.

"I mane ivery wor'rd of it."

"Oh, but why didn't someone say all this to me before! You mean she was—she was like other women—like Ag and Eileen and Ellie—she was like you——"

"She was betther than I iver was," Mrs Loughborough said humbly. "Whin ye think of her, Angela, think of someone who knew bitther sorrow an' bore it well, an' loved her child, an' tasted the full grief of parting."

Angela had crossed the kitchen now; she had her arms about the older woman; her wet face was against Mrs Loughborough's face.

"Oh, my God, I'm so grateful you told me this!" she said, laughing and crying. "Oh, God forgive me that I ever thought any different of her! It was living in that place where they were all so cold and hard, and thought the worst of everyone—that all girls were naturally crooked, and all women doing wrong! I'll never think of her again except to bless her and ask her to protect me. And there's nothing in my heart to be afraid of except to be good!"

"That's all, Angela. An' what 'll ye do wit' all yure money? Buy yuresilf a little home someday that you'd own?"

"I was never going to touch it! But now," Angela said radiantly, "d'you know what I'm going to do? I'm going to give it to Lizzie and Jerry Moore. He's crippled, you know, and he can only do odd jobs, and they're buying that double house in Long Island City. That 'll mean they have a home, and some rent coming in, and she'll not worry any more! That's what I'll do, and good riddance to it, and all my worries beside! Oh, Ma, I feel so light I could dance—I could go right straight up into the air——"

It was upon this last phrase that Tom came in, tired and grimy. His eyes brightened as he saw Angela's transformed face; his whole aspect brightened when he returned from ablutions in the bedroom to find Angela alone, setting his dinner upon the table in good wifely fashion, brewing him tea, sitting down opposite him to smile at him while he ate.

"Not goin' to church with Ma, hey?" Tom asked.

"Not tonight, no. I thought maybe you and I could go to a flick later, Tom," Angela said simply.

Meanwhile Mrs Loughborough had gone around the corner and up the snowy steps into the great warm edifice that was dimly lighted, that was stirring with well-bundled forms. Children were half walking, half running in the aisles, whispering, genuflecting ostentatiously.

When she got there, there were a good many people in the church. But she stayed on her knees a long time, and the big place was almost deserted when she went up the left-hand aisle to the altar and knelt before the statue of the gracious young woman in the blue robe, with a white veil falling lightly over her braided hair, and her arms outstretched to all the suffering, the sorrowful, the lonely and unfortunate women of all the world.

Before her the tiny lights of a hundred red candles wavered in the soft, incense-scented air. Mrs Loughborough knelt down and looked up at her.

"Mary, help an' save us all," she said in a whisper; "those wasn't lies I tolt her, dear'r. Ain't ye her mother as much as iver poor Kitty was? Haven't ye been guidin' her an' watchin' her for all of her life? That's all I tolt her. I said ye was good an' had done manny an' manny a favor for me an' for others; that's thrue, isn't it? Sure, where wud we all be if ye wasn't Mother to us, lovin' an' helpin' all along the roads we go? D'ye mind that I mixed ye up wit' another mother that's maybe long ago forgiven an' safe wit' ye for all time to come?"

The radiant vision made no audible answer. But in the dim candlelight there might have been upon her face a smile of infinite tenderness and understanding as she looked down on a homely old woman in a shabby winter coat, kneeling below among the troubled shadows of the world.

Grand Central Pickup

After a while the girl said steadily and audibly:

"Is there any chance of your taking me to dinner?"

Her neighbor glanced about him. He and she were alone on the end of the long railway station bench, although hundreds of home-going commuters, coming and going about them, made the spot one of the most populated and least isolated in the entire world. Satisfied, if still surprised, that she was speaking to him, he said simply:

"Why?"

The girl, an eager, handsome creature plainly but not shabbily dressed, edged nearer.

"Not what you think," she said eagerly. "I'm not hungry. I've—look, I've plenty of money; it isn't that. It's just that —I would so horribly like to go to dinner with someone!"

Her big white teeth showed in an appealing smile; her words rushed on.

"I'm working," she said. "I've got a good job! But—but it's spring. I've been sitting here wishing that someone—any one of all these people getting on and off trains—was going to meet me. It's so lovely to meet people, and hold out your hands, and laugh and cry, and perhaps have them kiss you! I think," she went on as the man watched her with a sympathetic smile dawning in his eyes, "I think that when I'm rich I'll hire someone to meet me places and rush at me and say, 'Mary darling!' "

"Is your name Mary?"

The girl's happy color rushed up and her eyes danced at

his tone. He was not going to snub her; he was not going to get up and walk away!

"No, but the girls people meet usually seem to be Marys, don't they?" she asked animatedly. "I've been waiting here almost since you were, I imagine," she went on. "Your friend isn't coming, is he? Was he due at six exactly? That's when you kept looking at your watch and at the clock."

"You're observant," the man said, smiling. "No, I don't imagine he's coming now. He was a small boy, and I was to take him to his grandmother for the Easter vacation. But probably they sent up the car for him and couldn't get hold of me to let me know. Shall we dine?"

He stood up and the girl stood up, and he got a fair look at her and saw that hers was a fine and an intelligent face. Perhaps she saw something in his face at the same time that impressed her, for she said in quick flushed apology: "Is this an awful thing to do?"

"Nothing awful about it. We're civilized people. We both have to eat."

"Was it your own small boy you were meeting?"

"No. I'm not married, Miss—— I don't know your name?"

"I'd so much rather you didn't, if you don't mind. And don't tell me yours. You can call me Miss Anything——"

"Why not Mary?"

"Mary, if you will. And tell me something to call you," the girl said, mounting the rise to the street at his side. "We'll have dinner and then say good night, and that 'll be all. I don't want to know who you are and I'm sure you don't want to know who I am. We'll disappear at about eight o'clock, like drops into the ocean, and never see each other again. But by just doing this," she ended with a momentary return to her eager, almost distressed manner, "you'll do me the greatest favor in the world. Really you will! You don't mind terribly, do you—what 'll I call you?"

"You might call me John. It isn't my name."

"John, then. I love the name of John! Back home I had a

friend—he wasn't a beau, he was in love with my chum, and she died of tuberculosis. His name was John."

"Where are we going? Where are your confederates waiting for me with the gas pipe?" John asked. The girl laughed.

"Not any place too swanky, but with music and lights and freesias and—spring!" she decreed. "Quiet, so we can talk."

"But if we aren't to know each other's names how can we talk? And how can I ever meet you anywhere and say 'Mary darling!' unless I know what you're doing?"

She did not answer. They had entered a big Park Avenue hotel now, and John was guiding her through the empty tables to a quiet corner where they could hear the soft music and watch the show without being seen. The evening was still early: it was not yet seven o'clock; unwonted soft twilight lingered in the streets and at the windows, and the scent not only of freesias, but of roses and stock and all the sweet spring flowers was in the air.

"Oh, this is so lovely!" Mary said at last, when they were seated near an open window and when she had loosened her plain coat to show a smart if well-worn frock with crisp lines of fresh white at wrists and throat. She stopped to sniff the violets on the table, looked about in immense satisfaction at the almost empty room, breathed deep in satisfaction. "This is exactly what I wanted to do!" she said. And then gratefully, with a flash of her wide smile for him, she added: "You're awfully kind to do this!"

"Not at all," the man said. "I had to dine anyway. Why not in the company of an attractive girl?"

"Yes, you had to say that of course," Mary said hastily, almost abstractedly, "but you're very kind just the same! I've been in an office and a boardinghouse and the subway all day—and all yesterday—and for weeks—and months," she said, appealing to him simply, "and I imagine I sort of lost my mind! You think I'm crazy, of course."

"No, I don't. I don't think you're crazy at all." He was a charming man, really, with his pleasant voice and his kind, courteous manner, she thought. "I can imagine how you felt, although I've never been in exactly that position," he said. "I've never lived in a boardinghouse, I mean. I've always had my family around me."

"Your family is probably wondering where you are now, then?" Mary said on a rising tone.

"Oh no, I'm quite alone now. I've an apartment up here on Fifty-fourth. My mother's—— There's nobody here but myself now. No," John said with his nicest smile, "I'm enjoying this adventure, and I wish you would!"

"If you only knew how I *am!*" She had removed her coat and had done something swift and adroit to complexion and lips and the waves of hair that showed under her hat; she was a handsome girl, but it was a fine rather than a pretty face.

"Well, let's talk," said John. "You were tired of the office and the boardinghouse and the subway. So what?"

"So I really didn't want to go home. I call it a boardinghouse, but it isn't, really. I wish it were!" Mary said. "It's just two old Germans, a man and his wife, both over sixty. There are only two boarders, myself and an old Fräulein who has a job as a companion; she only comes home once a week or so. It gets horribly quiet and lonely! The old lady—I call her Tante—is the sort that reads all the papers and does all the puzzles and talks about all the lost-and-found advertisements; she reads them aloud to the doctor. He's got bad eyes. And she cooks him noodles and sausages and things like that —all good, you know, but not exciting. But the house is clean, and the sheets are linen, and I only pay—I'd be ashamed to tell you what—and then they knew my mother, and they love me—they call me Liebchen, and that makes it nice. But it *is* dull!"

"What about the nice young man from the office who asks you to go to pictures with him?" John asked.

"Oh, he?" Her color came up in the pretty swift rush, as it had a fashion of doing. She laughed. "I tell him no. I'm not interested. Seriously," she said, "there isn't any such person."

"Why not?"

"Well . . . I don't know. But if there had been some nice man—I don't mean a sweetheart, but some good friend—waiting to take me to dinner, or a picture, or anywhere tonight," Mary expanded it, "I wouldn't have——

"And I don't know why I did," she interrupted herself to say, studying his face with a puzzled little smile. "Except that you looked—friendly, and not too young——"

"That's the first thing you've said that I don't like!" John protested. "I'm thirty-four. One still has an interest in life at thirty-four."

They laughed together and were friends, and suddenly to both it seemed pleasantly exciting to be dining together in the hotel dining room, with the lights softened and the music playing.

"Here we are," John said. "In a city of seven million, having dinner and talking like old friends, and not knowing each other's names!"

"And we mustn't know each other's names," the girl said with an alarmed look. "We must never see each other again. This is a complete adventure in itself. That's what makes it so romantic! It's an Arabian Night."

"I've been thinking," her companion said, "that names are strange things. If you told me yours it wouldn't mean anything to me, and yet I'd feel I really knew you. Not knowing it, I'm completely at sea. If you said Henrietta Johnson or Marjorie Bates it really wouldn't mean any more than Mary, but I'd feel that it did."

"The only thing that saves me from complete *shame* is that you don't know my name," the girl said seriously. "I think of myself, asking a strange man to take me to dinner, talking to him in a railway station, and all that saves me is to think, 'Ah well, he doesn't know me, and he never will!'"

"I know quite a few things about you," John said. "You're

smart and quick-witted and—and you're a lady, and you have a keen sense of humor. I think that's a good deal to know."

"You're very nice to put the 'lady' in, after my carryings on in the station," Mary said gratefully. "I don't suppose a man has any idea how awful it is to be a decent girl and not to know how to have any fun—to get started having fun. Any girl," she added thoughtfully, "any girl feels that once she got *started* she could keep the ball rolling. But how to get started?"

"I suppose that *is* a problem."

"Problem! And there are just a few years, you know, and they simply *race*. You're nineteen—and then you're twenty-four—and then you're thirty, like lightning!"

"You'd be—what? Twenty—what?"

"I'm pushing twenty-seven, as we say in old Ireland. I wish it was sixteen! But since we're not to see each other again you may as well know the stark, unvarnished truth."

Her eyes were grayish blue; the lashes thick and black. Her mouth was large; her complexion pale and clear except when she flushed; it was delightful to see the color rush up under its transparence. Her hair had a certain warmness in its brown, like cherrywood; she had a fine, thin, long hand, ivory-clean, with blue veins showing at the wrist. Her coat, her hat, her bag, her silk dress were all dark blue; she had pearls in her ears and a small string of creamy pearls about her round creamy throat. On her high cheekbones were a few fine pale freckles; her voice had a husky note in it. Leaning on the table, with the warm lamplight touching the lines of her chin and throwing the shadow of her eyelashes on her cheeks, John found her charming.

He told her his college had been Yale; they talked of books and of shows; at eight o'clock he left her for a few minutes and came back with two slim tickets fanned in his hand.

"We're going to see a play. I don't know anything about it!" he said. He sat down, laughing. "Did you think I was leaving you to pay the check?" he asked.

"I did have an awful moment! But I've money enough," the girl said. She resumed the look of rapture his question had for an instant interrupted. "Oh, not *The Beehive!*" she gasped. "I've not seen it. Oh, but how *wonderful* of you! You didn't have to do that!"

"I know I didn't have to do that. But you said you'd not seen it, and I've not seen it either. It seemed a good chance. What 'll we do if anyone recognizes us and says, 'Hello, Archibald,' or 'Hello, Susanna'?"

"Nobody 'll recognize *me,*" Mary said firmly.

"And I don't think anyone will me. We'll have to risk that, anyway."

"This is so much more than I either bargained for or deserved," Mary murmured as he put her into a taxi, "that I shall presently be advising all girls to pick up all men in all railway stations, and the national morals will go completely to the dogs!"

Much later, when they were walking back toward Fifth Avenue, under bright cold stars, she said in a suddenly serious tone:

"John, I don't know how to thank you for being so nice to me. I was down and out tonight. I have a job, I have enough money, I have a good home . . ."

"With noodles and potato soup and apple-strudel in it," he supplied as she paused.

"With all of those, and more too. But somehow it didn't seem to count tonight—all that I had. I wanted to feel young and popular and have an adventure! I went—I've often gone to the big station because everyone who comes and goes there is so thrilled, so busy. Meeting people, saying good-by; it's all so alive. I wanted to be alive too. And you've helped me, more than you'll ever know. I don't know who you are, but I know you were sorry for me and that you're kind—kind all through, and I—I do thank you!" Mary said, becoming a little confused and incoherent at the finish. "Now I'm going to take a taxi," she ended. "So it's good night and good-by. Only—just one more thing.

"You'll think this all over," she said, "as I will. Men talking to unknown girls, girls talking to unknown men—that's adventure, isn't it? That's adventure since things are the way they are between men and women, and since we all think of these things as we do. If we—if you, I mean, because I think I know what I'll do—if you really should want to see me again, come to that same bench in the station at that same time any—what's today?—any Tuesday. Perhaps I won't be there, but I think I will. Perhaps you'll come, but somehow I'm afraid you won't. But if you do, let's keep up the incognito. I don't want you ever to know that I'm the sort of girl who picks up men——"

He had been standing facing her, looking down, for she was not very tall, and holding her small hand in his big gloved one. Now he said:

"Ah, forget that silliness! What does that matter? I may not be able to keep our appointment," he went on slowly, and again he saw, in the light of the street lamp, the quick color rise under her clear skin.

"It isn't an appointment!" she said quickly, proudly.

"Well, whatever it is, I may not be able to keep it," John recommenced painstakingly, "because I may have to leave town."

"I *quite* understand." He might better have slapped her, and he knew it.

"On the other hand," he said, trying to lessen the hurt, "I may be sitting there patiently in the Grand Central for the next fifty-two Tuesdays, watching the clock, and no Mary!"

"But anyway, a million thanks!" Her tone was cold: she was crushed. She pressed his hand, stepped into the theater current of Sixth Avenue, crossed under the roaring elevated train. He saw her signal a taxi, jump into it. She was gone.

"A man talking to an unknown girl—that's an adventure, all right," John said half aloud. " 'Since things are as they are between men and women, and since we all think of these things as we do,' " he quoted her vibrant, eager voice. " 'Mary,' eh? Well, perhaps I'd better keep away from the Grand Central for a while on Tuesday afternoons."

For the next Tuesday afternoon he deliberately made a business engagement in Hartford. He got back to town at eight o'clock and walked into the station waiting room. A girl in a blue dress was waiting on the bench he already described in his thoughts as "our bench," but she was not Mary—not in the least like Mary. John's heart, which had given an odd plunge of dismay, delight and excitement, settled again. He thought about Mary every day, and several times a day; there was a peculiar thrill and heartbeat to the thought of her, but on the second Tuesday John was in bed with a heavy cold, and as six o'clock came about he merely looked at the clock, wondered if she were there waiting for him in the station, tried to read, tried to work out a puzzle, flung his magazine away, looked at the clock again and picked up his book.

On the third Tuesday he was there before she was; walking up and down outside the row of the benches, an unwonted agitation in his heart; expectation, fear, reluctance and hope all having their way with him. She would not come, of course; no girl in her senses, no girl with any pride—and Mary had lots of pride—would accept an affront such as he had given her, and forgive it.

But possibly, he thought suddenly, with an enormous sense of relief, possibly she had not been there for the two preceding Tuesdays, either. Perhaps she had been evading him as he had her. Mary. Mary. He said her name to himself and invested her with all the glory of the woman desired and lost.

In the end it was all very commonplace. She came in quickly and looked at the end of the long bench and, not seeing him, looked about, found him and came over to him with an outstretched hand and a smile. Just a nice girl, a working girl, in rather shabby but smart clothes; romance went out of the world for John, and everything was quite commonplace for a few minutes. But somehow, as they started off into Forty-second Street's traffic and crowds, his hand companionably steadying her arm, his voice at her ear where the hair curved under the blue hat, life came right again. Not sensationally, romantically, breath-takingly right; nothing like that. But it seemed good to have this girl Mary, and to be John, and to be together again. He had thought, in these three weeks, of many things he would like to say to her, and he had phrased them rather neatly to himself as he went through his quiet, rather solitary days, but the presence of the living girl was so vital, her answers, her reception of what he said so unexpected and so stimulating that John found himself being far more brilliant than his dream had been. He had to keep his eyes open to keep up with Mary!

They lingered over their dinner tonight until almost nine. Then Mary said that she was tired and didn't care for a movie. Could they talk a few minutes more and then separate? So they talked on for many more than a few minutes. Their oddly limited knowledge of each other only made the beginning of friendship the more absorbing; Mary could talk freely of her childhood in Glendale, in California; her father and brother still lived there, but her father had married again, and, while Mary liked her young stepmother, she had felt that she must break away and make her own life.

John told her in return of his little-boy days. He saw her smiling eyes film sympathetically when he spoke of the death of his mother, and had a moment of wondering exactly where all this was taking them, taking her and taking him. But Mary was a flashing conversationalist and she never let him stay on any one subject very long.

Always, under their talk, ran the thread of caution. Mary never betrayed herself. If John strayed close to revelations she would warn him lightly and quickly: "Look out—look out—don't tell me who your friends are at Oyster Bay!" It was at their fourth or fifth meeting that he told her that he was getting darned tired of it. Mary only laughed, unimpressed; she made no disclosures.

Then came the event that seemed like a miracle to them both. It was such a trifling thing; it was nothing at all really. Yet it filled them both with a happiness that was almost like awe.

It happened on a Saturday. Mary walked out of her way from the office to go through the station waiting room, and on the familiar bench sat John. That was all; yet that was breath-taking. It was one o'clock in the afternoon; they had had no appointment; they moved toward each other completely unaware that there was anyone else in the world; they linked hands; they smiled as if they never could stop smiling.

"How'd you know?" they asked each other. And on that day there was no question of what they wanted to do. They lunched at once, then they rode on a bus top out into the greenness of the spring, along the blue riverbank, and far down again through the arch into the park. And through the enchanted hours ran the additional enchantment, the knowledge that they had wanted each other at the same moment and had gone straight to the meeting place!

"I'd like to give you something in silver and enamel for your cigarettes, Mary," John said that day. "But I don't know what initials to put on it."

"Put 'Mary,' " she answered steadily; "then it 'll mean twice as much as any other name."

"If I thought you'd surely give me another chance to see you, surely, surely, surely—cross your heart and hope to die—I'd tell you something. Cross your heart and hope to die if you don't meet me next Tuesday and I'll give you a hint."

"Cross my heart and hope to die," the girl agreed cheerfully. But she had turned a little pale. "Tell me now."

"Well—no, I'll not tell you now," John said with a sudden change of manner. "I'll tell you Tuesday night. That's—this is Saturday—that's only two nights, isn't it? What are we doing now? It's nearly five. What about dinner tonight?"

"I have to work tonight. Truly I do." Her fingers pressed his. She turned away, was instantly lost in the river of men and women that was pouring homeward at the close of the warm, languid day. John looked for a moment for the well-known hat; it was no use. If he ever lost her this way in the big city he never could find her again! Too many girls, too many blue hats, too many street turnings . . .

On the following Tuesday, when they met, an untimely dusk had shut down over the spring city; the sky was close and leaden, a sulphurous warm rain was falling in thick sheets. Mary's raincoat enclosed her in blue glass; her hair was curled up by the rain, her cheeks rosy and fresh, and she was breathless.

"I've been running through it!" she exclaimed, grasping his hands. "It's simply fearful! You'll have to come home with me and eat noodles and sausages; we can't go anywhere tonight!"

"You wouldn't take me home with you?" John asked.

"No, I couldn't," the girl said, her manner changing, her smile fading. "I forgot."

"Sometime you'll forget and then I'll really know you, Mary."

"But that wasn't the agreement!" she reminded him jealously.

"I know it wasn't. I'll play fair. I've a plan for tonight too. I've ordered dinner already, and after dinner we'll listen to the fight—don't forget we've got fifty cents on the fight—and at ten o'clock I'll turn you loose in the great city. Come along!"

In the taxi, for the few blocks drive, Mary was very gay; she seemed actually to enjoy the dark night and the roar and splash of the storm. But at the door of the apartment house she paused.

"Oh, now listen," she protested, a wet shabby glove touching his coat sleeve.

"Now listen, what?"

"I think we go no further, my lad!"

"Listen yourself, Mary. It's a horrible night to go anywhere, and my place is snug and comfortable, and there's a fire. Mrs O'Brien, who comes in twice a week to clean, is engaged to stay and sit sewing in the bedroom until you go home."

"Mrs O'Brien?" There was infinite reassurance in the mere name.

"Come up and see for yourself. She's a fine woman too; she's the one to speak her mind if anything didn't suit her."

"You mean you actually asked her to stay?"

"I mean that when I saw what pitchforks it was raining, at about four, I went out to the kitchen and asked her if she could come back. She said she'd get herself a cup of tea and stay right on; she wasn't anxious to get out into it. So then I asked Himashira to get us some dinner."

"I'll find out your name, John," Mary said, still hesitant, but getting into the elevator with him nonetheless.

"No, you won't, unless you want to. I explained to Mrs O'Brien that you didn't know it and were very specially anxious not to know it. I told her that if you asked her she was, of course, to tell you anything you wanted to know, but that otherwise she would please keep—in a word, keep her trap shut!"

He was so pleasantly, so easily sure of himself! Mary said in her heart that she had never known anyone like John—handsome, groomed, lean, brown, masterful. There was a little twitch to his fine firm mouth when he was what she called "running her," a something masterful and affectionate and amused at her feminine struggles to escape, that stirred the deeps of her being and made every fiber of her thrill. He was wearing this expression now. "Don't be afraid, Mary," he said. "I won't eat you!"

"You have no business doing this, you idiot," Mary said in her heart. But it was heavenly, too, on this furious wet night, to follow him into the big luxurious rooms and see the promised fire blazing, to meet the imposing, black-clad Mrs O'Brien, respectable enough to chaperon a dozen Marys, and to sit watching Himashira as he dexterously laid a little table for two beside the fire. "Of all situations in the entire world," she said aloud, " this is the one a girl finds the most—superlatively—satisfying!"

"Well, it seemed to me the obvious and sensible thing!" John was as pleased as she. By the time the cups of soup came on, and the brown birds and the green salad, they were talking together easily, unself-consciously, and yet with a definite sense, too, that their friendship had taken a decided stride forward tonight.

"Alas," said Mary when the clock struck half-past eight and John was turning the dials to get the Philadelphia arena, "I can come to this doorway any time, now, and read your name."

"As a matter of fact you couldn't, for I have this apartment with a friend, and his name is the one downstairs. But you can have my name any time you want it, Mary."

"I don't want it, *please,*" she said hurriedly.

"You shan't know it then." They settled down into silence, listening to the fight. There was an interval of absorbed attention, and Mary said:

"It's a swell fight. I thought it might be a frame-up!"

"You're quite a fan, aren't you?"

"I like fights."

"You like everything I like, somehow."

" 'Then you must like yourself,' said the girl with a dimpled, provocative smile," Mary said smoothly.

"Delete that sort of thing," John answered in a lowered tone, not moving his eyes from the fire. "Somehow," he went on, "I think your name is Susan. It isn't, of course. It's probably a name I hate, like Marian. I somehow don't like Marian. It always sounds to me like a name the family picked because they didn't like real names like Margaret and Alice."

"Isn't it marvelous to be dining here in your enchanting apartment, and not to have the slightest idea who we are?" Mary asked. "We're reaching the end of the road, though," she added after a pause in which he merely glanced up at her, glanced away again and did not speak. "We can't keep this up. Let's—— I'll tell you what. Let's part tonight, and think this all over, and decide. And if we meet next Tuesday let's tell!"

"Next Tuesday is way off in the year 1984," John observed mildly. Mary laughed. "Suppose I were to ask you to marry me?" he added, almost as if involuntarily.

Things then began to go in a manner that Mary had not foreseen. She knew he had spoken almost against his will; she herself was suddenly quite at sea. She said unsteadily:

"I wouldn't advise that."

"Why not?"

"Because," Mary said, losing all bearings and entirely unable to think, "I rather think you're married already, aren't you?"

A silence, during which John, looking down at the fire, did not move. Presently he said quietly:

"What makes you think that?"

"You've—it seems to me you've indicated it in a thousand ways," Mary said stanchly.

"Suppose I told you that I was Richard Wilmartin," John suddenly began. In the silence they looked at each other.

"Richard—not *Dick* Wilmartin?"

"Richard Slocomb Wilmartin."

"Oh, you're not!" She was staring at him blankly. "Then you *are* married?" Mary said.

"Rather."

"But—but he has a mustache!"

"Had. You can shave off a mustache. I'm glad you know," the man said. "I haven't talked to anyone. I can talk to you. It's all an awful mix-up, or at least it seems like one. But it's simple enough when you understand."

"Your wife, then—I mean," Mary said, flushed and embarrassed, "Belle Pemberton. Weren't you and she supposed to be abroad?"

"I got back the day I met you. She's in France, with a dressmaker named Leon Le Gros."

"Oh no! Not after all—not after you'd——"

"You said that next Tuesday would have to end our affair or begin it all over again," he said after a pause. "Perhaps you're right. Perhaps we never should have begun it. You're the one that 'll have to decide whether we go on or not. I can't. I began all this as a joke; it's no joke now. I was married to Cassy Hawes, certainly, and then I was married to Harriet Archibald, and then I met Belle Pemberton. Everyone knows what happened—Pemberton was treating her like a dirty dog. She used to go on in *Tears, Idle Tears* with a black eye powdered up, and tears on her face, night after night! Everyone knows I sent her a blanket of gardenias for every performance and every matinee to pull up over herself in that last act, and everyone knows that I was a complete fool about her. She's one eighth colored; I knew it—it didn't matter. She's that kind of a woman!

"Well, my wife was found murdered in her bed a year ago. She'd left me, but I had a key to the apartment; they found it on my key ring. You know—everyone knows—what went on. They tried to frame me; they couldn't. I hadn't a particularly sound alibi, but the district attorney hadn't anything to go on. It didn't worry me. I knew I hadn't done it, and I knew who had. The fools had the whole thing in their hands time and time again and they let it slip. She was in court some days—the papers thought it was because she wanted the publicity. Publicity nothing; anyone looking at her could have told right then and there who was guilty!"

"She?"

"Pemberton. Belle Pemberton! Everyone still thinks I killed Harriet. Harriet was the sort of woman someone ought to kill. Rich—the steel people, you know—fat and soft and spoiled and flattered; no one ever got anywhere with Harriet except with flattery. She didn't know about anything else. She had one topic—herself. I divorced Cassy and married Harriet because she owned the handsomest yacht afloat. I'm boat crazy, and one day on Harriet's yacht fixed me. We were all at Biarritz—anyone who reads the papers knows that too. Harriet was seventeen and her income was two million a year. I hadn't a red. Well, I'm not so proud of that. But I didn't kill her. I walked out of that court as free as you are. But of course it was all ended. My life, I mean. I'm not the sort that goes in for uplifts and charities, profits by my misfortunes! I was having a swell time; I'll never have it again. I'm done. But it was Belle who did the shooting—why, she used that very pistol with the silencer from *Tears, Idle Tears,* and took it back to the theater the next night!"

"Oh no!" Mary breathed, her eyes wide in a pale face. "How'd she get in? I don't remember it all very well, but wasn't a maid asleep in the dressing room, wasn't there a man on the hall downstairs, and an elevator boy? Wasn't it up somewhere on the nineteenth or twentieth floor; could anyone have walked in without being seen?"

"Harriet was murdered on Sunday—the day there's no show; remember that? That afternoon Belle Pemberton, with a black wig on—she's tawny blond, you know—went to the Park Avenue Ducal Arms where Harriet lived, and asked to look at the furnished apartment just above Harriet's. Oh, I know what I'm talking about!" John interrupted himself to say impatiently, as Mary made a little incredulous sound. "She told me this herself! While they were going through it she slipped the lock in the back door. She only stayed a few minutes, said it was too expensive for her, went down in the elevator, tipped the boy and walked quietly out into the street and in at the side entrance of the place. She climbed the stairs comfortably—all the servants were out on Sunday afternoon; no one to bother her. She went in the back door and locked it. Then she waited until evening, went down the fire escape, watched her time, shot poor Harriet and went upstairs again. After a while she went down the back stairs and out into the night and home. No one ever suspected anything! They had that elevator boy on the stand for five minutes; he didn't count! Agent, hallboy, starter, elevator boys—they got through with them in fifteen minutes for the lot. They were after *me!* Where had *I* been? Well, I'd lunched with Miss Pemberton, and then we'd walked in the park, and then I'd left her at her door and wandered about, dined alone—no witnesses. Every newspaper in the city by Monday night had me in the electric chair. Meanwhile Belle was playing *Tears, Idle Tears,* and everyone in the house was whispering that I'd killed my rich dull wife for an octoroon!"

Mary's face was very white.

"I'm sorry," she said simply. And then: "Would you have gone to the chair?"

"No, they had nothing on me. I wasn't afraid. But she was. She was scared to death. *Tears* got started on a fresh run, but she had a nervous breakdown and after the trial we went abroad and were married. Then I found she'd been in love with Le Gros for months. I left them there."

"But oughtn't you—after all, you've a boy of eleven or so—oughtn't you clear it up for his sake?"

"He's with Cassy; she's a fine person. She'll take care of him and not let him take it too hard."

"What a story!" Mary said in a whisper.

"You're the first to hear it, the only one to know it. I never even told Yeats, my attorney. He said from the beginning that they couldn't get anywhere unless they could prove my having been there sometime that day, and all the men around the place knew me; they hadn't seen me for weeks."

"Just the same, you ought to be vindicated," Mary said warmly. "In the interests of justice . . . for the sake of the name of Wilmartin . . ."

"Oh, Lord, nothing 'll ever save the name of Wilmartin now!"

"But how did you get out of the country?"

"Simple. I've a Canadian cousin who looks exactly like me. I sent for Roger and he came down. He grew a mustache; I cut mine off. When we got ready to spring it Roger announced that he was going to Palm Beach—that I was, rather! The photographers flocked down to the Penn Station, and meanwhile I went on board the Europa, second cabin, and got away."

"What a *story!*" the girl said again.

"Mr Wilmartin—on the phone, please," Mrs O'Brien said at this point from the doorway. "In the library, sir. . . . Oh, my goodness, I've given away your name!" she added in consternation.

"Never mind, Mrs O'Brien, it's all right now."

"And it's eleven o'clock now," Mary said, "and I've got to go."

"Wait until I come back," John said. Suddenly he looked very tired. "I'll see you to a taxi," he said.

But when he came back she was gone. Mrs O'Brien could only report that the young lady had not said a word but that she had "sort of snatched-like" at her hat and coat, and disappeared. John snatched a hat and coat, too, and also without a word went after her.

The rain had stopped. Moonlight shone in the wet street. He was in time to see her getting into a taxi at the corner.

Mary's taxi turned downtown; she got out of it before a big building in which several floors were blazing with lights in the night. She went up into a hot big room filled with desks and dangling green lamp shades and typewriters and smoke and shirt-sleeved men, and through it, and into a glass-doored corner office marked "City Editor."

"I got my story, Walt," Mary said to a man at the desk. His feet came down from the typewriter level, his cigar came down from his mouth. His grimy face paled.

"Says you," he said in an awed voice.

"Says me," said Mary.

Three days later John had a letter from her. It was an incoherent letter, and stained with tears.

"John darling, darling, darling," wrote Mary. "You know now what it was all about—that I tracked you, and trapped you, and was lying all the time! John dear, I'm in despair—I don't want to live. You'd forgive me if you knew that my heart is broken, that everything I've ever tried to build up in myself is ruined, destroyed by me—myself. That I can never think of myself as a woman of honor again! My darling, I wrote their damnable story, and I wrote my resignation, too, and I took my check and tore it up before their eyes. Believe me, I begged them, begged them with tears not to print it; almost before I'd told Walter Nichols—on the city desk—what a scoop I'd bagged in the Wilmartin case, I was back there, begging him and Klein and Oliver for God's sake not to print it! Of course it was too late. They had the names, they had the facts, they were getting lawyers and the district attorney on the job then! And then, sitting at my desk—that same Tuesday night—I knew what I'd done! I knew that I loved you as no woman has ever loved a man before, that Cassy and Harriet and Belle didn't matter—that you were the breath of my life, were everything in the world to me! And I think that's why I did it, John. I think that under the excitement and pride of having landed the story was the feeling that I *could* do that for you—reinstate you with your friends, give you back something out of all the mess! But I'm not pleading for myself, except that somehow, somewhere, I must know that you've forgiven me. I don't mean that you could ever trust me again. We'll never see each other again. But someday I'll send you an address, and if you'll just wire 'It's all right, Mary,' I'll bless you to the longest day that I live! It isn't only losing you, my dearest, losing the right to comfort you for all the horror and the pain, but I've lost myself—the woman I respected and hoped such great things for!

"You see, I recognized you, John, that day in the station, and I'd been doing odd little columns for the *Gazette,* and they'd told me how badly they wanted the true Wilmartin story. It all came over me in a flash. 'If I can once meet him I'll get it!' I went back and told Walter Nichols that I had met you; he took me into Klein's office, and I had my little hour of being important! Last night—my God, was it only last night? I've not slept or eaten since—last night when you began to tell me, everything went out of my mind except my story. Newspaper people are like that. I said to myself it wasn't going to hurt you, and I'd gotten my story! I'd forgotten her and that you loved her—Belle, I mean.

"Darling, if I've ruined what was left of your privacy, I've ruined my own life too. I'm out of a job; you'll never find me. They haven't my address on the *Gazette;* we had to move a month ago because the old brown house was torn down; nobody knows where I am. You'll never know my name. I'm leaving town. Don't try to find me. I'm buried—I'm not going to see a newspaper or ever write a line for one again. But someday—for the sake of those Tuesdays that were happy days for you, too, and for the marvelous Saturday—forgive me."

"You write a swell letter, Mary," he said to her exactly eighty-one hours later. The girl in the library sprang up, facing him, her eyes wide. Her hand went to her heart, and the book she had been reading slid to the floor.

"Oh, John," she whispered. "Oh no—no!"

He had his arms about her. He was kissing her, and tumbling her hair, and holding her off, and kissing her again.

"Oh, John, how can you speak to me?"

"One swell letter," he said.

"You found me!" breathed Mary.

"Easily. Kiss me."

"John, but how!"

"You want that first? Well, you see, I'm a lonely sort of fellow, Mary, and everything you've ever said to me has made a mark. So when you gave me the slip—like a cheap French maid, by the way!—I realized that I had to find you or cut my throat, so I advertised in all the evening papers."

"But I haven't seen a paper! I came to my aunt here in the country—I've been gardening, and crying, and taking walks, I've been almost mad. I never saw any advertisement!"

"I didn't think you would. At least I took a chance you wouldn't. But you'd told me of your Germans in the boardinghouse; Tante and the doctor and the dog, Snyder. My personal said 'Tante, send me five dollars to Box Such-and-such, emergency, love to you, Doctor and Snyder." And I signed it 'Liebchen.' Remember that you told me they called you that, and that they read every line of the evening papers?"

"Yes, but they knew I'd come to my aunt in Bound Brook!"

"I chanced it they'd think you wanted the money and were up to something contraband, and—God bless their German hearts!—the next day there it was, registered and with a return address of course. I went straight up to Eightieth Street, and that was just two hours ago!"

Mary's head was on his shoulder; her arm was about him, and his arms both about her.

"Oh, this is heaven! You've forgiven me!" she breathed. "John, will they try her? Poor thing, I've let her in for it."

"Belle, you mean? No, they'll not bother her."

"Oh, say it, John, whether you believe it or not! If you knew what I've been going through! *Say* it."

"It's true. You see, I followed you down to the *Gazette* that night, Mary, because I knew—all along."

The scarlet color blazed in her face; there was never anything as lovely as Mary's color, coming up under the creamy skin.

"No, not all along," he corrected it. "It was really only toward the end that something—something sophisticated and smart about you made me wonder. Dick's had an awful lot of publicity, you know, and I've caught the overflow. We——"

"But *you're* Dick Wilmartin!"

"I'm not. I'm his country cousin, from Ottawa. Make a note of Ottawa, because we're going there twice a year. The minute I thought you were spoofing me, Mary, I thought of spoofing *you*. It made me a little sick to think you'd do it, and yet I couldn't blame any girl who had a chance to get a good story out of Dick. After all, he's had his fun with the ladies too! So I laid a trap, and I told Mrs O'Brien to come and call me at about eleven, and if you hadn't given me the slip I'd have told you right then. I was going to say, 'Don't hurry back to the newspaper, Mary. This is all fiction! For all I know, Dick *did* shoot his wife, perhaps with Belle's pistol. Or perhaps he got someone else to do it. Anyway, he's been acquitted, and she's tied up with her new man, and he's at large somewhere in France and probably getting married and divorced daily.'

"I was going to say all that, but you'd gone, and then I knew the fat *was* in the fire! I tore down to the street and luckily saw you. Remember it had been raining, and there weren't so many cabs about. But I got one and followed you, and I went in and had a talk with Nichols and what's-his-name, the city editor. I knew they couldn't rush the story—there are too many details to check—so I waited until you came downstairs, with your face red, crying, and then I went up. I squashed the whole thing. For all I know, there wasn't any empty apartment in that building. It was all fiction, I tell you! All made up!"

"Why, John, you *liar!*" Mary said simply, drawing his arm tighter about her.

"You should call me that! You, a spy, a deceiver, a girl who sold love for pelf!"

"We never can marry now. Think what we could call each other when we fight!"

"On the other hand, no one else can marry us, Mary. We can't let some fine man, some good woman, in on our secret."

Mary's eyes came up in sudden alarm.

"You're not married?" she asked.

"To the present, the past definite, the pluperfect, no," said John. "To the future, the subjunctive, yes."

"Let's—here, this is my uncle's chair, it's a marvelous chair, sit down, John," said Mary. "Let's get on to some other verb!"

Sinners

"WE HAVE TO KEEP IT kind of warm in here because of their not getting any exercise—they get chilly," the matron explained.

"Don't they get out?"

"Not this weather. And they sort of lose interest. . . ."

The matron glanced at the visitor, and the latter, a big, quiet-eyed woman in a once handsome, dowdy coat, looked back at her dubiously.

"They haven't got much ambition left when they get *here!*" the matron said with a laugh.

The other frowned faintly, as if in vague pain. She followed in silence through the big clean impersonal halls that smelled of coffee, disinfectants, air heaters and herded, overclothed humanity.

"I didn't get your name?"

"Huggett. Mrs Joe Huggett."

"And you're some kin to Lucas Rippey?"

"Some . . . ? Oh no. Just a friend." Mrs Huggett cleared her throat; her large, full, serious face had turned a little pale.

Some of the poor forlorn old men were reading shabby magazines in the winter heat of the assembly room; a radio was playing. Many of the occupants of the big apartment were merely staring idly into space—broken in mind, the visitor saw, as well as body. The warm air was thicker here, with the smell of clothing and bodies and food.

Lucas Rippey was a thin, blue-eyed old man, with white,

thin hair. He rose alertly, looked surprisedly at his visitor. When the matron had led them to a little side parlor and left them alone, he told Mrs Huggett smilingly that he could not remember the time he had had a caller before. His bright blue eyes twinkled at her delightedly.

"But I've only be'n here two years, and ain't settled down yet!" he confessed. "I worked, up to then. I got flu in the year 'twas so prevalent; the' warned me pneumonia 'd foller. And sure 'nough, it did!"

"Take a good look at me, Lucas," Mrs Huggett said heavily. She had seated herself, thrown back her widow's veil. "Don't you remember me?"

He looked at her keenly, still smiling.

"No'm. I'm sorry. But your face don't say nothing to me."

"I was Emma Kent," she said slowly.

The old man sat down himself now, suddenly, with an air of shock, and returned her steady, unsmiling stare. The light had died out of his eyes.

"Is *that* who ye are . . ." he said in a whisper.

There was a pause. Then the woman began:

"I've been hunting you for years."

"That so?" he asked, still in a dulled voice.

"Ever since I was thirteen years old," she resumed after another empty pause, "ever since I was thirteen years old—and that's all of forty years ago—I've been sorry."

A softer look came into the wintry, bright old blue eyes opposite her. Lucas Rippey began to shake his head regretfully, deprecatingly.

"I lied about you," the woman said flatly.

He cleared his throat and spoke without resentment.

"I've often wondered why ye did that," he admitted mildly.

"I don't know what got into me," the visitor said in a stony, quiet voice. "I don't know what does get into a girl, sometimes."

She paused, and he looked at her with respectful sympathy.

"I was running with Sue Clute . . ." she began again.

"Well, there!" he said, his face suddenly brightening as he seized upon the diversion. "I hadn't thought of them Clutes for forty years!"

"Sue had her picture in the paper, an' that was gall and wormwood to me," Emma Huggett pursued, resolutely, unhappily. "She was terrible pretty. I was just et up with jealousy, I guess."

He was considering it, his old head on one side, lips pursed and eyes narrowed.

"I never thought of that. I used to think you dremp' all you said," he murmured thoughtfully.

"No, I didn't dream it," the woman answered promptly. "I made it all up. I was dyin' to be important, to get noticed by somebody, like Sue had. The night Kane Madison was murdered I begun romancin' to my mother and gran'mother, an' the more they made of it, the smarter I thought I was. I don't know what in creation started me. But once I'd started, seems I couldn't stop."

"It's hard for us to explain our own acks, sometimes," Lucas said politely, in a pause.

"Hard?" she echoed in a tone that was itself hard. "Well, I've been tryin' to explain mine for forty years!" A shadow fell upon her plain good face. "You were in prison?" she asked reluctantly.

"Sixteen years."

"Oh, my God," Emma said in a lifeless whisper. "State's prison?" she added.

"State's prison."

"Was it awful, Lucas?"

"Yes, at first it was," he admitted, his eyes fixed on space as he remembered. "I wa'n't much more than a kid, and some of them men wasn't fit companions for man or beast. I was sickly too: I'd be'n raised in the Bayliss County Orphans' Home, you know."

"I didn't know that!" she said, stricken. After a moment

she added, "One minute, the last thing I was thinkin' of was you. The next, I was tellin' Ma and Gran'ma this long rigamarole about how I seen you up by the Madison place, runnin', and how you was buryin' something up near the birch grove in Holley's Woods. . . ."

"I never was anywheres near the Madison house that day," the old man offered as she paused. His blue eyes were fixed upon her with a sort of innocent, dispassionate expectancy. It was almost as if she were entertaining him with a story.

"You told 'em that in court," she nodded. For the first time anguish came into her voice. "Oh, why, why, why," she began, knotting her big, capable, work-worn hands together, "why didn't they believe you, instead of takin' the word of a crazy girl of thirteen! Mind you," she went on suddenly, "after that first crazy Easter afternoon, when I'd told my mother this yarn, I lay awake all night, and I made up my mind that I'd come out with the truth the next day, and tell them I'd been lying.

"But I couldn't get my courage up for it at breakfast, and at school, in recess, I kinder began to let it out to the other girls that I knew something about Kane Madison's murder. It was just too easy.

"Walkin' home from school, I remember, the wickedness of what I was doin' suddenly come over me, and I spoke right out loud, while I was goin' by Bassetts Pond. 'This has got to stop!' I says, as loud as that.

"But then when I got home Judge Robbins was there—the old judge himself, that us kids were all so scared of. And he held out his hand to me, gentle and friendly, and he says, 'Come here, Emma. You're only a little girl,' he says, 'and you don't understand the sinfulness of the world. Now,' he says, 'I want you should promise me that you'll not say any more about poor Kane Madison and the Rippey boy. Will you do that?' he says.

"Well, a great relief come over me, and I felt like I was saved. It never occurred to me that he was holdin' me as an important witness. I thought my share of the whole thing was over, and when the *Telegram* sent a feller out to get my picture the next day I was just as happy as I thought I'd be, gettin' my name into the paper. Judge Robbins had told me not to say nothin' more about anything, and yet I was gettin' all the excitement of bein' pointed out and talked about."

"You never seen me near the Madison house the day Kane was killed," old Rippey said definitely, after a pause, "becuz I wa'n't there."

"No, I never saw you at all that day," she agreed dully, the hard, shamed color in her face. "As a matter of fact I was up in our attic all afternoon, dressin' up and playin' lady."

"Huh!" he commented, thinking. The woman looked at him appealingly.

"I used to pray," she began suddenly. "I used to go down on my knees and pray that somebody would come out and prove that I was lyin'. But I couldn't do it myself!"

"I guess they'd have convicted me anyway," he suggested briefly.

"I don't know how they could."

"I was kind of a loafer," he remembered. "I was the kind of feller hard-workin' men like to git into jail."

Mrs Huggett sat looking at him heavily, dumbly. She sighed.

"I started life a charge on the state," the man said. "I didn't git out of the orphanage until I was fourteen. At twenty-two I was back on the state again for sixteen years. When I come out I was quite delicate, and the' sent me to Colorado. . . . Well, I worked some, there. But the state was payin' my rent, just the same. And now—here I am, back on 'em for life this time, unless all signs fail!"

Her alert eyes had brightened with sudden resolute interest.

"This time," she said, "I can get you out if you want to get out."

"How do you mean?" he asked, puzzled.

"Well . . ." She looked about the clean, ugly, disinfectant-scented room, her shrug indicated the clean, ugly, disinfectant-scented institution behind it. "Do you *like* it here?" she asked simply, in surprise.

His old face flushed painfully.

"No ma'am. Nobody could like it here," he answered firmly. "My pride—you may smile to hear me talk of pride——"

"I wasn't smilin'," Emma said, blinking and swallowing.

"The state's generosity I deeply appreciate," old Lucas Rippey said with his favorite forlorn attempt at literary flourish. "But I've by no means made up my mind to remain. I ain't sixty-four yet."

Emma Huggett was silent for a thoughtful moment, considering, with a faintly knitted brow and bitten underlip.

"I have a real nice ranch, down in the Santa Clara Valley," she began suddenly. "My husband got it from his folks. I have fruit and chickens . . . barns . . . everything."

"I guess that's down Linden Creek way?" he hazarded.

"That's in California," Mrs Huggett said briefly.

He widened his amazed bright blue eyes; he was pleased.

"Well, for pity's sakes!" he ejaculated. "That's always be'n a great word with me," he confessed. " 'California.' It has a real pretty sound. I've always thought I should like to see California."

"I hope you will," the woman said ineloquently. There was a pause.

"Ain't it some considerable distance away?" Lucas Rippey asked respectfully.

"It's well over twelve hundred miles by rail," she said.

"You be'n visiting back here?" he pursued, puzzled.

"No, I come to find you."

This left him speechless. He smiled his polite, appreciative smile.

"For forty years I've been sayin' this to you," Emma Huggett presently began in a determined voice. "I don't know as I ever imagined I would find you in a state home, or that we'd both be so well along in years. But I knew that somewhere, sooner or later, I'd be saying it.

"You spent sixteen years in prison for a crime you didn't commit, and it was my fault," she summarized it. "I don't know, Lucas, that anything in the world can make it up to you," she added, and there was a wistful softening in her heavy face as she looked at him.

"I guess I didn't 'mount to much, anyways," he said gallantly.

"That's neither here nor there; that don't lessen what I done," she persisted, tossing her head impatiently, as if she tossed his mollifying suggestion from her.

"Well, I always say I've had more time than most men for readin'," Lucas said cheerfully. "I'm a great hand for a book. Adventures—I seem to share 'em with the authors!"

"I'm well fixed," the woman said, not listening.

"And you live in California?"

"I was tellin' you. I've got a ranch—chickens and fruit—outside a place called Santa Clara."

He looked from the high institution window at barren fields level under January's snows.

"You don't have no snow there?"

"My alfalfa was three inches up this New Year's Day."

"For pity's sakes!"

"I had a big room fixed, off the kitchen, for my father," Mrs Huggett presently observed. "He had sciatica, and he couldn't climb stairs. I have a radio down there, and a Victrola, and an airtight. He was real comfortable there. I've got an old car you could drive. . . .

"I'd do for you," she said humbly, thickly, her voice trembling, and her big bare hands beginning to tremble too. "I'd do for you just as I done for Father. There's lots you'd like to do about the place. There's a Portuguese girl helps me with dishes and cleaning, but I'm one to run my own kitchen, and I'd like to have someone to cook for again."

"I don't know as I understand what you're drivin' at," Lucas said, clearing his throat.

"It isn't in any way making up to you," she persisted stubbornly.

"Why," he said kindly, pityingly, "what you done you done as a little girl. I wouldn't hold that against you! Nobody wouldn't. You seen a good chance to show off . . . children 'll do that. . . . That ain't nothing. . . ."

"I never thought, if I ever did find you, that you'd kill me, saying that," she observed as he paused. "I'll get you your ticket, I'll make all arrangements, and I'll meet you at San José station," she added.

Silence—a different sort of silence—deepened between them. The tears had come into her eyes, with the difficult words; tears stood in his bright old blue eyes as he answered her.

"Why, I don't hardly suppose you're asking me to leave the state home, Emma?" he faltered.

She made an awkward gesture, laughed thickly and briefly, frowned again.

"Well! You take me completely by surprise. . . ." said Lucas. "Well! This is surely unexpected. . . ."

"It's the one thing in this world that I want to do."

"Getting out, huh?" he mused. And there were already wings in his voice. He glanced out at the snow again; a radiator clanked in the warm, stuffy stillness. "I'd be glad to get out," he whispered, suddenly shaken. "This is a hard place to be . . . for a proud man." His voice thickened; he was still.

"I wouldn't be no burden to you!" he assured her, recovering.

"I wouldn't care if you were."

"Well, I wouldn't be. I could do a good deal of cartin', in that car—I can drive any make there is," he said eagerly.

"And there's nothing I don't know about chickens. Hosses—I haven't had so much dealing with them. But chickens—there's money in them. And I ain't a sick man, you know. I've always be'n a worker, only it was winter comin' on, and myself well along in years, and they being apprehensive that I'd take another chest cold."

"You won't get any colds in Santa Clara."

"California!" he said, rapt. "Well, I declare, I didn't know when I got up this morning—it shows how little trust we put in Providence—seems we never know what's coming!"

She sat heavily silent, watching him anxiously.

"I take this very kindly of you, Emma," he presently said, considering.

"It's like a dream to me that I've found you, Lucas, and you aren't dead, and I can maybe make up the hundredth part of what I done to you!"

"We ain't responsible for what we do as children."

"No, but we can pay for it, Lucas. I've been paying for forty years."

"Sho!" he said, distressed.

"If they'd sent you to the chair, then I would have spoke!" she burst out miserably. "There wasn't ever any doubt in my mind about that! But there were extenuating circumstances, and you was only tried for manslaughter. And meanwhile, they were all making a fuss about me—reporters and court—everyone. I kept trying, after I saw how terrible a lie I'd told—I kept trying to cut it down, and they'd praise me for that too.

"My folks moved away, but I made a girl back home promise she'd let me know what happened to you. But she never wrote me. And after that I tried to put you out of my mind and to forget the whole thing.

"But I couldn't. It rode me day and night. It come between me and everything right and sweet about my marriage and my children. There wasn't one of 'em born but I didn't look down at his little face and say to myself, 'I wonder if some hysterical girl of thirteen is going to swear *your* good name and your future away!'

"You spent sixteen years in jail for a crime you didn't commit. But I've been forty years in hell, Lucas. I used to pray that the Lord would make it up to you and punish me. But I never had the courage to come out and confess. No living soul ever knew what you and I know. I was afraid."

"I don't know but what I've had the best of it, Emma. I haven't ever be'n much of a success," the man said. "But I don't know's I've ever be'n afraid, either. You mustn't feel too bad."

"I want you to come and live in comfort and independence on my place," she said. "If I'm ever to have another moment of peace, it 'll be due to you. It's been burning in my soul for ten years that that was my way out."

"Well, you certainly are a good woman," he said slowly, in a silence.

"I'm not a good woman at all. I'm the murderer, not you. I hardly knew you, and I did to you what a savage wouldn't do to his worst enemy. There's no happiness I could give you that 'd clear *me,* I know that. But if putterin' about the farm, and feelin' that you were a free man, with something put by in the bank, in case I was suddenly took . . .

"If that 'd mean anything to you, Lucas, late as it is now to make amends, why, it 'd be a charity to me to let me do it!"

He blinked with wet, smiling eyes. But he spoke sturdily.

"If it 'd mean anything! Why, Emma, I don't know as folks realize just what this kind of a place is like, eatin' amongst a lot of paupers and beggars and fellers that aren't mentally straight. If I ask for a shirt or a sweater or a pair of pants, she unlocks the wardrobe and hands me out the first one she sees. I don't blame her, she's not got any reason to respec' me—but I haven't stopped respectin' myself, just the same. I don't know as you appreciate just how hard it is. . . ."

He stopped, smiling, with a circle of bright, hard red color in each of his withered cheeks.

"A man likes a little peace and privacy," he explained simply.

"I'm alone now," the woman said in a short pause during which they looked at each other. "My husband was a good man, but he was hard. He died awhile back; my boy died in the flu year. The other little feller died when he wasn't but four, and my girl married a missionary and lives in China. But I'm well fixed. I'm not complainin'.

"Only, there hasn't be'n a day of my life I haven't thought of you. I don't know that there's be'n an hour when I haven't remembered that hot Easter Sunday, back home, when Kane Madison was murdered, and when I, a smug little girl of thirteen, with long curls, stood up and lied away your life!"

"You wasn't nothin' but a kid, Emma."

"I knew better 'n that, though."

"I certainly," he said in a silence, "I certainly would enjoy livin' on a farm again. I'm country bred, and trees and fields seem to say something to me. Thoreau—a lady gave me a book by him. There was a man that had the secret of livin', Emma. Did you ever read his books?"

She was looking at him wistfully; there was something of humble entreaty, something of admiration, in her dull look.

"No, I never did, Lucas."

"Well, you'd enjoy 'em immensely," he said.

"There's just one thing more to say," she began abruptly, after a pause. "I want you to understand that the obligation in this matter isn't on your side. It seems to me you've already done more for me, Lucas, than I'm ever goin' to be able to do for you!"

Six weeks later she walked down to the barn, on a hot March morning, to tell him that lunch was ready. Supper was never anything but warmed-over biscuits and tea and fruit sauce and such nursery fare, but luncheon was a daily triumph for Emma, who was a master hand with chicken tapioca gravy and asparagus omelette.

The air was blue and singing this morning, and all about the white farmhouse the lilacs were in flower. The yard was pleasantly littered with ropes and planks and odds and ends; a bridal wreath had burst like a popcorn ball under the low window of Lucas' kitchen chamber, and up the slope of the hillside plum trees were white masses of bloom against a celestial sky.

The barn stood in a slight depression too shallow to be called a canyon; mighty oaks were scattered among the shabby old buildings; the windmill was flanked by towering, tasseled eucalyptus trees. A calf was blatting somewhere out of sight; chickens were talking and picking near the line of whitewashed farm buildings.

Lucas was sitting on a backless chair, mending something with a neat leather thong. The spring sunlight fell graciously upon his comfortable, relaxed old figure, in its muddy corduroys and thick sweater; he was whistling to himself as he worked, the Airedale attentive and adoring at his knee.

"If you aren't whitewashin' something, you're mendin' it!" Emma commented with an air of dryness.

"That Portygee broke his milkin' stool strap," Lucas explained.

"You're a great hand for jobs," she said, smiling in honest affection.

His delight in the little farm had made her see it with new eyes. Tom Huggett had been a sufficiently satisfied rancher, but there had been no romance in his attitude. Lucas, a broken old jailbird from the poorhouse, saw enchantment everywhere. One morning he was busily whitewashing, another hammering; on a third he drove the car into town and came back laden with chains, tools, seeds. The place seemed to gain an entity, a personal fascination, under his eager care.

Since Tom's death she had tossed her weekly copy of *Farm and Orchard* unopened upon a heap on the desk in the unused dining room. Lucas had fed upon these hungrily, had drawn her into discussions of pruning and hen houses. He wanted to try a hive, one of these days; he had theories about acacia honey. He was already "Uncle Luke" to the Portuguese who worked intermittently on the place; to half the village; Carolina, the kitchen maid, adored him.

He was happy, and Emma Huggett, watching him wistfully, as he expanded in this new atmosphere of comfort and liberty, felt in her own sore heart a certain satisfaction that was somewhat like happiness too. The old car was a very Cinderella coach to him; he worked over it, tinkered with it, kept it shining. His own books and lamp, his coffee cup with the pink roses on it, the instant allegiance of the dog, these were things in which he took untiring delight.

"Lunchtime?" he said when she had inspected the one-legged milking stool.

"If you're going to be a real farmer, Lucas, you ought to call it dinner."

"Well, that's right too." He walked along beside her through opened gates and corrals. "This feels more like June than March!" he said. And then suddenly, "Say, listen—listen. I've got a bone to pick with you! What's all this about?"

He drew from his pocket an envelope, a typewritten letter, a small, neat brown book.

Her heavy, sad face brightened only a shade.

"Oh yes!" she said. "Yesterday was the first. I put some money—fifty dollars—to your account."

"I don't need money!" he protested. "I've got some of that check you sent the superintendent. I haven't no more use for money here than Captain has!"

The dog leaped at the kindly old hand that dropped to his silky head.

"I'd pay a foreman more 'n that, Lucas."

"Why, but sho!" he said. "I eat my weight in butter and eggs every day. . . ."

"You don't eat much," she said quietly in the pause.

"It 'll just accumulate there at the bank," he said stubbornly.

"It's a good place for it."

"I want to tell you something that may make you feel good, Emma," the man said suddenly. "I've kinder wanted to say it for some time; I may's well say it now. I'd live the life I've lived all over again, to have it come out like it has now."

"There isn't any money in the bank that could buy your sayin' that," she said simply after a space.

"We don't know what governs our destinies," he went on. "What I'd have be'n without them long years of incarceration, who can say? I was destined to endure 'em, and you destined to eat your heart out with regret. But we don't know but what all's for the best. . . ." He stopped, innocently pleased with his own oratory.

She sighed deeply, frowned.

"You've got a sweeter nature than I have, Lucas."

"It don't take a very sweet nature to appreciate having health and liberty and some work to do," he suggested.

"Remorse is the thing that ages you and eats into your night's rest," the woman presently observed in her own heavy, hopeless way. "You might well forgive and forget, because you're innocent. But I keep going over and over it. Ma and Gran'ma were in the kitchen when I got home that Easter afternoon, and I'll never forget Ma's holding out the paper to me. 'See about Susan Clute, and her folks sendin' her East for violin lessons?' she says. Sue 'd always had everything I wanted.

"It kinda made me sick, the rest of that afternoon. I changed my dress and bathed my face and took a good long drink of water out at the pump, I remember, but I was just shaking inside.

"About six o'clock Mrs Tenney came running over, and she told Ma about Kane Madison being murdered. 'I'd like to know where Lucas Rippey was this afternoon,' she says in a scared sort of whisper, 'because everyone knows he and Kane were both after Thelma Cass.'

"Then I spoke up. Right out of a clear sky I says, 'Why, I saw Lucas Rippey up near the Madison place this afternoon!' I says. The minute I said it I knew I was done for. They both turned to me.

" 'Then you know where poor Kane was found?' Mrs Tenney says.

" 'It must have been somewhere near the house,' I says at random, not knowing whether she'd know I was lying then and there and say that the body was down near the railroad tracks or something. But no, she just looked scareder than ever, and she says, 'Yes. He was lying right across the door-sill.'

"After that I went on. As different neighbors came in I'd tell it all fresh. And when Judge Robbins come, the next day, I was as easy as an old shoe with the details about how you spoke to me, and how you were buryin' something and asked me not to say I'd seen you. . . .

"I was crazy, that's the only explanation."

They had halted in the shadow of the barn at the door-yard fence. The lilac blossoms near them moved in a soft breath of wind and were still. The spring sun shone down warmly upon the white-painted house and the new green of the high elms and maples. Larks went singing up from the grass in the green fields.

"I thought we was goin' to forget all this, Emma."

She laughed a brief, troubled laugh with a note of shame and gratitude in it.

"Yes, that's the sensible thing to do."

"I don't know as it matters much what you do with your life, long's you end it right," Lucas said thoughtfully.

"I know. But as if there wasn't trouble enough in the world, to send an innocent man to prison! Lucas," she added abruptly, in a quickened voice, "who *did* kill Kane Madison?"

"I don't know. We had a fight at the livery stable, all right, him and me," the old man said, "like it was proved in court. We fought over Thelma—she'd gotten into trouble, and he was sorter laughin' at me about it. I don't know when I've got so mad—all of a sudden.

"But that wa'n't all the score betwixt Kane Madison and me. Ever since I'd be'n a little feller in grade school he'd been bullyin' me. He used to twist my wrists. Sometimes my wrists would be sore for weeks, but I never dast to tell anybody. I hated him, all right; I *would* have killed him fast enough!

"This afternoon he come into Lenhart's stable while I was tendin' it for Len Lenhart, and he begun to ask me if I would like a message from Thelma. I wasn't never a regular beau of Thelma's, but she seemed awful sweet and pretty to me, and I couldn't bear to think of her bein' in trouble.

"He backed me up to the loft ladder, and he begun forcin' me up, and I struck at him with the broom handle—like they brought out in court—and I yelled at him that I'd kill him, all right. The lady in the cottage next door told all that true enough, and that I run out after him. . . .

"He run across the fields towards home. But I never followed him. I went up into the woods and laid down on the grass, all afternoon, hatin' him.

"But then who *did* kill him, Lucas?"

"Mysteries of the missin'!" he said cheerfully. "I always thought Millie done it, for all her carryin' on an' her widow's veil. It's a plot, all right!" He admitted himself that he was "great" on mystery stories. But then, Emma would muse a little enviously, he was "great" on everything. She was well past her half-century mark, but she had never met anyone like Lucas before, unless an occasional vital enthusiastic child were like him.

Everything delighted him, every waking, every breakfast, every hour of his busy puttering day was a separate delight. He discussed the chickens as if they had been human entities;

the old plow horses came over to the corral fence and rested their great shaggy heads there when Lucas was busy in the farmyard; the Airedale crushed his hairy length against Lucas' porch door at night and whined and muttered from time to time in a very ecstasy of love.

Miss Farmer ran out of the library with a new detective story for "Uncle Luke." Doc Brainerd, the veterinary, came out to the ranch and conferred with him. Thin little overworked Mrs Pointer from the next farm told Emma that the children were different creatures since Uncle Luke had begun to give 'em lifts in his car, and the very minister himself, ending a call, said warmly, "You've got the secret, Mr Rippey. I'm a young man, sir, I've got a lot to learn. You do me good."

It was only upon the famishing Emma that the healing dews did not fall.

"I see you as a little feller in the orphanage, Lucas. Missin' your mother, probably, wonderin' if you was ever goin' to have folks and a home of your own. And I see you gettin' out, a skinny little feller of fourteen, workin' for Smiley, the undertaker. What 'd that old skinflint pay ye, anyway?"

"Fourteen a month."

"Good grief! Whatever did you pay at Mrs Mason's for your room, then?"

"I paid her a dollar sixty a week. Her boy Silvester was in the same room."

"And you got your own meals?"

"Picked 'em up where I could. I used to go over to the station restaurant lots, and help 'em wash dishes."

"Silvester Mason wa'n't any too good company for you."

"No, he was a real demoralizin' influence, I always thought."

She would regard the sunshiny old thoughtful face wistfully, painfully.

"Nothin' hasn't ever embittered you, Lucas."

"No," he would agree, considering. "Don't know's it has."

"But wa'n't you thunderstruck when I, the minister's niece, come out with all that rigamarole?"

"Yes, I was, as I recall it. I was real surprised."

"It was my evidence that done it, Lucas."

"Emma, can't you forgive and forget?"

And Emma would laugh in desperation, seeing the sympathetic look upon his kindly, rosy old face.

"I tell you there's many a millionaire of sixty-five that 'd change places with me!" he assured her over and over again.

One very hot July noon he and she were alone, in burning summer silence, on the shabby, shadowy side porch. The night would bring coolness, indeed, would bring actual chilliness again, but it was hard, at the moment, to believe in anything but dry, parching, relentless heat.

The sky was whitish blue, the fig tree shadows seemed to pulsate with a green light. In the orderly dooryard pepper plumes hung motionless, filling the air with pungent scent; long strips of cream and russet bark fringed the towering trunks of the eucalyptus. Chickens were fluffing and complaining in the shadow of the stable lane; the windmill wheel was lifeless. Now and then the dog sighed, moaned faintly in his sleep.

Walled on three sides by the house and comfortably fenced on the open north side by heavy grapevines, the side porch was the coolest place on the ranch. It was mellowed by half a century of plain, busy living; its floor sloped a little, its unpainted woodwork was satiny from the touch of fingers. A shabby screen door connected it with the kitchen; a shabby single step with the packed hard earth of the yard.

Emma, always restlessly active, was stringing beans with quick, expert movements of knife and fingers. Her big hard hand would fill with the finished green strips, she would open her fingers to release them into a saucepan beside her. Her thick black hair was brushed back, crisp and wet; her full throat rose from a thin old cotton gown she called her "voyle."

Lucas was tinkering patiently with a yellow-jacket trap, bending the wire gauze carefully, whistling under his breath. He was in his shirt sleeves; sweat stood on his childlike old forehead, his thin silvery hair was plastered down with it.

He glanced at his companion now and then; stopped whistling.

"Heat's given ye kinder a headache, has it, Emma?"

She raised heavy eyes.

"No, I don't know as my head aches," she said slowly.

He worked on again in silence, and again gave her an uneasy look.

"Emma," he said suddenly. "There's something I want to say to you."

She glanced up expectantly; his tone was odd. Her hands were still.

"I've had this on my mind for some time," Lucas began again. His old face had reddened painfully. He hesitated, looking at her doubtfully. "This may make kind of a difference," he said and stopped.

"Whatever on earth are you talkin' about, Lucas?"

"You've be'n very kind to me," the old man resumed, forcing himself on. "And it's only right you should know."

"Know *what?*" she asked, nervous and impatient.

"Emma," he said, "would it surprise ye to know that I done it?"

She looked at him blankly, heavily, not in the least understanding.

"I mean—that you was right about Kane Madison," Lucas said.

The burning, difficult color of middle age spread to her own face now. Her eyes not leaving his, she automatically put aside her panful of beans and raised her fingers to press her throat.

"Yes sir, I done it," Lucas then stated flatly, in an expressionless voice.

"You . . ." she stammered, and swallowed with a dry throat. "You—why, Lucas Rippey," she added sharply, regaining her senses, "you don't know what you're sayin'!"

"Yes, I do, Emma," he persisted simply.

For a long moment she watched him steadily, almost fearfully, her breath coming quick and shallow.

"You wasn't anywheres near the Madison place!" Emma whispered at last.

"Becuz Kane Madison wa'n't killed at his own place. He was killed at Lenhart's barn, and he run all the way home."

Her eyes flashed as she considered this.

"'Twa'n't possible," she breathed, still watching him as if fascinated.

"That's the way it was, though, Emma."

"Oh, my God, my God, my God," she murmured, looking away. Her hand was clutching her heart now. Her lids had half sunk over glazed eyes, her breast moved painfully.

"I hit him with a pipe in Lenhart's," Lucas resumed. "He backed me up the ladder; he was ta'ntin' me about Thelma. I useter go kinder crazy whenever anyone ta'nted me like that. I useter go crazy even before I left the orphanage. The matron knew it. 'Don't get Lucas into a tantrum,' she useter say."

"Lucas, you never killed Kane Madison!"

"I say I did."

"You hit him on the head——"

"Down at Lenhart's, that Sunday afternoon. He run out the side door and went streakin' up through the medder. I run after him for a piece, yellin' at him that he couldn't talk to me that way, that I'd kill him. Then I come back, and I was scared. I knelt down and prayed, right there in the middle of the stable, that he wouldn't die."

"But the mallet, Lucas? The mallet they found in the Madison kitchen, that had blood on it?"

"Well, maybe it was ackshally used to hammer a steak with, like old Gran'ma Madison said. Anyway, I knew I'd hurt him considerable. There was blood on the pipe, all right.

"I got up from my knees scared to death, and I says, out loud, 'I've got to get out of here! I've got to get away,' I says. And then it sort of come to me that no, better hang around and act innocent. So I went out and washed the gas pipe at the troft and threw it down in the sun on the dry grass."

"Your sleeves was wet when they come took you!" she whispered, struck.

"Yes, from washin' the pipe. I washed my hands good, too, and then I prayed some more. My mother had be'n a great believer, and I says, 'I'll believe, too, if You get me out of this!'

"Well, I've come to believe!" he ended, with his wintry, sunny old smile. "But I had a long way to go before I found God."

"Lucas," the woman said, and her own voice was like a prayer. "Do you tell me you killed Kane Madison?"

"Emma, if it meant goin' back to the town farm, I'd have to tell ye——"

"Oh, let that go!" she exclaimed, suffocating. "Just tell me—tell me that you done it——"

"I do tell you I done it!"

"You killed him, only he got home before he fell?"

"He run across the medder, Emma, holdin' onto his head."

"They never thought of that!" she said, thinking aloud, remembering.

"They never thought of that."

"Then my lie," she began, trembling, ending a short silence, "my lie wa'n't all a lie, Lucas?"

"No. I got"—he cleared his throat—"I got what was comin' to me!" he admitted.

"Oh no," she muttered, shaking her head, covering her face with her hands and swaying to and fro. "No, it wasn't right. It wasn't right to give a little feller of twenty-two a life term, no matter what he done! And you from the orphanage, too, and delicate—like we all knew you were.

"But, oh—my—God, Lucas," she gasped, looking up. "I'm so grateful to you for havin' told me! I'm so *grateful* to you! I'm grateful to God!"

Her hands were over her face again.

"My God, I thank Thee!" he heard her say. "I thank Thee!"

When she sat down in her chair, arms dangling limply at her sides, eyes fixed on the hot white sky beyond the grapevines, she was panting, and he saw that her cheeks were wet.

"Don't mind me, Lucas," she said in an infinitely exhausted and gentle voice, with an unsteady smile. "Them's tears of joy. I'm happy. I don't know as I've been so happy since that Easter Day."

"It's be'n on my mind to tell ye."

"And I thank you, Lucas. You never did a kinder thing in your life."

"I wanted ye to know."

"Mind you," she said with sudden vigor, "it don't lessen my wickedness in lyin' about ye! No, it don't do away with that. But at least I didn't send an innocent boy to sixteen years in hell and ruin his life."

"You must of knew, Emma."

"No, I didn't, Lucas. I told them lies out of whole cloth!"

A long silence, hot and still all over the burning world that was beginning to smell of dusty apples and Isabella grapes.

Emma was breathing like a spent runner, sweat stood on her temples.

"The relief of it, Lucas!"

"It's goin' to make you feel different to me, Emma, that's what I'm kinder afraid of."

She had closed her eyes, her head flung back. Now she opened them. A smile—it was to him a new type of smile—on that sad, heavy face, suddenly brightened it. She did not speak, but she extended a brown, hard hand, and his fingers caught hers.

"You don't feel—hard, toward me, Emma?"

"Hard?" she echoed with trembling lips. "Lucas," she said, "I'm never goin' to feel hard again toward *nobody!*"

"I'm a criminal," he reminded her simply.

"Yes, but you paid. Whilst I . . ." she was beginning. "But no, I've paid too," she amended it under her breath. "God knows I've paid too! We both done wrong, Lucas. But through the infinite goodness of God we've found each other and forgiven each other, and that's all there is to it. You've done more for me this afternoon than I could do for you if I made you the King of England!"

Blinking, swallowing, her hands still shaking, she began to gather up her pans.

"Well, there, I haven't felt like this in dear knows when!" she said, laughing and crying at once. "I'm goin' in to wash my face and hands and brush my hair and get my bearin's. It seems to me like a new world, and I shouldn't wonder if 'twas a pretty good one, like you're always tellin' me."

The screen door banged behind her lightly; he heard the clink of the pans in the kitchen, and then her heavy step mounting the inside stairs.

Lucas sat on, on the shady side porch, tinkering with his trap, smelling the pleasant summer smells of dry tarweed and yarrow, wet, sprinkled roadside dust and ripening grapes. He began to whistle softly again as he worked. Once he spoke to the drowsing dog, who immediately rose, whimpered affectionately and pawed at the brown corduroy knee.

The old man smiled. He looked away, through a pattern of grape leaves, at the eternal hills, transparent and delicate today as opal-colored gauze. They seemed as light, as floating as the cloudless sky itself.

There was peace, there was content, there might even have been a trace of wise and subtle humor in his eyes.